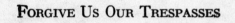

FORGIVE US OUR TRESPASSES

FORGIVE US
OUR TRESPASSES

BY

LLOYD C. DOUGLAS

Author of
'Magnificent Obsession'

GROSSET & DUNLAP
PUBLISHERS   NEW YORK
By arrangement with Houghton Mifflin Company

Forgive Us Our Trespasses

. . .

CHAPTER I

THE new-laid harvest straw beneath the faded red carpet rustled crisply under Martha's shapeless felt slippers as she padded across the living-room to the cluttered mantel.

With the quizzical grimace of long-neglected astigmatism she adjusted the steel-bowed spectacles that had been her mother's, had of a notion peddler for two dozen eggs and a pound of butter.

The wooden-wheeled clock — a noisy but amazingly accurate and exquisitely ornamented product of old Ferd's, while laid up one winter with a broken leg that had kept him two months sober — clacked irascibly at Martha that another blistering August morning was nearly five hours old. High time, indeed, that the day's work began. Not much wonder the Millers were poor.

Dragging her slipper-heels to the door of the spare bed-room which, in spite of her continued protests, Susan and Greta had insisted on occupying of late, Martha vigorously rattled the latch.

Glumly appeased by assurances from within, she returned to the dingy kitchen and peered into the kettle to see if there was enough water to prime the parching pump under the pear tree.

Then, kettle in hand, she plodded to the foot of the narrow stairs, and petulantly called:

'Julia!'

* * * * * *

Outstretched on velvet moss so soft and deep it yielded to every curve of her supple young body, Julia knew that

if she stirred, the least bit, she would never be able to re-
capture the complete satisfaction of this luxurious languor.

Doubtless it was too much to expect that an experience
so strangely sweet could be quite real. Sooner or later,
something or somebody would invade her peace. A tall
giraffe would saunter up and thrust his long nose into the
top of the banana tree. Giraffes ate bananas, didn't they?
... Or a big man with a blue coat and shiny buttons would
order her off.... Or there would be a peremptory summons
from afar to come at once!

Julia's unbuckled consciousness was already troubled by
the persistent echo of a distant call. It had seemed to come
from the depths of this tropical forest — a faint but urgent
cry for help. The voice had sounded tired, plaintive,
persecuted — just like Martha's.

But what would Martha be doing away out here in... in
Tasmania? Julia now readily identified her location by
recalling a picture in *The Pictorial Atlas*, her omnivorous
memory obliging her with phrases from the adjacent de-
scriptive text: 'Mountains heavily forested... magnificent
scenery... peaks of crystalline rock showing pink and blue
... frequent showers... luxuriant vegetation.' If this wasn't
Tasmania, it was some-place else too far off for Martha to
find. Martha never went anywhere, not even to Ligonier
on Saturdays. She always saw them off, standing there
under the big maple, mopping her tanned forehead with
the corner of her brown apron.

'Wish you was a-goin' along, Mat,' Hiram would drawl,
conscious that he only, by virtue of his clumsy championship of her dour eccentricities, could nickname her without
rebuke.

'No,' Martha would reply, sacrificially, 'somebody's got
to stay on th' place — what with them young turkeys and
all.'

Whoever was calling, Julia had an uneasy sense of guilt
over her failure to respond. Whether required to go or not,
she at least should have the courtesy to answer. Of course,

if it did actually turn out to be Martha — a most improbable event — she would have to obey. One always came when Martha called. Sometimes one came scowling and grumbling, but one always came.

Martha had an uncanny instinct for knowing when one must on no account be disturbed. Had one reached the most exciting episode in a story, Martha needed a few dry chips immediately to revive an expiring fire. Let the sunset be at that phase where vermilion was beginning to be laced with purple, Martha's accusing voice inquired from the kitchen door whether one expected to gather the eggs, or must she go out later and do it herself in the dark and all?... But this couldn't be Martha!

In just a moment, now, Julia would reply to the entreaty. She would draw a deep breath — though deep breaths were rather disconcerting, lately, for they seemed to make her plump, round breasts so much more mature than she was, herself — and try to exhale 'Coming!' so effortlessly as not to disturb this delightful lethargy. She would wait until the cry sounded a little more distinctly, and then she would answer, 'Yes, Martha... Coming!'

Evidently someone else had gone to the rescue, for everything was blissfully quiet again. That was good. So nice not to be bothered. Julia sighed contentedly as a big drop of warm dew dripped from the tip of a sheltering fern-frond and rolled slowly down her cheek.

She opened one eye cautiously — a mere tiny slit — to make sure the tall, slim, slanting date-palm was still there. It was; plainly visible through the vertical bars of her long black lashes.

Was this the one in the *Elementary Geography* or the *Child's Natural History*? No — it couldn't be; for the date-palm in the Geography had a gray monkey in the top, and the one in the Natural History was being climbed by a brown boy with arms as long as his legs, and sharp heels, scampering up out of the tiresome paragraph that read: 'The Malay is of pigmy stature, averaging 148–149 cm., with black skin and short woolly hair.'... No — this date-palm must be the one in the magic-lantern lecture, last winter, over at Hinebaugh's Schoolhouse.

As for the dripping rubber trees, with the waxy leaves that shaded her like hands folded above her eyes, Julia could locate them certainly. They were from the little conservatory at Fort Wayne... out in Spring Fountain Park... the day she didn't go to the show. And here they were in this immense conservatory — for this really was a conservatory. Julia smiled over her silly mistake. She had fancied herself out in the open... in Tasmania, maybe; and all the time she had been lying here on the moss in this conservatory, exactly like the one in Spring Fountain Park — only twenty times bigger!

But there was no mistaking these moist rubber trees. She had sat under them for a whole hour on a sticky green iron bench, that day last summer, when their family — all but Martha, what with the plums and all — had gone to Barnum and Bailey's circus; only she hadn't seen the show. She had indignantly left them standing there giggling foolishly on the crowded courthouse steps, craning their necks to follow the last of the little elephants at the tail of the pompous parade — the little elephants whose bulbous, bobbing, nodding heads seemed to be saying, 'Yes, yes — we're coming.'... (Yes, Martha... Coming!)

Hiram and Elmer had been so noisy and silly, and had attracted so much unpleasant comment, that she had suddenly rebelled against the further humiliation of going out to the show-grounds with them.

'Aw — come on!' Elmer had shouted, against the deafening shrieks of the steam calliope. 'Don't be a sissy!'

''S'matter with yuh?' growled Hiram. ''Shamed o' yer folks?'

Greta was laughing uproariously over Susan's comment, 'Wouldn't it kill yuh, Gret?... Father a-scoldin' the boys fer drinkin' so much, and him just able to stand up.'

Julia had been very sorry for her father that day, swaying

unsteadily in the broiling sun as he morosely watched the clanking, jingling, garish, pungent parade — his tanned face screwed up into tight little wrinkles, his shaggy gray hair curled in tight little ringlets on his temples, his blue eyes, deep-set, swimming with vertigo. She couldn't bear to see him ridiculed. He belonged to her.

'Please, Greta!'

Greta had grinned, and cracked her chewing-gum.

Julia had been strongly impulsed to slip her arm through her father's, and make off with him; to offer him a hand exactly like his, only smaller and not so brown; to smile into his eyes with eyes exactly like them, only younger and not so weary; to take him along with her — anywhere to be away from these unfeeling people who were not related to either of them except by the mere unfortunate accident that they all happened to belong to the same family.

At that very moment, however, he had turned on her reproachfully, stifled a hiccough that hinted at impending nausea, and muttered, 'You'd better let yourself go and have some fun once.'

'Fun?'

'Yes: their kind o' fun. It won't do you no good to be haughty. You might as well cave in — an' like it! I done it! So kin you! I even larnt to talk like 'em. If you don't want to be lonesome all yer life, you'd better ——'

That quite settled it!... Promising to meet them at the Pennsylvania Station at seven-fifteen (they had left old Florrie and the dilapidated surrey at Larwill and had come the rest of the way by rail), Julia had slipped through the sweaty crowd, her cheeks aflame.

Three blocks away she took the street-car — No. 52, a policeman had told her — an almost empty little green street-car that banged its bell furiously at the now de-mobilizing throng, demanding it to drag its roly-poly, waddling wife and gawky children and their yellow balloons and pink popcorn balls off the rails; had ground dizzily around sharp corners, and lost its few passengers — all but

Julia — finally reaching almost open country, where it took the bit between its teeth, tucked its chin against its neck, and galloped over a rusty, hummocky track, the trolley-wheel singing a painfully shrill note, until it brought up with a jerk at the shabby station-shed in Spring Fountain Park.

The grass was seared and badly trampled, and the dahlias were dusty and frowsy in their prim round beds. A black-lettered board pointed an index-finger toward 'The Conservatory.'

Julia had had the steamy, sweaty, stuffy, little green-house all to herself, that afternoon. Everybody else had gone to the circus. She had sat there on the sticky iron bench, hoping it wouldn't come off on her new pink ging-ham, dreamily transporting herself to the equatorial regions where all this rank, lush, stifled vegetation belonged, finding a strange kinship with it. She sympathized with these cramped, dwarfed, imprisoned rubber trees, and the gigantic ferns with dejected, drooping arms and wings.

And now, to Julia's annoyance, the cry for help was repeated. It came from just outside the conservatory door, this time. Would she, or would she not, come immediately?

The huge dome of the conservatory lifted and disappeared. It was exactly like the glass cover that protected the plate of soggy doughnuts from the flies on the high counter in Ruggles's Restaurant and Pool Hall at Cromwell.... Martha had taken the conservatory by the handle, and lifted it off. One could hear what she was saying now, ever so distinctly. Would she come, this instant, and help get breakfast for Susan and Greta, who, as she very well knew, had promised to be ready at half-past five to go with the other huckleberry-pickers to Wadham's marsh? And wasn't it little enough for her to do, seeing she had begged off from the berryin' to study her algebry, or whatever it was, so she would be prepared for that there County In-stitute, week after next, which everybody knew she hadn't any right to waste their money on — even if it was her'n,

a-teachin' silly paintin' lessons to women as ought to been
a-keepin' their children's buttons on — what with them so
hard-up and all? And didn't she have any natural feelin's
of——'

'Yes, Martha. I'm *coming!*'

Julia sat up, drenched with perspiration, stretched, inhaled an unsatisfactory draught of sultry, humid air, and
gazed out through the east window at a chrome yellow sun
that already threatened to break an August record. Next
Thursday's *Ligonier Weekly Banner* would probably say,
in big black headlines, 'HOTTEST DAY FOR TEN
YEARS!... Highest Temperature Since 1885 Recorded on
August the——'

August the whath?... August the tenth! Her birthday!
Would anyone else remember?

She reached out a long, slender hand for her stockings,
dangling over the back of a chair, and tugged them on.
After all, shouldn't she be glad she had a good excuse not
to go into Wadham's snake-infested huckleberry marsh and
have her arms and legs scratched with briars and nettles
while she fought deer-flies with an exasperation close to
tears, and shuddered with loathing at the sight of enormous
caterpillars, and wiped the slimy cobwebs out of her eyes
with sun-blistered, juice-smeared wrists?... Blessings on the
pesky algebra!

'J-u-l-i-a!'

'Yes, Martha. I'm coming!'

* * * * * *

Her entrance into the grim little dining-room was effected
with much difficulty. She could have wished that her first
appearance before her household, as an adult in good and
regular standing, might have been somewhat more impressive.

Circumstances had decreed that Julia must bump her
way crabwise through the obstinate swinging-door from
the smoky kitchen with a precariously poised platter of

bacon in one hand and the big battered coffee-pot in the other, while the family, glancing up from its first round of fried mush and sorghum molasses — with which munitions Martha had preceded her — wondered, not without warrantable anxiety, whether she would make port with all her cargo.

It was not to be expected that her lazy and surly brothers, much less absent-minded old Ferd — whose fork trembled in a long, slim hand that had been obviously intended for more esteemed employment than shingling barns and blowing stumps — would spring to her rescue. That would have been 'a-puttin' on style,' an affectation held in snarling contempt by Hiram and Elmer. Indeed, their sentiment on this subject was commonly shared by the entire male species, so far as she had been able to observe.

As for Greta, who, at twenty-two, had already well developed an impish talent for the enjoyment of other people's discomfiture; and as for Susan, whose twenty-seven virginal years and one hundred and sixty-seven pounds gave such alarming promise of unarrestable progress in both dimensions that she was frankly envious of her willowy young sister, Julia's predicament was clearly no concern of theirs.

Martha, seated with her angular back to the door, which now capitulated with a savage swish and a sullen bang, cleared a place at her elbow for the brown-stained coffee-pot, and dutifully remarked that this was Julia's eighteenth birthday.

While still in her teens, Martha had accidentally lost an upper canine. Morbidly self-conscious, her misfortune had worried her grievously; but there had been no necessity for replacing the missing tooth. By skillful practice, Martha had been able to conceal this disfigurement with the corner of her lip, a technique which had produced a meticulousness of articulation oddly inconsistent with the slovenly elisions and shockingly bad syntax demanded by her righteous passion to avoid 'a-puttin' on airs.'

'Yes; your little sister,' reiterated Martha, her choice of a pronoun indicating the maternal relationship she sustained to the family, 'is came of age.'

Brief, bucolic felicitations from the boys were mumbled through the mush, to which old Ferd — so stung with remorse over having no gift for her that he did not even raise his eyes — added solemnly that Martha could always be depended on to remember the days.

Depositing her awkward burdens, Julia stiffened to a martial stance, brought her full red lips to a determined pucker, tossed her curly head airily, and swept the breakfast-table with a look of pretended challenge, as if to say that she was quite grown up now and they must all have a care how they treated her.

A moment later she was repentantly reflecting that previous experiences might have warned her against indulging in this bit of playful pantomime. Julia's sporadic efforts to dramatize some situation for the amusement of her family had been uniformly unsuccessful. It would have been very pleasant, she often thought, to belong to a household quick to interpret and enjoy a little good-natured clowning. It was not that their stodginess and lack of sparkle evoked her contempt: she was too naïve to be contemptuous. Indeed, she had never known — except in *Little Women*, long since read to rags and learned by heart — any such family as the rollicking, bantering, make-believe crew that constituted her ideal home.

On one's birthday, however, it might reasonably be hoped that the family would waive its habitual taciturnity, and humor a whim; so, quite recklessly overplaying her premeditated skit, Julia glared at her brothers and sisters with a mock severity signifying her newly acquired dignity. But they had already returned to their bacon and mush; and, noting that no one of them — not even her father — showed signs of sharing her mood, she doffed her archness, rubbed a damp wisp of blue-black hair from her low forehead with the back of a shapely wrist — astonishingly like old Ferd's, only daintier — and slipped into her accustomed place on the end of the pine bench beside Susan.

'Reckon you'll be too cocky to live with, now yer old enough t' be yer own boss,' observed Hiram, who, on second thought, had decided not to leave Julia under the impression that he, at least, was too thick-witted to have taken note of her brief charade.

Equally unwilling to be considered incapable of clever deduction, Greta remarked to her plate that Julia would probably be leaving home, one of these days, to go on the stage.

Old Ferd hitched about in his chair, and for a moment Julia thought he was going to offer a comment.

'Julia's always been a-playin' she was somethin' else besides what she is,' said Susan.

'Well — she ain't harmed no one by a-doin' that,' growled Ferd. 'She come by it honestly enough. When I was her age, er thereabouts——'

'More coffee, paw?' inquired Martha, loudly, as if he were deaf.

'It's sure a-goin' to be a scorcher, Gret,' observed Susan, fanning her goiter with the bib of her apron, and peering through the open doorway toward the road.

'There goes old Len Bausermann with his pick 'n' shovel,' reported Elmer, following his plump sister's eyes to the highway.

'He'll be a-diggin' Granny Hartsock's grave today,' explained Hiram, without turning to look.

'A saint,' murmured Martha, unctuously, 'if they ever was one.'

'Who — Len?' chaffed Elmer. 'That consarned old chicken-thief?'

Susan and Greta laughed immoderately. Martha, easily offended when her piety was ridiculed, drew down the corners of her mouth, and pouted. Elmer explored a defective wisdom-tooth with a pointed quill, and grinned.

Old Ferd knew they didn't care to hear his story — **none**

of them but Julia. He could always be sure of an attentive listener in Julia, though sometimes she asked too many questions.

The family's rude indifference occasioned him no surprise. He had been on the defensive for so long in a home to which he contributed almost nothing, his small earnings claimed by Jake Heffel, that he had no right to be indignant over such discourtesies. He poured the thin coffee into his saucer with a shaky hand, crumbled bread into it, and sprinkled the dish with brown sugar, intent upon his occupation. Julia, toying absently with her food, studied his deep-lined, mobile face, confident that she was following his reminiscences as closely as if he had been given encouragement to recite them.

He was, she knew, skipping hurriedly over the Dresden part of it; the part that most interested her; the part that really mattered. She had never been able to construct a very clear picture of his boyhood home. The blurry impression she had of it was an accumulated synthesis of chance remarks accidentally dropped, and laconic answers to her importunate queries in the rare moments when he seemed willing to talk about his youth.

He would be out in his tiny shop under the big maple, standing at his home-made lathe, turning wooden pins for the mending of Squire Craig's harrow-teeth. The fine hickory shavings would come writhing and screaming from the point of his blue-hot chisel. He would pretend not to notice her, sitting on the old tool-chest, intently watching him.

'Let me treadle it, father. I like to.'

The huge oak balance-wheel overhead would lumber to a creaking stop.

'Mind you don't get yer foot caught under it, now!'

Julia would snuggle in between his arms and stand so close, her back to his breast, pumping the broad pedal that made the patched belt go snapping and crackling on the great wooden fly-wheel, threatening to bring it down on their heads; her father's warm, hairy forearm, tense on the chisel, moist with sweat and powdered with fine sawdust, brushing her cheek, almost as if he caressed her.

Panting with exertion, she would look up over her shoulder, and smile, when he signaled her to stop.

'You're more like her every day, Julia!' he would murmur, as the machinery idled to a standstill.

'Because my hair dips down to a point here in the middle?'

'That — and the deep dimple in your chin.'

'And she had the same kind of eyes that we have.'

'Exactly; that's where we got 'em.'

'The others don't have them, father.... Funny — isn't it?'

Thus drawn together in these brief intimacies, there would be some talk about her Grandmother Mueller — Ferd had changed his name to Miller, when coming to Indiana, because the people invariably mispronounced it; or was that the exact reason, Julia often wondered, when she had grown up — Grandmother Mueller who always seemed to be a mere slip of a girl, stooping over the flower-beds in the garden that was so ——

'How big was it, father — honestly: big as our potato-patch?'

He would chuckle derisively.

'Our potato-patch! Huh! Six — eight — ten times as big!'

Then there would be some vigorous prodding of memory for more information about the house. It was a great, rambling, stone house with tall, broad chimneys and many gables. Yes — his own room had a gable, and there was a window-seat with a rose-colored velvet cushion. Wrens nested in a little box under the eaves, and when it stormed, the branch of an elm swept the diamond-shaped panes of the mullioned window.

'And was there honestly a fountain in the middle of a big pool, father?'

'Yes — and lily-pads.'

And really goldfish, like you said?'

'Yes, daughter — but don't you think you'd better go and help Martha now?'

'And you would feed them in the mornings — and they always knew when you were coming, and swam close to the edge to meet you?'

Of late Julia was becoming painfully aware of their lost heritage. Her day-dreams were bounded by the high stone wall, made warm and friendly by the tall hollyhocks his mother loved. On summer afternoons she fancied herself sitting in the rose-arbor, hard-by the large, half-timbered workshop and studio where distinguished guests were so often entertained at tea.

'Tea! — in a shop?' she had exclaimed, the first time he had told her about it.

'But it wasn't a little shop like this here, Julia. Seems to me like it had five or six big rooms. I disremember, exactly. The people came to see the carvings; almost every afternoon, somebody. And there would be exhibitions, couple o' times a year. Lots o' people came then, from long distances, Paris and London.'

'Would they talk to you, father?'

'I was just a young feller.'

'Going to school?'

'No — I had a tutor.... But I was always a-hangin' around the shop, and I can't remember when I wasn't a-playin' with chisels, and a-makin' things.... Once I heard a Count — I disremember his name — a-tellin' somebody that *Mueller* on a rood screen made it worth more 'n' its weight in gold.'

And there was a river.

Julia felt almost certain, as she sat watching her father's slow motions with his spoon, oblivious of the dull prattle of his family's table-talk, that he was dreaming of that river. You went through a thick oaken door set in the garden wall. The door had heavy wrought-iron hinges, and was always locked o' nights with a key that must have weighed all of a pound. You went through the door, and there was the river. The banks were rounded and grassy, and a long row of tall poplars grew on our side, 'their leaves always a-flutterin' whether there was any wind or not.' He disremembered the name of the river, but 'one of the swans was called "William Tell."' There were boats, too; a couple o' canoes and a dory and a punt with a red and blue canopy ——

'How much did Lafe Shock git fer his gol-danged shoats?' Elmer was inquiring of Hiram.

'Four cents, I heared,' rumbled Hiram, puffing at his sputtering pipe. ''Bout enough to pay fer th' corn he'd chucked unto 'em.'

'Corn — hell!' scoffed Elmer. 'Them shoats never seen a grain o' corn. All they ever et was swill!'

'Lot o' good the Shock swill woulda done 'em,' sneered Greta.

'They was so gol-danged poor,' expatiated Elmer, 'that I bet Lafe had to soak 'em afore they'd hold slop.'

—— and a punt with a red and blue canopy; and, sometimes, in the evening, his mother sat in the punt, with her guitar, and sang ballads to him, very sweetly. No — his father never joined them. No — he disremembered what the songs were.

Now Julia was at sea with her father, standing beside him as he stoked his way, with blistered hands, on a slow boat; she was landing with him, bewilderedly, at Castle Garden. Much had happened since the swans and the ballads in the evening; but it was quite impossible to recover intervening events. His father had whipped him savagely when he was sixteen. He wouldn't tell her why; but it had something to do with his mother. She had cried desperately, and that night he ran away. The tutor had helped him get away. The tutor had gone away, too, that same night.

Judging by the confident tightening of his lips, Julia knew he was in New York now, apprenticed to Lamb's

Studios. Four years of that passed in a few seconds. Now he was hard at work on the big walnut eagle — his first important assignment — that was to be poised on a lectern for Saint John's in Philadelphia. Lamb's had taken him in on the strength of the Mueller tradition, and had given him every possible encouragement, undisguisedly rejoicing in his budding talent. Every day he was improving his skill; every night he was poring over his new books, determined to perfect his English.

Then came the war. Julia saw the clouds gathering on the seamed old face. It was all over now. He had gone back to Lamb's in a faded uniform topped by the absurd little cap with the stiff visor that he still wore, rather rakishly, on Decoration Day — a day Julia dreaded, for he always marched unsteadily, and joked a good deal, when he should have been silent and dignified.

Now he had returned to the Lamb Studios, stubbly, fuddled, and pungent, after a fortnight's spree. All was forgiven. Soldiers would be soldiers. Lamb's were disappointed, but hopeful. Why, Mr. Joseph Lamb, himself! — (Ferd had been too proud of that recognition to keep it a secret, even if its implications were not to his own credit) — Mr. Joseph Lamb, himself, had pleaded with him to straighten up, and be a man. Surely, nobody could have asked for a better friend, Ferd often remarked, than 'Mr. Joseph,' who, it was said, had given up his plans to enter the ministry because he thought he could do more for religion by adding something to its beauty. 'Mr. Joseph Lamb was a great artist!' Ferd would say. 'Yes *sir!*'

No — it wasn't the fault of Lamb's Studios if he had drunk himself practically into the gutter at a time when a returned soldier's dissipation was easily pardoned, but not so easily capitalized in a profession demanding the utmost steadiness of eye and hand. Ferd was so proud of his erstwhile craftsmanship and its stern exactions that he was willing to admit his own inability to meet its requirements, shamelessly confessing the cause of his failure, as if his **very** drunkenness, at twenty-four, was to be talked about in tones of respect, seeing it had been important enough to collide successfully with an esteemed art.

So — that chapter was finished, then, and her father had ceased being an artist. Julia recognized the exact moment when he 'took to the road' en route to Pennsylvania in quest of a distant cousin who owned 'a bit of a truck-farm.' Oddly enough, no exigency of poverty had ever induced him to part with the books he had bought in the golden days when he was so brilliantly succeeding at Lamb's. He had stored them in New York; had kept himself sober long enough to save the money required for their transportation to his new home; for, now he had a home. He had married the plump, shy, awkward, yellow-haired daughter of an improvident neighbor who indifferently operated a small sawmill, 'mortgaged, by Golly, down to the last cleat in the old pulley-belt.'

Julia knew how it always amused him to repeat that phrase. He smiled, now, and glanced up furtively to make sure the family's attention was occupied. She dodged his eyes and took no further risks with them until she was sure he was in 'pardnership' with his unthrifty father-in-law, who, hearing rumors of advantages to be had by moving to Northern Indiana, 'where everybody was a-makin' big money loggin' and gettin' out railroad ties,' had suggested the immediate migration of his populous, penniless tribe.

Ferd grinned again, rather wryly. Julia was not quite sure where we were in the story, now. Perhaps he was thinking about something he had never told her — something not very pleasant, perhaps; something not much to our credit, she feared.

He had taken along to Indiana their simple, mostly home-made, household gear, the precious books — English classics — which were to become a veritable Godsend to Julia! — and his only military trophy, his little brown jug. Occasionally, of a late Saturday night in Heffel's Saloon in Cromwell, when Ferd and his cronies had passed from the bragging stage to the distinctly maudlin, nose-trumpeting phase of bland confessions and remorses over their respective might-have-beens, he would pull himself together long enough to make a pathetic joke of his own disaster.

'Yep' — Ferd would say, grinning drunkenly through his tears — 'that was my only military trophy — that there little brown jug.'

He glanced up, now, out of the tail of his eye, and found Julia regarding him with rapt interest. A bit disconcerted by this intense scrutiny (sometimes Julia's penetrating knowledge of his moods and meditations annoyed him, just a little), he pushed back his chair, and muttered, partly to himself, partly to her:

'Yep — that's the way it goes.'

He gnawed off a large bite of Horseshoe chewing-tobacco from the plug he had rummaged from the depth of his overall-pocket, and, without a backward glance, strolled out through the doorway toward his shop.

Perhaps he would continue his reminiscences while he worked on the Snell baby's pine coffin; but he had already covered everything in his story that had any interest for Julia. Except for such minor episodes as the births of his five children, and the death of Minnie, six years ago, his history was an unpunctuated monotony of trivial jobs — building corncribs, replacing timbers in the forebay at Austin's gristmill, planing and hanging Squire Craig's screen-doors every April, and stowing them in the loft of the woodhouse every November — a chronicle as sterile of novelty as the legendary minstrel's redundant report that now another locust came and carried away another grain of corn.

Julia wondered, sometimes, whether her father ever missed her mother. It was obvious that he did not grieve for her. Minnie's biological contribution to Julia's character was no more in evidence than the influence of a hen on a golden pheasant's egg. Julia was all Ferd's.

Minnie had been an ignorant, whining, colorless, unimaginative creature, her quite astounding bulk disproving the adage that stout people are invariably optimistic. Save for the fact that she had been an economical housekeeper (as she had plenty of reason to be), and was thought to put up the best green-tomato pickles in the Oak Grove neighborhood, nothing important was remembered of her; not even by her own kin.

A litter of empty, overturned, glass fruit-jars on her grave in the Baptist Cemetery which, on the anniversaries of her death, the melancholy Martha stuffed with garden flowers, ironically testified to Minnie's previous relation to other natural objects in a world where she had dully foozled a chance to present society with a rehabilitated wood-carver of exceptional virtuosity, and had contented herself with the excellence of her piccalilli.

* * * * * * *

A clatter of wheels and harness drew Greta to the door.

'Fer Gosh sakes, Sue, if Bob ain't came with the hay-ladders on! Jolt the very stuffin' out of yuh!' She turned to the abstracted Julia. 'You'd better come, too, Miss Stuck-up! Here's that Schrofe boy what's so crazy about yuh.... Hoo-hoo, Bob! We'll be out in a jiffy!'

'Mebby you better go, Julia,' advised Martha, maternally.

Julia demurred. It was little enough time she had to review her algebra, even if she studied every minute.

Old Ferd, returning for a tin of water to cool his grindstone, arrived in time to take a hand in the argument.

'Give her a chance, Martha. I'd like to see one of us do somethin' to make our name a little more important than it's been.'

Martha picked up a double handful of dishes with a decisiveness of manner that promised an impressive exit, to be followed presently by a great clatter of pots and pans off stage.

'Well — all I got t' say is ——'

But the threatened tantrum was played to a thinning house. Ferd had found his tin cup, and was off with it. Susan and Greta were on the way to the wagon. The boys slouched toward the barn. Julia carried her plate to the kitchen, where Martha was sniffling ostentatiously, and vanished with a promise to make the beds, her sister's plaintive whine trailing her all the way upstairs. ''Pears like nobody in this house cares what I think about anything. Just a hired girl... without any pay.'

* * * * * *

Standing before the severely plain but expertly crafted walnut desk that her father had given her, last Christmas, Julia unlocked a drawer and re-read the precious document it contained.

The desk had become a symbol of the considerable difference between herself and her brothers and sisters. A source of anxiety and embarrassment at first, the desk had come to be a refuge and an inspiration.

On Christmas morning, having presented each member of the family with a fine, large orange, Ferd had made a mysterious trip through the snow to his shop, returning shortly with the desk. Julia's exclamations of delight had intensified the sullen silence. At supper, that evening, Greta's smouldering indignation blazed forth in an irascible comment to which Ferd quietly replied:

'She's the only one in this family that would have any use fer a desk. If any o' the rest o' yuh ever needs one, mebby I'll 'tend to it.'

This sarcastic explanation of the gift did little to conciliate them. So much constraint was traceable to the episode that Martha told Julia she had better take her new desk upstairs and keep it out of sight. Susan added that she, for one, would never darken the door of Julia's room while it was there.

But, however painful the situation, at the outset, it developed for Julia a privacy she had never enjoyed before.

By common consent, the family left her to herself, implying, a dozen times a day, that she considered the rest of them inferior, twisting her every remark into allusions to their ignorance.

'What shall I do, father?' she inquired one day, in the shop. 'They're always trying to act as if they're not as smart as I am.'

Ferd grinned, and blew the sawdust off his chisel-handle.

'They don't have t' put on, very much, t' play that.'

'But it makes me so miserable!'

'Well — don't cry.... That's what yuh get fer a-bein' smart. Smart people's always miserable. Old man Solomon said that — er somethin' about like it.'

'Was he miserable?' asked Julia, with a tearful little smile.

'Gosh, yes! He was the smartest man that ever lived!' Ferd sat down on the tool-chest, laid a dusty hand on her knee, and grinned mysteriously. 'Julia, are yuh sure you've found all the drawers in that there little desk? One of 'em ain't got no handle.'

Her eyes brightened.

'No,' she whispered, excitedly, 'I haven't found it. Will you show me?'

He had found it for her the next time the family was out of the house — a narrow drawer set in the center of a row of six open pigeon-holes and faced by a little pilaster carved to imitate a longitudinal section of a Corinthian column.

'That there's it,' pointed Ferd, hugely enjoying Julia's flutter of excitement. 'No — it don't come out that way,' he said, when she had unsuccessfully grappled with the ornament which defied the best efforts of her finger-tips. 'Nobody could ever get it out a-doin' that.'

'Do show me, father!'

He had proceeded then in leisurely fashion, immensely relishing her suspense, to demonstrate the strange magic of the secret drawer.

'Now, if you ever want to put anythin' out o' sight, Julia,

commented Ferd, with a comradely wink, 'you'll know how to do it; and it'll take a heap o' tinkerin' with this here desk fer anybody else but you to find out how that drawer opens.'

Julia was ecstatic.

Her close inspection of the desk had led to another discovery: Ferd had carved the name 'Mueller' on the beveled edge of the little receptacle for ink-bottles and pens.

'I'm so glad you did that, father. That makes the desk still more valuable, doesn't it?'

Ferd flushed with pride.

'It's the only time, Julia, since I cut the name under the wing of an eagle what holds the Bible in a big church in Philadelphia. It's the same way my father cut his name — and his father — and his father's father.... It's a good name, daughter.'

Standing now before the desk, Julia withdrew a document — much too long to fit into the secret drawer — bearing the impressive seal of the Great State of Indiana and signed with an affected flourish by the Noble County Superintendent of Public Instruction, authorizing her to teach an ungraded school for the term of One Year. Beside it, in the long envelope, was the covering letter containing a pressing suggestion that the recipient plan to attend a five-day Institute to be held in Albion, the county seat, in late August, chiefly for the benefit of inexperienced teachers.

'Please, God,' whispered Julia, wistfully but shyly, for they were not very well acquainted, 'let me have a school!'

Nobody in the Miller family exhibited any piety but Martha, who was presumed to have enough for all. Martha's conversation was sprinkled with scriptural allusions, her stock of texts featuring the punitive phrases promising the ultimate rebuke of the proud, the 'froward' (whoever they were), and the stiff of neck. Julia, gifted in parody, occasionally employed these solemn exhortations herself, with *ex tempore* improvisations and amendments which amused her, and sometimes frightened her, too; for, she reflected, if there really was a hell, surely the fabricator of any such flippancies was reserving a warm berth.

When Martha, in her thin, flat voice, caroled from the kitchen, 'I'm washed in the blood of the Lamb,' Julia invariably shuddered, swallowed hard, and muttered, 'Ugh! — how nasty!'

'Please let me have the Schrofe School,' wheedled Julia, clutching her precious credentials tightly in one hand and with the other pressing her eyes hard to make sure they were closed firmly enough to satisfy the requirements of Deity, who was sure to be suspicious of her sincerity, 'so I won't have to come home except on Sundays. But — any school will do. Please, dear God, let me hear from one of them pretty soon. It would be so nice to have word on my birthday. Please!'

Somewhat startled by the inflection of this final word of entreaty, which hinted at an intimacy with the Almighty which, she was aware, impertinently presumed upon a very sketchy relationship, Julia added, humbly ' — Unless, of course, it should not be in accordance with Thy Holy Will.'

* * * * * *

What have yuh got yer Sunday hat 'n' dress on fer?' inquired Martha, when, a half-hour later, Julia passed through the kitchen, book and slate in hand, pausing to remark that she was going down by the creek where it was cooler.

'I thought I might walk over to Oak Grove, when I am tired studying, and see if there is any mail — about a school, you know.'

'Mighty sight o' studyin' you'll get done with that on yer mind. Better to a-gone berryin', like I told yuh. Anyways, all the schools are a-took by now. 'Pears to me like ——'

Without waiting for the rest of it, Julia walked out of the kitchen, quickened her steps immediately she was out of sight over the slope behind the barn, tossed her algebra and slate into the grass at the foot of the big willow that overhung the stream, climbed to the highway, and set out at a swinging stride toward the village two miles to the west — two miles by the road, but subject to considerable discount if one cut across Squire Craig's stubble-field, just beyond the Baptist Church, and took the path through the woods along the widening river, pent by the Austin milldam.

There were two high fences and a padlocked gate to climb, and occasionally the Squire's ill-tempered ram contested the audacity of trespassers, but Julia was impatient to peer into the tiny pane of dirty glass — No. 8 — in the Post Office which occupied a few square feet in the front end of Baber's General Store.

Halfway across the stubble-field, Julia's steps became shorter and less confident.

Seated, with his back to her, on the top rail of the fence that bounded the woods, was a young stranger, fashionably dressed, his shoulders slumped as if he were lost in serious thought; in trouble, perhaps.

Julia reflected that if he were to straighten himself out to full length he would be very tall.

The stranger's perch must be quite uncomfortable. Julia surmised that he would not remain there long. If she dallied, he might proceed, unconscious of her approach. She stopped, toying with the idea of retracing her steps, but the sun beat pitilessly upon the dazzling yellow field, and the cool maples promised a relief irresistible. Her heart quickened as her pace slowed. She pulled off her dowdy hat, made of cheap lace over a wire frame, and patted the damp curls at her hot temples.

Now the young stranger had turned, and, over his shoulder, was regarding her arrival with frank interest. He stepped down from the fence, on the grove side, consulted his watch, and smiled. It was almost as if he had been waiting for her, thought Julia; as if they had arranged to meet, and she was late. Had he decided to play, she wondered, that they were keeping an engagement? Could it be possible that there was anyone in the world like that? It would be such fun.

Would he not think her a bit stupid if she stared stonily into his friendly eyes, pretending to be offended, pretending to be haughty? Was it not one's duty to be cordial to strangers? Even Martha, prude that she was, believed that one might be 'entertaining angels unawares.'

Julia had never seen that sort of a smile on a boy's face. It signified nothing but a proffer of friendliness from one young human being to another. It left out of consideration the negligible fact that they were not of the same sex. How different from the awkward, crooked grin of the typical gum-chewing youngster who maneuvered to one's side at a boisterous barn-dance and paid one a clumsy compliment while turning to wink at some equally boorish bystander, as if to say, 'I'm a-tryin' to see how fer I c'n git with her!' — as if their relationship implied that she was willing it should be rated an obscenity. She had often been half-ashamed she was a girl.

Julia was within a few yards of the fence, now, making no pretense of indifference to the presence of the tall, athletic chap who awaited her, watch still in hand.

His smile was so disarming that her red lips parted in an honest recognition of the first of its kind she had ever seen worn by a contemporary male. Her ingenuous response to it was quite free of self-consciousness or embarrassment. Toward this handsome, urbane, self-possessed boy — clearly not of her world at all, so far as outward appearances went — she sensed a strange kinship which, she believed, it would have been unworthy of her to deny either to herself or to him.

It was what she had been longing for, all her life, wasn't it? Hadn't she dreamed of an acquaintance with some congenial spirit in whose company she might be... herself? Why dissemble? She owed something to that dream.

'It's much cooler over here,' he said, offering her both hands, when, having lightly climbed to the top of the fence, she sat facing him, fanning her flushed cheeks with her crumpled, frumpy hat.

'I know,' said Julia.

She took his hands without hesitation or coyness, and joined him.

'But we must keep an eye out for my Uncle Jasper's pet sheep, Otto the Seventh,' he said, as they fell into step on the path. 'Otto has a vile disposition, and the run of this grove.'

'Yes,' said Julia, 'I know.'

He ventured a sidelong glance, as if to inquire whether his new friend had exhausted her conversational possibilities, and met an enigmatic smile.

'Had I kept you waiting long?' she asked, with an earnestness that puzzled him.

He turned about and faced her so soberly that Julia repented her whimsical audacity. Did nobody in the world know how to take a little joke? Was she the only one, after all, who had any instinct for impromptu drama? She took a step forward. He detained her with a light touch on her arm.

'Yes,' he said, rather huskily, 'I have been waiting a long time... for you.'

'Don't spoil it,' said Julia, entreatingly. 'We were only playing, weren't we?'

CHAPTER II

FOR the first time in the history of the Schrofe School it was being taught without benefit of whips and dunce-caps.

The innovation caused some stir. Discipline had been much less savage in recent years under a succession of female teachers, but the present policy of complete disarmament was viewed with anxiety.

'Fer the girl's own sake,' agreed the younger mothers, whose support of her had been swiftly won by the affectionate interest bestowed on their little tots, 'them bigger boys oughta be kept in hand. They'll run her out afore Thanksgivin'.'

Ham Ditzler, who had put in six exciting winters behind that desk, more than a decade earlier, and now divided his time between odd jobs of plasterin', paperin', paintin', an' butcherin', in the casual employ of his erstwhile pupils — ('danged degradin' work') — offered to bet (amount of wager unspecified) that the Miller girl would never finish out her term, a prediction which came true, though not for lack of firmness in her schoolroom.

Abner Schrofe, Chairman of the Board of Trustees, when joined in his barn by the four other members, one rainy Sunday forenoon in early October, silently shucked corn during their recital of the public's apprehension based on criticisms offered by the veteran pedagogue.

Upon the conclusion of their remarks, Chairman Schrofe listed heavily to starboard and deftly poured a considerable quantity of tobacco-juice down a convenient rat-hole, thus setting himself at liberty to express the opinion — conciliatorily phrased in terms consonant with the dignity of his office — that Ham Ditzler was nothin' but a damned old sore-head.

Encountering no opposition to this statement, not even from Zeke Trumbull, Ham's son-in-law, with whom he

made his home, Abner further deposed that there was more
brains in Julia Miller's little finger than Ham Ditzler had in
his hull body, adding that he would respectfully entertain a
motion a-sayin' it to be th' sense of this here board, duly and
properly assembled, that Miss Miller's services was 'sadis-
factory.'

Hez Brumbaugh said he would so move, and suggested
that the Chairman inform Miss Miller of their action.

Jake Waters, who since last spring had owed Abner the
final Eight Dollars on a Guernsey heifer, 'lowed that Ham
Ditzler — after all's said and done, and a-takin' him by and
large — was purty much of a gol-darned old blatherskike
whose idears wasn't wuth hell-room.

At Zeke's suggestion, this was taken by consent. He
modestly demurred, however, when delegated to convey
this sentiment to his father-in-law, feeling that it would
have 'more weight' coming from someone else. The de-
corum of the board being slightly disturbed by this remark,
it grinningly adjourned to the hog-pen to inspect the new
'Poland-Chiny' sow that Abner had purchased at the recent
Whitley County Fair.

'Please, Mr. Schrofe,' pleaded Julia, next morning, after
Abner, delighted to have an official errand at the school-
house, had told her he was on his way to settle Mr. Ditzler's
hash, 'leave him to me. Don't hurt him. I'll think of some
way to accomplish the same thing without humiliating
him.'

Ham, already silenced by a hint from Zeke to the effect
that if he knowed which side his bread was buttered on he
would let up on the Miller girl, bewilderedly accepted her
invitation to make a little talk to the school on the afternoon of Columbus Day, on which occasion he astounded
himself and the assembled mothers by confessing the difficulty that an old-timer has in a-keepin' up with th' march o'
progress.

An able craftsman of home-made philosophy, Ham spent
many meditative hours evolving what he thought was a

brand-new theory for the achievement of this here thing they calls success, chattering so volubly about his discovery that it became a community joke.

His convictions on this subject were never better expressed than on the late afternoon of an eventful day in May when, riding home from a service at the Oak Grove Baptist Church in company with Zeke and Lola and their swollen-eyed little daughter Goldie, Ham observed:

'It all goes fer t' show that this here thing they calls success is the fruit of self-confidence.

'If yuh know yer bigger 'n' yer job, and c'n drop the dang thing whenever yuh like and do somethin' better, the people yer a-workin' fer seems t' know it without yer a-tellin' 'em. They take orders as if they was a-spoke by Jehovah, so long as they know yuh know there's sumethin' in prospec' fer yuh a dang sight more important than a-foolin' away yer time with the likes o' them!

'If a teacher, f'rinstance, thinks he's got about all that's a-comin' to him, and has to mind his p's and q's er the Board'll set on him, he just natcherly has t' whale hell outa the brats to make 'em behave.

'If he c'n get along without rules er whips er threatenin's, it's because th' scholars knows that he don't have t' care a tinker's dam whether he keeps his job er not, seein' he c'n leave 'em, if they don't like it, and do somethin' better.... And I bet that's the secret o' success in all th' walks o' life, in ev'ry day an' generation.'

Ham leaned far out of the open surrey, where he shared the back seat with Goldie, and improved his impaired articulation by relieving himself of a large quid of tobacco, wiped his stubbly lips with the back of a brown hand, and continued:

'You take this here parson, over in Wayne, what's been a-sayin' lately that th' story about Jonah ain't so, d'yuh reckon they'd let him stay there and be as honest as that if they didn't know the hull town knows as how he's had an invite to a big church in Chicago? Not by a dang sight!

They just grin when he goes after the Old Testyment fer
a-sayin' that th' Lord God drownded all them heathens fer
spite... 'cause they know that if they holler he'll tell 'em t'
take their danged ol' church b' th' bell-clapper, 'n' go t'
hell!'

'Sh! — Pap!' admonished Lola, without turning. 'What
kinda talk... right afore little Goldie, too!'

'Well — I wisht I'd a-heared some talk like that when I
was about her size,' muttered Ham, remorsefully. 'Mebby
I'd amounted to somethin'.'

'I wonder,' inquired Zeke, 'why didn't this here smart
preacher in Wayne take that there bigger job in Chi?'

Ham was fidgety with eagerness to explain.

'Now yer a-gettin' to it! That just goes fer t' show how
smart this feller is! If he went to Chicago, where mebby
he'd be exac'ly the size of his job, er mebby a little smaller, he wouldn't be able t' tell 'em where t' get off at. He
likes a-bein' where he c'n tell 'em, if they object t' his
preachin', that they c'n take their danged ol' church b' th'
bell-clapper,'n' ——'

'Pap — that'll do now!' snapped Lola, adding, growl-
ingly, 'Can't we never talk about nothin' else but things as
riles Pap and makes him swear, right afore little Goldie?'

'All th' same,' finished Ham, doggedly reverting to his
original proposition, 'if Julia Miller hadn't 'lowed, all th'
time she was a-teachin', that she was a-goin' away purty
soon t' be a rich man's wife, I bet she'd a-had t' lam them
sassy young rake-hells all over th' schoolhouse, five times a
day!'

Little Goldie wept noisily.

'Shet up, Pap!' commanded Lola. 'Hain't yuh got no
proper feelin's at all?'

* * * * * * *

Sometimes, during those early autumn days, Julia's happiness almost suffocated her. As often, it terrified her. Was
Martha's grim and hateful philosophy correct? Did people

always have to pay the piper? Was this ecstasy the sort of thing you inevitably had to settle for with interest compounded?

Sudden waves of black depression briefly but increasingly inundated her dream-world. Was she living in a fool's paradise? Would the clock presently strike twelve, and send the prancing horses scampering back to rejoin their fellow-mice? Nonsense! She must pull out of this! How silly! Was ever anyone more fortunate than she?

She became very sensitive on the subject of her happiness, eager to keep her radiant spirits within bounds so that Fate would at least give her credit for all the humility and gratitude she would muster. Diligently occupied with the unaccustomed task of disciplining her emotions, sternly warning them to keep their distance from her eyes, her lips, her voice, her hands and feet, Julia was unaware of the outward effect of these suppressions.

'Julia has growed up, almost overnight,' muttered old Ferd.

'Who'd a-thought that Julia Miller would age so fast?' remarked Mrs. Abner Schrofe. 'She's a *woman!*'

The effect of Julia's self-discipline in the cause of propitiating Nemesis was an unconscious exhibition of that magnetic and covetable type of personal poise not to be had cheaper than at the price of a stoical imprisonment of kinetic energy bruising its fists against the bars and pleading for its right to shout and dance and sing.

Eager to offer any forfeit to fend off the Day of Judgment, Julia had decided to room and board at home, involving a daily tramp of nearly six miles. It was a very real sacrifice, in anticipation; for, in looking forward to her new work, its most alluring promise had been the escape it offered from an irksome home environment.

School had been in progress barely a week, however, before Julia began to doubt the efficacy of her splendid sacrifice. The atmosphere at home had improved. The boys were shaving now, every other day, in honor of the young

school-mistress who appeared at their breakfast-table
trimly clad for her day's work. Susan and Greta crimped
their hair, starched their aprons, and conceded the boarder
a right to the exclusive use of her own trinkets. Her father's
gratitude for the money she had engaged to pay touched her.
Martha's awkward tenderness and solicitude slightly embarrassed her. What a difference a little money made in the
general line-up of human relations! Julia smiled, with new
understanding, over the story that had gone the rounds
about Widow Mercer, who lived near Bippus, ten miles
east.

Mr. Mercer, an enthusiastic Maccabee, had left her Two
Thousand Dollars in fraternal insurance. There were four
sons, all concerned that this large fortune should not be dis-
sipated. They suggested that their mother divide the money
among them, and spend her time living in their homes as an
honored guest.

'No,' she had replied, quietly. ''Pears to me like an
elderly lady with Two Thousand Dollars would be a much
more interestin' guest than an old woman with nothin'.'

It made all the difference in the world, money did!

One day you were 'Julia?... Julia!... *Julia!!* Come here,
this instant, like I told yuh, and peel these potatoes!'

One short week later you were 'Julia, you just let Susan
peel them potatoes, and you go set down till supper's ready.'

Nor was this refreshing change at home Julia's chief
ground for satisfaction. She was grateful for the opportunity to be alone, two hours daily, with her enchanting
memories and high expectations. The vigorous walk quickened her imagination. Fully a third of the trip to school was
taken through tall timber on a picturesque wagon-road that
negligently waived the right o' way to close-meshed clumps
of flaming sumac, and an occasional obdurate oak — a narrow ribbon of a road, carpeted with freshly fallen leaves
frost-sensitized to autumnal rays filtered through the live-
lier half of the prism, and crisp under her nimble feet.

On the return journey, Julia was always the school-teacher, it being part of her discipline to restrict her thoughts to her professional obligations.

On the early morning trip, however, she was all Zandy's! Her capacity increased for the vivid recovery of her deliriously happy experiences with him. To the very minutia of detail, Julia reconstructed every tone, posture, and gesture associated with those dreamy, unreal afternoons under the shade of the river-willows behind the Baptist Cemetery, not more than a dozen yards from her mother's grave, and the few almost painfully rapturous hours that had transfigured dull and dusty little Albion into the City Delectable!

The first half-mile of the out-bound trip, which brought her to the Baptist Church, where she turned to the left on the busy Larwill Pike, was invariably taken, at that early hour, without encountering any traffic, either on foot or wheel.

Except for the shrill scream of some excited water-bird on the river, and the lonesome clangor of a cow-bell registering the impatience of horns entangled in a wild grapevine down in the glen, there would be no sound but the rhythmic crunch of frosty gravel under her competent heels.

Julia's precious recollections proceeded in orderly sequence. Sometimes — let her do her utmost to concentrate on the opening chapter of the almost incredible story — her memory would insist on turning whole handfuls of pages; but, tugging herself free of the culminating episodes that mattered most, she would pursue events chronologically. She always wanted to be through with the early part of the story before she reached the busier mile of pike, for the full enjoyment of their first encounter demanded a few merry roulades of bantering laughter — her own: Zandy had been so serious. And, besides, she liked to be in the thick of the dark woods when she arrived at the Albion part of it!... Dear, dear Zandy! How tender! How precious!

Julia's reminiscences always began at the fence where they had met on the morning of her birthday. Now they were ambling slowly through the grove. They had left the path, and were wandering toward the river. She was still en route to the Post Office, but they were off the path.

'You have a first name, too?' (I have told him mine.)

'Alexander.'

'Quite long and dignified.' (I think I must not do that, any more. He doesn't like teasing. He is so serious.)

'So was my grandfather. It was his name. Everyone calls me Zandy. My sister began it when she was a little tot, and I was a baby.'

'Do they call you Zandy at Dartmouth, too?'

'Mmm.' (Zandy says 'Mmm' when he means yes; not 'Umm-humm,' the way our people do. Martha thinks it queer when I say 'Mmm.') 'College students are not very formal. Even the profs have nicknames.'

'Do they know it?'

'In time. They don't seem to care. We had a big Scot in Math, last year, with an enormous mustache. He discovered that he was "The Walrus," and pared it down. When that didn't help, he shaved it off.'

'And then he wasn't a walrus, any more?'

'Oh, yes, he was still a walrus.... I say, Julia, I'm going to like you, most awfully.' (I knew, then, that it was true. Zandy was going to like me. He couldn't have said it, that way, and not mean it.)

'What is your sister's name?' (I think it better we should talk about his sister. I'm afraid my face is red, and my heart is just pounding!)

'Alison.... She's married.'

'Does she live in Cincinnati, too?'

'She lives in a Pullman car. Her husband is Roland Forsythe.'

'The famous tenor?'

'Mmm... and tanker.'

'You mean he drinks?'

'Like a fish.'

'Is that why your sister goes along?'

'Exactly — but Alison doesn't mind. She likes excite-ment. And she thinks Providence has appointed her to keep a great artist sober. She married him for that.'

'And she can't?'

'Not much of the time.'

'But how can he sing?'

'You don't have to be sober to sing! A good many people never do sing unless they're ——'

'It doesn't always work that way. Some people get glum and mean.'

'Roland doesn't. He's mean when he's sober. But it'll get him, some day. Leaky heart.'

'How I hate it!' (I almost tell him why, for he's sure to find out.)

Now they had reached the gate at the farther side of the woods, and Julia had climbed it, leaving Zandy to wait her return from the Post Office. She had discouraged his going along, reluctant to amuse the loafers who would be sitting in front of Eph Mumaugh's blacksmith shop.... Now she was back.

'Look, Zandy!' (How natural it seemed to call him Zandy.) 'I've got a school! — the Shrofe one! — the one I wanted!' (He takes the letter, and our hands touch.)

'Writes like a ten-year-old boy, doesn't he?'

'He probably never went to school much.'

'I'll bet he can multiply bushels by dollars.' (We are down at the river, again, sitting on the grass.)

'That's where I'm weak... figures. I think algebra's awful!' (I tell him all about having to go to Albion for the Institute.)

'I'll help you. It's easy.... Explain it to you in an hour.'

'Will you, honestly?' (Zandy gives my hand a little pat. That was the first time.)

'This afternoon!'

'But I mustn't take your time. You'll be busy!'

'What would I be busy at? It'll save my life.' (His father is sore at him because he's decided to be a writer, instead of making nails, and he's changed his course in college, and his father has sent him to the country, all summer, as a punishment, instead of taking him along to Europe, as he had promised.)

* * * * * *

Most of the early part of the story would have been covered by the time Julia reached the woods. She had walked rapidly on the pike, and could afford to take the rest of the trip more leisurely.

Now they were sitting on the river-bank behind the Baptist Cemetery. It was Thursday, late afternoon. They had known each other three days. She was reclining against the bole of a maple, using the opened algebra to protect her back from the rough bark. Zandy had just finished reading her the *Rubáiyát*. What a wonderful voice he had! So tender! Her eyes were wet.

'Let me have it a minute. I want to see that verse about ——' She reached for the book.

He took her hand.

'Anybody would know at a glance, Julia, that you were meant for some kind of creative art.'

'How would they?'

'Your thumb!'

'What's funny about my thumb?' she had asked, searching his deep-set, gray-green eyes.

'Bends back so far.... Open your hand, dear.... Wide.... See?'

'Does yours?... Let me look.... Why, the very idea!... Is that what makes you think you can write?... Our hands are very much alike, aren't they?'

A little shiver of excitement always came over Julia when she reached this part of the story.

'We're alike in more ways than that, precious!'

She had made a little effort to retrieve her hands. Zandy had taken both of them in one of his. When he kissed her, she did not resist. How everlastingly right it seemed! She had shared his kiss, a bit clumsily. They were both quite stampeded for a moment. She hoped he would kiss her again: perhaps she could do better. It was rather embarrassing to feel that one had been so awkward. She had done much better, the next time, maybe because it was not so hurried.... Zandy's kisses! They made your heart so big there wasn't room in your chest to breathe!

He had walked back with her, that day, until they could see the chimney of her house. When she stopped, meaning that he mustn't come any farther, he said, 'What are you doing, tonight?'

* * * * * *

It proved to be an eventful evening. Julia volunteered to accompany Martha to prayer-meeting. At the door of the church, however, she said, 'I think I'll run over to the Post Office, first.... I've a letter that should be mailed to Albion, about my room, you know.'

'I thought you had did that,' said Martha. 'You'll not be back afore meetin' is out!'

But Martha seemed relieved. Julia knew that her sister preferred not to have other members of the family present when she testified to the submissiveness of her burden-bearing. It reflected no credit on her home, where, it was implied, she took all the hard knocks with little to show for them but a chastened spirit.

'You'll not go through them dark woods, will yuh?' Martha cautioned. Julia promised.

Zandy was waiting for her, by the fence where she had first met him. He kissed her lips, her eyes, her hair.... They were made for each other, weren't they?... They would plan to spend their lives together.... Why not?... Didn't she love him?...

Someone was blowing out the malodorous kerosene lamps in the church when Julia returned across the stubble-field with Zandy, the shrill rendition of 'God Be With You Till

We Meet Again' warning them their tryst was over. They stopped in the darkness for a final embrace.

'It won't be long now, sweetheart.'

'Oh, Zandy; I'm so happy!'

The little group on the church porch was separating, Martha's prim voice conspicuous above the others.

They walked home almost in silence, Martha mentally putting into rehearsal the testimony she meant to give, next time; Julia wondering what Martha would be saying if she knew that Zandy Craig was going along with her to Albion where they were to be *married!*

Late in the night, Julia, wide-awake but calm, wondered if she were playing the game squarely with everybody; with her father, with Martha, with Zandy's father, who made nails and was so gruff and domineering; with Zandy's mother, who already had a girl selected for him.... But, as Zandy had said, they had their own lives to live. Her father, her sister, his father, his mother — had they not been given a chance to live their lives, as they liked?... Maybe not.... It was all very confusing. Life was complicated.

'We will do what our hearts tell us is exactly right, darling,' Zandy had said. 'Nobody in the world has a right to keep us apart. We will keep it a secret, now, but, one of these days, when they see how happy we are, and how right it all was, they will be glad.'

* * * * * * *

Old Ferd remarked at supper, one Saturday evening in early November, that he had met Abner Schrofe, that afternoon.

'Ab says,' reported Ferd, proudly, 'that Julia is the best teacher they ever had. I'm a-goin' to tell her when she comes down. It's no more 'n' right she should hear it.... What's a-keepin' her?'

'She's been a-lyin' down most o' th' afternoon, paw,' said Martha. 'I'm afeard that long walk every day is a-pullin'

Julia down, now it's come rainy. She hasn't looked good fer quite a spell.'

'She was a-cryin' when I looked in to call her t' supper,' said Greta. 'Funny fer Julia to be a-cryin'.'

'I'll go up,' said Martha. 'Here, Susan, dish them turnips.'

Julia recognized her sister's step on the stairs, raised up on one elbow, dabbed at her eyes with a soggy little handkerchief, tucked a letter under her pillow.

'No — I'm quite all right, Martha. Working pretty hard, you know. Just... sort of unstrung. No — I don't believe I could eat a bite; not now. Maybe, after a while. Run along. It's nothing.'

Martha clumped down the stairs, and the letter was unfolded again.

'What a misfortune, darling, if things are as you fear. If it had happened a little later — wouldn't we have been glad? Maybe it isn't that. Try not to worry.

'All one hears about now is the big game with the Chicago Athletic Club on Thanksgiving. Father and mother are coming East for it. How I wish you could be here! Big doings!

'If it's what you think, darling, can you go on, a little while, as if nothing had happened? How long? Maybe I can have a heart-to-heart with my father. But he's pretty hard, you know. Savage old thing, when disappointed. I'm afraid he'd take me out of college. That would set us back. If I can get through this year, the rest will be easy.'

* * * * * *

Julia had fainted at the Friday afternoon program with which school closed for the Christmas holidays. The room was packed with visitors and stuffy with festal decorations. When the exercises were all but over, Julia crumpled in a pathetic heap on the floor. Young Jason Schrofe, whose attentions she had regarded so casually that he had quite lost hope, drove her home in his sleigh.

'That settles it,' said old Ferd. 'She's not a-goin' to tramp through them snowdrifts any more.... You must find a place to board, Julia, closer by th' school.'

She smiled wanly and shook her head. She would be all right. No use wasting the money.

She had hoped that the cruel exertion might... somehow ... solve the problem. In any event, the long walk daily helped to distract her mind. She might go mad, otherwise. ... How long would it be until people noticed?... What would those all-knowing young mothers think of her fainting?... How much torture could she stand in these cruel stays?

'It fairly breaks my heart, darling,' Zandy had written. 'There you are, worrying your dear little head off; and here I am, starting home for the holidays, unable to bear even a wee bit of your trouble... and discomfort, too, I suppose. I don't know much about such things.'

'The dear boy,' thought Julia. 'He doesn't know, of course. He probably thinks a woman just knows it's going to happen, on a certain day, and — when the time comes — it happens. And I don't know much more about it, except that I'm afraid I can't keep it a secret much longer... not even for Zandy's dear sake.'

* * * * * *

Zandy was in line for the Perkins Medal in oratory. On no account must that event be jeopardized.... Could Julia, he wondered, manage to carry on until the oratorical contest was over? February third, it was. How about it, Julia, darling?

Julia would certainly try. Zandy must not be disqualified for that medal. Perhaps his father would be that much more kind, if he won it. But, dear boy, let's arrange to tell them the very minute the contest is over! It's getting serious! Please!

It so happened that on the very night when Zandy was laboriously composing a letter which began, 'My dear

Father Miller (for I really want to call you Father Miller, because your Julia is my wife; though I'm afraid you will be annoyed, a little, that we haven't told you earlier about our wedding)' — Greta had whispered to Susan, and Susan, white-faced, had whispered to Martha, and Martha, trembling with fear and indignation, had entered Julia's room without knocking.

Julia was outstretched, her dark-circled eyes were closed, her hands lay supine, palms upward, on the counterpane. Martha looked at her for a long time before she spoke. She swallowed, noisily.

'You might as well make a clean breast of it,' said Martha, hoarsely.

Julia opened her eyes and smiled.

'In the drawer of my desk, Martha. Here's the key. That long paper. That's it. My marriage license.'

'So you run off and got married, did yuh?'

'Well — not exactly... run off. We were married during the County Institute.'

'And you was in Albion, a-livin' with a man, while we thought you was a-goin' to that school that cost all o' Thirty Dollars!'

'He was my husband — and it was my money.'

'Humph! He don't seem to set much store by yuh... a-leavin' yuh to face the music. What's his name?' Martha adjusted her steel-bowed spectacles, and stooped under the lamp. 'Alexander Craig... who's that? You don't mean t' say it's that rich Craig's boy what was here last summer a-visitin' at the Squire's?'

Julia nodded.

'It's a heap the Craigs would do fer a Miller! You wait til your father hears o' this. He'll make that young rascal sweat! He'll have th' law on him!'

So — at long last, Julia had no further need to punish her desperately ill-treated body. Ungirded — physically, mentally — she felt that her worst troubles were behind her. They could say what they liked, they could do what they would — she had made her last agonizing trip to the school-house. There was some comfort in that, at least.

Old Ferd was torn between grief and anger. He wanted to pour out his rage without delay. He would write to that lousy whelp and tell him, for once, what somebody should have told him long ago — that he was a low-lived coward, a dirty blackguard, and — and — if he ever darkened their door, except to bring the money to pay for Julia's sickness, he would be pitched out!... And he did write that, and more, pounded a stamp on the envelope with a fist that looked amazingly like Julia's, only not so white, and stalked, half-blind with hate, to the Post Office, where he was regarded with fresh interest, the loafers in corduroy coats and felt boots noting his state of mind and winking at one another out of the tails of their eyes. He was aware of it. Everybody knew, damn them!... There was a letter for Julia. She always got the mail, herself.... He would tear it up, and throw it in the river. The sleety gale sobered him, somewhat, on the way home. He did not destroy the letter.

* * * * * *

'A couple of years from now, darling,' wrote Zandy, a week later, 'we will have forgotten all about this. At the moment, things do look pretty dark, don't they? I was all ready to come when I had the letter from your father. He is in a great temper; hardly to be blamed, of course; talked of shooting. Anyone else but your father, I would debate that subject with him. But all I could do for you now would be to stir up a tremendous row and probably make everything more difficult for you.

'I postponed writing to my father until last Saturday; couldn't think up just the right way to approach the matter. He is always so autocratic and hair-triggery. I did the best I could to make him see things. There is a wire from him this afternoon, hundred words, saying he is done with me. That, of course, only means he is very sore. He may come around all right. But not very soon. You have no idea how stubborn he can be

'So — meantime, I can't stay in school. My mind is too upset, anyway. I shall be out of funds, too. In fact, I'm out of funds now. The month's allowance is just due, and he isn't even going to send that. I've made up my mind to bum my way through to the Coast. This twenty is all the money I have but five dollars. You can depend on me to send you some more as soon as I have it. Don't be discouraged, dear. I intend to succeed. Success is more a gift than an achievement. Some people are born to succeed. I am one of them. You will share. Keep that in mind through these hard days. I shall soon send for you, and we will be happy together forever.'

* * * * * *

With confidence unshaken, for there was a peculiar contagion associated with Zandy's optimism that gave her courage, Julia watched the last of the snow disappear.

Everything was going to come out all right, as Zandy had predicted. He had started West to find work and make a little home. Then he would send for her... for *them!*

Every few days there came another postal card... from Detroit, Chicago, Davenport, Denver, Spokane. Zandy was on the way.

Presently the lilacs were opening, and the air was vibrant with the hum of all sorts of awakened winged things. Julia could hear the occasional scream of her father's chisel doing a shrill aria to the accompanying rumble of the big wooden fly-wheel.

'Poor old darling,' she thought, tenderly. 'He's worried about me, and trying to keep his hands busy... dear, shaky, old hands.'

'What's father making, Martha?'

'Will yuh let on yer surprised when he gives it t' yuh?'

'Mmm — but maybe you'd better not tell me if it's a secret.'

'A little cradle,' whispered Martha. 'Mind yuh don't let on.'

Julia wept a few happy tears. Her father had forgiven her, then. That was ever so much better. It would come out all right, as Zandy had said.

When Doctor Engle came, next day, he was shortly after joined by Doctor Marshall, a specialist from Fort Wayne. Jason Shrofe had driven him up from Larwill.

Doctor Marshall had quiet blue eyes and wore a brown suit that fitted him. He did not talk much, and hardly asked any questions at all. Julia had great confidence in him and felt no shyness in his strong, competent hands.

The charge was twenty-five dollars, and when Julia had counted it out — after Doctor Engle had handed her the pocket-book from her desk — she was pleased to find that there was just enough; a twenty, a two, and three ones. Doctor Marshall looked at the money and the empty pocket-book, and said not to bother about paying it until she was well. He would send her a bill, some day.

'Thank you,' said Julia, gratefully. 'I'll pay you as soon as I'm up.'

'That will be soon enough,' said Doctor Marshall.

Martha came and sat on the edge of the bed, after the doctors were gone, holding Julia's throbbing fingers. Martha had shown the doctors out, and Julia had heard them talking, downstairs, for a disturbingly long time. Martha's face, always an open book, was troubled. It twitched, as it did when she was worried.

'What is it, Martha? You talked to them. Do they think I'm very sick? They don't think I'm going to — they don't think maybe I'm not going to get well, do they?' Julia's words came slowly, and as from a considerable distance.

Martha pressed her bony knuckles hard against her cheek and swayed slowly back and forth.

'They're a-doin' everythin' they knows how, Julia. We must all put our trust in th' Lord 'n' His precious promises.... Can't yuh let yerself just rest on His Blessed Name?'

Julia turned her face away and stared hard at the white wall, her eyes wide, frightened.

'Would yuh like Brother Miner t' come over from Cromwell 'n' talk t' yuh, Julia? It might be quite comfortin'.'

Julia shook her head, and there was a little convulsive shudder of her shoulders. Sighing audibly, Martha drew up the sheet over the quivering shoulders, laid the back of her rough hand against the hot neck, and quietly left the room.

A violent storm was rising in Julia's breast — a devastating tornado of rebellion. Why had Fate played this ghastly trick on her? What had she ever done to earn this dull tragedy? What chance had she had from the beginning? Why had Destiny set her down in this stupid house — her mother a whining fool, her father a shabby old drunkard, her brothers and sisters nothing but clods and dolts?

And that wasn't the worst of it! Fate had opened the door a little way and pointed toward liberty. Love — great love — had come! Why hadn't Fate left her to the tiresome little drudgeries that were the common lot of people badly born? Why this mocking glimpse of freedom?

In her broken-dyked passion, Julia's scorn swept over everything and everybody associated with her disaster. Her father! What right had this drunken old man and his slatternly wife to bring her into the world at all? And this smug, surly, ignorant, superstititious old sister — calmly inviting her, in this hour of break-up, to like it!... to put her trust in the Lord! Mighty little He cared! Nobody cared! Least of all — the Lord! If He saw it, at all, He probably grinned! Another good joke! — saith the Lord.

Martha was back now, seated again on the edge of the bed, wetting her thumb and leafing the thin pages of a book. Julia dully turned her eyes and recognized the cheap little Bible she had earned for faithful attendance at Sunday School when she was nine or ten. Martha was doubtless hunting for some more of those precious promises. What a dull, uninteresting old thing those precious promises had made of her!

Clearing her throat and settling her spectacles more firmly on her thin nose, Martha held up the Bible at an angle that would better the light on the fine print.

'No, please, Martha,' muttered Julia. 'Not now — please!'

'I'll just leave it here, then,' said Martha, regretfully. 'Mebby it'll be a sort o' comfort just t' have it under yer pillow.'

She was gone now, leaving Julia with the precious promises within easy reach. But the storm was by no means spent. With white-knuckled little fists and tightly clenched teeth, rigid lips wide apart, Julia stared up defiantly. In a moment she gave way to the passionate indignation that was all but driving her mad. The precious promises! Bah! ... God — and the Bible — and prayer — and the angels — and miracles — and faith that would remove mountains! Bah!... She groped under the pillow, clutched the book, opened it in the middle, utterly blind with hot tears and crazed with desperate anger, and began to claw at the pages with her nails. She buried all her fingers in the book, and tore, and ripped, and crumpled, making snarling little mutterings deep in her throat.

'*That!... and that!... for You!*' she panted. (Rip!) '*And that!... and this!... for Your...* (Crunch!)... *precious ...promises!... Look!... if You can see... You cruel Thing ...what I'm doing to your Holy Word!... Now! There!... send me to hell!*'

Completely spent by her exertion, Julia lay as one dead under the litter of ragged, crumpled desecration, her shuddering sobs all but subsided; and, fatigued beyond endurance, drifted away from the shameful scene, and slept.

When she woke there was a dim light burning on the table. Her father was sitting on the low rocking-chair by the bed, elbows on knees, his fingers tangled in his shaggy gray hair. Remembering dully, she felt about on the counterpane. Nothing there. So it was only a bad dream, after all. That was good. Her fingers touched a rumpled

scrap of paper. It was not a dream. She laid her hand on
the torn paper and closed on it.

Roused by her stirring, Ferd glanced up, and their eyes
met. Julia's were inquisitive.

Ferd shook his head, and smiled wanly.

'It's all right, Julia. I cleared it up. Nobody seen it.
Guess you was a little out o' yer mind fer a spell.'

'I'm dreadfully sorry, father,' she murmured, penitently.
'It was... an awful thing to do.'

Old Ferd caressed the white hand nearest him. With the
other, Julia absently rolled the fragment she had found into
a tight little ball.

She fell to wondering whether there was anything still
legible on the scrap; and, if so, whether it would be some
frightful forecast of doom for sinners. Well — she deserved
it, didn't she? She recalled her curiosity about the sentimental mottoes that came on thin, narrow, sticky strips of
paper wrapped around cheap taffy at the County Fair....
Funn⸍ how people took stock in the silly fortunes told that
way.... She remembered a discussion between Martha and
Becky Slemmer, one day, over the 'messages' they had
had by tossing the Bible open at random and reading the
first verse at the top of the page.... Martha had come by
many a precious promise accidentally... poor Martha....
Becky had laughed over some of hers, and Martha had
hush-hushed her, warningly. Becky said you couldn't make
much out of it, anyway. One time, after a big quarrel with
Zelma in which they had bit, scratched, and pulled hair,
she had gone to the Bible for guidance, and the magic verse
at the top of the column said, 'She is loud and stubborn.'
Becky was sure, at first, that the Lord referred to her sister,
but she wondered afterward. Martha said: 'No — Becky.
The Lord wouldn't send a message t' Zelma through you.
He must 'a' meant somethin' personal.'

'Shall I get yuh a cold drink, Julia?' Ferd was inquiring.

'Please, father... and turn up the light a little, won't you,
before you go down?'

*　*　*　*　*　*

'You're ever so much better this morning,' said Doctor Engle, cheerily.

Julia smiled contentedly, and nodded.

'You're overcoming this toxine, Julia.'

'What's toxine, doctor?' she inquired, interestedly.

'Poison.'

'Yes,' said Julia, thoughtfully, 'I have overcome it.'

'Well — maybe not all of it yet,' he cautioned, stroking his cheek, 'but ——'

Julia's dry lips puckered determinedly, and she nodded her head with an air of deep conviction.

'All of it,' she said, firmly, 'all the poison is gone.'

That afternoon, to Martha's astonishment and disapproval, Julia demanded pen, ink, paper, and privacy. Protestingly, the weary and worried woman propped her sister up with pillows, and closed the door.

Summoning all her depleted energy, Julia wrote a long letter addressed to her unborn child. The writing was uneven and sprawling, and the lines sagged at the right end, more and more, until the last ones ran nearly off the pages in a pitiful little toboggan toward the corner.

Everything she knew about Dresden was in it; high pride for the things that were Dresden; high hopes for the heir to the Dresden tradition.

Everything she knew about Zandy was in it; poor, bewildered Zandy, so frightfully misunderstood, and showing up so badly when he really had it in his heart to do the right thing.

'I'm going to hide this letter, and hope that you find it some day, in case anything happens to me. You'll not find it, perhaps, until you're big enough to want to take things to pieces and see how they were put together. I hope you won't find it even then. I hope you won't find it until you're old enough to have had a few harder bumps than just falling out of your cradle.

'I've discovered a secret. It's going to take me through what I have to face. If I live, it's going to make me over

into something else than I've been. If I die, I'll die happy.
I'm going to tell you what I've found. It's the only thing
I have to leave you. If you'll take it, and make use of it,
you may need no other fortune.'

It was a difficult letter to write. The uncanny experience
that had been hers, during the preceding eighteen hours,
was not easy to explain. But Julia did the best she could,
and with the last physical resource left from the fatigue of
writing, she groped her way dizzily to the little walnut desk,
with a great effort opened the secret drawer, deposited her
letter, and returned to her bed, exhausted.

* * * * * *

After her grinding agony was over, Julia slept, and woke,
and slept, and dreamed.

In the late afternoon, she became slightly delirious.
Martha caught fragments of it, and wept quietly.... Roses
overhanging a trellis at the doorway of a little bungalow...
Zandy being welcomed with outstretched arms that quickly
fell inert from fatigue.... Then — there was a garden...
a high, gray, stone wall... and in the wall there was a door
... and beyond the door, a river.... Martha sobbed chok-
ingly, and turned the iced towel on the hot forehead.... And
on the river there was a punt... with a red and blue canopy
... and the sound of a tender voice, singing... and a guitar.

When she awoke again, it was almost dark. It was apparent to the watchers that Julia was mildly curious about
the presence of the whole family.

Doctor Engle was seated at the bedside with his fingers
on her wrist. Her father stood stiffly beside him, his hands
clenched. Martha slowly waved a palm-leaf fan, supporting
her weary weight on outspread fingers laid against the head
of the bed. Susan and Greta stood at the foot, staring wide-
eyed. Hiram and Elmer were in the doorway.

Julia's eyes slowly traveled over the group, finally coming
to rest on old Ferd whom she inspected with gravity. She
attempted a little smile for him — a solicitous little smile

that seemed to say, 'What a lot of trouble I'm making you. So sorry.' Ferd couldn't face the stiff little smile any longer; closed his eyes, walked to the window, wept.

Julia had kept her secret too long. Through hot, parched lips she asked Martha if she would please take care of the baby. Greta drew a sudden racking sob, and sank to the floor. Susan raised her up and tugged her out into the hall.

'His name,' murmured Julia, valiantly battling with the oncoming fog, 'is Alexander Ferdinand.... But — Martha — if that's too long a name... for such a little boy... you may call him Zandy.'

* * * * * *

It was late afternoon. They had just returned from the service at Oak Grove Baptist Church, and its sequel in the Cemetery. The long row of hitching-racks had been quite inadequate. Barely a third of the people had been able to enter the church.

Martha had whispered to the undertaker, and he had laid one of the sprays on their mother's grave, hard-by. Jason Schrofe, observing that his flowers had been chosen for this tribute, tarried, after the others had moved away, and replaced it.

Susan and Greta were busying themselves in the kitchen, sympathetically assisted by neighbors whose voices, restrained but endeavoring to be cheerful, drifted up the stairs where Martha, having laid her borrowed bonnet and veil on Julia's primly made, white-counterpaned bed, was stooping over the cradle.

Old Ferd tiptoed into the room, and Martha glanced up.

'Look at them long fingers,' she said. 'Like her'n.'

Ferd handed her a yellow envelope.

'One o' the Schrofe boys fetched this over from Cromwell.'

Martha opened it, read it through, silently, her lips forming the words, and gave it back. Ferd stared hard at the message from Seattle.

COURAGE DARLING IT WILL NOT BE LONG NOW
GOOD JOB   ZANDY

He tossed the telegram on Julia's bed, and stumbled out of the room, whimpering like a punished child.

* * * * * *

That night — as if the Millers had not already furnished enough sensation to satisfy the community — Ferd hanged himself from a rafter in the vacant stall next to Florrie.

Hiram had gone out to throw down some straw, and saw It, from the mow-ladder, slowly revolving. Martha, hearing a hoarse shout, ran from the kitchen and found her brother retching violently. It seemed a long time before they found a box high enough to stand on.

'I was a-feared o' this, all along,' groaned Martha.

Greta kept screaming, hysterically, while she tugged at the rope of the dinner-bell that clanged ominously from its perch on the roof of the milkhouse.

The barnyard filled with neighbors carrying lanterns. Milt Mumaugh volunteered to drive to Albion for the coroner, and put his three-year-old roan mare to a gallop.

It was a warm night, but they felt chilly and built a fire to sit by while they waited. About midnight, the wives of the watchers served sandwiches, cake, and coffee.

Abner Schrofe and Doc Engle sat on the doorstep of old Ferd's shop, smoking and slapping mosquitoes.

'Baby a-goin' t' live, Doc?'

'Looks like it.... Poor little devil.... Maybe better off if it died.... Not much of a future for it, I'm afraid.'

'Well — as fer that,' drawled Abner, 'yuh never c'n tell.'

CHAPTER III

'AND now, Ferdinand' — Reverend Miles Brumm pursed a public smile — 'perhaps you had better mount your new pony, and see how he sits.'

'Please, Uncle Miles, I don't want to.'

Ferdinand's voice was barely audible, but to the congregation assembled in the parsonage barn-lot there was no mistaking the determined shake of his curly head.

Consternation prevailed in the audience, composed of half the children in Zanesdale, and what Mr. Brumm would have considered on Sunday morning as 'a goodly company' of adults.

A medley of encouragement, ridicule, insufferable patronage, and downright contempt volleyed at the embarrassed boy.

'Aw, gwan! Ride him!' ... 'Don't be scairt of him, Ferdinand; he won't throw yuh!' ... 'He's yourn, hain't he? Git on 'im!' ... 'Shucks! — feared of a Shetland pony!' ... 'Yeah — tame as a kitten!'

Ferdinand hung his head, abstractedly crushed an ant with his bare toes, and was painfully conscious of the rapid beating of a bulging vein in his neck.

'Bet he cost a hundred dollars!' appraised Nathan Himes, who had joined the procession when it passed his drugstore.

'Hundred dollars!' scoffed Bill Trask, the station agent; 'that there saddle 'n' bridle cost more 'n' a hundred dollars!'

'My land!' exclaimed Sophie Trask, proudly relaying her husband's versatility to the huddle of women by the big gate, 'Mr. Trask says the saddle and bridle alone must 'a' cost more than a hundred dollars! What must the pony be worth?'

Nobody paid any attention to the comment except young Mrs. Himes (her as was one o' them Sheriff Effendorfer girls from over beyond Maples; so stuck up — all of 'em —

their noses was out o' joint), who, behind her hand, re-marked to Clara Sellars, the lately-from-Wayne peroxide-blonde milliner (less said the better), that the Trasks always knew so much, to which Miss Sellars replied, in a disgusted undertone, 'Don't they give yuh a pain?'

Mr. Brumm, aware of the unanimous curiosity about the pony, to which his young nephew had now added spice by his reluctance to exhibit a natural interest in it, felt himself in an awkward situation. He had been unprepared for the episode that had plunged his family into the public eye. No chance had been given him to collect his thoughts or confer with Ferdinand in private.

It was the lad's tenth birthday. At breakfast he had re-ceived a large, inexpensive pocket-knife from his uncle, a sticky, acrid-smelling, red-and-green *Child's Illustrated Bible* from his aunt, and three lead-pencils in a slim paste-board box from Angela.

He had put down the apple he was munching, and had gone about, as the custom was, dutifully kissing the donors — Uncle Miles, first; for Uncle Miles was always served first with whatever happened to be in distribution; and then Aunt Martha, who moistened a finger and brushed back the unruly lock that dipped to a point in the center; and then Angela, whom he tried to kiss on the cheek, for Angela's kisses were wet, and he had a disinclination toward them which he hoped she would realize, one of these days, without too much injury to her feelings.

At that mellow moment — for, however stiffly the family ties were habitually starched, there were festal occasions when something like spontaneous affection had its innings — there was a vigorous rap at the kitchen door. Straighten-ing his frayed cravat, Mr. Brumm had answered the sum-mons. A stranger's business-like voice was heard.

'Mr. Brumm? ... How do you do, sir? ... Very well, sir. ... My name is Thompson. I'm from Chicago; that is, I'm from the Winnetka Stock Farm. Our people has had orders to deliver a pony here for Master Craig ——'

Through the open door came the rumble of many voices. Angela wiped her shapely lips on her sleeve and hurried to the window. Ferdinand stared hard at Aunt Martha, listening intently.

'He lives with you, don't he? ... It's a birthday gift from his father. ... It's Mr. Craig's instructions from Seattle. ... I've just got in with it, expressed from our place in Winnetka. ... The pony's out here in your lot, delivered in good shape, as you'll see, and if you, or the young gentleman, will sign these papers, I can catch the nine-seventeen back to the city. ... Right here you are, sir, on that line; and here, too, if you please. Thanks! ... Quite a crowd we gathered up, coming through the village, eh? Guess it's the first time a pony ever came to this town on a passenger train.'

Aunt Martha had taken off her brown apron and joined her husband at the back door, nervously smoothing her hair with both hands.

Ferdinand, blinking rapidly, and tapping his front teeth with a restless thumb, squeezed past his aunt, and ventured out upon the back porch, quite overawed by the gathering crowd.

Uncle Miles, with a pumped-up air of heartiness, as if he himself were being presented with a thoroughbred Shetland pony by his admiring fellow-townsmen, breezed forth to the barnyard, delightedly intoning, 'Well — well — indeed! ... A great surprise, I'm sure! ... A pony! ... Well — well!'

It was the crowd that remembered the pony was Ferdinand's.

'Heigh! Ferdinand! Come on out! Look what yuh got!'

'Must I, Aunt Martha?' asked Ferdinand, his face twitching.

'Of course, silly!' shouted Angela, clutching his hand and dragging him along.

'Fancy that great big boy having to be tugged out of the house to see a pony!' scoffed Clara Sellars.

'He's only a kid,' explained Mrs. Himes. 'Awful big for his age; tall as his half-sister, and she must be all of fourteen. I s'pose he's just shy of so many people.'

Very much embarrassed, Ferdinand allowed himself to be propelled through the crowd. He drew a stiff, reluctant smile, reached out a slim hand, stroked the pony's velvet muzzle, and was generously rewarded for the tentative caress, the pony sniffing inquisitively at his pockets and licking his hands.

'Aw — look — ain't that cute?' The women cooed appreciatively, and beamed on Aunt Martha, who had joined them, murmuring apologies for her looks and all. They told her she looked quite all right, they were sure.

Miss Sellars, pretending interest in the half-finished sweater that Mrs. Himes was carrying under her arm, whispered, 'Did yuh ever see such an old frump?'

'Awful pious, I guess.'

'Can't people be pious without ——'

'No,' said Mrs. Himes, 'Sh! — Listen!'

'Well — Ferdinand ——' said Uncle Miles.

'No, Uncle Miles.' His deep-set, gray-green eyes were perplexed, and his face was contorted as he gnawed his lips. He stepped back, and glanced about as if looking for a way of escape.

Mr. Brumm wiped his brow with a large handkerchief. It would hardly do to send these parishioners of his away with so great a mystery to discuss.

'Don't you like your pony?' he stammered, in a tone that affected to express the general surprise.

'Of course!' Ferdinand's voice was husky under the strain. 'But I mustn't have it! I can't have it! You know why!' Hot tears sprang to his eyes, and he scurried through the speechless crowd, disappearing into the house.

'Ferdinand's a little nervous and excited,' explained Mrs. Brumm, primly, but obviously shaken by the unfortunate event. 'He wasn't expecting a pony, you know, and what with so many good friends coming along, and all ——'

'That's it — that's it,' said Mr. Brumm, who, upon Ferdinand's retreat, had moved toward his wife to learn what explanation she was offering for this strange conduct. 'Ferdinand will be quite himself, presently.'

'Yeah — I bet there's a skeleton in the Brumms' closet, all right, all right!' muttered Miss Sellars. 'They're badly fussed — both of 'em!'

* * * * * *

Ferdinand, face downward on his bed, could hear the children's excited shouts as they took turns riding the pony about the barn-lot. ... It sounded now as if they had taken him out into the road. 'Please let me next, Angela!' ... 'I said first, Angela!'... 'These stirrups is too high!'

He heard his uncle's heavy footsteps on the stairs.

'Now, my boy, what's the trouble?' Uncle Miles was serious.

Ferdinand stifled a racking sob.

'You know I can't take anything from *him!* ... Sure — I love the pony, and I want it awfully... but I wouldn't take anything from *him — not if he gave me a million trillion dollars!*'

'But you didn't have to show off like that before all our people! What do you suppose they'll think?'

'I don't care what they think,' growled Ferdinand into the damp pillow. 'It's none of their business, is it?'

'They'll make it their business to find out.'

Uncle Miles sat down on the edge of the bed, Ferdinand moving over with a great effort to make him room.

'You are a strange child, Ferdinand, to feel this way about your father.' Uncle Miles laid a hand on the twitching shoulder. 'I hardly thought it possible for a child of your years to be capable of as much hatred as you ——'

'But *you* hate him, don't you, Uncle Miles? Aunt Martha hates him!'

'Hate is an ugly word, Ferdinand. Neither your Aunt Martha nor I hate anybody in the whole wide world —· not even your erring father. Whatever mistakes he may have made in letting your young mother suffer and be misunderstood and maligned...and die...it will do you no good to carry a grudge — especially now that he wants to be friendly.'

At this, Ferdinand broke down completely, and cried piteously.

'He waited for ten years!...Not one word from him! ...Even if you and Aunt Martha did hate him, I kept hoping he would write to me when I got big enough to read. ...But I swore, last Christmas morning, I would hate him...forever!'

'On Christmas morning!' Uncle Miles was horrified. 'What a day to choose for a pledge to everlasting hate!'

'Good as any,' grumbled Ferdinand.

Uncle Miles took a turn or two up and down the room, tugging at his black burnsides.

'Well — if you're sure you don't want the pony' — Uncle Miles' tone was conciliatory — 'we'll sell it. Perhaps that would be more prudent, anyway. You've shown pretty good judgment for a small boy. We can't afford a pony, and our people know it. You would only make the other children envious. It's out of keeping with everything else we have. ... Suppose we sell the pony, and put the money in bank for your college education: how's that?'

'But — Uncle Miles!' — Ferdinand's voice rose shrilly. 'That's all the same, isn't it? I don't want anything he's got! I won't have his ponies, or saddles, or colleges, or anything! He same as killed my mother! Aunt Martha said so! I'm going to write and tell him so! You see if I don't!'

'Now — now!' soothed Uncle Miles. 'You wouldn't do that.'

He patted Ferdinand on the head and walked slowly out of the room and down the hall to his study, where he slumped into the shabby morris chair by the window and meditatively twisted the burnsides into pencil-points.

Every three months since his marriage to Martha Miller,

seven years ago, he had received a draft for two hundred
and fifty dollars from his prosperous brother-in-law. It
exceeded his salary.

Indeed, his decision to marry Martha Miller — which he
tried later to tell himself was based on the fact that she,
albeit unsightly and eccentric, was an excellent housekeeper, a paragon of piety, and singularly devoted to his
motherless little Angela — had been hastened upon her
confiding to him that the baby Ferdinand was something
other than a liability.

'It's very sacrificial of you, Miss Miller,' he had said,
that April afternoon on his return to the Miller home for a
brief glimpse of Angela, who, since the revival he had conducted at the Oak Grove Baptist Church in November, had
been happily in Martha's care — 'it's very fine of you to
have assumed, so cheerfully, the burden of your unfortunate sister's child: very unselfish, indeed!'

Martha had smiled, cryptically.

'I must be honest with yuh, Brother Brumm. Of course,
I would 'a' took care o' Julia's baby, like I promised, even if
young Craig had disowned it. ... But — he remembers.'

'Indeed?... Does him credit, I must say. ... Does he remember substantially, may I ask, Miss Martha?'

'Two hundred and fifty every quarter.' Martha seemed
satisfied with the effect of her announcement. 'Reg'lar as
the clock.'

'A thousand dollars a year, Martha, for the keep of a
baby?'

Martha nodded, smiled, folded her arms, rocked gently.

'I had a promise from Craig' — she leaned forward and
lowered her voice confidentially — 'shortly after our poor
Julia passed away. He had wrote a-sayin' was there anything he could do, though at the minute he hadn't much to
do with, he said, and I reckon that was true. ... Give the
devil his due, I always say ——'

'I'm sure you would, Martha!'

He recalled Martha's prompt reaction to the note of

tenderness in his voice. She had smiled appreciatively, puckered her lips self-deprecatingly, touched her hair, rather gingerly; for it was the first time she had done it up over a rat — not one of the larger rats, to be sure, such as the bulky Susan affected; a mere mouse, indeed, compared to Susan's — and was obviously not quite at ease with her graying foretop so heavily shadowing her eyes.

'But — and so — then —— Oh, yes; then I wrote him as how poor Julia had gave me th' baby t' bring up, and that I meant t' do so, well as I could. If he ever wanted t' send me anything toward its keep, all well and good, I said, but the baby was mine. I told him as how it was Julia's last words, and it was, almost. I asked him t' promise he would never try t' take little Alexander away from me, or even write to him when he grew big enough t' understand; fer it might make him discontented and all... *and he promised!*'

'Alexander? I thought the child's name was Ferdinand.'

'Well, you see Julia had wrote a letter, a couple o' days afore she died, and if the baby was a boy it was to be Alexander. So Craig always calls him Alexander. ... We just couldn't; not after what he'd done, 'n' all. ... Anyways, that's the baby's other name.'

Mr. Brumm had proposed marriage to Martha, that evening, and had been accepted with a coyness he had hardly suspected her capable of in the face of her nun-like, ascetic piety.

On the day of their wedding in December — Mr. Brumm had just returned aglow over the quite brilliant success of his three weeks' revival at Partridge Crossing, Illinois — certain small items of business were under discussion. He and Martha were out walking in the snow on the highway, safe from the hostile curiosity of the family in whose opinion that slick feller Brumm was a-tryin' t' lay his miracle-workin' hands on th' baby's money, an indictment they had hinted at, in his presence, and freely discussed within easy earshot.

Martha had beamed over the prompt victory she had

won in gaining his consent to look for a settled pastorate and discontinue his itinerant evangelistic career. Her solicitude over his endurance of cold beds, unwholesome food, and long journeys touched him, even if — as he suspected — there was another reason, quite as good, for her request. As the wife of a minister, Martha hoped to enjoy whatever refracted glory shone upon that office. There would be small comfort sitting at home, unrecognized, with the care of two small children — Angela was seven, Ferdinand three — while her crusading spouse spent blocks of weeks in distant parts.

With this triumph scored, Martha was prepared to be generous when Miles (it was becoming easier to call him Miles) suggested that he would deeply appreciate it if their future negotiations with Alexander Craig might be conducted by himself. It would be much more pleasant, all 'round, if he, as head of the household — and would not little Ferdinand be the same as his own son, now? — were entrusted with this business.

Pursuant to that agreement, Martha had promptly written to Seattle notifying her young brother-in-law of her marriage and stating that hereafter Mr. Brumm was to be considered custodian of the child's funds, adding that the arrangement would undoubtedly make Mr. Brumm even more interested in little Alexander. She hadn't said why.

Shortly before little Ferdinand was eight, Mr. Brumm had received a letter from Craig — they had always referred to him as Craig; not Mr. Craig, which would have denoted an unearned respect for him, or Alexander, which would have seemed more friendly than they felt — inquiring whether it would be considered a violation of his covenant if he wrote to his son on the occasion of his next birthday. The letter was typed on the expensively embossed stationery of *The Puget Sound —— Editorial Department*.

Mr. Brumm, who enjoyed letting himself go, a bit, with

a pen, had written a reply which, after many revisions, pleased him.

'We live very simply here, as becomes the family of a village clergyman, on small pay, ministering to a by no means well-to-do community composed of persons who for the most part make their own clothes and grow their own food. Your son's wants are few. As you are aware, we have thought it imprudent to inform him of your benefactions. Did he know that we are receiving generous amounts of money on his account, it would unquestionably alter his relation to our household, both in his mind and ours. It would make for constraint, and, perhaps, a breakdown of the discipline which every small boy, however tractable, requires.'

There was a great deal more of it, running into all of four pages, redundantly cautioning Mr. Craig that any affectionate gesture toward his son, at this time, would make the child restless in his humble home, and reminding Mr. Craig of his promise to Mrs. Brumm 'never to disturb the existing relationship while she lives.'

Mr. Brumm had had no reply to that letter which, he felt, deserved adequate recognition, considering the amount of time and labor he had spent on its composition. The quarterly remittances continued to arrive unaccompanied by any personal message. On each occasion, Mr. Brumm receipted with a brief note, reporting on the boy's health and advancement in school, always optimistically.

As for young Ferdinand's opinion of his father, they had tried to shape it properly by making the relationship seem as remote as possible. How else, indeed, were they to insure the child's contentment?

Reflecting on it now, in the light of this morning's dismaying episode, Mr. Brumm wondered if they had not slightly overdone their efforts to portray Craig as a selfish, cowardly scapegrace who had fled in terror from the gravest of obligations. He was aware that Martha had spared no ugly words in recounting for Ferdinand the pitiful details of a tragedy which had become an obsession in her cramped mind. Would this hot-headed boy actually write to his father, provoking an open breach, perhaps an investigation? It was a comfort to remember that Ferdinand did not know his father's address beyond the bare fact that he lived in Seattle. But was that a comfort? Mr. Brumm wondered if a letter addressed to Alexander Craig, Seattle, might not be delivered.

* * * * * *

Meantime, while Mr. Brumm toyed absently with his beard, there was a dull rumble of conversation drifting in from Ferdinand's room, where Aunt Martha was endeavoring to set everything right. From the boy's protests, it was to be gathered that she was not meeting with much success.

'I was just a-sayin' to Ferdinand' — Aunt Martha rose from the low rocking-chair, and leaned against the foot of the bed as Uncle Miles strolled in — 'that we mustn't have any more fuss now about this pony business. It's gone plenty far enough!'

'Well,' said Uncle Miles, casually, 'we'll think it over and decide what's the best thing to do. Ferdinand's going to be reasonable, I feel sure.'

His shoes squeaked as he went downstairs. Aunt Martha sighed audibly, and followed him. Ferdinand, fatigued by the emotional storm, yawned, stretched, slept.

After a brief conference in the kitchen, Uncle Miles harnessed the glossy bay mare to the jump-seat buggy, while Aunt Martha, in their downstairs bedroom, changed to her white lawn with the black spray.

'Angela,' she called, 'your father 'n' me are a-goin' to make a call on Sister Sprecker.'

In deference to Ferdinand's distress, Angela had cheerfully consented that the pony should be stabled, and was sitting on one foot in the porch swing deeply absorbed in *The Last Days of Pompeii*, which, after many unsuccessful attempts, she was devouring with interest. The book was lowered to her lap for a moment. Odd — making a visit on Saturday afternoon. Father always reserved Saturday for study.

Aunt Martha did not explain that she herself was to be left with Sister Sprecker, who lived on the pike halfway to Bluffton, while Uncle Miles continued to town for the purpose of sending a telegram, which he could not prudently dispatch from Zanesdale, inquiring of the Winnetka Stock Farm whether they would buy back the pony and equipment. She tiptoed upstairs, and returned to the front screen-door, bonneted and black-mitted for her journey.

'Ferdinand's asleep, Angela. He's been so stirred up 'n' all. Get him a piece when he comes down. We mayn't be back much afore sundown. You peel th' potatoes, 'n' make a good fire about five o'clock.'

Briefly disengaging herself from panic-stricken Pompeii, Angela mumbled acquiescence and hoped they would have a good time.

She was a flaxen-haired, large-eyed, precocious youngster whom her father regarded as a valuable asset in his profession. A great deal of attention had been paid to Angela when she was a mere tiny tot by the adoring widows and elderly maidens in whose indulgent care she had been lodged, in at least a score of small towns, while her father was pursuing his evangelistic ministry, previous to his second marriage.

Sometimes she sat beside him in the pulpit, an enraptured and undeniably touching picture of cherubic innocence. Not infrequently she was adverted to, with a tender gesture, when the preacher spoke feelingly of the uninquisitive faith to be found at its best in the heart of a child.

At eight, Angela had sung, 'I'll Meet Mother Over There,' in a sweet, unaffected, little voice that had utterly devastated with emotion the large crowd on the last night of Mr. Brumm's memorable revival at Unger, shortly after accepting their call.

More than a hundred souls were saved during that revival; and at least a score, already saved, experienced the second blessing. Little Angela herself had publicly professed a receipt of the second blessing, on that final night of the revival, somewhat to her parent's confusion; for this degree, while not explicitly restricted to an adult constituency, had not — at least within his own purview — been undertaken by anyone of Angela's immature years. There was nothing he could do about it, however; certainly not at the moment, seeing with what a spontaneous wave of hysterical exultation the child's bland announcement was accepted. In fact, it was Angela's second blessing that had brought the month's 'big meetin'' to an almost painfully triumphant crescendo insuring her father's standing in the community for five successful years.

As was to be expected, Angela, thereafter, was looked to, on occasions when emotion ran high, for a tender song, a fervid testimony, a sugary little prayer — demands which she met so adequately that even she herself could not have failed to realize the value of her talent, had she been infinitely more reticent than she was. Everybody predicted a bright future for Angela. It went without debate that she could expect to be mightily used by the Lord. Aunt Martha occasionally hinted to her husband that it would be a pity if Angela's head should be turned by so much praise; but, observing that his smug smile left something unsaid on the subject of envy, she did not venture to press the matter.

No endeavor had been made to capitalize Ferdinand's piety which was of a much less showy type. He had displayed no prophetic gifts. At Christmas and on Children's Day he spoke short pieces and participated in dialogues, always without enthusiasm or promise of future distinction either as an apostle or platform orator. Privately he despised these exhibitions, and consented to be a party to them only when his loyalty to his uncle was challenged. Especially did he loathe the dialogues. Overtopping by a head all the other boys of his age, he appeared the dolt in a line-up of brighter juniors, albeit some of them might be older than he. It was a sore trial, indeed, when it came his turn to hold up a little white pasteboard card bearing the letter D, and recite, shamefacedly, amid the pardonable titters of the congregation:

> 'I am the Daisy that grows in the spring,
> Sweetly adoring the love of our King.'

Presently all these letters would spell

GODS LITTLE FLOWERS

and he could stumble awkwardly to his seat beside Aunt Martha, who, smiling benignly, would wet a finger and brush back the lock that had come all the way from Dresden.

Ferdinand accepted Angela's opulent faith at face value. It never occurred to him to be jealous of the marked attentions she received, wherever they went, sometimes in quite glaring contrast to the attitude people manifested toward him. He rejoiced in her well-deserved popularity. He liked Angela. The hazard of childish quarrels between them had been reduced to a minimum by the fact that no question of property rights ever arose. Until recently, Angela had contented herself at play with her dolls and dishes. Ferdinand, when not whittling sticks, amused himself with his small set of smeary rubber-type. They kept out of each other's way.

Of late, however, Angela had been taking more interest in Ferdinand. At first he had been flattered by these friendly attentions; though, on the whole, he rather liked her better when she left him to his own devices. Sometimes she came out to the bench, behind the woodhouse, and sat by him while he whittled toy furniture out of soft pine; sat very close, often hampering him.

Angela confided in him very freely now, as if he were her own age. One of these days she was going to be an evangelist. She could do it now if they would let her. Not only would she do a great deal of good, but she could earn some money. She could have nice clothes. 'And I'll get you a really good printing-outfit, too, Ferdinand. You want one very much, don't you?'

And when he said he certainly did — very much — she would kiss him, and say: 'Never you mind. I'll get you one that you can print a little newspaper on. Wouldn't that be fun?'

* * * * * *

Ferdinand was roused by Angela's voice down in the parlor, singing, 'That Will Be Glory For Me,' to her own accompaniment on the melodeon. He was debating whether he should not go down and ask Aunt Martha for a piece of pie, now that he had slept through dinner-time. It was almost three.

Suddenly the music stopped abruptly. Angela was calling from the foot of the stairs.

'Ferdinand!'

'Ye-es.'

'You awake now?'

'Um-humm.'

'What are you doing?'

'Nothing.'

'Lonesome?'

'No — but I'm hungry.'

'Want me to bring you a piece of cake and a banana?'

'Well — if you want to.'

She came presently and sat down beside him on the bed, licking sticky fingers.

'Don't you want any?' asked Ferdinand, his mouth full.

'I just had some. Did you know that father and Aunt Martha have gone away for all afternoon?'

'No.... Let's go down and play croquet.'

'I'm so sorry you had such an unhappy birthday, Ferdinand.' Angela's voice was husky. 'I could have cried

for you, this morning. Do you feel better now?' She put
an arm around him and pushed him back on the pillow.

Ferdinand made a brave show of not being annoyed
when Angela bent over him, burying her hot face in his
neck, and blinding him with her tousled hair.

'Let me up, Angela. You're smothering me!' shouted
Ferdinand. 'I don't feel like romping.'

'I'm not romping,' whispered Angela, trembling.

* * * * * *

Ten minutes later, Angela, with very red cheeks, went
to the melodeon and continued where she had left off at
the third verse of 'That Will Be Glory For Me,' hoping
that Ferdinand's stubbornness meant he was too dumb to
understand, or, having understood, would not uninten-
tionally give her away.

The front doorbell rang loudly, and Angela, still scarlet
and shaky, answered it. Mr. Trask had brought a telegram for Ferdinand. Whatever was Ferdinand doing with
telegrams?

She rushed upstairs with it. He was standing at the
window, drumming absently on the pane with his knuckles.
He did not turn.

'Look what you got!' Angela hoped the message would
be pleasant, at least diverting.

He clumsily opened the envelope and mystifiedly read
the telegram several times before its meaning became
quite clear. It was signed by the Winnetka Stock Farm.

WE HAVE BRUMMS WIRED PROPOSAL TO RESELL
TO US PONY AND EQUIPMENT DELIVERED YOU
TODAY STOP IF YOU DO NOT AGREE WIRE IM-
MEDIATELY COLLECT

'What is it?' Angela was bursting with curiosity.

Ferdinand crumpled the message in his fist, and shuffled
past her toward the stairway. There he paused, his face
working, his eyes brimming with angry tears.

'You're all a lot o' cheaters!' he screamed.

Angela stood in open-mouthed amazement.... So unlike Ferdinand to explode like that!

He clumped down the stairs, savagely shouting: 'I hate all of you! Do you hear me? I hate everybody in th' whole damn world!'

Angela brightened.

'He won't tell, then,' she reflected.

Ferdinand flung himself out of the house, banged the front gate, pulled his cap far down over his red nose, dug his fists deep into the pockets of his pants (cut down from a pair of his uncle's), and stamped sullenly up the road toward the railroad track, only three hundred yards away. The east-bound Erie Flyer was just due. It always stopped at Zanesdale for water.

Sometimes Ferdinand strolled down to the station and stood close beside the dripping water-tank when, at exactly three-thirty-six, the huge locomotive paused, gasping rhythmically, while the torrent poured into the capacious tender, the fireman on the coal-pile, holding the rope, calmly smoking his pipe, unmindful of his happy privilege.

Most of the fast trains thundered through Zanesdale with a terrifying racket. Ferdinand never failed to experience a surge of hot indignation over this arrogant contempt for his town. He knew it wasn't much of a town; had contempt for it himself; but it was annoying to have the utter insignificance of Zanesdale thrust upon him nine times a day.

He would not have time to run down to the station, now, even if he had been in a mood for running: besides, he didn't care to answer any questions that Mr. Trask might ask, so that he might be able to tell Mrs. Trask the sequel to the pony story which she would promptly explain to the town.

He climbed on top of the gate-post at the corner of Harsh's melon-patch — his favorite vantage when watch-

ing the long, black, proud Pullmans flick by, each adding
its own little 'Psst!' of disdain; and watched Number Nine
(he knew all the trains that way) slow to a screeching stop.
There was a long hiss of escaping air from the brakes; an
acrid smell of greasy, hot metal. The diner was directly in
front of him. Little tables with candles on them. A man
and a woman, with a black waiter hovering over them.
Too late for dinner, too early for supper: this must be
'tea.' People in stories were always having 'tea.' Ferdinand drew down the corners of his mouth and hated the
man and the woman, though he knew she was a pretty
woman. He hated the obsequious waiter, and mumbled,
audibly, 'Damn nigger!'

The train moved slowly on, so slowly that the locomotive was exasperated by the sluggishness of the heavy
Pullmans, and barked a staccato of short, angry demands
that it had better get to business, now, or we'd be late
again pulling into Washington. Ferdinand climbed down
from the post, made a detour around the rear of the
melon-patch, and entered the barn through the back door.
The pony looked around over its shoulder, stopped munching its mouthful of hay, and blew a long breath that made
its soft nostrils flutter.

He advanced slowly and laid a hand on the pony's flank
which twitched as if the light touch had tickled; moved
forward another step and took a wisp of tawny mane in
his fingers; was about to pat the friendly pet on the nose.

On sudden impulse he drew back and muttered, 'No —
I tell you — *No!*'

Retracing his steps through the back door, half-blinded
by tears, he stood for a long time gazing abstractedly into
the muddy water of the miasmic, green-scummed little
pond that belonged to Flook's Tile Factory; amblingly
circled the barn, and moved toward his little workbench
behind the woodhouse.

He took the new knife from his pocket, turned it over
several times, opened it, closed it with a sharp click; and,

deliberately drawing his long arm back to full torsion, he sighted carefully — his lower lip pinioned by a row of uncommonly straight teeth — and threw the knife all of forty yards with such velocity and precision that it landed with a mighty splash exactly where he had intended.

Ferdinand grinned. It was an ugly grin that did something to him on the inside — a brand-new sensation which defied his childish analysis, but seemed to be made up of such ingredients as, 'Damn them all!'...'I haven't a friend left in the world!'...'I've got to go it alone!'...'I *can* go it alone!'...'I *will* go it alone!'... '*You see if I don't!*... *Damn you all!*'

CHAPTER IV

FERDINAND arrived home at five, gayly whistling an improvised tune.

He was in unusually high spirits today; for Miss Carle, who had specialized in Creative English at Wellesley, and was hopeful of teaching it in a college, some day, had detained him again after school to discuss his latest composition as seriously as if they were equals in age and experience.

'But, Ferdinand,' she had cautioned, 'really, you're quite shockingly cynical, I'm afraid... for fifteen!'

He would have liked to leave the question of his age standing just that way, but when she added, 'You're not any older, are you?' he felt obliged to tell the truth.

'I'll be fourteen next May.'

'My word!' ejaculated Miss Carle. 'Owlish as Omar, when you ought to be out playing marbles.'

'I guess I grew pretty fast,' Ferdinand admitted, shyly.

'And pretty sour, too,' laughed Miss Carle. 'But you can write, young fellow! Just be a bit careful how you whirl that battle-axe! You might hurt somebody, and be sorry.'

It was evident, at home, that something important was afoot.

Aunt Martha had crimped her hair and was tidying up the house. Apparently all the major feats of putting to rights had been attended to, for she was now at the final stage of patting the sofa pillows and rearranging the trinkets on the mantel — the shepherdess he had carved, a year ago, the china cat that someone had given to Angela when she was five, the oval slab of polished stone that Uncle Miles had picked up on a vagabondish trip long ago in the Petrified Forest. A fire had been neatly laid in the grate, though it was only the second of October and unseasonably warm.

'Mr. and Mrs. Joel Day are coming to call, this evening,' explained Aunt Martha, impressively. 'Mind yuh don't leave yer things a-lyin' around.'

Angela, softly humming while she pressed the skirt of her blue dress on the ironing-board in the kitchen, broke off to say, as Ferdinand thrust a long slim hand into the cooky-jar, 'Mustn't scatter crumbs. The Days are to be here, tonight.'

Upstairs, Uncle Miles was found straightening books on the shelves in his study. Ferdinand paused in the doorway, half-minded to tell him that Miss Carle had encouraged him about his writing. He was bursting to tell somebody. On second thought, he decided that Uncle Miles might think him boastful.

A neat stack of opened letters lay on the corner of the desk, otherwise bare except for an engagement-pad which occupied a conspicuous position in the middle. The letters were making-believe they were the current mail of a busy man of affairs, the edge of an old telegram protruding slightly from midway of the deceitful pile.

Doubtless Uncle Miles meant to slip up here with Mr. Day for a half-hour's confidential chat about church business while Aunt Martha, in the parlor below, endeavored to infect Mrs. Day with a more passionate interest in the missionary box, the ultimate unpacking and distribution of which, Ferdinand grimly hoped, would put some body in Paouting-fu to at least half the bother that the recruiting of its miscellaneous contents had already cost him.

He was seldom inquisitive about Uncle Miles's activities, but the engagement-pad caught his eye. He felt the makings of a grin at the corners of his mouth, and dealt with it severely.

A mere glance at tomorrow's crowded program should be sufficient to inform a sharp-eyed deacon that the new minister was not only industrious and popular, but was a person of orderly mind and much experience.

October 3

8–9 . . . . . Correspondence
9–10:45 .Study
11 . . . . . .Mercy Hospital (Mrs. Penfield)
12:15 . . .Luncheon YMCA Com. on Evangelism
2–4 . . . . .Pastoral calls on Brucker, Winona & Swift Sts.
4:30–6 . .Study
7:30 . . . .Midweek Service
8:40 . . . .Conference with S.S. Officers

'Don't disturb anything, Ferdinand,' remarked Uncle
Miles, importantly. 'Mr. Day is coming out, after supper . . .
and Mrs. Day . . . to make us a little visit.'

Ferdinand said he wouldn't, and retreated to his own
room at the end of the hall, grinning broadly.

There were a great many things about his transparent
Uncle Miles — affectations, pretensions, petty deceptions —
which, while they had shocked and distressed him at ten,
were only amusing, now. He had quite outgrown his earlier
illusions about absolute integrity as an indispensable to
anyone engaged in the spread of religion. His observations
had led him to suspect that there was as much duplicity
practiced in Uncle Miles's profession as in any other business, the main difference between sacred and secular callings
being that in the latter a man had at least a sporting chance
of getting something out of it worth the time and trouble.

Still — Ferdinand was obliged to admit — they had done
very well, as ministers' families went. The three years on
the rim of Fort Wayne had been good for them. Uncle Miles
— what with Angela's undeniably valuable coöperation —
had been very successful. The two of them had made themselves known soon after their arrival in the big town. Together they had put on noon meetings in the large railroad-
shops, where Uncle Miles had invited soot-smeared me-
chanics, munching their apple pie, to remember the faith of
their mothers — all of whom were presumed to be dead
and in glory — and Angela, assured of manner and easy to
look at, had sung mellow ballads in keeping with her father's

exhortations, accompanying herself on a portable organ which she played so effortlessly that many of the younger workmen wondered if she were actually pumping the thing with her own feet; and, having maneuvered their position to the satisfaction of their curiosity on this point, had remained steadfastly regarding the robust girl's well-turned ankles with an admiration she did not appear to resent.

After that, it had been easy to book engagements at Young People's social affairs in the down-town churches. At first Uncle Miles had imagined that his sentimental little talks, replete with touching anecdotes, were coming into demand; that Angela's contribution merely provided a unique embellishment to his addresses — a delusion he was gradually relieved of, however, as more and more invitations were extended to his gifted daughter alone. But, for all that, Uncle Miles had prospered beyond all reasonable expectations, and the call to the small church in Indianapolis had been no more appreciated than deserved.

They were still poor; not so poor as they had been, back in Zanesdale, but required to practice rigid economies. Aunt Martha, to whom frugality was a virtue, if not indeed an obsession, had succeeded in making poverty a noble estate.

For a long time they had been paying for a 'little piece of real estate' in Keokuk, Iowa. It had never occurred to Ferdinand to inquire what the 'little piece of real estate' consisted of, whether houses, lands, or business blocks. It had always been a 'little piece of real estate,' which, although involving much correspondence and many receipts of long envelopes from Keokuk, could not amount to very much on their wages, even though they skimped valiantly to make the payments on it.

Ferdinand made almost no demands upon the family purse, considering it no more than his share of the burden to wear the cheapest of clothes — though Aunt Martha didn't try to make them herself any more — and went about, uncomplainingly, with empty pockets. A stated allowance had never been thought of in their family. If Ferdinand wanted a five-cent pencil-tablet, he asked Uncle Miles for a nickel, please, to buy a pencil-tablet; and, to Uncle Miles's credit, the nickel was always forthcoming without argument or reluctance.

Angela had not yet achieved her ambition to appear as the head-liner in a revival. Uncle Miles, finding it quite impossible to leave his local duties for so long a time, and unwilling that Angela should attempt so responsible an undertaking by herself, had put her off; though he kept saying, when she pressed him, that they would surely do it, one of these days; or, if they couldn't, he would see what might be arranged for her 'next winter — perhaps.'

She had been growing almost rebelliously restless when the call to Indianapolis had eased the tension. She would be making new 'contacts' — Uncle Miles's redundant use of this word 'contact,' especially when he made a verb of it, always annoyed Ferdinand, who was unconsciously becoming something of a stylist — and doubtless 'opportunities would develop' if Angela would only bide her time; as indeed they had, for it had been barely a month now since their coming to Indianapolis, and Angela had already been pleasantly spoken of in the newspapers three times (and unpleasantly spoken to in the High School Principal's office twice for her bland nonchalance in respect to Cæsar's Gallic Wars).

It had not yet occurred to the Music Committee in Uncle Miles's church that Angela, who had quickly assumed the position of leading soprano in the choir, deserved a cash competence, for no such appropriations had ever been considered; but, on every hand — or at least almost every hand — one heard her appreciatively mentioned as having had much to do with the unprecedented attendance at church services.

Women declared at the Aid Society that they never had any trouble, now, getting their menfolks out of bed on Sunday mornings.

A few of the more conservative were for putting vestments on the choir, something they had never discussed before Angela joined it. One woman, convinced that the congregation, which was almost militantly non-conformist, would not consent to gowns on the choir, wondered — though it took a good deal of courage to say it, even in the privacy of a group of three — whether it might not be tactfully suggested to Mrs. Brumm that Angela was really a bigger girl than she thought; to which another woman, equally moved to candor, replied, 'No — we mustn't do that. It would do no good, anyway. Angela is just one of those people who, no matter how much they have on, always look as if they'd left something off.'

As for Ferdinand's attitude toward his uncle's bustling ministry, and the luxuriant Angela's aspirations, it stopped with merely wishing them well. Aunt Martha had long since discontinued her direct appeals to him to prepare himself vocationally to follow in his uncle's footsteps; and Uncle Miles, who had frequently besought the Lord, at family worship, to lead 'this lad into the ministry of the gospel' — mostly to please Aunt Martha, Ferdinand always thought — had lately omitted this supplication from his invoice of the family's wants.

Of course, there was no use pretending he had no interest in what went on at their church, for Uncle Miles's profession was singular in that neither he nor his household was ever for a moment free of it. The church was all they lived for. It was at once the hub and the rim, the corona and the periphera of their thoughts and conversation. Such friendships as they had, if not actually originating at the church, eventually brought up there — tentative, temporary, shallow-rooted friendships, for at any minute they might pack up and move elsewhere.

Three years had made structural changes in Ferdinand. They had spread some substantial and nicely distributed flesh on his gangling frame, the additional weight seeming to have given him more self-confidence. He was still rather shy, but had almost outgrown his earlier tendency to a morbid self-dissatisfaction which, at ten, had made him painfully sensitive, touchy, and inclined to mope.

It had been a long time, now, since he had participated in a family scene, contenting himself — when they glanced apprehensively in his direction on occasions brimming with the raw materials of argument — to draw a twisted smile, which, although he had never seen it, he suspected of being somewhat unpleasant. Situations that had once fetched out of him a squeaky and savage indignation, popping off to the ruination of a meal, and hurling him out of the room, and tossing him onto his bed where he would lie for hours hating all visible creation, including himself, were now handled with an indifference so closely akin to contempt that the family sometimes wished he had not tied down the safety-valve.

Aunt Martha, particularly, viewed this change in Ferdinand with prayerful anxiety. Much as she had deplored the lad's occasional releases of volcanic protest — mostly protests against the quite irksome and unquestionably silly inhibitions which she herself laid upon him; for she insisted that at ten he should carry himself like an experienced saint of seventy, while she rigged him in babyish sailor-collars and fussy girlish waists not worn by any child over five, a manner of dress that promoted his misfortune in being oversized to a farce so ludicrous that even he, murderously angry as he was, sometimes laughed himself into wild hysteria over his own appearance in the mirror, a storm usually followed by a fit of rebellious weeping — he often wondered if Aunt Martha did not secretly enjoy such emotional hurricanes.

On several memorable occasions she had knelt, with Ferdinand sourly crouched beside her (venomously despising them both), and prayed aloud — her wailing petitions punctuated with convulsive sobs — that 'this wayward orphan, whom Thou in Thine Infinite Wisdom, hast entrusted into our care and keeping, may be just brought under the influence of Thy Blessed Spirit.'

All that was over, now. Aunt Martha had herself under much better control. Whether the benign rainbow that arched her had arrived to signal the biologic fact that she had graduated from her riproaring middle forties, or whether the promotion from a bucolic atmosphere of country-village piety into the relative sophistication of bigger towns and association with 'city folks' had pushed in a few of the shriller stops in her turbulent spirit, Ferdinand did not know.

Perhaps it was these early experiences of the utter breakdown of emotional discipline that had produced in Ferdinand a mounting contempt for home theatricals. Unquestionably, these unbridled seizures of Aunt Martha's had been bad for him. They had made him despise any sentiment that threatened to evoke tears. He had wept himself out in early childhood.

At thirteen, plus, these deep lesions had healed, but not without leaving some impermeable scars on the lamina of young Ferdinand's soul at the very points of exposure most frequently bombarded in a home where prayer and piety, sentiment and emotion, were all in the day's work.

Adversions and appeals to Deity were, in Ferdinand's opinion, merely an unscrupulous and unsportsmanly method of having your own way in dealing with people who might be so weak-minded as to believe that you and God were at one as to the soundness of your cause. If you couldn't get what you wanted out of the other fellow by wheedle and whimper, purchase or threat, vituperation or violence, you bade him listen while you took it up with the Lord in prayer. You closed your eyes, and, in the lugubrious tone of one making funeral arrangements over the telephone, prosecuted your case while your helpless victim knelt beside you hotly wanting the courage to say, 'Either you're a fraud, or your God is a rascal!'

Ferdinand no longer took any stock whatever in prayer — either in the family worship kind of prayer that besought the Almighty to make you sweet-spirited and obedient to

His Holy Will, five minutes after you had stubbornly objected, at breakfast on Saturday, to spending the whole afternoon helping old Mullins clean out the church furnace, when you had been looking forward all week to a bit of carving on the fire-screen you meant to give Miss Carle on Christmas; or in the public kind of prayer that asked God to touch the generous hearts of this dear people (Gosh! how he loathed those smug antiques that stood in prim rows in Uncle Miles's prayers!)... and incline them to give sacrificially to some pet scheme they were being badgered into against their wishes.

He had been trying lately not to think about it at all; saying to himself that in any other environment than his the whole matter of religion in general and the activities of the church in particular would be giving him no concern.

Until recently, he had suffered frequent torments, as he watched his feverish disdain burning out to smoking cinders. Could it be that he had 'quenched the Spirit'? Uncle Miles was forever warning his flock against the cold apathy that meant one had committed the 'unpardonable sin.' These past few weeks, he had almost left off torturing himself with these morbid reflections. The 'unpardonable sin' was just so much more nonsense — all of a piece with everything else they ranted about and wept over and grudgingly subscribed to.... A lot o' bunk!... Tripe!

* * * * * *

Ferdinand tossed his books on the bed and clatteringly rummaged in the disordered lower drawer of his battered, second-hand, taffy-colored desk for a shoe-brush and the box of blacking. He, too, would be expected to help entertain these precious Days whose threat of a visit had set them all scouring and preening.

Poising one foot on the edge of the untidy drawer, Ferdinand grimacingly recruited a mouthful of lubricant and spat viciously into the noisomely pungent blacking-box. He, too, would be required to come down, with his hair roached high to show he had an intellectual forehead, and smirk for this rich and brittle Mr. Day, who, because his deceased father had organized Uncle Miles's church and paid for most of it, was in a position to make them all jump through the hoop — and like it.

He would have to sit there for an hour and a half, posing for an angel; just as if he gave a damn whether these wonderful Days liked him or not. He smeared the dauber side of the brush into the blacking, and anointed the toe of his shabby shoe.

Angela, of course, would sing for them in her most luscious manner. If the guests didn't ask her promptly, Aunt Martha would direct the conversation into that quarter. 'Yes — Angela has been a great help,' she would say, in her precise, company voice, 'what with her singin' 'n' all.' 'Won't you sing something for us now, dear?' — this Mrs. Day would beg, probably hoping she wouldn't. But you could count on Angela.... Well — so much the better. While that was going on, he wouldn't have to do anything.

Ferdinand banged and bumped and smeared the shoe-brush against the desk-drawer as he insured himself against being sent back to 'polish the heel as well as the toe' — meanwhile carrying on with his sour prognosis of the evening's entertainment.

Angela, having more than satisfied the customers with her recital, closing it with an extended rendition of 'Crossing the Bar,' would smile, fold the music, push in the organ-stops, and slowly revolve on the hair-cloth stool to receive the inevitable 'My! — ain't that grand?'

And then this Mrs. Day — a feathery, fussy old dame, no doubt — would turn to him.... Ferdinand raised his other foot to the ledge of the drawer and again paid his respects to the vile blacking-box.... Ducking her big-plumed head, coquettishly, and grinning as if she were peering under the hood of a perambulator, she would inquire, 'And what do *you* do, Master Ferdinand?'

That's what she would say, and the way she would say it.

He had never seen her, but he knew. He had seen Mr. Day. Mr. Day had met them at the train. Uncle Miles had known he would, for he had written promising to do so. And there he was, sure enough, standing on the platform where the day-coach passengers alighted. Mr. Day had known they would be riding in the day-coach, though he himself wouldn't, of course.

Ferdinand had had no difficulty picking him out of the crowd on the platform — a square man, with square shoulders, square hands, square feet, square head, square mouth. He was to be their boss, because he had lots of money. Mr. Day had shaken hands all round and led the way to a shiny new Cadillac. Ferdinand hadn't liked the back of Mr. Day's square head or his square knuckles on the steering-wheel, though he was bound to admit that Mr. Day inspired respect. Mr. Day owned them now, same as he owned his Cadillac. Uncle Miles sitting beside him, with his arm stretched along the top of the seat, as if he were getting ready to hug Mr. Day, was already saying, 'Yes, yes; to be sure, Brother Day: ab-so-*lute*-ly!'

Ferdinand transferred his suspenders to his Sunday pants and emptied his pockets on top of the desk.

'Perhaps you sing, too,' Mrs. Day would suggest, 'like your sister.' And then Aunt Martha would heave the long sigh that meant she was going to explain how Angela wasn't his sister, a story that Angela would interrupt presently to reply to Mrs. Day's query.

'Ferdinand whittles,' she would say, crossing swiftly to the mantel for the little shepherdess. And Mrs. Day would gurgle, 'You don't mean to tell me! Look, Mr. Day, at this perfectly ex*quis*ite piece of carving!' And Mr. Day, deliberately finishing the long sentence he was on, and steadfastly looking at Uncle Miles from under his square eyebrows — just to show he was the kind of a man who mustn't be interrupted — but reaching out his square hand to signify that he would be pleased to take up Mrs. Day's case as the next order of business, would presently pinch his

glasses onto his square nose, owlishly inspect the shepherdess, and say, as he handed it back, 'Nicely done, I'm
sure.'

Ferdinand was tumbling the contents of the top bureau-
drawer, looking for a clean collar that had no frayed edges.

'He prints, too,' Aunt Martha would add, proudly,
though she was forever chiding him for wasting his time with
all that type-settin'. Before she and Angela were through
with it, he would be sent upstairs for 'that meenoo and
program' he had made for the Annual Canvass Dinner at
Fort Wayne, last winter. And Mrs. Day would squint at it,
and twist in her chair to get a better light on it, and borrow
Mr. Day's glasses; and Mr. Day would suggest that Ferdinand might do a lot of the church printing, 'just for good
practice.'... Gosh! — how he hated these hellish exhibitions!

* * * * * *

Ferdinand put his Harvey's Grammar face down on the
desk and listened for the doorbell. It would soon ring, now,
for he had heard the car-doors slam, opulently. It rang,
sharply, as if Mr. Day were saying, 'Don't keep us waiting!
I paid for most of this house, myself!'... and Uncle Miles
was opening the door, his hearty 'Well — well!' meaning,
'I know you did, Brother Day, and I came running fast as
ever I could — ab-so-*lute*-ly!'

They were all talking at once, now, and drifting through
the hall into the parlor. Mr. Day was remarking dryly
that the floors needed to be gone over, and Mrs. Day —
who sounded quite elderly — was asking Aunt Martha, in
a high key, how she was finding the house, anyway.

Presently, Angela came to the foot of the stairs and
called him. He would have to go. He gave his hair a final
scrub with the brush, scowled into the mirror, and started.
Hopeful of slipping into the room so quietly they would
hardly notice his arrival, Ferdinand made as little noise as
possible on the way down.

Slowly negotiating the last few steps, he was able, by the

location of their voices, and a panoramic glimpse through
the wide doorway, to place their positions — Aunt Martha,
first; then Mrs. Day, a white-haired, little old lady, old
enough to be Mr. Day's mother (as indeed she was, he soon
discovered); then Mr. Day, on the brussels sofa, polishing
his glasses with a large silk handkerchief, Uncle Miles
sitting close beside him with a hand on Mr. Day's knee.

Another step located Angela, close to the melodeon, of
course, talking animatedly, and, for her, rather affectedly,
to some unidentified person not yet in the picture.

Ferdinand cautiously moved forward and brought gradually into view a slim, modishly shod foot and a generous
glimpse of the first silk stockings he had ever seen, a pair of
gracefully crossed, tailored knees, a shapely arm negligently
thrown back across the top of the chair — it was a dining-
room chair, put there for him, and she had evidently preferred it to the patent rocker which stood vacant — her fur
boa tossed back from her shoulder.

Nobody like that had ever been in their house before.
Ferdinand hadn't yet seen her face — it would require some
courage to do this next step — but he knew she did not
belong to their world, at all. Something in her posture told
him that.

'Come on in, Ferdinand,' called Angela, pleasantly, in the
tone of thirty addressing six, which made him know the
stylish stranger could not be very old, if Angela was playing
grown-up.

Summoning all his valor, Ferdinand stepped to the door
and found himself staring — open-mouthed, he feared —
at the most beautiful woman he had ever seen. She smiled,
a slowly widening smile, which seemed to mean they were
already friends of long standing, bending her head forward
and looking at him from under long black lashes, her lips
puckered a little, teasingly, as if to say, 'I know you don't
want to come in here and be bored; but — let's have it
over.'

Ferdinand's heart skipped a beat, and then made up for

it with a hard bump that put him quite out of breath and
made his voice unsteady when, reluctantly detained by
Aunt Martha's hand on his arm, he paused to speak to
Madam Day and Mr. Day, who obligingly made short
work of him to resume their briefly interrupted remarks.
All the previously inactive minerals in Ferdinand's blood
responded to the first potential magnet he had ever approached, his natural shyness giving way to a new sensation
of actually belonging to someone!

She did not rise or offer her hand when Angela said,
'This is Ferdinand, Mrs. Day.' People, when introduced,
always stood up and gravely shook hands. Eighty rose to
shake hands with eight. Mrs. Day merely tipped back her
pretty head, so he could see the fringe of glossy little black
curls under her big picture hat, and smiled, with red lips
parted.

He could not speak for an instant. The routine phrase,
'Pleased-t'-meetcha,' which he had been obliged to mumble
so often that it was all one word, would not come. It was
inappropriate. He swallowed, rather noisily, and said,
'I'm glad — I'm glad to — I'm very glad!'

'By Jove, boy,' she drawled, 'I really believe you *are!*'
She pointed to the vacant chair beside her. 'Do you always
say such delightfully nice things?'

Angela, hopeful of smoothing over his unsuccessful
attempt to manage the usual formula, explained maternally: 'Ferdinand is so shy, Mrs. Day. He always
hates being introduced.... You can sit in the rocker,
Ferdinand. Mrs. Day thought she would like this straight
chair better.'

'Yes,' said Ferdinand, still in a trance, 'she would.'

He sat down, and while wondering if it would be all
right for him to look her straight in the eyes again — wanting to, but afraid he would stare at her — he gazed interestedly at her hands, wishing she did not have gloves on.
She leisurely unbuttoned them and began slowly to take
them off, tugging at one finger-tip after another. He

glanced up, a bit abashed, and they both smiled, under-standingly.

'I'm always wondering about hands, too,' she said, lazily. 'Your sister has been telling me what interesting things you do with yours; but I think I could have guessed — now that I see them.'

Ferdinand instinctively spread them out, glad now that he had taken pains with his nails.

'You make things, too,' he ventured. 'Maybe you paint.'

'Rather badly. I've been having better luck, lately, dabbling with wood-cuts. That's great fun!'

'I expect you have lots of carving-tools.'

'Too many! I keep experimenting with all these dif-ferent-shaped chisels, and never use any one of them long enough to——'

'Hard wood?' queried Ferdinand, professionally.

'Oh, dear, no; not yet! I've just begun it, you see.'

'I have tinkered with some little designs,' confessed Ferdinand, modestly, 'but I don't know what they look like.'

Angela, recovering from her amazement over the taciturn Ferdinand's easy talk, put in, 'He hasn't a press, Mrs. Day — nor hardly anything to work with.'

'Pine?' asked Mrs. Day, having briefly turned her head to acknowledge Angela's comment.

'No — oak and walnut.'

Mrs. Day's finely modeled eyebrows lifted a little in surprise.

'How would you like to come over, some day, and see what I have been doing? Perhaps I might trade you a reamer or two for some good advice.'

'I'd like to!' Ferdinand flushed with pleasure. 'But I don't think I could tell you anything that you don't know.'

'Saturday — maybe?'

'Yes — after dinner?'

'No — I'm to be out for dinner. Come about two.'

She belonged, Ferdinand realized, to a different world from his drab little island where the conversation never rose above the dull tittle-tattle of domestic drudgeries in homes like theirs, and the equally stupid prattle about rummage sales that were to finance a new cement sidewalk around the church and mend the plumbing in the basement. Hers was a world that had dinner at night instead of noon, an unselfconscious world that spoke correctly without stiffness, that moved with dignity but without embarrassment, a world that leisurely went out to the diner for 'tea.' The difference between her world and his swept over Ferdinand, not to his discontentment, but to his almost painful wistfulness. He felt that she had recognized him as eligible to citizenship in her world, and was glad.

'That's agreed, then. I'll expect you,' she said, rising, as Aunt Martha — still talking primly to Madam Day, and nervously smoothing her shapeless black skirt — moved toward them, apparently intending to draw Mrs. Day, whom for excellent reasons she was obviously shy of, into the adult section. 'Your father can tell you where we live,' concluded Mrs. Day, with another smile that sent Ferdinand's damaged heart racing.

Aunt Martha's curiosity spoke in her strained face. Aunt Martha's face was never under very good control. Bulletins announcing her every doubt, anxiety, hope, and fear were posted about her restless mouth and myopic eyes immediately upon arrival. At the moment, Ferdinand knew what was going on in her mind as certainly as if she shouted it. She was engaged in a struggle, attempting to be obsequiously courteous to Mrs. Day because it was incumbent on her to be deferential to Brother Day's Mrs. Day, while endeavoring to warn Ferdinand — with one fleeting glare of stern disapproval — that he was on no account to be permitted to come under the influence of this frivolous, worldly creature whom Brother Day — so steady and sensible about everything else — had had the misfortune to marry.

Conversation broke off, in the other corner of the room, in acknowledgment of Mrs. Day's arrival in their midst. Brother Day stiffly stood at attention, tapping his nose-glasses on his thumb-nail. Uncle Miles tardily scrambled to his feet, pulled down his vest, and said, 'Well — well!' just as if Mrs. Day had quite taken them by surprise, dropping in unexpectedly.

Madam Day snapped the massive silver latch of her black leather bag several times, and pursed her lips resignedly.

Aunt Martha proffered her chair and drew up another. They were all ready now, it appeared, for Mrs. Day to explain why she had intruded.

'Ferdinand has promised to come and see me,' she said, in a tone that hoped she was giving his parents pleasure —'to talk about wood-cuts.'

'Very good of you, Sister — er — Mrs. Day,' beamed Uncle Miles, in the voice he used when patronizingly commending a shy testimony offered at prayer-meeting.

Mr. Day elevated his chin, stroked the back of his bald head, gazed critically at the ceiling, and tapped his lean knee with his glasses. There was the suggestion of a frown creasing his forehead. Ferdinand wondered if the frown did not mean that Mrs. Day should first have consulted Mr. Day before making her proposal.

'Well' — said he, judicially —'perhaps the lad had better be encouraged to do something more useful than fiddling with wood-cuts.'

Aunt Martha, cannily reasoning that, while Brother Day might enjoy handing his wife a surly rebuff, he probably wouldn't thank anybody for being so impertinent as to applaud him, remarked: 'Ferdinand comes natural by his taste fer wood-carvin'. His grandpa's folks in th' old country was all wood-carvers. When he come t' this country, he changed the name to Miller because his family

name was hard fer folks t' say. Their name was Mueller
— M-u-e-l-l-e-r.'

'I wonder if they were related to the very famous family
of Muellers in Dresden. Do you know, Mrs. Brumm?'

Aunt Martha, hugging her angular elbows and rocking
gently, nodded with pride.

'My father was born in Dresden in the house of Fred-
erick Mueller. He was the great-grandson of Hans Mueller.'

'Indeed!' exclaimed Mrs. Day. 'What a heritage!'

'Ye-es,' agreed Mr. Day. 'Very interesting.'

Angela had slipped over onto the chair recently vacated
by the charming Mrs. Day.

'Awfully odd, isn't she?' whispered Angela.

'Hunnh?'

Ferdinand was barely conscious of her comment, so intent was he on the developments in his own case, now under
discussion on the other side of the room.

'Odd!' repeated Angela, guardedly, behind her hand.

Ferdinand reluctantly detached his gaze from the object
of his adoration, and regarded Angela with an inquisitive
stare.

'How do you mean — odd?' he said, absently. 'I think
she's the most wonderful person I ever saw!'

CHAPTER V

'LOOK, Janet!' Ferdinand laid the limp proof on the imposing-stone, folded his smudged arms, and glanced over his shoulder for her approval. 'Rather good, wouldn't you say? How fortunate we could use one of those quaint, diamond-shaped colons on the very first page.'

'Perfect!' Janet Day hovered close, snuggling a hand affectionately under his elbow, her cheek pressed lightly against his broad shoulder. 'Old Thomas Caxton would be green with envy. Really, Dinny, you're marvelous!'

'It's you that's marvelous, Janet. I would never have known anything about this, but for you.'

For a moment she neither responded nor turned away; stood soberly staring at the first page of what was going to be General Bryce's annual Memorial Day greeting to the diminishing survivors of his brigade — a sixteen-page brochure done in two colors on hand-laid Italian vellum, the price no object, for the General was rich. It was the most pretentious thing they had attempted.

Janet had been very quiet and pensive today. Twice, as they had encountered each other, face to face, in the narrow quarters of the little printing-shop that cluttered the whole south bay of her attic studio — screened off to segregate its inevitable untidiness — Ferdinand had been made uneasy by the entreaty in her brown eyes. Janet wanted to ask him something, and didn't dare. Janet wanted to tell him something, but was afraid. Had he done something to grieve her? What could it have been? He had failed her somehow: in what? But no — it was rather as if she, herself, was on the defensive.

Her competent fingers tightened their warm grasp on his arm. Perhaps she was going to talk about it now.

'No,' she said, preoccupiedly, 'you would have done all this, anyway, sooner or later. However, I'm glad I have had a little part in it.... I want you always to think well of me, Dinny. You've been such a dear, and I'm so proud of you.'

Impulsively he lifted her hand to his lips, an act that surprised them both, a little. Ferdinand despised sentiment.

'What is it, Janet?' he asked, gently. 'Something bothering you?'

'Now you've ink on your nose, Dinny,' she laughed, a bit nervously, he thought. 'No — it's nothing. Just moody, because it's raining and dark. I didn't intend it should rain, today.'

'Well — if you're sure that's all. I was afraid you were unhappy. I didn't do anything, did I, Janet?'

Shaking off her dolorous mood, and facing him with a twisted little smile, Janet slipped her palms slowly upward on his well-muscled arms, grasped his ear-lobes in her slim fingers, made a gesture of chastising him, and murmured, 'Of course not, simpleton.'

He had called her 'Janet' from the first; ever since that enchanted Saturday, now more than three and a half years ago, when, shy and excited, he had followed the solemn butler over the deep-pile Oriental rugs from the impressive front entrance to the broad, winding stairs, and along a narrower corridor to narrower stairs leading into the huge attic room.

'Master Brumm, ma'am,' the man had said, leaving them.

Under a large north skylight, young Mrs. Day — who had not been absent from Ferdinand's thoughts, waking or sleeping, since the night he had met her — sat on a tall three-legged stool before a composing-case, distributing type, her high heels hooked on a rung. Her heavy black hair was braided in one long plait. She wore a short skirt, and a long, green, open-throated jacket with capacious pockets, the costume diminishing her age and urbanity until she was quite another person than the queenly Mrs. Day whose black voile nearly touched the floor, whose white lace yoke had brought up in a tight, ribbed collar that almost reached to her dainty ears, her slim height emphasized by the big black hat with the orange velvet tips, on the night she had made their house, and all the people in it, outmoded and shabby.

Except for the slow, half-teasing, puckery smile with which she turned to welcome him, this girlish Mrs. Day might have been someone else than the mysterious goddess who had been playing the deuce with his imagination and staling his appetite for dinner.

Slipping down from her high stool, she had thrust her hands deep into the pockets of her smock, her head tilted as if in critical judgment of a picture.

'You seem ever so much bigger, taller,' she said. 'How old are you?'

'It's this collar, I think,' Ferdinand had replied, soberly. 'Going on fourteen.... Aunt Martha would have me wear it.'

'Who's Aunt Martha? Does she live with you?'

'But you met Aunt Martha. Mrs. Brumm is not my mother.'

Mrs. Day's shapely arm was thrown up suddenly in a gesture of happy discovery emphasized by a vigorous snap of the fingers, her face alight.

'By Jove!' she shouted. 'So — that's the answer to the riddle!'

'My mother died when I was born,' explained Ferdinand.

'And your father — what became of him?'

Ferdinand was very sorry that the subject had arisen. He had come, eager and inquisitive, hoping to see Mrs. Day's wood-working equipment; and here we were, wasting precious time.

'He's living... out West... I never saw him.... You're putting the type back in their boxes; aren't you?' Ferdinand drew nearer the case. 'May I watch you do it?'

'Oh — we're going to talk about wood-cuts,' said Mrs. Day. 'But, first, sit down. Tell me some more about yourself.'

'There isn't much,' he replied, gloomily; but he took the big club chair she pointed to, and began to tell her what little he knew. Seated on a low ottoman at his feet, she listened intently, asking brief questions when he paused. There was, after all, a good deal of the story. It was a whole hour before Mrs. Day seemed satisfied, and they sat silently.

'I think you should have kept the pony,' she said, after a long pause. 'That must have hurt him, dreadfully.... And you never wrote to him?'

Ferdinand drew a long sigh, with a convulsive catch in the middle of it, and abstractedly twisted Mrs. Day's soggy little handkerchief into a slim rope. Her understanding sympathy and affection had loosed a long-pent flood of suppressed misery. He smiled, feebly.

'That's the first time anybody ever defended my father,' said Ferdinand. 'Why should I have written to him? He never wrote to me.'

Mrs. Day rose, and, walking slowly to the dormer window, stood looking down at the busy street.

'I'm guessing that there's some more of that story... that you never heard,' she said, impressively.

Then there had been some hot chocolate and cakes, and Ferdinand became quickly absorbed in Mrs. Day's explanation of the new printing-press which her good friend, Mr. Oscar Zimmerman, had lent her. Mr. Zimmerman had made quite a hobby of art-craft printing; had done some beautiful things; now he had tired of it; had sent her his entire equipment for use while he was abroad.

'He will be so interested in you, Ferdinand. I wrote him you were a Mueller descendant, and that I intended you should have a go at these things — wood-cuts, art printing, etchings.'

They became very well acquainted, that day. Ferdinand's name was too bulky and mature, and was abbreviated to 'Dinny,' which seemed to make him rather light-hearted, as if his name had weighted him.

'You may call me Janet, if you like,' she had suggested.

'If we're going to play together with these things, you'll probably be teaching me, very soon, and I mustn't be much older than my teacher, you see, or it might discourage me.'

'I never knew anyone named Janet, before,' said Ferdinand. 'I'm glad.'

'Dinny, you say the most adorable things... and all unconsciously, too. That's the best part of it. You're developing into a young courtier; I can see that.'

* * * * * *

Ferdinand was also developing into a young liar, he feared, after he had answered all of Aunt Martha's pressing questions relative to that first visit with the problematical Mrs. Day. Naturally disposed to be suspicious of well-groomed femininity, Aunt Martha was troubled. Ferdinand was required to reproduce the afternoon, item by item. How was Mrs. Day dressed? Was Mr. Day at home? Was Madam Day present? What did she have to say? What all happened?

Ferdinand promoted himself, that evening, from the mere happy estate of apprentice to a beautiful crafts-woman. He achieved the dignity of a great story-teller. Baron Münchausen would have been proud of him. Amazing himself by the increasing glibness of his tale, he invented a conversation he had had with Mrs. Day that represented her as most ardently concerned about the welfare of the church, albeit she never attended, due to a slight heart affection which made it dangerous for her to expose herself to strong emotional appeals; garbed her in a somber dress, laid a gray shawl about her shoulders, had the audacity to put her hair up in curl-papers; located her workroom in the busiest part of the great house; caused servants to stand by her, handing her the things she needed in her work — and wound up with an account of his hostess's admiration for Aunt Martha and Uncle Miles and Angela.... Fearing he had been extravagant in this, Ferdinand decided to risk nothing further and excused himself on the pretense of having to study.

But Aunt Martha was never quite at ease over Ferdinand's two and three afternoons a week — and all day Saturdays — with Mrs. Day.

'I never did like the looks o' that woman,' she would say, anxiously, to Mr. Brumm. 'You wait!... We'll see!'

And when, at length, having waited, they saw, she muttered, grimly pleased that her forecast had been so prescient, 'Didn't I tell yuh? Didn't I warn yuh? Where were yer eyes?'

* * * * * *

Dinny carefully unwound the inky string from the type-form and went about the extraction of an upper-case H that seemed a bit defective.

'Rather rubbishy sentiment; wouldn't you say?' he called across to Janet, bent over a wood-cut with a big reading-glass in one hand and a slim reamer in the other, putting stripes in a wind-blown flag.

'Oh — I don't know,' she replied, as from a considerable distance. 'It's about what one would expect, isn't it, from a mellow old gentleman, trying to be lyrical about war; trying to remember and forget at the same time, like the proud but poor old lady in London who went out to sell papers, mumbling, "Times, tuppence! Times, tuppence! Lord, I hopes nobuddy 'ears me!"... And no one will actually read this, anyway, you know. They'll be saying, "What a *lovely* piece of printing! Whoever did it? And especially these bee-ootiful ornamental capitals, and this incomparable tail-piece! Just look at that *flag!*"... That's what they will be saying, Dinny.'

'That's rather cynical... for you, Janet,' laughed Dinny. 'I'm always the one that's scolded for being more concerned over the way things look than what they mean. You must be deteriorating.'

He ran the sticky, snapping, black brayer over the face

of his corrected galley, and began pounding another proof-page onto it with a plane.

'I think words get their definitions, not from the dictionary, but from the private sentiments of the people who use them,' continued Dinny, philosophically. 'Take the General's word "misunderstandings." That's what caused the war — "misunderstandings." Fact is, they all understood one another too well. People are forever calling their quarrels "misunderstandings." Nonsense! So long as they were misunderstanding, each one could give the other credit for a bit of ignorant honesty. But when they begin to understand each other, they call out the troops and distribute the gunpowder.'

'You amuse me, Dinny,' drawled Janet, intent on her occupation. 'You would never have thought about that, at all, if you hadn't been annoyed because "misunderstandings" is too long to look well in a line of twelve-point Caslon set to fourteen ems. It's just when they begin to inconvenience us that we find fault with words and have hot debates over them. We think up shorter synonyms that look better on whatever page we're making up, and then imagine we've discovered a new idea, or expressed a pleasanter thought. If "licentiousness" is too unwieldy, we change it to "liberty."'

'"Parsimoniousness" *is* easier to set, if you call it "thrift,"' agreed Dinny, willing to go on with the game, but a bit bewildered over Janet's choice of an illustration.

'It all depends upon who's talking,' she added, absently, 'and when. "Liberty" is a pretty word, isn't it?'

'I should think these old soldiers,' pursued Dinny, didactically, 'would never want to hear another word about war. It must give them the heebie-jeebies in the night. I saw a team of farm-horses run off with a mowing-machine, when I was a little boy. The man fell off the iron seat, and got tangled in the knives. The scared horses turned short when they came to a fence-corner and had their hind legs nearly chewed off, not having sense enough to stop. I see it yet, sometimes, when I'm slow going to sleep. It's the most reliable of all my pet horrors. Wouldn't you think these old veterans would be just as happy not to be reminded of screaming horses with eyes dangling on a string, dragging their insides after them in long muddy ropes; and neighbor boys with the white splintered ends of bones sticking through their bloody pant-legs, and sticky globs of warm brains——'

'I say! Dinny! Stop it! What a ghastly imagination!'

'I'm going to fetch it to market, one o' these days.'

'Going to be a butcher?'

'Going to write a book... called "Balderdash." Chapter one — patriotism; two — religion; three — I haven't quite decided on three yet, but it's to be something about the superstition that people with money have a right to play wheel-barrow with everybody who works for them or lives with them. Ever play wheel-barrow, Janet?'

'Yes, I think so. How do you play it?'

'Well — you get down on the floor, on your hands, and I pick you up by the feet and push, and you either have to walk on your hands or bump your nose.'

'Oh, yes — I've been playing that, all my life. Nice game!'

For a little while, Dinny rattled on with his sour diatribe against war, Janet remotely keeping track of his excursion.

It hadn't been quite true that she'd always been playing wheel-barrow. Father — God bless him — had been infinitely tender and considerate. How he had humored her every wish — hers and her mother's. Maybe that was why he could leave so little when he died; almost nothing, indeed, but extravagant tastes. She could have seen it through; but not her mother. Mr. Day had proposed such an easy solution. 'You'd be a fool, Janet,' her mother had said. 'It's a chance in a lifetime.' What a pity her mother had died, seeing the sacrifice had been made to please her.

'All this sweet hokum of the General's about "shot-and shell,"' Denny was declaiming. 'He's singing hymns about the varnished shot-and-shell piled in pyramids at the foot of the Soldiers' Monument. If he really wants to give the old fellows a thrill, why doesn't he remind them of the slippery shot-and-shell — all ooky and slimy with ——'

'I heard you, Dinny, the first time!... Hand me that slide-rule, will you, dear?... But, you see, that's the way to keep patriotism alive.'

'Patriotism's tripe!'

'Yes, Dinny.... Come over here and see my flag. Is that any better?'

He bent his five-feet-eleven over her soft shoulder, leaning his weight against the table on an ink-smeared hand.

'Fine, Janet! Much improved!... Now you take my Uncle Elmer; not meaning that he was worth a hoot before he went to Cuba, but just supposing he was. Gets himself all hotted up about his patriotic duty when somebody pounds a drum; sobs into his beer; hep-heps to Havana in boots two sizes too small for his big feet; curries the Colonel's horse; comes home with dysentery from eating spoiled meat that the get-rich-packers unloaded on them; and... Janet — perhaps you might give the eagle's left wing just a bit more spread... and expects to spend the rest of his life lying about in the shade at the Soldiers' Home. Patriotism — rot!... Look out for those stars, Janet! You'll have a deuce of a time putting them back in, you know, once they're out!'

'I know, Dinny. By the way,' she laughed, 'that's what the General's little book is about; isn't it? He believed that. Once the stars were out, it would be hard to put them back in.'

'Rubbish! Sentiment!'

'Then why are we doing this, at all?'

'Because I'm earning money to go to college this fall.' Dinny turned back to his table and carefully peeled off a new proof.

'Speaking of college — has your uncle relented?'

'Him — relent? He's more convinced than ever. Says

he has already assured old Dean What's-His-Name that I'd come to Magnolia; says it would do him a terrible lot of damage in the conference, or whatever it is, if I went to a godless State University. Everything's godless that Uncle Miles doesn't happen to know about. Odd jumble of conflicting ideas in Uncle Miles's head. I'd give something for a picture of the inside of it. Long ago, he was out in Arizona and visited the Petrified Forest. Never gets done talking about it. Picked up a piece and brought it home. Fondles it, and says, in a stage whisper, "That's *a million years old*, my friend!"... But, on Sundays, it's only six thousand years old, so it won't antedate the sun, moon, and stars.'

'Don't be too hard on him, Dinny. He can't contradict Genesis, you know. His whole flock would stampede.'

'I'll bet Mr. Day wouldn't follow along in that stampede,' said Dinny, eager as usual to find something meritorious in Mr. Day, seeing Janet had to live with him — a sore trial, he suspected. Or, was Dinny championing the cause of Mr. Day because he feared that Janet was thinking too much about Mr. Zimmerman, who was at home again, and so frequently visited her?

'No,' replied Janet, gravely. 'Mr. Day wouldn't follow in that stampede. He never follows. He'd lead it.'

'But — you don't mean to tell me Mr. Day believes that old Jewish myth about the universe being created in six days!'

'On Sundays, when he's in church — yes.'

'And the yarn about Adam... and Eve made out of Adam's rib?'

'Oh, yes; he believes that, every day and no matter where he is — especially about the rib.'

'Meaning... you're a rib, Janet?' queried Dinny, laughing, but half-wishing he had not said it.

'One of the shorter ones, Dinny.'

'They're called "floating" ribs.'

'How do you mean — "floating"?... Loose?'

'Oh, no,' scoffed Dinny, pretending pride in his superior knowledge of physiology, 'they never get loose.'

'I should have known that much; shouldn't I?'

'You probably never thought about it before.'

'Don't be too sure about that, my son,' she said, in a tone that worried him a little. It wasn't like Janet to be so mysterious. He couldn't quite understand her, today. Even her immediate change of topic was not at all reassuring.

'So — I suppose you'll be going to Magnolia, then.'

'I'm in for it, all right. However, I am not particularly interested in science, so it doesn't matter much. The Lit. course at Magnolia is probably no thinner than in many a bigger school. Professors in English Comp. can't tell you how to write. If they knew how to do it, they'd be doing it; wouldn't they? All I want is a chance to do some reading, on my own hook, and plenty of time for scribbling. I can have that at Magnolia. They're much too hard up to enforce any discipline. I can go my own gait.'

'I'm going to miss you — terribly.' Janet left her work, and stood beside him. Her eyes were troubled.

'That's the only thing about it, Janet. I don't know how I'm to get along without you.'

She walked to the window and stood looking out.

'There isn't very much more I could do for you, Dinny; is there?'

'You're the only real friend I ever had, Janet.' He put down the brayer and joined her at the window. 'Sometimes, I've wondered if I wasn't leaning too heavily; monopolizing you.'

'It's been the other way about, dear,' said Janet, soberly. 'I've monopolized you. You haven't been interested in the girls of your class in school.'

'Pooh! They're nothing but silly little gigglers.'

'Maybe you wouldn't think so if you made any effort to know them.'

'You're all the girl I want, Janet,' said Dinny, lightly.

'That's just the trouble. It isn't good for you. I'm not

your girl; nor am I your sister, or your mother.' She faced
about, and abruptly changed the subject. 'Oscar — Mr.
Zimmerman — wants you to have the stuff he lent us; all
the Caxton and Cheltenham and the rest of it, and the
seven-by-nine press, and this fancy Caslon, too. He says
you're to take it along to college with you. He hopes you
will set up a little shop and make it pay your way. Rather
nice of him; don't you think?'

'Very!' said Dinny, trying to sound grateful. 'But
weren't you going to use it, any more?'

'No — not after you leave, Dinny.'

He wasn't quite sure whether he wanted to be under such
obligation to Mr. Zimmerman. True, it would be of no consequence to the rich bachelor globe-trotter whether Dinny
used the printing-equipment or not. Otherwise it would
probably be idle in a storage warehouse. But he disliked
accepting anything from Mr. Zimmerman. He was candidly jealous of Mr. Zimmerman, of his easy grace, his urbane manners, his charming personality, his casual allusions
to the places he had seen — Singapore, Calcutta, Moscow
— mentioning them in about the same tone Dinny might
have used when speaking of Oak Grove or Zanesdale or
Unger. He often wondered if Mr. Day were jealous, too;
not that he cared, greatly. Perhaps Mr. Day's private feelings were modified, somewhat, by the fact that Mr. Zimmerman was one of the heaviest stockholders in the Day
Wholesale Provision Company. Money made a lot of
difference.

'Dinny' — Janet's voice was a bit uncertain — 'we're
getting awfully crowded and cluttered in this room.
Lately, I've been thinking we might move our printing-
stuff to larger quarters. I looked at a room yesterday. It's
in the Woolford Block on Superior Street ——'

Dinny remembered that Mr. Zimmerman owned the
Woolford Block, and with difficulty suppressed a scowl.

'—— and I can get it for a song. Suppose you run in,
next time you're down-town, and see what you think of it.'

She took up her purse from the table, and handed him a key.

'Number 306. Go in on Monday, after school, and look it over.'

Dinny was in no position to debate the matter. He nodded, and took the key. It was growing dark, though only five-thirty, and the rain was falling in torrents.

'Take my umbrella, dear.'

'Thanks, Janet. I'll telephone you, when I've seen the room.'

'Good-bye, dear.' She reached out her slim hand, and looked up, fleetingly, into his perplexed eyes. It was so unlike her to offer her hand. They never shook hands. Dinny took it, rather confusedly, and was at a loss what to say.

'I'm afraid you're dreadfully worried about something.' Dinny swallowed hard, and put his hands lightly on her shoulders.

''Bye, Dinny!' Impulsively she threw her arms tightly around his neck and kissed him on the lips; then, turning quickly away, walked toward the window, stood with both hands outspread on the broad sill, a mere silhouette in the gathering gloom.

That was the picture he retained of Janet for a dozen years.

With another long, anxious look, he reluctantly went out, and closed the door.

*　*　*　*　*　*

On Monday afternoon, he went to inspect the room in the Woolford Block; went without interest, and weighted by an unaccountable depression.

The room was not empty, as he had expected. All their printing-equipment was there, installed in orderly fashion, ready for work.

On the imposing-stone was a receipted bill for three months' rental. At the bottom of the paper, hurriedly written in pencil, were a few lines in Janet's tall, slim letters:

God keep you always, dear Dinny. Forgive me for going away. I'm not really bad, Dinny. It's just that I'm tired playing wheel-barrow.

He gazed woodenly at the message for a long time, with an aching throat and burning eyes. Then he tore it into small bits, savagely stuffed the scraps into his pocket, went out, locked the door, and clumped slowly down the stairs.... Janet was no better than the rest of them. They were all cheaters! Damn them!

CHAPTER VI

AFTER a wheezing ascent of four steep flights in the wake of his young employer and guide, the gruff expressman had unshouldered Ferdinand's small, old-fashioned trunk, with a groan of relief and reproach, and had ambled off down the bare, resounding dormitory hall grumblingly fingering the four dimes and seven nickels that totaled his exact charge.

Obedient to some atavism urging him to establish a claim to his new property without delay, Ferdinand laid his coat and collar on the sagging bed, and went through the preliminary gestures of making himself at home. The room was cramped, shabby, and incompletely furnished, but it was his, and the feeling of possession was pleasurable.

The convex lid of the antiquated trunk was thrown back against the dingy wall, and the welcome task of unpacking proceeded; his meager, outmoded wardrobe, a handful of books, a dozen cheap towels, and the case of carving-tools, over which there had been such a row, Aunt Martha's eloquent disapproval rending the Yuletide peace and reaching an impassioned climax in her unexecuted threat to carry the expensive gift back to that there high-'n'-mighty Mrs. Day with her own hands.

'With love to Dinny from Janet.'

It was the engraving on the silver plate inside the velvet-lined lid that had detonated Aunt Martha's tightly corked resentment against a mysterious (and probably questionable) friendship which had ripened without benefit of her sanction, and was increasingly fulfilling her dire prediction that the attachment would wean Ferdinand away from his 'humble home 'n' all that it stands fer.'

And what right had this Mrs. Day to be 'Janet' to a mere half-grown boy, inexperienced, unworldly, and calfishly infatuated? What kind o' 'love' was this, we'd like to know, that had the impudence to flaunt itself in the face

of his family? And since when had his name been changed
to 'Dinny'?... 'Dinny' — indeed!... *Dinny!* — well, we'd
see about that!

Ferdinand sat down on the edge of the weak-spined bed
with the silver-mounted box in his hands.

Queer — wasn't it? — how an inanimate thing, pieced
together of wood and screws and glue, silver and velvet
and steel, could take on a personality possessed of so many
sensitive, changing moods? One day you couldn't bear to
look at it for the worry and chagrin it had caused you.
Next day you loved it so tenderly it made your throat
thick. Another day you despised it for reminding you of
a tragic disenchantment that had all but killed you.

The box of carving-tools and his mother's little walnut
desk; living things, they were!

The desk!... One winter Sunday afternoon when he was
seven, in a promptly repented unveiling of cankered memories, Aunt Martha had told him the story of the desk;
just the bare, ugly, shameful facts about the storm of
jealousy it had provoked, a storm which Aunt Martha
deplored but partly justified.

'I always said yer grandpa never should 'a' done it.
He might 'a' knew it wouldn't set right with th' rest o' th'
family; not that I ever cared, myself. I had t' work too
hard, goodness knows, ever t' spend any time a-settin' at a
desk. But Julia was always his favorite. It broke his heart
when she died.'

'And grandpa died, too, that same night, Aunt Martha,
didn't he?'

Aunt Martha had nodded, shuddered, and laid another
stick on the fire.

The desk had come along when Aunt Martha had left
'th' old home,' her brothers and sisters pressing no claim
to a share in it. As a little lad, he saw it only when they
moved from one house to another; and not even then, for
it had remained thickly wrapped in the dusty burlap in
which it had been shipped to Unger.

Shrouded, it had lived in dark corners of attics, damp corners of cellars, a thing neither to be used nor thrown away. It was almost as if they carried his mother's corpse about with them.

When they had moved to Indianapolis, Ferdinand had asked for it. Consent was rather grudgingly given. He had one desk, hadn't he? However, Aunt Martha supposed he had a right to it, if he wanted to crowd his room with it. Sometimes he wished he had not insisted. He almost never used it, and when he did he felt depressed.

Perhaps he had better ask Uncle Miles to ship him the desk.... Dinny drew a wry smile. He could put the case of carving-tools in the drawer of the desk, and let them settle their problems between themselves. Now that he was in college, there would be plenty of other things to occupy his attention. New friends and fresh interests would lay his ghosts.

But, what about these new friends; these fresh interests?

The past three hours had been a disappointing surprise. 'College' was not quite as he had pictured it, a comradely, democratic, open-hearted aggregation of irresponsible youngsters, bent on getting acquainted with one another by the shortest routes.

At almost every station stop, en route from Indianapolis to Magnolia — so close to Cincinnati as to think of itself as a suburb — young people boarded the train. Doubtless they were going to college; perhaps to Magnolia. A few suitcases were adorned with pink and white stickers, pennant-shaped, cheering for the school. Already he was entertaining a growing sense of loyalty and pride.

For the most part, however, the pilgrims bound for Magnolia, if they greeted each other at all, seemed shy and restrained; a mere nod, 'Hello, Buster; back to the mill?' ... 'How 'r' yuh, Prichard; good summer?'

But this was the day-coach, and these the day-coachers. The distinction gradually dawned on Ferdinand. For some time he had been curious, when the train stopped in the

larger towns, over festive sounds on the platform well to
the rear. At Richmond, he strolled to the steps, and,
leaning out, saw a score or more of well-dressed, high-
spirited people, old and young, bidding good-bye to a
handful of students, gathered at the entrance to a Pullman,
the white-jacketed porter busy with their baggage.

He went back through his own car, and overheard their
cryptic banter as they scrambled up the steps, the porter
banging the vestibule doors behind them. These, too,
were Magnolians — the real, traditional college students
of song and story, larkish, noisy, devil-may-care. He wished
he had committed the extravagance of riding in the Pullman. It would have made all the difference. Not quite,
however, he reflected — not in these clothes.

A month afterward, burning with hot resentment against
the discrimination that had bled his pride white, Ferdinand marveled that nearly four years of intimate association with a person so sophisticated as Janet Day had
contributed almost nothing to his knowledge of that other
world to whose citizenship he aspired.

Analyzing their relations, however, he saw that it was
neither his fault nor hers that the friendship had done so
little for him in this respect. Such community of interest
as they had was based almost exclusively on their shop-
work. Ferdinand had never taken a meal with her except
the sandwiches, cakes and tea, casually enjoyed during a
few minutes of recess from their occupation. Janet was
always dressed in an inky, paint-daubed smock, her hair
down her back; he was always in his working togs. They
rarely talked of anything else than their immediate con-
cerns. Janet had not given him a ticket to the world of
smart people.

Alighting from the train, Ferdinand confronted a gay
scene. A spirited crowd — modishly dressed, bareheaded,
beautiful girls, and white-sweatered, flannel-trousered,
handsome fellows — cheered and chaffed the recruits
descending from the Pullmans; their classmates, no doubt;

old acquaintances: but no — fully half of them were obviously newcomers, like himself. Solicitously in tow of the old-timers, they were now being presented to the welcoming throng. A phalanx of motor-cars was drawn up along the platform, engines noisily churning and clamoring to be off, drivers' seats occupied by debonair greeters, sons and daughters of the other world, the world that rode in Pullmans and came to meet people who rode in Pullmans.

Ferdinand had not been expecting anyone to meet him, and therefore had no occasion to be disappointed; but he was overcome with a feeling of such loneliness as had never afflicted him before. He took up his battered old suitcase, made some inquiries of a policeman whose amused attention was grudgingly distracted from the real people's festivities, boarded a street-car, reached the campus — a gently undulating grove of oaks and elms, zigzagged with winding paths of white, hard-tramped gravel-ribbons that negligently wandered about from one main entrance to another of the dozen or more nondescript buildings of brick, of stone, of cement, of wood, in attempted imitation of every known school of architecture and ranging in age all the way from raw newness to pathetic dilapidation.

He had anticipated, without relish, the quiet chat he would probably have with Dean Sloke. He would be shown into Dean Sloke's office, when his turn came.

'Ah — so you are Ferdinand Brumm, the nephew of my esteemed friend, the Reverend Miles Brumm of Indianapolis, who has been a valuable supporter of Magnolia. We are glad to have you here, Mr. Brumm. Now what can we do for you to make you comfortable?'

Ferdinand was pointed to the Registrar's office. He saw that there was no necessity for seeking an interview with Dean Sloke. There was a long line of bewildered freshmen, leaning an elbow against the long, tall counter. No one of them in any way resembled the urbane youths who had been so hilariously received at the station. Surely they

had had time to arrive here, by now. Mailed advice had
counseled freshmen to come to the Administration Building immediately upon arrival. Where were these others?
But perhaps there was a special room for their accommodation. Maybe the freshmen who came to town in Pullman
cars were handled in some distinctive manner, or at some
other hour.

He took his place in the line, and, advantaged by his
height, surveyed his neighbors. The girl in front of him
was a nervous, home-made, little thing; the boy whose
broad, square back obstructed her view of the distant goal
had the black-tanned neck of a farmer. The criss-cross
furrows on the neck announced that their bearer was
older than the others by four or five years. He'd been
ploughing deep and saving his pennies against the day
when he might come to college.

Ferdinand was half-ashamed of himself over this critical
invoice of his companions. Come to think of it — this was
his own crowd, after all; wasn't it? By what right was he
assuming a supercilious attitude, in his mind, toward these
yokels?

At length he had reached the impressively business-like,
barricaded throne of the Registrar and his self-consciously
competent assistants. He answered a few crisp, inquisi-
torial queries, wrote his name on three or four blanks
which were promptly and soundly smacked with a big
rubber stamp, counted out forty-two dollars at an adjoining wicket for which he received another emphatic whack
on his credentials, moved forward to 'Rooms,' paid another
fee, earned another whack, took his key, picked up the old
suitcase he had been pushing along with his foot, and milled
through the crowd to the doorway. It moved back, a little,
to make room.

Nobody had spoken to him except the perfunctory
clerks, nor he to any; though there had been a few shy,
bucolic grins accompanying the 'Beg your pardon' which
went along with sundry unintentional jabs of elbows in the
jostling line-up of rookies.

They were a very ordinary lot of people, he thought, on both sides of the counter. Those back of the counter were a bit more seasoned, had learned their tricks, had developed something of the arrogance so appropriately worn by petty officials peering through wickets and sourly handing dipped pens to the public for its signature; but there was no essential difference between the green clodhoppers on this side the barrier and the ripe clodhoppers on the other.

As he had stood there waiting, Ferdinand wondered if Magnolia wasn't trying to impress the new arrivals; trying to make-believe she was a big university. Where was this warm, home-y friendliness that bubbled on the comradely pages of the college catalogue? Was all this swanky, big-business-y, card-index-y, cash-register-y atmosphere, this frowning fussiness, this cool official insolence, this elaborate hocus-pocus of labeled wicket-windows and ostentatious thud of rubber stamps a lot o' bunk? His instinct told him the whole affair screamed of insincerity....'Just a friendly, home-y, little college' — hell!

* * * * * *

Ferdinand answered a vigorous rat-a-tat-tat of knuckles and admitted one who, promptly identifying himself as Orville Kling, junior, resident across the hall, candidate for the ministry, leader of the college band in need of new material, and Religious Editor of *The Blossom*, requested pay, in kind, at his first full stop, for his generous tender of a biographical sketch.

With less to tell about himself, Ferdinand made short work of his own story. Pressed for further disclosures, he admitted he had no idea what he would 'take up.' No — not the ministry; he was sure of that much.... Well — he had no taste for it, no fitness for it, and, to be frank, no interest in it. Kling thought this odd, considering Ferdinand's home environment.

'Hope you'll come down to the Y rooms, second floor,

tonight at seven,' suggested Kling. 'Just an informal little
get-together of the fellows to meet the new Frosh; a sing-
song, brief devotional service, some short prayers, a few
snappy talks; all through by eight.'

'Thanks,' said Ferdinand, graciously, but without enthusiasm.

'That's the spirit,' approved Kling, anxious to ex-
hilarate Ferdinand's wan interest. 'It makes all the difference, later, if you begin your college life right.'

Ferdinand nodded obligingly, and conceded that this
must be true, but his acquiescence lacked fervor. Bent on
saving a soul from anæmia, Kling rose to defend his moral
precept. Hands deep in his coat pockets, and rhythmically
elevating himself on his toes, he dealt seriously with Ferdinand's limp aspirations to make a right start.

'Yes, sir — it makes all the difference, you'll find. The
whole four years depend on the first week's contacts.
Down there on Sunnyside Avenue, the upper classmen are
teaching the new fraternity pledges to smoke a pipe, scorn
the barbs, and beat the profs.... Up here, we have different
ideas. You'll start right, won't you, Brumm?'

'You mean — at a prayer-meeting?'

'Well — that kind of a beginning would make for
safety; wouldn't it?' queried Kling, slightly accelerating
the tempo of his adroit bouncing up and down on his toes.

Ferdinand grinned amiably, and walked to the window,
leaning against it; long, rangy arms folded.

'I'm pretty well up on prayer-meetings, Mr. Kling.
I've been raised on them. And — as for safety, I have all
my credits in that, too.... I mean to be friendly, and I'd
like to meet the fellows, and I appreciate your asking me,
but ——'

Kling stopped his bouncing and drew a long face.

'But — you won't be there.'

'I don't think so.'

Kling smiled bravely, shook his head regretfully, seemed
reluctant to leave. His eye wandered about the room.

'Play on anything?' he inquired, brightening.

'No — I'm not musical. Sorry.'

'Thought that might be a clarinet. We need another clarinet.'

'It's a case of carving-tools.'

'Carving-tools.... I never saw any. Mind if I look?'

Ferdinand's consent and the snap of the latch occurred simultaneously. Kling glanced up and smiled.

'They call you "Dinny," don't they?'

'Ye-es.'

'Rah, rah, rah — Dinny Brumm! That's what we'll be hearing next fall. You'll be going out for football, of course. They wouldn't let a big fellow like you escape.... Janet your sister?'

'Yes.... Is the athletic field close?'

Kling pointed north with his head, deeply interested in the shining tools.

' 'Most everybody's there now, watching the varsity warm up. Want to go over? I'm going.'

Ferdinand begged off with an excuse that he had a few errands in town.

'Well — so long, Dinny. See you later.'

* * * * * *

Supper was at five-thirty, the tenants of the dormitory preferring it early. Ferdinand was not hungry, nor was he keenly disposed to risk further interrogations about his plans for the evening. Waiting until the clangor of the second bell and the last clatter of descending feet had subsided, he put on the rather yellow and battered straw hat that Aunt Martha felt would do quite well enough, though he had entertained some doubts, walked quietly down stairs, down the slope, and turned to the left on Sunnyside Avenue. The broad verandas of the fraternity houses were filled with bareheaded students, some standing, some lounging in the big wicker chairs, some sitting on the railings swinging white-flanneled legs. Ferdinand was conscious of their amused attention, as he passed the Beta House — the last on the row, opposite which one took the street-car.

A merry voice sang out, accompanied by good-natured chuckles, and followed by a mature growl, 'Cut that out, Reddy! What th' hell!' —

'Hey, Reuben! How's the weather up there?'

Ferdinand scowled, flushed, and gave his full attention to the approaching street-car. He wondered if he wasn't going to hate Magnolia.

After supper, at a downtown restaurant, for which he had little relish, he went to the office of *The Morning Star*, and made his way to the Managing Editor's desk. He was a little more sure of himself in this environment, and presented his cause without nervousness.

'What experience have you had?' asked Mr. Brophy, tilting back in his chair, and scrutinizing Ferdinand not unpleasantly from under his green eye-shade.

'I've been doing amateur and semi-professional art-craft printing for some time. Since early June, I was on the display ads with *The Ledger*, Indianapolis.'

'How could you work evenings, and go to college?'

'I think I could manage, sir. No classes in the afternoon.'

'You'd have to be on from seven to ten-thirty, six nights a week... all but Saturday.'

'I could do that.

'Take this out to the composing-room, and set it.'

Ferdinand nodded, took the ad-copy, and pushed his way through the metallic racket of linotypes to the row of cases in the corner. It was the first time he had felt at home in Magnolia. The smell of ink revived his spirits, straightened his broad shoulders. Mr. Brophy followed him along, and spoke laconically to the grizzled foreman who nodded without looking up or removing his pipe.

'You may begin tomorrow evening, if you like,' said Mr. Brophy, an hour later, glancing over Ferdinand's shoulder.

'Ninety cents an hour. Six nights; seven to ten-thirty. Time and a half for overtime. Pay on Mondays. Right?'

'Right!... Thank you, sir.'

After a while, the foreman strolled over.

'Pretty fair, for a dub,' he growled, fetching his *r*'s rolling up from far back under an Irish pharynx. 'Mr. Brophy says you'll be goin' to college, day-times. Sure it won't be too much for ye, me boy?'

Ferdinand lowered his half-filled stick, and warmed to the genial, ruddy-faced Timmy Fagan. No — he could do it, all right. Liked it. Besides — he needed the money. Couldn't stay here without some kind of a job.

'You're luckier 'n 'most, t' have a trade,' said Timmy. 'Most uv 'em has to wait table and wash dishes at th' frats.'

'I'd see myself doing that!'

'Well — somebody's got t' wait on th' rich boys 'n' girls, 'n' see that they have enough t' eat, when they come in from their tennis, all tired and hungry,' drawled Timmy, his eyes wrinkling with delight as he noticed the flexing of Ferdinand's jaw-muscles. 'But,' he added, 'I can see that you'd rather somebody else 'tended to it.... And — now that we're speakin' o' meals, maybe you'd like to come over and have a bite o' honest Irish hospitality on Sunday, say, after the eleven o'clock Mass which you won't be to, bein' a heathen. The missus'll be glad, and th' kids, too. You'll be lonely like, for a while.'

Only an ungrateful snob could refuse such an invitation, thought Ferdinand. He accepted gladly, promptly; but, a moment later, and all the way back to the campus, where the dormitory windows gleamed with a welcome he wished he might respond to with more warmth, he was uneasy over his promise to old Timmy. Timmy, God bless him, had him all wrong.... Right, of course, about thinking he would resent the necessity of a job to wait table for these precious young well-to-do's, but quite wrong in thinking that he wanted to hold himself in sour aloofness from them.

It was the world they lived in that he most wanted to explore! And how was he ever to invade that world if he approached it via Sunday dinners at the Timmy Fagans'? Perhaps he'd better trump up some excuse.... But Timmy was no fool. Timmy mustn't be hurt.

However — no use worrying about it. Nobody need know. The Fagans probably had no college connections, at all. The 'kids' would be freckled little Micks — a half-dozen, maybe, who would show him their toy aeroplane... and that would be the end of it. 'Such a nice time, Mrs. Fagan!... Thank you, Mr. Fagan.... Yes, indeed, Mr. Fagan, I'll be glad to!... Good-bye, little Fagans!'

* * * * * *

He couldn't help being so tall that his contemporaries presumed him able to get forecasts of the weather, but he could help looking like a Rube. Pursuant to that resolution, he went into town, the next day, strode up to the counter of the best clothing store, and possessed himself of a natty new suit of blue serge.

His immediate college bills had been paid, and there was more than a hundred dollars in his pocket — earned by himself, every cent of it! Why shouldn't he do what he liked with it? His wages were assured. They would amply cover his expenses, with a comfortable margin.

Ferdinand paid for the suit and spent the remaining forty-eight dollars of the hundred he had allotted to this adventure in a neighboring haberdashery. Uncle Miles, he knew, would have scowled and remarked that even friendly little colleges have a 'subversive' (pet word of his) influence on youth; and as for Aunt Martha, she would have had — if aware of his amazing profligacy — a fit.

* * * * * *

Up early on Friday, arrayed in all his new finery — the blue, double-breasted suit that squared his shoulders, the soft gray fedora set at a sporty angle on his freshly groomed head, russet shoes, smart fawn shirt, tie a shade darker matching the handkerchief that peeped from his breast pocket — Ferdinand found he still had half an hour to spare before his first encounter with the class in English Composition.

Yesterday there had been mere lesson-assignment sessions in Beginner's Greek with old Appleton who promised to be a hard taskmaster; Algebra under nervous and self-conscious young Peters who would be lenient (it was devoutly to be hoped); and Latin under the meek and obsequious little Harwood, commonly spoken of as The Bearded Lady.

He would bone in Greek not only because he really wanted to learn it but was afraid of Appleton — a sarcastic old savage. He would toddle along in Cicero, Latin being a cinch for him. And as for Algebra, it could go to the devil along with the inexperienced Peters who was clearly too frightened over his new responsibility to pay much attention to anybody else's dilemmas.

But English Composition was quite another matter. This was going to be a bread-and-butter affair. Ferdinand knew he would be writing, all his life; writing for a career, writing for wages. No fooling, here.

He could have wished that Professor Grover's sketch in the catalogue had hinted at a wider experience. A degree from some well-known university would have added luster to his biography.

That Professor Grover had not been much of a nomad was obvious. Never had he been taken up, in foreign parts, for vagrancy. He had stayed on home base and kept himself unspotted from the world.

Topping the list of courses offered by the English Department was an impressive and extended survey of the Grover equipment.

WILLIAM ERNST GROVER, A.B., A.M., PH.D., LITT.D.

So far; so good. But the rest of it indicated that Professor Grover's mileage was disturbingly low.

Educated Magnolia Public Schools; Magnolia Academy (grad. 1878, with high distinction); Magnolia College (A.B., 1882, *m.c.l.*, Class pres. and hist.; winner Rebecca Winters Dutton medal); Master of Arts (Magnolia College, 1885. Thesis: 'Prehistoric Mounds near Magnolia'); Ph.D. (Magnolia College, 1889. Thesis: 'Magnolia Under Doctor Swits'); Litt. D. (Magnolia College, 1896). Author: 'Magnolians Who Made Their Mark' (Magnolia College Press, 1899), 'Fifty Years of Magnolia' (Magnolia College Press, 1902), 'Forward, Magnolia!' (Magnolia Ptg. and Engv. Co., 1910).

Three cheers for good old Magnolia; eh, Professor Grover? Ferdinand would have grinned had he been less disturbed over the prospect.

The time came when he did grin; shouted with laughter; slapped his leg and yelled with delight. That was while engaged in composing the article on 'Rhododendron College,' midway of his junior year. He sold the article to *The Iconoclast*, receiving, two months later, in the same mail, a check for one hundred dollars from the editor in New York, and a crisp request for an early interview with President Braithwaite of Magnolia.

'It might have been more discreet,' said President Braithwaite, endeavoring to suppress a twinkle, 'had you gone to the fauna rather than the flora for a fictitious name. "Rhododendron" made it a bit obvious, you know.... This about the Pyncheon chickens — facetious enough but cruelly unkind!'

'I had had the chickens in mind for a long time, sir,' said Ferdinand, on that occasion. 'It simply had to be said.'

He did not say how long, but the fact was that this idea had first occurred to him on the morning early in his freshman year when, with a few minutes to spare before going down to his first class in English Composition, he had put aside *The House of the Seven Gables* which he had been reading, and had glanced at the college catalogue's sketch of Professor Grover.

Apropos of 'Rhododendron's' policy of recruiting her Faculty exclusively from the ranks of her own alumni, Ferdinand, the junior, wrote:

'Concerned as this institution is over the mental and moral improvement of the outer world, particularly such parts of it as must be reached by water, it occurs to some of us that Rhododendron College might well consider a philanthropy nearer home.

'Year after year, proud of her children, Alma Mater has refused to permit their acceptance of chairs in other schools.

'Yale, Harvard, Princeton, Columbia — does Rhododendron not owe it to these institutions, all of them doing good work and undeniably excellent in their way, to encourage their efforts not only by consenting that a few of our alumni may join their faculties, but by inviting some of their more distinguished sons to accept minor posts on our instructional staff?

'Not a Rhododendron alumnus on the faculty of any other college! Not a single professor at Rhododendron bearing a degree from any other school!

'Should it be said that our policy of intellectual inbreeding insures the integrity of our academic tribe, and guarantees against the debilitating invasion of alien blood, it may be replied that dangers lurk in the way of such aloofness.

'Witness, for example, the tragic plight of Hepzibah Pyncheon's poultry. Generation after generation, they had carried on, gloriously free of any exotic contamination, dourly scornful of the frivolous vulgarians in neighboring coops. And did not the fateful day arrive at length when these same Pyncheon chickens stalked about, spurless, combless, and without plumage; still proud, still grave, still haughty, but lacking the sense of humor necessary to the laying of an egg, to say nothing of the thermal dynamics required to hatch one?

'Featherless, eggless — but not crowless. Even when

they were too feeble to scratch, either for provender or
reasons of personal hygiene, they still raised their voices in
the old pæan of praise that they had been kept free of
foreign taints. They had the pip, yes; but, thank God,
they were not mongrels!'

* * * * * *

Discovering, to his dismay, that the new russet shoes
were much too snug, Ferdinand hurriedly divested himself
of the entire ensemble, resolved that he would wear none
of it until he could wear it all.

Professor Grover was kindly patronizing, playfully
paternal. The class would begin by submitting, on Tuesday, a fifteen-hundred-word theme on 'Early Impressions
of Magnolia.'

As the class straggled out, Ferdinand overheard a col-
loquy in the hall. The Pullmans were talking it over, as
they ambled toward the main doorway.

'Freddy says the old boy always asks for that, the first
day. He says if you dash off a lot o' rot about the great
honor and privilege, and all that sort o' bilge, you're solid
with him for keeps; says if you write that when you saw
the campus for the first time you just sat down on the grass
and cried out loud, you'll be a Phi Beta Kappa when
you're a senior.'

'Phi Beta Kappa! D'you mean they've got a ——?'

'Don't be a silly ass!... Phi Beta Kappa, my eye!'

* * * * * *

The elder of the two Fagan kids was a girl with the black-
est hair, the bluest eyes, the whitest skin, the evenest
teeth, and the most heady smile that Ferdinand had ever
seen done into one picture of glowing, high-school-girlish
vivacity. Patrick, Kitty's brother, was fifteen.

Timmy Fagan's elder kid was going to resemble her
mother, one day, as to amplitude of charms; you could see
that. At seventeen, however, this threat, that at forty-two

Kitty's physique would probably be redundant, evoked no pity.

The dinner was all that it had promised to be, and more; a gay meal, Ferdinand at his best, glad he had come.

It was over now. Young Pat had left for a ball game. Timmy's eyes began to swim in response to custom's demand for the Sunday afternoon nap. Mrs. Fagan's housewifely conscience had conveyed her to the kitchen, scorning the volunteered assistance of her attractive child.

They sat in the swing on the little side porch overlooking the trim, tiny garden. Ferdinand was actively in the market for the companionship Kitty was so ready to bestow. He had been quite desperately lonely, almost ill of loneliness.

'You haven't seen our beautiful park yet,' said Kitty. 'You'll like it, I think. It's very nice, and there's a big lagoon with boats. Lots of people go there, Sundays.'

They stood for a long time at her gate, laughing, bantering, occasionally lowering their voices to brief seriousness, on their return at five-thirty.

Ferdinand regretfully looked at his watch.

'Good-bye, Kitty,' he said. 'Next Sunday, then.'

'Okay, Dinny... 'Bye.'

There was a deliciously lilting circumflex accent over the ''Bye' that rang and sang in Dinny's ears, all evening, as he stood at the case and stuck large, boastful type certifying that Wemble's would be doing the city of Magnolia a good turn, tomorrow, with some unprecedented values in sheets and pillow-cases.

CHAPTER VII

'No use,' said the nurse, decisively. 'He won't see you.'

'He's got to,' growled Dinny.

'Oh, I don't know as he's got to,' countered Miss Lash, suddenly defiant. 'The police couldn't make him talk. What makes you think ——?'

'Sister' — Dinny drew an ominous frown — 'you go back to Mr. Peter Andrews and tell him *The Star* knows all about it, anyway ——'

'Thinks it does, maybe,' scoffed Miss Lash.

'Which comes to the same thing, so far as tomorrow morning's report of the accident is concerned, he'll find. I'm here to let him correct us on any of the minor details. It's ten o'clock, and we've no time to fritter.'

'You certainly have a lot of crust — for a kid.'

'You ought to know,' grinned Dinny, companionably. 'Just a kid yourself.' The accusation was ridiculous. Miss Lash was not seriously annoyed, however, and the little nose she made at him developed into a smile.

'I'll try him again,' she said, in the manner of a fellow conspirator.

Dinny was covering his first assignment as a reporter. Mr. Brophy had urged him to work full time through the Thanksgiving recess, the display ads being particularly heavy at this season.

'And if you have nothing better to amuse yourself with in the evenings,' added the editor, 'you may share Anderson's police beat with young Maloney. Anderson's off to see his Alabama relatives. You've been hankering to try your hand at reporting: here's your chance.'

Mr. Brophy had been prompt to make his promise good. The Thanksgiving vacation had begun only today at noon, a general hegira leaving the campus all but deserted. Happy to have a congenial occupation, Dinny worked on the ads all afternoon and early evening. At nine-thirty, Timmy Fagan called, 'Mr. Brophy wants ye.'

'You're just leaving for the Protestant Hospital, young feller' — Mr. Brophy tossed him a memorandum scribbled on a card — 'to interview an old man, mysteriously shot in the leg; has no police record, good citizen, but won't talk. Make him tell you.... Scatter along, now, and see what you're good for.'

'Mr. Andrews says you can come up,' announced Miss Lash, amiably. 'I told him he'd better get it off his chest; but don't pester him, will you? He's a fine old man, and wouldn't hurt a fly. I won't have him persecuted.'

'It seems he's told you,' deduced Dinny.

She raised her brows, smiled archly, and led the way, Dinny following with long, confident strides.

'Very sick?' he inquired, as they traversed the third-floor corridor. The pungent reek of antiseptics and spent ether were doing odd tricks with Dinny's unaccustomed nostrils, and the hoarse, unhuman moans of some patient groping out of anæsthesia shortened his steps. Miss Lash grinned.

'No — or you wouldn't be seeing him; superficial wound, no infection, he can go home in a day or two. But' — she paused at the door — 'I'll not have him hectored; understand? If he doesn't want to talk freely, that's that, and there's your hat. Promise?'

Mr. Andrews's gaunt old frame was so slight that the bed seemed unoccupied except for the benign face on the pillow. He shyly projected a thin, white hand from beneath the sheet, cleared his throat nervously, and drew a timid, embarrassed smile.

'Nurse thinks I may as well tell you,' he murmured, with a weary sigh. 'If I don't, you'll probably make it worse than it is, though it's none of the public's business, far as I can see.'

'The public,' sympathized Dinny, taking the chair Miss

Lash had pushed up for him, and sensing with satisfaction the revival of his self-confidence, 'is an old hen.... And the newspapers are impudent gossips.... And reporters are a pest.... But — such things being as they are — how *did* you get shot in the leg?'

'My next-door neighbor, out in Lambert Park, is Mr. Charles McCutcheon ——' The old man sighed again, deeply, as he watched the name sprawling across the reporter's untidy wad of copy-paper; but, having burned his bridges, there was no retreat. '—— A longtime friend of mine. We both work for the Buckeye Implement Company. We have a croquet-ground together, a small garden, and in the winter we play chess.'

'He has been to see you, I presume,' encouraged Dinny.

'No — er — well, yes; but I had them say I was too sick. ... I'll be coming to that, in a minute.'

The weary old voice droned on, reminiscently. Charlie was a widower, you know; he, a bachelor; nobody else mattered; went down town in the morning on the same car, lunched together, pretty nearly inseparable.

''Bout two weeks ago, Charlie's daughter — the one that lives in Pinckney, and doesn't like me very well because I monopolize Charlie — gave him a St. Bernard pup to keep him company, a big-footed, empty-headed, destructive beast that tore up Charlie's house, all day — what time he wasn't tearing up mine — and howled like the devil all night. I could see that Charlie was worried, but he kept saying the dog would settle down and feel at home presently.

'And so, yesterday — wasn't it, nurse? — Charlie had gone down to Tiro to spend the night with William's folks; wedding anniversary, or something. You see, I hadn't slept for more 'n a week. Guess I was kinda out o' my head. Charlie had him out in a kennel at the far end of the lot; but, Gosh! that hadn't helped any.... I had an old revolver that hadn't been fired off for ten years or so. Three o'clock, I was pretty desperate, and put on my pants 'n' went out there. Somehow the hammer got caught in my pocket ——'

'You could have made up a story, couldn't you?' inquired Dinny, solicitously.

'I'm not very good at that,' replied the old man. 'Besides — my leg hurt pretty bad. I managed to get in before it had bled very much, and 'phoned for the doctor. He brought me here — and that's all there is to it. You can print it, if you want to, and all the neighbors will despise me — and Charlie will never speak to me again.'

'What did you do with the gun?' asked Dinny.

'Threw the darned thing in the cistern.'

'Excellent! Now don't you worry any more,' soothed Dinny, patting the emaciated hand. 'We'll see you through it.'

Dinny caught a car and hurried back to *The Star*, eyes bright with inspiration, so eager to document his scheme for the easement of good old Andrews that it never occurred to him there might also be some inquisitiveness on the part of *The Daily Eagle* concerning this mystery. That night, Dinny recognized for the first time unmistakable signs of his talent as a potential novelist. He warmed to his task. It was an unusual story, and toward the last of it they were snatching unfinished sheets out of his typewriter and rushing them, page at a time, to the linotypist.

Next morning, December twenty-second, subscribers to both papers were amazed at the difference between the two accounts of this strange affair. According to *The Eagle's* report — a mere stick on page seven — Mr. Andrews had accidentally shot himself while endeavoring to pot his absent neighbor's noisy dog, a minor injury from which he was rapidly recovering.

The Morning Star — (first page, with a carry to three) — offered a long, dramatic story of Mr. Andrews's heroic silence about the shooting. In his delirium, however, the brave old fellow had muttered, 'Don't shoot again, lad.... I haven't any money except what's there in my pocket-

book.... You can look, if you like.... Take it — and hurry
before somebody comes.... I won't tell on you, boy.... It
would break her heart.'

From these broken fragments, *The Star* had adroitly
built up a tale of romance and adventure impressive enough
to stand in the museum alongside the mastodon — all lath
and plaster and imagination, except the third dorsal verte-
bra and two molars. Chivalrous old Andrews! Brave old
Andrews! Attacked in his little home by a marauder, he had
recognized the wayward son of an old friend.

Nobody knew, nobody was likely ever to know — for
Andrews seemed determined to keep his own counsel —
what a wealth of romance lay undisclosed in the heart of
this kindly old bachelor. Ambitious as she was to print all
the news, *The Star* had quietly withdrawn from the bedside of this valiant knight, challenged to match his sports-
manship by declining to press the matter any farther.

That afternoon, industriously distributing big type,
Dinny, out of the tail of his apprehensive eye, observed the
approach of his boss, paper in hand. He redoubled his
zealous interest in his occupation. Mr. Brophy was at his
elbow now, but Dinny did not look up. It was a very busy
day.

'My son,' said Mr. Brophy, reproachfully, '*The Eagle*
will probably try for a goal from the field with your Andrews
story, tomorrow morning. They'll make us look like a cage-
ful of monkeys.'

'I've been thinking a little about that, too, sir,' admitted
Dinny, confidentially, 'but, you see, the tale they tortured
out of old Andrews, late last night, was concocted in sheer
self-defense. He was resolved not to tell the straight story,
so he made one up, on the spot, to satisfy their greedy
curiosity. He would have done the same for me, if I had
badgered him. Takes all the blame on himself! Risks the
good opinion of his neighbors, risks his job at the shop,
throws away the lifelong friendship of Mr. McCutcheon....
Shoot McCutcheon's pet? Nonsense! You wait until the

people see the picture of saintly old Andrews, in bed at the hospital, near death's door, staring up out of those big, wistful ——'

'Hell! — they're going to discharge him this afternoon.'

'No, sir. I beg your pardon, sir. They had thought of it, but the nurse and I agreed it wouldn't do. I was out there and told them *The Star* would pay for all it cost to keep him a week, at least.'

'He won't stay. Even if he does, he'll talk.'

'No, sir. The nurse says his room is rapidly filling up with flowers and baskets of fruit. And Mr. Kellerman was there, making a fuss over him ——'

'You mean old man Kellerman?'

'Yes, sir — president of the Buckeye — he was there; and Norton of *The Eagle* tried to see him, but Andrews sent down word to him that they'd practically forced him to tell them the tale he'd made up. The nurse says he likes our version of the affair ever so much better, though he told Mr. Kellerman he didn't think it was very sporting of us to print what he said while he was unconscious.'

'Well — I'll be damned!'

'So will Doctor Cummings,' drawled Dinny, 'for he told me he would. And, as for that ——' He hesitated, grinning.

'So will you, I presume,' assisted Mr. Brophy.

'*The Cincinnati Democrat* was there, taking pictures, when I left.'

'Well,' said Mr. Brophy, 'it's your affair. Carry on with it. This is going to call for a lot of expert lying, so I'll let you manage the campaign. I've been in the newspaper game for twenty years, my boy, and you're the biggest liar I have ever known.'

'Thank you, sir,' said Dinny. 'D'you think maybe I'd better go out there again?'

'Yes,' replied Mr. Brophy. 'I think maybe you had; and if old Andrews weakens and tells the truth, you needn't ever come back.'

Timmy Fagan had silently joined the party, obviously enjoying himself.

'Timmy,' said Mr. Brophy, 'I'm going over to head-quarters for a chat with Chief O'Brien. I'll be back in half an hour.'

'Yes, sir,' said Timmy, 'but it's all right, Mr. Brophy. I was over there at noon, and he's called 'em off the case. He sent you this long, black cheroot, sir, and said to tell you those greasy Republicans on *The Eagle* could whistle for any more dope on the Andrews shootin'.'

'You editing *The Star* now, Timmy?' asked Mr. Brophy, lighting the gift, dubiously.

'Well, sir' — Timmy lowered his voice, confidentially — 'we couldn't let th' boy down, sir, seeing it was his first offense. I told the chief he was a fine lad, and I'd seen him at Mass, last Sunday.'

'Nonsense, Timmy. Brumm's not a Catholic.'

Timmy smiled, omnisciently, and turned toward his stone table.

'My Kitty's attendin' t' that, sir.'

* * * * * *

Dinny Brumm's freshmanhood at Magnolia which, at the outset, had threatened to be drab and uneventful, was not altogether unsatisfactory.

Startled, after five days, by the realization that he was likely to become a lone wolf on a campus where everyone else had entered into budding friendships — his nightly employment, and his boarding at a restaurant in town having made it quite impossible for him to be sociable — Dinny resolved to mend matters by spending an hour, late afternoons, on the athletic field. He could at least relieve himself of the just accusation that he wanted no friends and preferred to go it alone.

At three o'clock on Wednesday, therefore, he had presented himself at the freshman wing of the 'training quarters' in the inadequate old gymnasium, where, without ask-

ing any questions or announcing his purpose, he was glee-
fully welcomed by young Assistant Coach Roberts and the
awkward assembly of prospective gridiron heroes, the tallest
of whom he overtowered.

His whole time having been occupied by other more important matters, Dinny had never taken any active interest
in high-school football, but from the first moment of his adventure with the pigskin he seemed to have an instinctive
feel for the game.

What came later to be referred to by sports writers as his
'reckless courage,' was in evidence that first day, possibly
attributable to the fact that the savagery of hard tackling,
on the open field, appealed to his mood. The utter futility
of life had laid so low an estimate on the claims of personal
safety that Dinny was indifferent to bruises or the hazard
of broken bones.

When, at five, two teams were lined up by Coach Roberts,
Dinny observed that the personnel of the combating squads
could easily be identified even in their muddy, handed-
down toggery. As usual, the real people were on one side,
giving battle to the people who didn't matter much. The
real people had naturally gravitated, some chemical affinity
pulling them together. He found himself playing right
tackle on the team that didn't matter much. The Pullman
cars were to recognize the Day Coaches to the extent of using them for experimental purposes — to try out their own
strength, speed, and skill.

There was quite an accumulation of sentiment in Dinny's
mind on that subject, and in the ensuing thirty minutes of
play he expressed it so convincingly that, toward the end of
the game — which attracted a vociferous crowd of specta-
tors who found the battle of the 'frosh' more exciting than
the experienced maneuvers of the varsity on the adjoining
gridiron — there seemed to be a unanimity of consent, on
the part of the opposition, when Dinny took the ball, that
he might go down the field with it, undetained.

Perspiring, and secretly exultant, Dinny divested himself

of the tight-fitting old mole-skins that reeked with the acrid memories of many celebrated engagements, his team-mates and foes respectfully assisting. As he left the gymnasium, he found himself walking alongside Barney Vaughn, against whom he had played in the line. Barney was friendly, inquisitive. Where had Brumm been keeping himself?

'You must drop in and see me,' said Barney. 'I'm at the Custer Cottage, Sunnyside Avenue. That's where the Sig pledges live, you know.'

'No — I didn't know where they lived,' said Dinny. 'I don't even know what "Sig pledges" are,' he added. 'Red-headed ones, maybe?'

Barney ran his fingers through his untidy mop of bur-nished bronze, and laughed. Then he was serious.

'I'll bet somebody's been getting your goat, Brumm. You played like it. My Uncle! but you were a brute. Look at that elbow o' mine, will you?'

They overtook a couple of seniors, strolling back toward the campus — seniors of the Pullman car variety.

'Yeah,' one was drawling, 'the barbs were running circles around 'em. Who is this Brumm fellow, anyway? How-come we heard nothing about him? Hell of a scouting com-mittee we've got, this year.'

'That's what comes of letting the Sophs attend to it,' re-plied the other. 'We'd better have Bristol look this bruiser up, and tow him into camp.'

Barney winked, companionably, at Dinny, as they passed the self-assured strollers.

'Stock going up, eh?' chaffed Barney, out of the side of his mouth. 'Couple o' my brethren, those ginks.'

'Why didn't you speak to them?'

'Frosh aren't supposed to: you knew that, didn't you?'

'Democratic little school, isn't it?'

At the foot of the slope, their ways separated. Barney urgently renewed his invitation. Dinny evasively mumbled excuses: no time to visit, nose to the grindstone. Thanks, all the same, old man. See you tomorrow.

* * * * * *

On Friday morning, as Dinny entered the rapidly filling classroom of Professor Grover, and looked about for a vacant chair, the long arm and beckoning fingers of Barney Vaughn summoned him to a seat in the back row, where he was received with friendly smiles. He realized at a glance that he was in a Pullman car.

Professor Grover, who did not have to eat a whole egg to determine whether it was bad — a quip he often repeated without bothering to enclose it in inverted commas — reported that the papers submitted on Tuesday were, in the main, satisfactory. They would be returned, with notations, to their makers, at the close of the hour. (On the back of the last page of his essay, in red ink, Dinny read, later, 'well conceived, meritorious for perspicacity, clarity, and force.')

However, pursued Professor Grover, deliberately, it was not to be supposed that all the papers were of equal value; and, for the benefit of those who hadn't quite caught the idea, he would ask that one of the more excellent themes be read at this time.

Experience had taught him — Professor Grover pulled a benevolent smile — that it was usually embarrassing to the author when called upon to read his own piece aloud to the class. He would therefore request — he adjusted his glasses and glanced down at the unfamiliar roster — he would therefore request Miss — er — Adams to read the paper he had chosen as among the best.

A bit flustered, Miss Adams detached herself from her immediate environment, rather self-consciously approached the sanctum with much nervous jingling of bracelets, bangles, and other light hardware, faced her audience rosily, and began to intone her unknown classmate's anthem of praise to Magnolia in a dulcet tone so cooingly mellifluous that covert grins were exchanged among the more sophisticated.

Barney Vaughn leaned toward Dinny, pressed the back of his hand against the side of his mouth, and whispered, unctuously, 'Gawd is love.'

Dinny grinned, feebly.

The tender passion of the impromptu score which Miss Adams was fervently attaching to the sticky sweetness of the libretto produced a strange effect upon the class. By the time she had turned the first page, the dullest dolt in the room had his open palm against his mouth, apparently engaged in a battle for air.

Professor Grover smiled, hopefully, as if promising that it would eventually come out all right, and moved slowly back and forth in his chair, his outspread hands rhythmically rubbing his knees. It was easy to see, however, that he was worried. He had only read into this piously grateful tribute to the college far enough to see that it was definitely committed to a loyalty of high degree. He hadn't noticed, at the moment, that it was quite so superlatively silly as it now appeared, set to the sloppily sentimental adagio affected by Miss Adams whose mark for the semester's work in English Composition he had now determined upon in terms of three flats.

Dinny's flair for satire was not an achievement, but a gift. He had not deliberately planned the early pages of his impressions of Magnolia with a view to disarming the reader in order, later, to smite him with a volley of ridicule.

About midway of page four, it became evident in the mounting flush and occasional hesitations of Miss Adams that even she, herself, infatuated as she was with her elocution, had begun to suspect the increasing digression of the text from the melody, and realized the enormity of the farce to which she was unwittingly contributing the ultimate touch that gave it perfection.

She was reading now the early impressions of the freshman as he watched the masterful manner in which the rubber

stamp was affixed to impressive documents, the stony stare
of experienced officials which heightened the newcomer's
respect for a college of such magnitude that its most insignificant underlings felt the dignity and superiority of their
honored trust, the crispness of their laconic 'Next window,
please, for that.'

Barney inclined toward Dinny, at this juncture, and
guardedly whispered, eyes intent upon the reader, 'Some
body's been pulling the old man's leg,' to which the awe-
stricken Dinny added, absently, 'The paralyzed one.'

They were hearing now about the democracy of a friendly
little college, the one place in the world where social caste
was regarded with the scorn it properly deserved in the
opinion of all people to whom the Almighty had vouchsafed
even the bare elements of humor.

Dinny sighed, rubbed his red cheek, and reflected that his
essay was quite too long. The class must be frightfully tired
of it by this time. He glanced at Professor Grover and
imagined that the roving eye flashed him a baleful threat of
hard times. Pulling himself together and affecting nonchalance, he turned cautiously to Barney and remarked, lips
barely moving:

'The old boy should have eaten one more spoonful of this
egg before he served it.'

Barney thoughtfully dug deep in a trouser pocket and
came up with a penny.

'This says you laid it,' gambled Barney.

'Vulgar display,' whispered Dinny, loftily.

Professor Grover was fussily rummaging through the pile
of papers.

'Just a moment, Miss — er — Adams,' he broke in,
huskily.

Miss — er — Adams lowered the paper and looked up for
further orders.

'I think we have heard enough of this essay, now, to
gather what must have been in the mind of the writer. It
seemed only fair that any slight irritation or disappointment

should be recognized. Happily, such sentiments are held by a very small minority. Magnolia does not assume responsibility for the irascibility of newcomers who expect immediate preferments…. We have here another paper, written in a better temper, which I shall ask Mr. Bristol to kindly read…. Thank you, Miss — er — Adams.'

'"To kindly read,"' observed Barney, 'shows the old thing to be human, anyway.'

Dinny wiped his brow, and nodded with the pensiveness of a convalescent consenting to a proffered pill; then rallied enough to reply, wanly:

'This must be a rough day on the sea.'

* * * * * *

During the first two months of Dinny's residence in Magnolia, Kitty Fagan frequently had occasion to come to *The Star*, early evenings, with important messages for her father, the delivery of which would be but the work of a moment.

Not wishing to appear ungracious toward Timmy's lonesome young friend, she would wave a hand, fingers twinkling; and Dinny, resolutely blind to the amused interest of a score distracted from their gainful occupations in the composing-room, would meet her halfway to his case and amblingly accompany her to the door where they would pause and chat amiably for a moment. He always worked half an hour overtime, on his own hook, to make sure he had not visited with Kitty at the expense of the company.

By the middle of November, Kitty's emergency messages for her father had all been delivered, and *The Star*, suddenly bereft of these pleasant interludes scheduled to be played about eight-thirty, twice a week, became mildly curious.

Bert Snyder, on machine No. 1, observing Dinny emerging from the coat-room at ten, sharp, one night, dressed for the street, re-lit his corn-cob pipe, tossed a hot slug bearing the cryptic phrase 'etaoin shrdlu' into the bubbling pot, and ventured his guess to Stub Harley, on No. 2, that Timmy had advised her not to come up any more. Stub thought it more likely that Mr. Brophy had set down on it. Pinky Gormer, assistant telegraph, hung a few smeary pages on each of their hooks, and bet there had been a quarrel.... But nobody knew and, after a little while, nobody cared.

On the fourth consecutive Sunday at the Fagans', Dinny realized that he was being gradually, unprotestingly assimilated. Noting that the living-room which gave directly on to the front porch was unoccupied, he did not rap on the screen-door, but opened it and made his way through to the kitchen.

'We heard you coming, Dinny,' said Mrs. Fagan, too intent on the beautifully browned chicken she was taking from the oven to give him better attention than a fleeting smile. 'I can't think what's come over that gate.'

'Where's the oil-can?' inquired Dinny. 'I'll touch it up.'

'I know,' said Kitty, putting down the bowl of whipping cream.

'Let him find it himself.... It's up on the sewing-machine, Dinny, in the back room.' Mrs. Fagan vigorously beat the potatoes. 'Don't look around in there. It hasn't been picked up.'

Timmy met him halfway up the stairs, and said it was too warm for a coat.

Kitty's attitude became proprietary.

'Dinny doesn't want that much sugar in his tea.... Dinny mustn't have another piece of pie, father. It's bad for his wind. If we're going to make the team, we'll have to go easy on the pie.... Dinny, we really must look after those poor fingers: that nasty acid. Can't they use something else on their dirty old type?'

On the fifth Sunday, Dinny met the four of them on the imposing front steps of Saint Vincent's at eleven o'clock. It was his first experience in a Catholic church. He knew next to nothing about that institution, and suspected that what little he did know was untrue. Of course, he took no stock in his own family's estimate of it, aware that their passionate prejudice had been slowly percolated through a filter of ignorance and contempt — a musty old filter clogged with nearly four centuries of gritty deposits precipitated from neighborhood brawls and border wars.

In the questionable judgment of Uncle Miles, whose proud boast it was that his feet had never crossed the threshold of 'Rome,' the Pope was 'the Anti-Christ.' Dinny had but a vague idea who 'the Anti-Christ' was, beyond his natural deduction that it was a cryptic epithet never employed in eulogy.

Aunt Martha maintained that practically all Catholic churches were secret arsenals, their subterranean grottoes stuffed with rifles and ammunition. She wagged her head ominously when she predicted the day of 'a great uprisin' that'll make th' rivers run red.' This was, on the face of it, mere drivel and nonsense. You could tell, because the rivers were to run red. Aunt Martha was always quite definitely off the rails when she talked in terms of red or any of the collateral hues. She always got excited, hysterical, and incoherent when she discoursed on Sin, which was scarlet, or Salvation, which was crimson.

As they mounted the church steps, pressed close on either side by pilgrims of all sorts, Dinny felt himself a member of the Fagan family. There was something tender and intimate in this new relationship. He would sit in the Fagan pew. He would belong to them, for an hour, in bonds of a common wistfulness. Not that he expected to get much out of it further than the satisfaction of sitting quietly with them. Doubtless he and Kitty would share a hymn-book. There would be a long, tiresome sermon, but they would not have to listen to it. Perhaps he would touch Kitty's fingers, when the clergyman inveighed against some sport or pleasure, and they would steal a pious glance at each other, tongue in cheek.

The instant they entered the dim, vasty nave, Dinny found himself quite alone. His Fagans had vanished, their places taken by four strangers who suddenly went about the business of dipping finger-tips in the huge marble shell, touching themselves with an adroitness that could not possibly have been achieved through experience, but must be accounted for by some instinct which Dinny knew he did not possess.

The supple grace of their genuflections set them apart from him and all his kind. The only movement he had ever seen, comparable to it for artless dexterity, was the sweep of a lithe tiger's breast against the bars as it reached the end of its brief journey and turned to pad softly but determinedly to the other corner of the cage.

He followed these people, dressed like the Fagans, halfway down the broad aisle, where, pausing, they dipped again, not by conscious effort, but as if each of them had been gripped by some current flowing from the wood of the pew-end, so that when their fingers touched it, they responded — galvanically.

Kitty glanced sideways and offered him a fragment of a smile — a mere, transparently thin cross-section of a smile — as she slipped swiftly from the seat to her knees beside Pat and her parents. Dinny lumberingly joined her on the bare narrow rail on which they knelt, ashamed of his awkwardness. Adjusting his joints with much difficulty, he distributed his weight so that his elbows on the top of the pew might ease the discomfort of his knees. When all this had been attended to, he glanced down at the profile of the rapt face beside him. The smart little white hat with the blue ribbon looked very much like Kitty's hat. The firm, round, white chin was amazingly like Kitty's lovely chin. The steady fingers, gently moving from one bead to another on her rosary, resembled Kitty's competent fingers. But Kitty had escaped. This girl beside Dinny was a foreigner. Kitty and Pat and good old Timmy and hospitable Mrs. Fagan had left him forlorn, chagrined, and lonely on the beach while they, diving with the skill and precision of graceful seals, had whisked away into their Sea.

Kneeling thus on the hard pebbled beach of that mysterious Sea in which the Fagans were so confidently at home, the sublimity of it all began to lay hold on Dinny Brumm. He realized now that something inside him had been calling, faintly but urgently, all his life, demanding exercise, sustenance, liberty; something aquatic that couldn't walk on the hard ground.

They were back in their seats now, but the mesmeric spell did not lift. They rose, they sat, they bowed, they crossed themselves with sure, deft strokes, Dinny trying to keep pace with them in the rising, and sitting, and kneeling, feeling himself a mere stumbling baby trudging with short, drunken steps in the wake of experienced track-sprinters.

Now the congregation hummed briefly with swiftly flowing, unintelligible fragments of liquid sentences, sentences prodded out of it by stately challenges addressed to the great white and gold and flickering altar by an ornately garbed figure. The celebrant was attended by small boys in vestments, who needed no telling what to do, boys who anticipated each impending phase of the ancient drama, boys whose very backs seemed to disdain such childish fripperies as marbles, tops, and kites, having forsaken all that was secular to pledge their life to all that was sacred.

Presently it occurred to Dinny that these strangers whose pew he shared might be as well pleased with their guest if he made no further ridiculous attempts to imitate them in their worship. The next time they sat, he resolved to remain seated.

He looked about. It was the first occasion on which the Gothic had ever spoken to him directly. The Gothic beckoned him to attempt a spiritual journey.

Dinny's eyes rested on the beautiful window nearest him, a multi-colored window crowded with brave events upheld and flanked by miniatures of enhaloed saints — enraptured saints bearing massive keys and open books, bearded saints leading submissive lions, beardless saints led by victorious lambs with a fore-foot sustaining a shouldered banner; crowns and crests, shields and swords, cups and censers, purple grapes and yellow wheat-sheaves, and hilltops tipped with spires.

His eyes traveled up until the window narrowed to a pointed arch that led the way to the base of a flying buttress. He gave himself willingly to its graceful curve, and followed along past innumerable sign-posts — all pointing up... Up... *Up!* — each arch, and tip, and spire daring him to leap to another... higher... Higher... *Higher!* — until visibility was lost in the shadows overhead.

Perhaps that was the way Religion really ought to be, thought Dinny. No wonder the Catholics had lasted so long without the necessity of change, reorganization, reappraisals. The old Church invited you to look up. That was all she asked. She made no promises that she could reveal the Ultimate. It was up to you... how far you could see. You looked up — and the Church carried you from one aspiring arch to another until you could go no farther, not because the arches ended, up there, but because your frail sight could no longer follow them into the Mystery whose depths they plumbed.

Meantime, the rhythmic tide of the venerable ritual came rolling, rumbling on in strong, confident waves — music out of a Past that was also a Future; music that took no account of infinitesimal weeks and months, but dealt with a thousand years as if it were only a day; music that never even glanced down to see whether you were following an ox-drawn plow or addressing parliament from a throne, much less noticed whether you rode in a Day Coach or a Pullman; spoken music, drifting from within the chancel, chanted music, drifting from the choir overhead.

For a period there was much made of a small jeweled case, set into the altar; hushed silences bounded by the silvery tinkle of a bell; deep, deep reverence between the silvery tinkle of the bell.

The sweetish-brownish aroma of incense hung in the air, invisible in the nave, though above the heads of the celebrants it drifted like a torn tapestry — a very old, brown

ish-gray tapestry. To Dinny's unaccustomed nostrils the
elusive scent was an indissoluble combination of mingled appeals to the most spiritual of all the senses. He tried without
success to analyze its weird effects upon his imagination. At
first it seemed to possess a certain medicinal quality —
faintly stimulative. No — it was not a stimulant, but an
exultant, insisting upon the exultation produced by calm acceptance, confident repose.

There was something primitive about it, too; something
woodsy, as if it exuded from the enshadowing trees beneath
whose branches valiant men of old had knelt to worship —
trees which the Gothic had preserved in stone.... Dinny
wondered what strange magic the incense was conjuring in
the trained, consecrated nostrils of the transported Fagans.

Aunt Martha had scorned the institution that tried to
worship in a heathen language.

'Nothin' but gibberish!' declared Aunt Martha, who
knew only her mother tongue, and that imperfectly.

Dinny did not find it so. In the mounting radicalism of
eighteen plus disillusionment, he was ready to do bump-
tious battle with any detailed invoice of 'I believes,' hawked
in the language of the clearing-house and the market-place.
But there was a sudden tightening of the throat, a burning
of the eyelids, when the sonorous phrases came welling
forth from the dimly lit chancel:

Et in Jesum Christum... Dominum nostrum... qui con-
ceptus est de Spiritu sancto... natus ex Maria Virgine...

You didn't have to believe it: you just knew it was true.
His eyes groped into the vaulted roof. Up there, out
there, beyond there — what? When you had it all explained for you in the patter of the machine-shop, the language of the garage, the department-store, the football
field, you waved it away and muttered, 'Stuff and nonsense!' It was a different matter when sung to you in an
otherwise unused tongue, through an aromatic veil of incense:

... carnis resurrectionem... vivam æternam!...

That was the glory, then, of this Catholic religion. It didn't ask to be understood, as Chemistry asks to be understood.

Perhaps that was the whole trouble with Uncle Miles's religion. It explained everything, succeeding only in making itself absurd. Its speculations were hard and-fast facts to be weighed on the scales, poured into a test-tube, shaken over a flame.

Not much wonder, thought Dinny, this Catholicism had carried on.... Every so often, turbulent little sects had spewed themselves out through the heavy bronze doors of cathedrals to quarrel and dogmatize; obliged, when their fury was spent, to build cheap and ugly little imitations of the eternal thing from which they in their willfulness had fled.

Every new generation of the self-outcast had revised the imitation. Never were they done tinkering with it, reconditioning it, modernizing it, making it over 'to meet the new day.' And — meantime — while their most progressive engineers dug deep under the thing to install new heating, climbed high on the thing to equip it with a tighter roof, repainted it, relandscaped it — The Everlasting Church stood fast!... 'sanctam Ecclesiam Catholicam!'

That was the Sea!

All the time the inquisitive and heady were busily building their little dams, and draining their miasmic ponds, and changing the courses of their impotent, muddy, little creeks, the Sea had steadily throbbed to the tune of the stars without so much as a by-your-leave to any earthly powers. That Sea did not even pause to smile at the snarls and fist-shakings of the engineers. The Sea did not know they existed!... Dinny Brumm devoutly hoped he could learn to navigate that Sea. He went out of Saint Vincent's, into the October sunshine, tentatively committed to the great experiment.

'How did you like it?' asked Kitty, smiling a little, but wide-eyed with genuine concern.

'I really can't talk about it, Kitty,' he murmured.

She grasped his arm for a moment, and patted his sleeve lightly.

'"*Dominus vobiscum*," Dinny!' recited Kitty, gently, gratefully.

'What do I say now — anything?'

'You say, "*Et cum spiritu tuo*," Dinny.'

He repeated the words after her, adding, 'dear.'

* * * * * *

That afternoon — a golden-russet, burnt-sienna afternoon — they climbed the high hill overlooking the city park. The southerly slope of the hill was a cemetery. It was a full quarter-mile to the nearest white stones; a half-mile to the broad granite arch of the old-worldish gateway flanked on either side with clumps of cypress trees.

Dinny was reflective, eyes moody, lips pursed, as he reclined on an elbow, Kitty sitting cross-legged beside him, endeavoring to punctuate the long silences with sprightly talk.

'Wise old owl,' she pouted, 'come out of your trance.'

Their eyes turned toward the cemetery gate, far below. Some secret order in uniform was creeping along, led by a brass band, en route to bury a brother... Chopin's Funeral March... As the band passed under the broad stone arch and through the cypress trees, a whole half-dozen measures were completely obliterated. Kitty supplied the missing passage, keeping time with martial bobs of her bare black head, her pretty cheeks distended as if she blew the notes on the big, shining tuba that presently led the way out into the sun.

'Pumm, pum-te-pumm, pum-te-pum, te-pum, te-pum,' pummed Kitty, soberly.

The cortège was marching out into the glow, now, but the dirge was still in the gloom, candidly hopeless of anything to come of this dignified enterprise further than the wretched anti-climax of ropes and shovels and the bouncing of clods on a box.

Dinny lay outstretched on his back, gazing straight up, listening to the wisps of the despairing march which Kitty continued to accompany, softly. Now it was quite stilled again for an instant, while the band rounded the other side of a massive cliff. Presently there swept up the hill a great wave of hope. 'Nevertheless!' sang the dirge. *'Nevertheless — I tell you!'*

Kitty scrambled to her knees, facing Dinny, her eyes bright, dancing, her pretty teeth sparkling, keeping time with both hands, fingers outspread, chanting, happily:

'Tra-la — Tra-la — la-la-la-la — la — tra-la' ...

'You actually believe that; don't you?'

'That it's going to come out all right? Sure! Of course! Don't you?'

'I think I do... when... when it's said in Latin.'

'I don't quite get you, Dinny.'

'Well,' he drawled, dreamily, 'I think the belief in everlasting life is silly... but *"vitam æternam"* is sound.'

'Funny boy,' laughed Kitty. 'Old owl!'

Then he told her almost everything he had thought about, that morning in church. On the way down the hill, she promised to ask Father Donovan for some little books he might read, though Dinny was not sure he wanted them.

'I'm contented,' he said. 'Besides — I would have trouble reading them. Latin's tedious... in large quantities.'

'Oh — but this will not be in Latin,' explained Kitty.

'Maybe we'd better leave well enough alone,' said Dinny, thoughtfully.

* * * * * *

Two disquieting books came into Dinny's hands, within three hours of each other, on the next Thursday night.

The first was lent by Father Donovan and delivered into the hands of Dinny, at his case, by Kitty Fagan — a book he opened at one A.M., in his room, and perused for a scant five minutes. Then he closed it with a snap. He had read the English — the modern, workaday English, under the

pitiless glare of electric light — the English explanation of
The Mysteries.

Here was the 'Profession of Faith' for converts:

'I., N. N., having before me the holy gospels, which I
touch with my hand and knowing that no one can be saved
without that faith which the Holy, Catholic, Apostolic
Roman Church holds, believes, and teaches, against which I
grieve that I have greatly erred ——'

Dinny ran his eye down the page:

'I believe in one only God in three divine Persons, distinct from, and equal to, each other — that is to say, the
Father, the Son, and the Holy Ghost.'

How often he had heard Uncle Miles tangle himself up in
the labyrinthian mazes of this incomprehensible 'three in
one' business — as if it mattered; as if anybody knew.

'I believe in the true, real and substantial presence of the
Body and Blood, together with the Soul and Divinity, of
our Lord Jesus Christ, in the most holy Sacrament of the
Eucharist.'

That's what the little jeweled case was about. The Lord
Jesus Christ was in there. They took Him out, and then
put Him back in again.... Uncle Miles had some queer
ideas, too; but ——

The rest of it Dinny merely glanced at.

'I believe in the seven Sacraments...

'I believe in Purgatory...

'I believe in the Primacy, not only of honor, but of juris-
diction, of the Roman Pontiff, successor of Saint Peter,
Prince of the Apostles...

'I believe in the veneration of the Saints and of their
images.'

'And' — the book was closing now, and in an instant it
would be shut with a sharp slap — 'I believe in everything
else that has been defined and declared by the sacred Can-
ons and the General Councils, and particularly by the
Council of Trent ——'

Dinny didn't know what the 'Council of Trent' was, but

it was with the 'Council of Trent' that his spiritual exploration terminated. It was seven years before he smelled incense again.

He undressed, and went to bed with the book Mr. Brophy had lent him at midnight. Mr. Brophy had asked him along to lunch, for on Thursday nights he always worked overtime, ads being heavy in the Friday morning edition of *The Star*.

They went to Clancy's, which closed at eleven, in accordance with the law, and remained open until one to accommodate the Fourth Estate, certain other discreet, and Sergeant O'Shane, who paused at Mr. Brophy's table to exchange the customary:

'Annything new, Misther Brophy?'

'More fighting in Ireland, Sergeant; that's all.'

'And that's not news, Misther Brophy.'

'Dinny,' said Mr. Brophy, when Clancy, himself, had put down on the bare table a plate of Swiss cheese, rye bread, and two steins of beer, 'did you ever read Hardy's *Jude the Obscure*?'

Dinny, his mouth full, shook his head.

'I'll lend it to you,' said Mr. Brophy, taking the book from his pocket and pushing it across the table.

'Thanks,' mumbled Dinny. 'What's it about?'

Mr. Brophy made up a cheese sandwich, painstakingly.

'It's about a tremendously ambitious youngster who wanted a college education, so he could be somebody, and threw a wrench into the machine by marrying out of his class.'

'And so he didn't get to be anybody?'

'He didn't even get a college education.'

'Why do you want me to read it, Mr. Brophy?'

Mr. Brophy shrugged a shoulder.

'It will do you good to get acquainted with Thomas Hardy... vigorous style... sound workman.'

In bed, now, with the book, Dinny became absorbed in the tribulations of Jude's boyhood — strikingly like his own, in spots. He read until four, lowered the book, stared for a long time at the wall, sighed deeply, and turned out the light. It had been a long day. Dinny had grown much older, since sunrise.

CHAPTER VIII

MAGNOLIA students, unable to return to their homes, were
welcome to the seven o'clock dinner at the President's
house on Christmas.

That no bones were made about the purely philanthropic
nature of this affair was blandly certified by the technique
of recruiting its guests. The bulletin boards, a few days in
advance, announced that if these stranded would make
themselves known to the Y.M. and Y.W. secretaries, they
would receive personal invitations.

It was easily to be deduced, from the character of the
agencies thus serving as a clearing-house for this social
function, that its guest-list would consist largely if not
wholly of barbs; for, almost without exception, the fraternity
and sorority element had no truck with the Y.M. or Y.W.
beyond the dollar perfunctorily disgorged during the early
October campaign for their maintenance. The Greeks were
not, as a rule, religious.

Tradition held that these Yuletide festivities, however
praiseworthy in their altruistic intent, lacked brilliance.
Indeed, when a seasoned Magnolian — whether Greek or
barbarian — was hard pressed for a simile adequate to
bound some experience of boredom *in extremis*, he was apt
to liken it to the Braithwaites' Christmas Party, even if he
had never attended one himself and might have added but
little to its incandescence if he had.

Dinny had missed the affair, a year ago, truthfully offering the excuse — though he could have invented one — that
he was obliged to work at that hour.

Nothing was more remote from his intention than attendance at this year's Christmas conviviality in the big, square,
dormer-windowed, brick house which dominated this end
of Sunnyside Avenue, dignified aloof from the long row of
Greek chapter houses — for it was set in spacious grounds

— but obviously mothering them and sharing with them the same Strozzi lamp-posts in the broad green parking, four to the block, on either side, as if the Old Lady, upon installing hers, had said they might as well provide similarly for the children.

But it now turned out that Dinny was to be one of the guests at the annual barbarian spread.

Encountering President Braithwaite, whom he sincerely admired, Dinny impulsively pledged himself to attend the feast. They had met in the almost deserted hall of the Administration Building on the morning of the twenty-second. The college session had closed.

'Not going home, Brumm?'

'No, sir; not this time, sir.'

Dinny did not feel it necessary to add that he was done going home; never expected to go home again; had, in fact, no home to go to since the receipt of Angela's astounding letter, a month ago, easing her burdened soul of a confession that, while rummaging in her father's desk, she had discovered evidences of long-continued misappropriation of funds rightfully Dinny's — a defalcation in which Aunt Martha was a silent but culpable accomplice. Angela, deeply stirred in a revival staged by the celebrated 'Buster' Brown and the incomparable song-leader, 'Merry' Merriweather, had experienced 'the third work' — an altitudinous degree of sanctification involving the wholesale confession of sins, venial and mortal, in which salutary enterprise she had, after a manner of speaking, spilled the beans.

'The money,' wrote Angela, in an affected back-hand on reeking pink paper, 'must have stopped coming about two years ago.

'I think my father must have begun to be scared, about that time. Your father probably wanted to arrange to send you to college, though I couldn't find that letter in the package.

'The only one on that was dated more than two years

ago. It was written on a New York Central train. It said,
"If it is true my son has no inclination to go to college and
has a good job and bitterly resents any further help from
me, there is nothing more to do.'"

Savage with indignation, Dinny rapidly composed and
destroyed a half-dozen letters — three to the rascally old
Uncle Miles; two, slightly less ironical, to pious Aunt
Martha; concluding with a real masterpiece of shocking
sacrilege to the thrice-blest Angela. Having thus documented his sentiments in regard to the elementary decencies,
and the mysterious ways of Providence in delegating the
propagation of sweetness and light to ambassadors so
nonchalant on the subject of common integrity, he screwed
the cap back on his fountain-pen, and called it a day's work.

Presuming, correctly, that Angela's purgation demanded
her having it out with Uncle Miles and Aunt Martha,
Dinny thought he would wait until these unctuous de-
faulters had had time to concoct some ingenious explanation. But they, judging by their silence, were waiting for
his offensive; so, communication was cut off. As Christmas neared, it occurred to him that, aside from the greeting
cards he meant to mail to Mr. Brophy, old Peter Andrews,
and the Fagans (whom he rarely visited now, Kitty having
impatiently transferred her affections to young Mike
Slattery, a handsome and promising department manager
in the Crystal Laundry), he had no occasion for shopping.
Dinny hoped Aunt Martha would not trouble herself to
send him anything. But it would be quite like her to do so
— a sappy book of preachments, perhaps, written, pub-
lished, and peddled by the Reverend Bouncing Bilgewater,
or some such moron.

'Then you will be coming to our Christmas dinner,' said
the President, genially.

'Oh, yes, sir,' declared Dinny, with grateful enthusiasm,
'Thank you very much, Doctor Braithwaite.'

Almost from his first day, Dinny had found himself
wondering how little Magnolia, so narrow and reactionary,

had invited a man of President Braithwaite's broad sympathies and urbanity to direct her affairs. And how had Doctor Braithwaite ever persuaded himself to lead a cause so unpromising?

It was common knowledge on the campus — even the freshmen chattered it — that the President was in hot water, the conservatives furnishing the fuel. The President had been elected for his skill as a money-getter. But for that he would have been ousted long ago. But for that he would never have been called from the Financial Secretary-ship of little Minton, in Wisconsin, a despairing toy college that he had rescued from the grave. Minton had called him to that job in the very nick of time to save him from a heresy trial at the instigation of his Conference. As a minister, he had been too modern, nobody but the young people following him.

'Everybody knows ——' Orville Kling, still Dinny's dormitory neighbor, and now President of the Y., had come over, last week, to borrow a pot of mucilage; for, as Religious Editor of *The Blossom*, he was always out of paste. 'Everybody knows,' declaimed Kling, fresh from a meeting of his cabinet, in which Doctor Braithwaite had been put in the pan, 'that he's an out-and-out higher critic!'

'Critic of what?' inquired Dinny, absently, intent on the trail of an irregular verb in his Greek lexicon, 'Critic of *what?*' he repeated, 'and higher than *who?*'

'You wait! ——'

Disdaining the persiflage, Kling slowly closed one eye and tipped his head far back, hinting at inside information he dared not reveal.

'You just wait until Braithwaite has finished this two-year drive for the Half-Million Endowment Fund. The Board will give him his walking papers!'

'Not very sporting, I should say,' observed Dinny.

Kling hooked a leg over the corner of Dinny's table, rested an elbow on his knee, and beat time to his oracle with an impressive forefinger.

'The conservation of Christian faith,' he intoned, 'is not a sporting proposition.'

'I had noticed that,' drawled Dinny, not very pleasantly.

'What I say is,' continued Kling, warming, 'if Braithwaite wants to make a dash for this so-called liberty of religious thought, let him do it — but not while he's on the payroll of an orthodox institution.'

'Like Martin Luther, for instance?' queried Dinny.

'That's quite a different matter,' growled Kling, pacing to the window and backing up defensively against the sill, 'Luther, as it happened, was right!'

'But the conservatives didn't think so,' amended Dinny, 'or did they? I'm not very well posted on that.'

'No — I don't suppose you are,' muttered Kling, meaningly, 'though you ought to be, considering your background.'

Dinny impetuously pushed back his chair, and was on the point of offering a sarcastic discrimination between 'back-ground' and 'back-fire,' but thought better of it, and turned again to his lexicon.

Kling strode heatedly toward the door.

'Here,' said Dinny, 'you've forgotten the mucilage.'

'Thanks,' said Kling, stiffly, 'I think I can find some.'

'Sure you can find your scissors?' teased Dinny, grinning.

'I suppose you think that's witty, son.' Kling had his hand on the knob.

'I think it's a scream, Brother Kling,' retorted Dinny, '*all of it!* — the Board of Directors, Christian faith, home background, the Y.M.C.A., *The Blossom's* Religious Column, and — and the paste-pot and the scissors! ——'

The door banged with a resounding wallop.

' —— and you, too,' finished Dinny, addressing the infuriated footsteps in the hall. 'You're a scream, too!'

* * * * * *

At three, still uncomfortable over his promise to attend

the Christmas party, which was going to be dull with an exceeding great dullness, no matter how the Braithwaites might tear their hair to make it interesting, Dinny went skating in the park.

There was nothing he enjoyed so much. The day was perfect, air crisp, tonic, the sky turquoise, the sun bright.

He recognized no one on the pond, but it required no company to complete his satisfaction.

With long, lazy strokes, he traversed the quarter-mile longitudinal stretch of the steel-blue lagoon, delighting in the ease of a locomotion that always gave him the sensation of flying. There was a unique exhilaration in the ability to let oneself go; to lean back confidently on the promise of that strange centrifugal energy developed by 'the outer edge roll' — a confidence more exacting, and better rewarded, than the faith of the floating swimmer.

He glanced without much interest at the indifferent skaters as he swept past them. Most of them were huddled in small parties, hacking away with short, stumbling steps, what time they were not clawing at each other for support, or spilling themselves, or shrieking hysterically over the misfortunes of their neighbors, or fussing with their straps. Magnolia was a bit too far south to breed able ice-skaters.

Presently Dinny sighted a tall girl, apparently alone, who knew what she was there for. My word! — what a competent young eagle she was! He wheeled, and followed her at a respectful distance.

She was slender, but beautifully formed; exquisite from the top of the brown fur toque that matched her curly hair to the flashing blades of the high-laced skating-boots which intriguingly disclosed attractive segments of gleaming silk between them and the short brown skirt. Her gauntleted hands — long, strong hands — were outspread at the tops of her hips as if they signaled the measured strokes like a coxswain. She clasped them behind her back, now, as if they had nothing whatever to do with it.

The girl had leisurely slowed down, at the end of the pond, finishing the lap with a series of incomparable 'eights.'

Observing that she was quite absorbed in her own affairs, Dinny did not linger to join the admiring circle that collected rapidly to view her skillful maneuvers, but drifted negligently away toward the farther end of the lagoon. Turning, there, he noticed with satisfaction that she had detached herself from her little theater and was again on more extensive flights. He hoped she would come on. Pursuing a small orbit, in reverse, Dinny waited. His heart gave a hard bump as she swept closer. Her face was radiant with vitality — a patrician face, thought Dinny; a portrait face, finely modeled brows, sensitive nostrils, red lips curved like the bent bow of a medieval arbalest. Little curls peeped from under the fur toque, softening the lines of a gallant forehead.

She smiled, as one artist to another.

'Very good ice,' she said, casually, in a tone that made Dinny think, if she sang — and surely she did — it would be contralto.

'You skate beautifully,' said Dinny.

Her slightly raised brows and parted lips accepted the candid tribute.

'You should know,' she replied.

'But you didn't learn it in Magnolia,' Dinny hazarded, flushed a little by her bland compliment. He held out his hands, invitingly.

'Shall we?'

'Why not? I'd like to.'

She had hardly consented before they were beginning to drift, crossed hands clasped, into a long, indolent roll that inclined their tall, lithe forms so far off balance none but the expert could have trusted to it.

Their wake was a double row of graceful fern-fronds, laid down almost end to end on the glassy lagoon. At first the fronds were twenty feet long and sixteen inches apart. Then they lengthened to thirty feet and narrowed to thirteen inches, for Dinny had drawn her closer, and she had instantly responded.

They moved as one body, their rhythm perfect. Sometimes the long twin fronds seemed pointing directly toward a mighty collision with a group of wobbly-ankled gigglers; but, without signaling each other by so much as a pressure of the fingers, the welded pair of ice-artists would bend the arc of the fronds and sail past with the grace of a yacht acknowledging the sudden puff of a capricious breeze. Preferring to sense to the full the ecstasy of reckless swallows, they had not attempted conversation, but their thoughts had been active.

It had required no deduction on Joan's part to identify her overtowering companion as a Magnolia athlete, for there was a huge pink *M* on his white sweater. Dinny was still in the dark, his curiosity mounting.

'What's the letter about?' she asked, when they idled to the first stop at the eastern end of the pond where they had met.

'Football — but this is a lot more fun, don't you think?'

'Yes,' she laughed, 'but I never played football.... You must live here — or you would have started home.'

'No,' replied Dinny, 'do you?'

'Yes... Are you coming to our Christmas party?'

'I certainly am!' said Dinny, fervently. 'Whose party?'

'I'm Joan Braithwaite.'

'I should have known,' said Dinny. 'But you're always away. University of Wisconsin — isn't it?... I'm Ferdinand Brumm, Miss Braithwaite.'

'Oh!' Joan's pretty mouth rounded in happy surprise. 'So you're the lad that galloped the sixty yards with all Camford hanging on to you! I read about it.... You're "Dinny"!'

'Thanks!... But it was only the last three or four yards that they all got on.... Like to do it some more?'

'How many of them were there — actually?' laughed Joan, taking his proffered hands.

'I believe they had eleven on their team, that day,' said Dinny, thoughtfully. 'It may have been a few more. Camford is frightfully unscrupulous, you know.'

They chatted, amiably.

Yes — she loved Wisconsin, but her father was insisting on her coming to Magnolia, next year. Dinny expressed his sincere regrets.

'I mean, of course,' he amended, 'I'm sorry for *you*, having to leave your friends... and Magnolia will be quite a change, you know.... Not much doing here.'

'Oh, I won't mind — much,' said Joan; adding, after a considerable pause, 'The Gammas gave a nice party for me, last night — that's my sorority, you know.... By the way — where were *you?*'

'I'm a barb,' drawled Dinny.

'Oh... I didn't know.... Pardon me, won't you?' She endeavored to cover her confusion with a contrite little laugh as she added, 'I didn't know the — the non-fraternity men called *themselves* "barbs."... I thought they quite bitterly resented the word.'

'Why should they?' asked Dinny, dryly. 'We know that when the fraternity men call us "barbs," it's just a bit of friendly chaffing — same as when we call them "Greeks." We haven't the courage and vitality to be barbarians, and they don't know any Greek. Why — if their badges weren't of different shapes and colors, they'd never know when they met a brother.'

'Frightfully satirical, aren't you?' Joan's tone was crisp.

'It's the best thing I do,' boasted Dinny, in mock seriousness. 'I've been commended for it by Professor Grover, a couple of times. In fact, he gave me *E*, last semester, in Creative Composition. *E* stands for Excellent, doesn't it?'

'Oh, yes,' consented Joan, 'and it stands for some other things — when it's grading satire and sarcasm.'

The twin fronds on the ice behind them widened a little.

'What — for instance?' Dinny wanted to know.

'No matter,' said Joan, idly. 'Forget it.'

'But I quite insist. You had something you wanted to say.'

'I'm afraid it isn't very polite,' ventured Joan, 'but doesn't *E* stand for Enraged — and Embattled — and Embarrassed — and ——'

'And — what? ——'

'Envious.'

'You're quite frank,' said Dinny, after an instant of recovery.

'Well — you would have it, you know.... I told you I didn't like irony.'

'But — you like humor, don't you?... and if there's anything funnier than a bunch of college students taking on airs because they're "Greeks," I'm sure I don't know what it is. You'd think they would tumble all over themselves getting into old man Appleton's classes. We barbs have Homer all to ourselves. Oddly enough, old Appleton is a barb, himself!'

Joan disengaged her hands, a little before they reached the end of the pond. Her face showed disappointment.

'Does it make you happy,' she asked, soberly looking him straight in the eyes — 'to be... that way?'

'I've had very little occasion to be happy,' parried Dinny.

'You mean here?... at Magnolia?'

'I mean everywhere... and always,' said Dinny, suddenly sincere. 'If I were to tell you ——'

'Do you want to?' Joan's tone deepened, and her dark brown eyes searched his rugged face.

'No,' he answered, brusquely, adding, suddenly contrite, 'Thank you — all the same. I think I'd — I wouldn't mind telling you — if it weren't such a dull story.'

They simultaneously felt that their little visit was over. Joan glanced at her wrist-watch. Dinny squinted at the declining sun.

She reached out her hand.

'I'll be seeing you, then, on Christmas?' she said.

Dinny felt very lonely as she glided away. She was the most superb creature he had ever seen.

* * * * * *

President and Mrs. Braithwaite were warmly effusive as they welcomed him in the wide doorway of their spacious parlor.

Joan was standing a little to one side, within the room, talking animatedly with Barney Vaughn, who seemed in unusually high spirits. Dinny had forgotten that Barney, who had passed a dozen universities en route from Phoenix, Arizona, to Magnolia — to the never-flagging curiosity of all, unaware that his father was a Magnolian — might be a guest tonight.

He had not talked with Barney since last May. They had briefly informed each other about the weather, when they happened to pass on the street, unless they sighted each other early enough for one of them to cross over and avoid even this laconic exchange of cool civilities.

The constraint that stiffened their previously close friendship dated from Dinny's refusal to become a Sig.

The Sigs had not bidden him promptly. Within a week after his first appearance on the athletic field, the Delts had spent two hours with him, reciting the honored names of alumni (none of them Magnolians, as it happened) who had gone forth to hold aloft the good old banner, and the Pies had offered to share their refined salt, but he had politely declined. Barney had urged him to wait.

The Sigs were a good while getting around to it. His work at *The Star* kept him occupied, and made it difficult for him to be sociable. The preliminary overtures of the Sigs were made somewhat listless by the fact, which developed in casual conversation when Barney had him in as his luncheon guest, that he would be unable to conform to many of their regulations for the disciplining of 'the frosh.' The Custer Cottage was already crowded to capacity with their pledges.

The bid was not issued until early December, Dinny learning, later, through an outburst of confidence on the part of Barney, who had had it from Curly Sprague, a soph, that Spike Davis had held out for some time, threatening to blackball Dinny, if it came to a vote. Spike had been talked into consent on the night after the Thanksgiving game with Camford in which, as fullback, he had kicked the goal that tied the score and rent the sky. He was feeling very much at peace with all mankind, and a bit drunk; so he waived his objections, and agreed to Dinny's election.

Dinny was unsure whether he wanted to accept the belated invitation. He confided his dilemma to Mr. Brophy, one night.

'You'd better, I think,' counseled Mr. Brophy. 'Otherwise you're rated a barb, and that will be awkward for you, not only while you're in college, but — always.'

So — Dinny had accepted the little button symbolic of the tardy honor the Sigs conferred, and merged into the pack, to his considerable inconvenience, for the new relationship levied irksome requirements. He bolted his six-thirty dinner at 'th' House,' dashed for a street-car, and arrived at *The Star* usually ten minutes late, requiring double-measure overtime at his own expense. He never had time to eat a dessert, except on Saturday.

The fraternities initiated their freshmen during the first week of June. The Sigs did not initiate Dinny.

Each candidate, according to custom, was assigned a special test of his nerve, or an earnest of his eagerness to become a Greek. Barney was to stand in front of The Palace Theater, one night, from eight to eight-thirty, with a hand-organ and a monkey — a salutary lesson in humility, though he had been cuffed about almost enough to have cured him of any uppishness. Chuck Rawlins was to present, on the occasion of his initiation, a live sparrow, the Sigs offering no suggestions for its capture, but insisting that his approach to the classic shrine, minus a live sparrow, would be undesired. Porky Bennet was to attend the Pan-

Sorority tea, that afternoon, as Carmen, the Sigs volunteering to furnish the tambourine from their property closet.

Spike Davis was chairman of the committee on initiation. Most of the stunts had required no imagination on his part, having been bequeathed, through many generations of Hellenic forbears.

Dinny's special assignment had cost Spike several contemplative hours. Cocky young Brumm had taken his honors too lightly; had dodged too many disciplines on the ground of his employment in town. Furthermore — though this factor Spike would have denied with fists and fangs — Dinny had played exceptionally good football at fullback on the frosh team. The local sports writers had made no riddle of their belief and hope that next fall, when he was eligible, he would add luster to the varsity. Even Woods, reviewing the season in *The Cincinnati Times-Telegram* (recently popularized and circulation-boosted through its absorption by The Craig Syndicate), had remarked, of next year's prospects, 'Magnolia has an excellent chance at the Conference pennant, what with her strong line, and the long-legged Dinny Brumm, who will have reached the age of responsibility.'

All these things being as they were, Spike had something unique for Dinny to do as proof that he was worthy to wear a Sig pin.

'What's eatin' you, Spike?'... 'You can't have him do that!'... 'Snap out of it, old son. That's much too thick.' Thus did the seniors try to talk him out of it. But Spike held his ground. It was his show, wasn't it? He was running this affair, wasn't he? Brumm had it all coming to him, didn't he?

Dinny was to carry a football under his arm, to all his classes, for a week. It was to be the one monumental pigskin on which Jim Faucett, the frosh captain, had vaingloriously inked the scores of their games with other classes — most of which triumphs had been freely conceded to Dinny's fleetness and ruthlessness at fullback.

'I can't do that, Spike.' Dinny shook his head, deter-minedly.

'Very well,' said Spike, loftily. 'That's that, then! If you want to be a Sig, you know what you've got to do. Think it over.'

Barney Vaughn came to Dinny's room, that afternoon, troubled.

'Dinny — you've got to, you know,' pleaded Barney. 'They've talked to him, but he won't budge.'

Dinny sat toying with a paper-knife, his brows knitted in a brown study.

'He told me to find you.' Barney's voice trembled a little. 'And come back with an immediate reply.'

Dinny rose, presently, tossed the paper-knife on the desk with a clatter, thrust his hands deep into his trouser pockets.

'No, Barney; there isn't anybody at Magnolia who can give me such an order — and if there was anybody who could, it wouldn't be Spike Davis.'

'But ——' Barney was half-frantic. 'What am I to do? ... What shall I tell him?'

Dinny took the little button from his lapel, laid it in Barney's hand, and said, slowly, but without heat:

'You can give this to Spike, with my compliments, and tell him to go to hell.'

'Do you realize, Dinny, what this is going to do to our friendship — no matter how I feel about it, personally?'

'I'm afraid I do,' muttered Dinny. 'That's the worst part of it, of course.'

'Want to sleep over it?'

'No — that's final. I shan't change my mind.'

'Awfully sorry, Dinny.... Good-bye.'

* * * * * *

Mrs. Braithwaite, buxom, black-gowned, maternal, pro-ceeded to adopt Dinny, who had been the last to arrive, engaging him in a conversation which she endeavored to pivot around himself, somewhat to his anxiety, for any discussion of his home and his people was distasteful.

Joan and Barney had moved away, joining the group clustered about Miss Gresley, whose parents were missionaries in India. She would rejoin them, after her graduation in June. Miss Gresley was always an object of interest, frequently appearing at missionary teas and church affairs in Hindu costume which became her more than the clothes she wore now.

Dinny wanted very much to speak to Joan; hoped she would presently welcome him. But dinner was announced at that moment. Tall, genial, handsome Doctor Braithwaite excused himself to find Miss Gresley, who, as the farthest away from home, was clearly eligible to sit at her host's right hand.

'I am going to take you with me, Mr. Brumm,' said Mrs. Braithwaite. Dinny offered his arm.

It was not until they were all standing with their hands on the tops of their chairs, waiting for whatever of ceremony was in order, that Dinny noticed the position of Joan at the right of Barney, who sat next to Miss Gresley. Their eyes met, briefly, and Joan accorded him a little nod of recognition.

The President suggested that they sing a verse of 'Holy Night,' after which they sat, fully three fourths of the score of shy guests immediately and concertedly helping themselves to a nervous sip of water, as if to say that they knew what *that* was for, anyway, whatever baffling dishes might challenge their social experience later.

'You met our Joan, didn't you, Mr. Brumm?' Mrs. Braithwaite had dipped a spoon into her fruit cocktail. 'She told me. So nice you could skate together. She quite enjoyed it. See — she's looking this way now ——'

Dinny glanced in Joan's direction, not quite sure whether the smile was for him or her mother. Barney, at the moment, was speaking to Miss Gresley.

'Of course you know Mr. Vaughn. You are classmates,

aren't you? Joan met him, last night, at the Gammas' reception. I'm so anxious for Joan to make some good friends, for she's coming to Magnolia, next year. Her sorority sisters were so kind to her, last night.'

'Yes — they would be, I should think,' assented Dinny, hopeful that the conversation might soon veer away from the reception. Apparently it occurred to his hostess, at that moment, that Hellenic activities might not be of interest to him.

'The Y.M. and Y.W. have just lovely parties, too,' she said, 'don't you think?'

'So I'm told,' replied Dinny, in a tone that evinced about as much personal knowledge as if she had remarked on the exceptionally large pineapple crop grown last season on the Island of Oahu.

'You're a naughty boy,' chided Mrs. Braithwaite, smiling. 'I don't believe you go to them, at all, and they're really very pleasant affairs.'

'I work nights, Mrs. Braithwaite,' explained Dinny; and, when she had inquired for particulars, he told her, their conversation broken, now and then, by her brief exchange of talk with Orville Kling — though he was mostly occupied with Miss Naylor, the Y.W. secretary — and Dinny's futile efforts to find some mutual interest with sallow, little Miss Upton. His eyes roved about the table, and when he reached Joan, they exchanged a steady look of inquiry, as if she still asked, 'Does it make you happy — to be — that way?'... and as if he countered, 'Why should you care?'

'But you have almost no social life at all, Mr. Brumm,' lamented Mrs. Braithwaite. 'What a pity you are tied up to such an exacting schedule.'

'It's no great matter, Mrs. Braithwaite.' Dinny lightly dismissed the dilemma with a slight shrug. 'I rather enjoy my work on *The Star*. And — as for society — well, I'm not eligible to it, you see. As a matter of fact' — he lowered his voice, confidentially — 'I came into this town in a day coach.'

Mrs. Braithwaite laughed a little, glanced about the table, fleetingly, and replied, 'But so did most of us, I fancy.'

'I dare say,' agreed Dinny; adding, 'You understand.' Again his eyes wandered toward Joan, who met him with a level gaze that continued to ask, 'Does it make you happy?——'

'I do understand,' said Mrs. Braithwaite, as if they were done with riddles, 'and I'm sorry, and something ought to be done about it — but I'm sure I don't know what.'

After dinner, Kling announced — bouncing up and down on his experienced toes — that, at the request of the President, they would sing a few songs. Miss Noble, invited to the grand piano, carefully put her handkerchief down on the ledge of the key-board, and accompanied 'On, Magnolia,' to Kling's encouraging direction, all joining with loyal enthusiasm. Then they sang 'America,' with unusual heartiness, for patriotism was in the air, and 'God Save the King,' as a second verse, for the 'neutrality' of early autumn had been buried under the falling leaves and the snow. Kling suggested 'The Marseillaise,' which they hummed, uncertainly, no one knowing the words very well.

Dinny was not quite sure which wing of the party he belonged to, after the dinner. Mrs. Braithwaite had signed him to remain by her, just a little to his discomfiture, for perhaps she was making an effort to pay him special attention, in atonement for the indifference of her sort toward the social redemption of day-coachers. But Dinny felt remote. On the other side of her, the President, Joan, and Barney represented the kindly condescending element that viewed the party as finely bred settlement workers look on at the games promoted for the uplift of slum brats.

In all fairness, Dinny reflected that he was supersensitive on this subject; told himself that what appeared to be conscious superiority on their part was nothing but an acknowledged inferiority of his own. But the situation was awkward, and he wished himself well out of it. He felt like an overgrown child, sitting with adults, at a children's party.

Kling, who appeared to be the spokesman for the guests, ventured upon a little speech of gratitude on behalf of them all. Pleased with the success of his remarks, he pulled out the tremolo stop, and, gradually increasing the tempo of his teetering up and down, jambed his stubby hands deeply into his coat pockets, achieving the posture and meter that presaged an early outburst of emotion.... Of course, none of us was forgetting, in the midst of our Christmas gayety, the bereavement and suffering of our hard-pressed neighbors beyond the sea, waging valiant warfare to protect civilization against the ruthless selfishness of The Hun.... Kling was roundly applauded.

'Terrible — isn't it?' Mrs. Braithwaite turned to Dinny, her brows knitted in painful reflection.

'You mean the war?'

'You're a bad boy,' said Mrs. Braithwaite, reproachfully.

Kling now suggested that they have a few words from the President, and sat down, smiling expectantly.

Doctor Braithwaite rose, rather soberly, thanked them for coming, invited them to drop in when they liked, through the lonely vacation days.... It was true, as Mr. Kling had indicated, that our happiness should be tempered with sympathy for the millions defending themselves in an unnecessary war. We would be justified in extending sympathy, also, to the millions who, through no fault of their own, were being pushed into a conflict, as aggressors, for which they had no personal inclination.

'The thing we want to avoid — or postpone as long as possible — is the attitude of hatred toward the Germans,' went on Doctor Braithwaite, deeply earnest. 'Germany has contributed too much to the enlightenment and beautification of the world to be dismissed, lightly, as an enemy of civilization.... These lurid tales of atrocities may, or may not, be true. I, for one, do not believe them!'

Dinny pounded his hands, the others tardily and rather doubtfully joining in the applause for politeness' sake.

'I see you agree with Doctor Braithwaite — about the war,' said his hostess, upon the conclusion of the President's brief address. 'It's not the popular thing, I'm afraid.'

'I'd agree with Doctor Braithwaite — no matter what he said!' declared Dinny, fervently. 'He's always right — and I know he's right about this.'

'Thank you, Dinny!' she said, softly, adding, 'You won't mind if I call you "Dinny"?... I'm afraid Mr. Braithwaite will find only a minority willing to share his views.'

'He doesn't need to care — a man like him!' declared Dinny, with assurance.

Mrs. Braithwaite shook her head, uneasily.

'People are growing more and more militant,' she said.

The party was breaking up, now. The Braithwaites attended to their duties as hosts. Joan was shaking hands with the girls, as they filed out and up the stairs to recover their coats. Barney had escaped. He and Dinny had not exchanged a dozen words.

'Going up the hill?' inquired Kling, breezily, still under the influence of his success as an impromptu speaker.

Dinny assented, without enthusiasm.

Joan moved toward him, her eyes troubled. Overriding the antagonism that had developed between them there was a curious intimacy in their attitude as he bent to listen to her swiftly spoken confidence. It was as if they had known and trusted each other for years.

'Don't say or do anything to encourage my father in his — his attempt at suicide!' pleaded Joan. 'He's dead wrong, and he's going to get into trouble! Don't lead any more applause that might make him think he has backing. Please!'

'How do you know he's wrong?' Dinny's gray-green eyes challenged her brown ones with a steady look.

'Indiscreet, then,' she compromised, impatiently. 'My

father ——' Joan lowered her voice almost to a whisper. 'My father has quite enough problems on his hands, just now, without incurring any more. You like him, don't you?'

'More than any man I ever met!' said Dinny, with fervor.

'Well — so do I,' murmured Joan, 'and I'm not going to let him ruin himself if I can help it.'

Dinny offered his hand.

'Good-night — Miss Braithwaite.... Sorry my little gesture of loyalty to your father has distressed you.'

Joan's brown eyes fired, angrily.

'I don't like sarcasm,' she muttered, 'and I think you're perfectly hateful, Dinny Brumm!'

Dinny's hand was still extended. She seemed determined to ignore it. Her hot eyes winked rapidly as she faced the faint traces of a conciliatory smile — half-reproach, half-indulgence — on Dinny's lips.

Impetuously, she took his hand, for a fleeting instant, and turned away.

* * * * * *

'What did I tell you?' exhorted Kling, as they trudged up the slope toward the dormitory. 'The man's positively dangerous! You'll find' — Kling measured his syllables with a didactic hand — 'that when a man's religious faith breaks down, it isn't long until his patriotism isn't much good, either!'

'Looks like it's going to snow again,' observed Dinny, with exasperating unconcern.

'And *you* want to be careful, too, young fellow,' warned Kling, ominously.

'Meaning *what?*' growled Dinny, dangerously, with a savage clutch at Kling's sleeve that flung him almost off his feet.

Amazed at this unexpected onslaught, Kling was speechless for a moment, and then said, nervously, 'I'm not going to fight you, Dinny, if that's what you want.'

'Oh — so you are a pacifist, after all,' taunted Dinny. 'Well — you needn't fight, this time, if the idea of it alarms you, or violates your convictions; but' — he clutched Kling's overcoat collar in the strong grip of his long fingers —'if I ever hear of you dishing out any more of your damned impudence about Doctor Braithwaite — ever again — in public or private — I'll beat hell out of you, whether you defend yourself or not! Have you got that, now, so you can remember it?'

He left Kling standing there on the path.

Without turning, he proceeded on up the hill, climbed to his room, slammed the door, disrobed, and wrote two letters, the second addressed to the Reverend Miles Brumm.

Dear Sir:

I have instructed the Speedway Moving and Storage Company of Indianapolis to call at your address for a small walnut desk of mine, formerly the property of my mother.

You will be good enough to let the moving people have the desk for immediate shipment to me, at my expense.

This, I think, will terminate our business and other relationships.

Any fear you may entertain relative to the possibility of an effort on my part to recover the money you stole from me, can be safely dismissed.

In view of the fact that my contempt for Mr. Alexander Craig is all of a piece with my contempt for you, I would not press the claim.

No reply to this letter is expected or desired.

Yours truly

FERDINAND BRUMM

CHAPTER IX

MAGNOLIA COLLEGE was considered good copy during the academic year of 1915–16.

It was a period when any recognition on the front page, crowded with heavy artillery, marine disasters, massacres of millions, and the multisonous clangor of a world on fire, required more racket than small church schools were accustomed to add to the cosmic din.

Even the Associated Press, sated with sensation, conceded, at the close of her second semester, that Magnolia — for sixty-three placid years an earnest little violet, staking her last shy petal on the nobility of diffidence — had done her bit in leaded black-face.

In the fall, Magnolia spectacularly won nine smashing victories on the gridiron with scores that dizzied her competitors, no one of whom got within ten yards of her goalline. Egged on by sports writers, she tentatively booked an exhibition game with Harvard to be played the next September, an engagement which was canceled in the spring, Harvard having lost interest, Magnolia having lost Dinny Brumm.

On New Year's Eve, the Recitation Hall burned to the ground, unquestionably the work of an incendiary, public opinion agreeing that some ardent 'preparedness' fanatic had thus expressed his sentiments toward a college so spiritless as to permit an uncompromising pacifist to direct her destiny.

On March tenth, the most widely known member of the undergraduate body, whose long legs and reckless courage had been primarily responsible for Magnolia's brilliant achievements in football, was expelled for adorning the President of the college Y.M.C.A. with two black eyes and a split lip.

The prosecution, appealing to the increasingly popular

cause of patriotism, made large capital of the fact that the
plaintiff had come by his injuries as a result of an impassioned address in behalf of his country's injured pride. The
defendant's spirit of disloyalty was further evidenced by the
recent appearance of his article in *The Iconoclast*, a discord-
ant organ of protest, in which the author had heaped con-
tumely upon his Alma Mater, and shown a disposition to
bite the hand that fed him.

The defense endeavored to show that the attack on Mr.
Kling's person was an honest, albeit overenthusiastic, reprisal for certain damaging remarks made in reference to
Doctor Braithwaite. It further ventured to prove, politely
as the circumstances permitted, that the statements of
Mr. Brumm in *The Iconoclast* — though admittedly phrased
in the pardonable superlatives of rampant youth — were
unfortunately true.

The faculty jury, Professor Grover, chairman, was out
only five minutes.

Had it been Kling who was being fired, the press might
have passed over the matter with negligent observation.
The expulsion of Dinny Brumm was quite another affair.
The Cincinnati Times-Telegram, in particular, wanted to
know all about it, and set forth Dinny's cause with so much
unction that the Magnolia Board of Directors was deluged
with letters and telegrams inquiring, in varying degrees of
indignation, whether the college had lost her mind.

On March thirteenth, a student mass-meeting was held.
The use of the college chapel — Magnolia's only adequate
assembly hall — having been denied for this purpose, the
auditorium of the City Building was secured. Unwittingly,
the promoters of the event thus recruited not only the attendance of almost the entire student body (the Sigs refusing to participate), but augmented the audience by several
hundreds of interested towns-people whose concern for
Magnolia's welfare was largely based on her athletic activities.

Mightily cheered and heartened from the packed galleries, which included not only ardent football fans with nothing at stake beyond their own enjoyment, but anxious representatives of the Chamber of Commerce, the Better Business Association, and scores of influential resident alumni, the undergraduates, after an accelerating tempest of fervid oratory, voted as one man for the rescinding of the faculty's action and a prompt reinstatement of Dinny Brumm.

A few of the more audacious wanted a trailer affixed to the peremptory resolution, threatening a general strike in the event of refusal on the part of the faculty to conform to student opinion. This, however, was voted down, the Magnolians, as a whole, recovering their habitual prudence even in the tumult of revolution vociferously fanned by the town.

On March twentieth, after an all-night session of the faculty and the Board of Directors, Dinny Brumm was restored to his previous rating. A mild proviso was attached demanding that Mr. Brumm settle for Mr. Kling's personal repairs and the mending of sundry articles of furniture which had impeded the celebrated fullback in his task of chastising his neighbor — it having leaked out that Dinny had already made these reparations.

On March twenty-first, Dinny left Magnolia to accept the position offered him by wire from Mr. Steinberg, the Managing Editor of *The Cincinnati Times-Telegram.*

The Athletic Association, getting wind of Dinny's offer and acceptance, hastily organized plans to see him off with a procession led by the college band, but he had already gone when the committee rushed to his room to disclose the nature of the vindication they had arranged for him; was, in fact, sitting in Mr. Steinberg's office, listening to the latter's expectations of him, at the very moment when the committee was scouring Magnolia in quest of him.

The bone of contention having been thus providentially dragged from the arena, the Board of Directors again assembled to focus its attention upon the President and in-

quire diligently of itself whether, in view of all the controversy stirred by his pacifistic opinions, it might not be better to set him free to preach his unpopular gospel of non-
resistance on his own hook, undetained by any further obligations to the college.

The Board split squarely in two on this issue, the objec-
tors maintaining that a considerable number of important
'prospects' whose contributions to the Endowment Fund
would depend upon the retention of Doctor Braithwaite,
were awaiting the outcome of this affair with a concern that
might affect Magnolia to the tune of a hundred thousand
dollars, or so.

Notwithstanding this meeting was conducted *in camera*,
every member under pledge to give out no interviews, the
discussion, the decision, and the underlying cause thereof,
were good for a first-page column with a throw to three,
next morning, in the public prints.

On May nineteenth, President Braithwaite delivered the
address to the graduating class of the Theological Seminary,
in which he lost the support of the well-to-do conservatives
whose influence had previously fended off the attacks of the
swashbucklers.

Later, at the funeral, it was remarked on all sides that
Doctor Braithwaite was not quite himself while delivering
this 'unfortunate' speech. He should have been in bed; was
running a temperature of 101°.

At the hour, however, no alibis were offered, and the address was judged on its demerits. Doctor Braithwaite proceeded vigorously to reappraise the preacher's job for the
edification of the fledgling prophets.... We were entering
upon a Reformation of the Church comparable to that of
four centuries ago. The bulk of the old beliefs were irrelevant. The oncoming generation would be so disinterested
in them that it would never even glance in their direction.
The old credos were as dead as Queen Anne.... We had done
with musty metaphysics, at least for the epoch with which
we would have to do, and would concern ourselves so ex-

clusively with kinetic energies that speculative philosophy could safely retire to the sanctuary of the museum.... The only service any longer possible for the old theology would be rendered in the capacity of an ancient landmark from which explorers might plat the curve of Christian progress.

The Board went into conference, late that afternoon, and passed a resolution requesting Doctor Braithwaite's resignation. But he was too ill to be handed the document, next morning, for he had developed a grave pneumonia.

On the following Friday, he died. It was quite obvious that the minority who agreed with him would say he died a martyr. It was equally obvious that the majority, who had thrown him out, would refer to him as a sincere, misguided radical whose disaster was easily to be accounted for: he had broken loose from the old moorings. Let this be a lesson.

A few of the elderly invincibles muttered that it was a judgment of God. One bushy-haired apostle, large of lung and expansive of gesture (eight years later elected Sublime Cyclops of the Ku Klux Klan in that region), ventured to preach, the following Sunday, on 'Vengeance is Mine: I will repay, saith the Lord.' Hopeful of riding into public notice on the shoulders of a corpse, he sent his manuscript to *The Star*, which, on the indignant Mr. Brophy's orders, was printed exactly as written, inclusive of all the bad spelling, bad grammar, and bad temper which distinguished it as a flagrant example of passionate ignorance.

It was an eventful year at Magnolia College. Hitherto it had been her proud boast that in her quiet corner she had preserved the faith once delivered to the saints. Having bred no speedy hares, she had gone in for steady tortoises, promising that great merit occasionally accrued through a race won by the plodder whose brilliant competitors had gone to sleep, on the course, overcome by sheer boredom. The highest mark ever accorded the winner of a Rebecca Winters Dutton Medal had been scored by an essay entitled 'Obscure Martyrs.'

Little Magnolia, in the fierce glare of the spot-light, felt stark naked, and was ashamed.

* * * * * *

But if the college year was a succession of dramatic events so interesting to the public that Magnolia's carryings-on were fetched in, every morning, off forty thousand doorsteps, along with the milk — events in which Dinny Brumm continuously figured either as an active principal or an unwitting accomplice — the season was replete with unpublished episodes vastly more upsetting to this junior's peace of mind.

Having worked full time on *The Star* through the three months' vacation, Dinny's economically administered savings were augmented to the point where he felt safe in launching upon his junior year without a job.

With more leisure in prospect, he had accepted the associate editorship of *The Blossom*.

Had the barbs been able to move concertedly, they might easily have had their way in all the college elections relating to non-academic activities, for they outnumbered the Greeks three to one; but, lacking such unity, they were usually trounced by the sophisticated minority. This time, the Sigs and the Pies had failed to get together on a slate for *The Blossom* staff, each offering a favorite son. The sororities took sides, the Gammas, as usual, lining up with the Sigs, the Lambies throwing their vote to the Pies. The barbs elected their ticket.

Gates, the impecunious senior editor, less concerned about becoming famous as a journalist than for the commercial success of his paper (the staff receiving a modest rake-off, if the year's business justified a bonus), encouraged Dinny to assume unrestricted liberty on the editorial page.

Faithful to its innocuous name, *The Blossom* had ever been a frail and shrinking organism, a mere amplified bulletin of collegiate announcements and uncritical comments. Its platitudinous editorials roused no breeze. Such spoofing as it indulged in usually applied to budding romances on the campus, calfish persiflage worthy of a high-school 'annual.'

Grinning with satisfaction, Dinny milled the college paper into a giant cracker that went off, every Thursday afternoon, with a loud bang. After the first issue, *The Blossom* sold on the news-stands over in town, and was warmly discussed in the faculty meetings. Gates raised his advertising rates on unengaged space.

The Cincinnati Times-Telegram reproduced, in its Sunday supplement, *The Blossom's* first long editorial entitled, 'What Every Freshman Ought to Know.'

Satirically featuring the unsurpassed spirit of friendliness, democracy, and smug insularity of Magnolia College, which rejoiced in its self-containment and its ability to make of its student-body 'one happy little family,' the editorial proceeded to explain the fraternity system for the benefit of bewildered newcomers.

'Less than one fourth of our students,' continued the editorial, 'are domiciled in large, imposing residences on either side of two sacred blocks at the western end of Sunnyside Avenue. Here dwell the Greeks in dignified sequestration from the raucous shouts of the proletariat.

'On each massive front door there are secrets carved in classic Greek, and on each roof is a mortgage presumably printed in the baser argot of the contemporary banking-house.

'You are advised to ask no questions about these institutions or their tenants. If they recognize you as a Greek, they will tell you. In that case, their secrets will be entrusted to you, and you may be assured that they are secrets, and no mistake; for when a senior who knows no Greek confides a Greek secret to a freshman who knows no Greek, it is guaranteed to remain a mystery. You will also be encouraged to carry with you to your ancestral home a generous portion of the venerable mortgage and drape it a-straddle your father's chimney. If he is of a grateful mind, he will realize the honor thus brought to your tribe.

'If, unfortunately, you are not of the stuff instantly identifiable as Hellenic, make no struggle to simulate a virtue which cannot be achieved by personal effort. In almost any pawnshop in town you will see jeweled fraternity badges on exhibition. To purchase and wear one of these emblems would not improve your rating.

'Neither will it aid you, in this endeavor, to enroll in Greek courses with the hope of promoting your eligibility, for the tongue of Olympus is a native gift with our fraternity and sorority people, and you will rarely meet one of them in the inquisitive groups that cluster about the feet of Professor Appleton.

'Pass quickly through the Delphian groves, when you must needs venture upon Sunnyside Avenue, lest you be blasted by anathemas from some Corinthian portico.

'And when — as sometimes happens — you are snubbed and snooted by the Greeks, because you are a barb, if it so be that the gods have blest you with even the atrophied vestigial remains of any sense of humor, permit yourself the luxury of breaking forth with wild spasms of "inextinguishable laughter."

'If you are a co-ed barb, so much the worse for you. It ill becomes a girl to be a barbarian. You are not built for it. Submissively accept your unkindly fate. Defer to your more sophisticated sisters when you encounter them on the campus. Step off the path, and humbly address them in their own language. Many of them have never learned to speak English correctly, and it will be a pleasant courtesy if you salute them in Greek.

'While it may be superfluous, perhaps impertinent, to suggest a suitable amenity, *The Blossom* will cheerfully furnish upon request, a brief salutation to be employed on such occasions. We do not guarantee, however, to provide applicants with the English translation.'

* * * * * * *

Of all the people who relished Dinny Brumm's sour diatribe, nobody more keenly enjoyed it than Professor Ernst Martin, for eighteen years master of Geology, Archæology, Anthropology, and sundry other brittles.

Professor Martin's odd gait, due to a club foot, and amazing tricks of facial expression, acquired through diligent dealing with a stammering tongue — (sometimes he hung on a dead center in the middle of a sentence, and whistled himself out of it, to the utter devastation of persons unacquainted with his slight disability) — amply explained why, at fifty-two, he was a dry old bachelor.

Long-time faculty wives could well remember when 'Ernie' had laid frank and futile siege to every good-looking girl within hobbling distance.

Convinced, at length, that he was at his best when in pursuit of inorganic objects of nature, Professor Martin had reluctantly renounced romance in so far as it related to himself, but he had never relaxed his interest in the heart attacks of other people. His library shelves were crammed with love stories, the more ardent of them re-read until he knew them by rote. He was a devotee of the movies, and at least twice a week followed the sinuous grace of his favorite stars with hungry eyes.

But nothing afforded him more pleasure than to observe the brief and covert exchange of wistful, exploring glances in his class-room. He had become so adept as a heart-diagnostician that he believed he could tell, almost the first day of a new semester, what pairings-off were likely to develop.

It was the shy ones who interested him most, the pairs who sat farthest apart, never entering or leaving the room together, until — one day — oh, joy! — the tortured stag would maneuver to the side of the flustered doe, as the herd filed out of the room, and Ernie's secret forecast had come true.

Sometimes he would mate a pair so sluggishly moving toward each other that he was exasperated beyond endurance. On one occasion, he had waited a whole year for signs of advancement on the part of two diffident young things, who were forever looking at each other, and, caught at it, would quickly busy themselves in some other quarter. Unable to be patient any longer, Ernie contrived an errand that would speed their affair.

His class in Anthropology was taken to 'the mounds,' near Pinckney. The gate was locked. He sent the timid pair to the owner's house, a half-mile away, over a narrow, rocky path, and through a tangle of uncleared forest, for the key. They were gone an hour, and when they returned, they were no longer on foot, but floating in a gossamer golden cloud. The stag's shoulder was white with powder, and the doe's ears were pink with embarrassment. But they had remembered to bring the key. It was a great occasion.

By far the most baffling problem that had yet engaged Ernie's attention was the annoying current case of Joan Braithwaite and Dinny Brumm who were now members of his junior section in Anthropology.

In Professor Martin's expert opinion, if ever two handsome thoroughbreds had been destined from all eternity to find each other — even if they had to meet halfway round the globe — these tall, proud, self-sufficient personalities were that privileged pair.

It was a small class, seventeen in all, accommodated by the first semi-circular row of chairs in the room whose walls were eventful with high glass cabinets stuffed with meteorites, stalactites, fossils, pottery, and plaster casts of extinct animals and approximate humanity of uncertain date.

'If my l-lectures bore you,' Ernie was accustomed to say, at the opening session of a class, 'there are p-plenty of interesting trinkets to look at, a c-ca-casual inspection of which would do you no dis-s-s-service.'

Joan had chosen the chair at the extreme end of the curved row, Dinny had taken the seat nearest the door. The intervening chairs were occupied by average examples of *Homo sapiens* in its commonest variety, worthy

and well-meaning young persons, no doubt, but clearly of
a different biological category from the two who, at opposite ends of the row, were so definitely of a higher species
of primate. The amusing, the infuriating thing about it was
that neither of them seemed to know what anybody should
have been able to observe at a glance.

There was that good-looking young cub, Barney Vaughn,
for example. *He* knew it. Vaughn was pathetically infatuated with Joan. Anybody could see that. But Vaughn
avoided Brumm. Once Ernie thought Vaughn had pur-
posely snubbed Brumm in a brief clash of opinion in a
class discussion.... Why did Vaughn have an aversion for
Brumm? Obviously — Vaughn knew, by instinct, that
Joan Braithwaite was Dinny Brumm's property!... Ernie
was furious.

After a few sessions of this class, Professor Martin became increasingly excited over his secret discovery that
the calm disinterest of Joan and Dinny was more calculated than a mere mutual indifference. There was something between these two. Their avoidance of each other
was intentional. They were not strangers, but enemies.

At ease in his woolen dressing-gown, with his bad leg outstretched on a neighboring chair, Ernie read the editorial,
that Thursday night, in *The Blossom*, and laughed aloud. It
was Brumm, of course. None of the others would have
risked it. None of the others could have done it, had he been
as audacious as the devil. It was Brumm! My Uncle! —
what a savage disposition the young beast had!... Then the
corners of Ernie's mobile mouth drew down, and his thin
brows met.... The surly piece was funny enough, God
knew, but Dinny shouldn't have done it. Wasn't Joan
Braithwaite the acknowledged queen of the whole sorority
outfit? What did the chap mean by jumping up and down
with his big feet on the soft white neck of Joan's exclusive
social tribe?

For a full hour he sat tugging his lip, relighting his pipe,
occasionally grinning, faun-like, sometimes shaking his head

despairingly. At length he arose, limped to the grate, poked
the fire, and muttered, grimly,

'D-a-a-a — dammit... I'll t-t — try it! It w-w-worked
w-w-w — once!'

* * * * * *

On the following Wednesday afternoon, the class in Anthropology made the annual excursion to view the mounds.

It was a comforting late October day, hazy and lazy, blue
and white on top, purple around the edges, brown under-
foot. Blackbirds were noisily mobilizing for the southern
expedition. Gray squirrels were working overtime storing
their warehouses. Red-headed woodpeckers were drilling
deep for drowsy hide-aways. The woods glowed with
smouldering embers of summer, and the narrow black
stream that had carved a rough toboggan through the limestone cliffs ran swift and cold.

The seventeen budding scientists, conducted by Professor
Ernst Martin, were glad to be out in the country. At one
they had met for the twelve-mile trip on a jerky, jangling,
little accommodation train to Pinckney. The sexes had seg-
regated in the dusty coach. Barney Vaughn, seated pro-
prietarily beside Joan, made himself agreeable to the cluster
of girls. Some of the men read newspapers, others stared out
at the windows.

Dinny sauntered to the rear platform, where, watching
the grass-grown ties and rusty rails squirm through the hills,
he was presently joined by his preceptor, who nodded
amiably and seemed, by the companionable twinkle in his
sharp little eyes, to be threatening an intimacy. They stood
for some time, swaying with the motion of the train, eyes
intent on the reeling hills.

'B-Brumm,' shouted Professor Martin, against the racket,
'as a s-sour old barb, permit me to c-c-congratulate you. It
was very c-c-clever.'

'Thanks.' Dinny grinned down into the bright, beady
eyes. 'Great scenery, down this way, isn't it?'

'Especially at this season.... B-but it would have been even more c-c-clever if you hadn't done it.'

'Somebody had to,' defended Dinny, suddenly clutching the thin arm of his master as the train whip-cracked around a hairpin curve. 'It was long overdue.'

'T-too bad it had to be you,' shrilled Martin. 'Y-you might have c-c-capitalized your p-popularity.... N-n-no use baiting the d-d-damn frats.... And there are some m-m-mighty fine girls in the s-sororities.... T-t-take a g-girl like Mmmm-iss Braithwaite, for example. W-well w-worth c-c-cultivating, I should say. N-n-not mmm-any like her!'

'Plenty of nuts, this year,' observed Dinny, pointing to a clump of tall hickories, vanishing around the screeching bend.

'Y-y-yes... j-j-just what I was s-saying!... N-not all of 'em on t-trees!... I'm g-going back inside. T-too c-c-cool out here for me.'

Dinny turned, and regarded his professor with fresh interest.

'It's a rough road,' he said, smiling.

'I-i-it always was for m-me,' rejoined Martin, meaningly. 'B-but it ought to be easier f-for you.' One little eye winked, sardonically.

Dinny felt that something was expected of him, though if the fantastic little geologist thought a confidence was in order, he was going to be disappointed.

'You're fond of riddles; aren't you, Professor Martin?'

Martin chuckled, nodded vigorously, and shouted over his shoulder as he retreated:

'Y-y-yes — and I've s-solved a f-f-few!'

Now what did the uncanny little devil mean by that?... Something up his sleeve, no doubt.... Had women on his mind.... Unhealthy imagination.... Meddling matchmaker. ... Damn fool.

Arrived at the dingy wooden station in Pinckney, they straggled off toward the path that led a mile toward the grove of the Indian mounds, Martin hobbling ahead, cane-whisking at brittle milkweed pods, the girls single-file behind him, Barney Vaughn leading the male contingent, occasionally pressing solicitous attentions upon Joan as if she needed assistance on the rugged stone ledge of the ravine. Dinny brought up the tail of the procession, quite conscious — he had had one fleeting glance from her, as they entered the train — that he was in high disfavor with the only person in this party that mattered.

At length a path diverged from the ravine and ambled toward the left, through a seared meadow strewn with huge boulders. In groups, the expedition crossed leisurely toward the high-fenced grove. At a considerable distance, keen young eyes learned that the place of interest was somewhat lacking in hospitality.

NO TRESPASSING! THIS MEANS YOU!

'W-w-what's this?' exclaimed Professor Martin, indignantly, as they gathered in front of the padlocked gate. 'Mr. B-Bowers assured me it would be left open for us. I m-must g-g-go for the k-key. The sh-short way to his house is d-d-down the ravine. N-n-no — I shall deputize a c-c-couple of you to go. It w--would take me too long. W-we must not be delayed.'

With the critical air of making a momentous decision, he deliberately took a careful invoice of the company, obviously contemplating the appointment of an important committee. His little eyes shone. They devilishly rested, for an instant, on the expectant face of Barney, wistfully posing for an Eagle Boy Scout who had not yet had a chance, today, to do a good turn.

Dinny could hardly believe his ears. What had possessed the ugly little jackass to hurl them at each other's heads in this ruthless fashion? He glanced apprehensively at Joan, but she had quickly recovered. She smiled, graciously enough, left the group of girls, and joined him. Professor Martin had suggested that Mr. Bowers might be glad if the President's daughter and the varsity's best-known star were sent to ask the favor. If they had no objection, would they go and get the key?

'Martin's a nice little arranger,' said Dinny, when they were out of earshot.

'Yes,' returned Joan, frostily, 'charming idea.'

'You don't have to talk to me, you know,' explained Dinny, indifferently.

'That's good,' returned Joan, quickening her steps.

In sullen silence, they retraced to the ravine. Joan briskly led the way along the narrow ledge, bending forward the stiff branches of intruding shrubbery, and not caring what became of them.

'Perhaps you'd better let me go first,' called Dinny.

There was no reply. Joan hurried on.

'And look out for those loose stones!'

It happened, presently. Joan, with a startled exclamation, disappeared over the edge. She was attempting to rise from her knees in the shallow, rock-strewn stream, when Dinny reached her.

'Now you've gone and got yourself in a mess, haven't you?' scolded Dinny, reaching out both hands toward her. She ignored them, and tried to scramble to her feet.

'You needn't bother,' she protested, hotly. 'I don't want your help — a bit!'

'Yes, you do,' he drawled — 'and quite a lot of it. You've hurt yourself. Haven't you?'

She nodded, reluctantly, like a defeated child, and reached up for Dinny's hand.

'Help me over to that flat rock, won't you?... No — not that way!' Dinny was gathering her up in his arms. 'Take my hands, please. I can manage, if you steady me.'

Joan took one short step and unsuccessfully tried another, shook her head, held out her arms. Her lips were white. Dinny lifted her clear of the water and deposited her gently on the little limestone island.

'It's my knee.... It hurts dreadfully.' She was trying to keep her voice steady, but she was trembling.

'Think it's broken?' Dinny knelt beside her, anxiously. 'Can you bend it? Try.'

Her eyes were tightly closed, and her face was drawn. She began slowly unrolling her stocking.

'Rather I'd go away?' Dinny swallowed, nervously, and felt foolishly helpless.

Joan eased back on both elbows, dizzy with pain, too sick to inspect the purpling bruise. Dinny wet his handkerchief in the cold stream, and was about to lay it on her forehead. Anticipating, she took the handkerchief, and dabbed at her temples, clumsily.

'Does it — look broken?'

Dinny carefully examined the damaged knee, resolutely telling himself he was a cad if he failed to concentrate his attention on the immediate field of Joan's injury. It was not broken, he reassured her, but it was frightfully bruised. Perhaps the sharp pain would ease up, presently.

'But you mustn't stay here any longer,' he decided, promptly. 'I'll take you to this Bowers place, and we'll have a doctor.'

'You can't,' objected Joan. 'Better leave me here, and get some help.... Oh — what a beastly nuisance!'

Had anyone been watching, thought Dinny, the pair of them must have made an amusing spectacle as he waded downstream, carrying Joan — huntsman fashion — on his back, her head drooping forward over his right shoulder, her curls tickling his ear, her warm cheek close against his. His left arm circled under her knees, his left hand firmly clasped her right. With difficulty he repressed a grin, and wondered if she was too uncomfortable to realize the absurdity of it all.

For the first fifty yards, nothing was said, Dinny picking his steps, deliberately.

'Am I jolting it too much?' he inquired.

'I can stand it,' said Joan, 'if you can.... I'm sorry.... I was hateful.'

'You were going pretty fast,' reproved Dinny. 'It was rather reckless.'

'I was furious!' Joan's voice registered directly into his ear a justification of her imprudent speed. 'He had no business asking me to go... with you.'

'Well — why did you?' growled Dinny, sourly. 'I'm sure I made no bid for it. I was surprised when you came along.'

'Couldn't make a scene — could I?' demanded Joan.

'Of course you could.... I don't believe you're above making a scene.... I never knew a woman who didn't like a — like a chance to exhibit her resentments.'

Dinny plodded along for several steps, conscious that he was carrying an explosive, and wondering how long it would be until the detonation occurred.

'Yes,' mocked Joan, acidly, 'I expect it's a lot you know about women — as irresistible, and polite, and ——'

'You see that little bridge ahead?' interrupted Dinny. 'I'm going to put you down, if you can stand on one foot, and try to hoist you up.... Pardon me — you were saying ——'

'I was saying' — Joan bit her words into hot little shrapnel — 'that you're a beast... and I don't like you!'

'There's no reason why you should,' muttered Dinny.

Hostilities were briefly suspended during the process of mounting over the rocks to the foot-bridge. Joan independently made her way alone to the end of the railing, and looked wistfully in the direction of the stone house, a hundred yards away.

'Well — here we go again,' said Dinny, cheerfully, ready to resume his burden. 'It won't be far now.'

'I can't see why you wanted to write that mean thing,' complained Joan, after Dinny had lifted her to his back.

'Just for devilment.'

'Sure it wasn't for revenge?'

'No.'

'"No," it wasn't? — or "no," you're not sure?'

'I'm not sure it wasn't.'

There was a long silence. Dinny was almost to Mr. Bowers's little lawn, now.

'I wish you weren't... that way,' murmured Joan, in a tone of genuine regret.

'Why should *you* care?' drawled Dinny, with cool indifference.

He carefully lowered her to the porch steps, where she slumped down, spent with the fatigue and strain of their trying half-hour. Dinny stretched his arms at full length, drew a deep breath, readjusted his scarf, ran his long fingers through his damp hair.

Late that night, as he sleeplessly reviewed the afternoon, alternately glowing with the memory of Joan's physical warmth and chilled by her hostility, he wondered what he might have said in reply to her tardy rejoinder had the front door not opened, at that moment, with Mrs. Bowers hurrying out, all sympathy and concern.

'Why should *you* care?' Dinny heard himself saying, in a tone of sarcastic self-depreciation.

Joan had looked up, wide-eyed, lips parted, searching his face with the undisguised candor of a child inspecting a total stranger.

'I — don't — know,' she said, slowly, her lips trembling a little. Then she glanced toward the opening door. 'Thanks, Dinny, for helping me.'

Mrs. Bowers had rung down the curtain on this disturbing scene, murmuring solicitous little cries of motherly interest, and Dinny felt his immediate responsibility transferred to her competent hands. He waited until the telephone conversation assured the early arrival, by motor, of President Braithwaite and a physician.

The men were playing ball in the meadow, when Dinny returned with the key. The girls were seated in the shade. Martin was consumed with curiosity, the brief explanation failing to satisfy.

He endeavored to corral Dinny into a corner, later, on the train. When all hints and subtleties of inquiry had been adroitly parried, he threw delicacy aside and asked a direct question.

'D-d-did you have to c-c-carry her?'

Dinny's eyes narrowed as he stared absently into the questing little gray beads that flashed a hungry wish.

'Miss Braithwaite said she needed no assistance,' he replied, dryly.

Ernie gave it up then, mumbled something about the stuffiness of the atmosphere, and hobbled aimlessly out to the sooty back platform, where he hung on to the begrimed iron railing and gazed moodily into the gathering dusk.

'H-h-hell!' he muttered. 'D-d-damned ungrateful c-c-cub!'

* * * * * *

So few swans had fledged in the Magnolia duck-run that the approaching visit of Congressman Philemon Bascom, '98, resident of Washington and Dubuque, was an event demanding celebration.

The Honorable Mr. Bascom had consented to deliver the principal address at the formal opening of the new Science Building on the afternoon of March thirtieth.

That the reception in his honor, on the night previous, might be loyally backed by undergraduate interest, the faculty had appointed a student committee of five to coöperate with their elders and betters in making arrangements.

Wesley Tinker, President of the Hellenic Council, was to represent the fraternities. Dinny Brumm was easily the most conspicuous figure among the barbs. Sophia Wise, temporarily in the public eye as winner of the recent essay contest, would speak for the girls who knew no Greek secrets. Joan Braithwaite naturally epitomized the sorority element at its best. Orville Kling was asked to appear in behalf of the theological students.

At the committee meeting, held in the library at the President's Mansion, lent to Joan for the occasion, an hour and a half was spent, that first Thursday night of March, in a rubber-stampish approval of the 'tentative suggestions' sent from the faculty 'as a basis of discussion.'

Hopeful of enlivening the stupid and perfunctory chatter of obsequious acquiescence, Dinny ventured the opinion that a reception was no place for a long program of speeches. Would it not be sufficient for Doctor Braithwaite to welcome the honored guest, briefly, and let the guest say 'thanks.' Why all these amateurish student harangues. There would be plenty of oratory touched off next day, at the impressive dedication.

Kling, whom Dinny suspected was over-eager to represent the seminary on the reception program, promptly sustained the policy of offering the student body a chance to express itself.

'Speaking for the theologues,' he declared, determinedly, 'I think the faculty's wish in this matter should not be questioned.'

Unable to resist the temptation to tease, Dinny soberly remarked:

'One might imagine the theologues would be quite relieved if they were not pressed to participate.'

'How so, may I inquire?' demanded Kling, bristling.

'Well' — explained Dinny, with a nonchalant gesture — 'this reception impinges on the opening of the Science Building, doesn't it?'

Kling truculently protested that he didn't care to enter into any controversy, but could assure Mr. Brumm that the Church was heart-and-soul in sympathy with Science — 'of the right sort.'

Dinny wished, a moment later, that he had been content to let the matter rest there; but, resentfully remembering Kling's impudent attacks on Doctor Braithwaite's liberalizing beliefs, he decided to jab the harpoon a bit deeper.

'How do you mean — "the right sort of Science"? — the kind taught in Genesis, maybe?'

Kling's ears were red, and he folded and refolded his notepaper, angrily.

'I did not come here, sir, to debate theology with a — an atheist.'

'In that case,' said Dinny, conciliatorily, 'I withdraw my suggestion.... Let the theologues express themselves, by all means.... I would like to propose that Mr. Kling be asked to speak on "The Contribution of Orthodoxy to Scientific Research."'

'You're trying to be funny.... Aren't you?'

'Of course — *I* think it is funny. But I wasn't sure that *you* would. May I apologize for underrating your capacity for humor?'

Tinker, the chairman, rapped on the table with his knuckles.

'Now — if you two will hire a hall, sometime, the rest of us will be happy to attend. For the moment, you're both out of order, I think. Let us proceed with our business.'

The meeting adjourned, presently. As Dinny passed Joan, who stood in the doorway of the parlor, she whispered, 'Wait.'

When the others had gone, she returned to the parlor, where Dinny, standing by the table, was leafing a magazine.

'Dinny — I wish you wouldn't.'

'I'm sorry,' he said, contritely. 'But that chap's always needing a trimming... and never getting it... not properly.'

'Oh — I think I know why you feel that way.' Joan motioned toward the divan, and they sat. 'Mr. Kling has been very annoying in his attitude toward my father.... I think you like my father, don't you?'

'You know I do, Joan. I would do anything for him!'

'Then — don't try to fight his battles. I don't want this to sound ungrateful, Dinny, but it won't help my father for you to be on his side.... Because — well, you see, you're too often on the *wrong* side! And you are so dreadfully savage and sarcastic that you infuriate people!'

'Very well,' said Dinny, slowly, 'if you think it annoys your father... for me to be loyal to him, I'll not intrude again.'

Impulsively Joan laid her hand on his, and exclaimed, impatiently·

'Now — there you go!... That's just what I mean... that ironical... cruel —— ' Hot, angry tears welled in her eyes.

Dinny rose, glanced at his watch, smiled.

'We won't quarrel,' he said, indulgently.

Joan stood, facing him, eyes flashing.

'Yes, we will, Dinny Brumm! You've been perfectly hateful! I don't know what all's happened in your life to poison you so, but if you don't get rid of it — somehow — you'll be wretched forever!... And so will everybody else that's... that's interested in you... at all.'

Unable to think of an appropriate reply, and stirred to frank admiration of her militant pose, Dinny grinned, appreciatively.... Gad — she was a superb creature!

Joan turned away, utterly exasperated.

'I won't keep you!' she snapped, hotly. 'Good-night.... The maid will show you out.'

Dinny followed her toward the doorway.

'Joan,' he called, 'please — don't be angry.'

She hesitated, turned, waited.

'I didn't mean to hurt your feelings,' he said, gently.

He reached out both hands, and looked down repentantly into her reproachful eyes. She took his hands, and regarded him with an expression of pity.

'Why do you do it — Dinny?' she said, pleadingly.

'Because' — Dinny was serious, sincere, contrite — 'because I can't help it!... I was started — all wrong.... The world's full of — full of bunkum, and I can't help laughing at it.... I fancy I shall keep on laughing at it, until I die.... That's the way I'm made.... I'm sorry, sometimes, and wish I wasn't that way.... But — you mustn't trouble yourself about it.'

She loosed her hands, slowly, and stood looking down at the floor.

'Good-night, then,' she said, huskily, with a wan little smile.

'Good-night — Joan — dear.'

Very tenderly, Dinny drew her, unresisting, into his

arms. She laid a soft palm on his cheek, and looked up into his face.

'Oh, Dinny,' she whispered, 'please... please!'

He bent to kiss her. She shook her head, buried her face in his breast. Dinny gently touched her hair with his lips His voice trembled a little when he spoke.

'I'll try, dear, to be good,' he said, sincerely.

'Honest?' Joan was smiling through her tears. She raised her head slowly, rather shyly, cheeks aflame.

'Honest!' promised Dinny, tightening his embrace.

Joan closed her eyes. The hand that was laid against his cheek moved slowly upward, caressed his hair, circled his neck.

Very gently, Dinny's lips sought hers. It was a chaste, comradely kiss that he offered her, symbolic of a resolution to cultivate a more amicable spirit. Only on such terms, he felt, would Joan permit this intimacy. Passionately in love with her, it was difficult to discipline that kiss.

To Dinny's amazement and exultation, Joan met the endearment in quite another attitude than that of a pleased reformer enheartening a penitent to keep his vows. At the touch of his lips, she responded as to an electrical contact, drew a long, convulsive breath that confessed the depth of her emotion, and the kiss she gave suffused him with an ecstasy he had never known.

They clung to each other for a full minute before Joan, her lips still on his, shook her head ever so slightly, and then, with a contented sigh, laid her cheek affectionately against his shoulder.

After he had gone to his room, that night, Dinny sat for a long time on the edge of his bed staring straight ahead, trying to reconstruct each separate instant of that exultant experience. Had any other girl than Joan Braithwaite consented to — much less joined him in — a kiss like that, he might have wondered a little about her.

But, because the girl was Joan, the warm, tingling memory of it carried a peculiar possessive, protective tender-

ness. His eyes were wet. Joan belonged to him! He walked
to the window and looked out, down the hill, at the big
house, loving it because it sheltered Joan.... Dear Joan!

* * * * * *

The next afternoon at the Athenian Literary Society,
which Dinny rarely attended, believing it worth a fifty-cent
fine to spare himself the irksomeness of sitting through a
protracted session of parliamentary wind-bagging, Kling
made a patriotic speech.

As an alumnus, he was there on invitation, and glad to be
back in the spacious room, where, he averred, he had
learned to speak on his feet.

His attacks on Doctor Braithwaite were ostensibly
cryptic, at first, but as he warmed to his theme, the clumsy
devices of indirect accusation were abandoned. It was an
insolent address. Dinny hotly scowled through it, promising himself that Kling would have to pay for his surly impudence.

That night, he executed the threat he had held over
Kling, so blind with indignation he gave no thought to consequences. What Joan might think of it did not occur to
him.

Next day, the campus hummed with the story. Dinny
called up Joan, but she was not at home.

On Monday, current copies of *The Iconoclast* were in circulation. Dinny had sold it many weeks earlier; had almost
forgotten it. But Joan, without considering how much time
must have elapsed between the composition and publica-
tion of this brutal effrontery, avoided him when they met
in the hall; ignored him in the class-room.

He dropped her a note, attempting explanation, but was
indiscreet enough to jest about the article as 'a hang-over'
from his 'unredeemed estate.' The note, plus the spreading
rumor that Dinny had made savage war on Kling, so distressed Joan that she was at a loss to know what to reply.
While she debated, the faculty moved in the direction of

punishment for Dinny. Her father's affairs were already sufficiently complicated. Any attempted reconciliation with Dinny, at this moment, might add to the President's problems. She waited.

Almost before she realized the swiftness with which Dinny's case had become a *cause célèbre*, he had left town. He telephoned to her. Mrs. Braithwaite answered.

'May I speak to Miss Braithwaite?'

'Who is speaking, please?'

'This is Dinny Brumm.'

'Miss Braithwaite is not in, Mr. Brumm.'

Her voice was not unkind, but Dinny interpreted.

Considering how much variegated disaster menaced Doctor Braithwaite, from all sides, it was obvious that the family was better off without any further traffic with Dinny. He appreciated the situation, and felt almost sympathetic with Joan's mother. She had done the right thing.

CHAPTER X

LOUNGING with athletic arms negligently disposed along the back of a slatted, sun-drenched iron seat in Central Park, overlooking undulous acres of verdant velvet, the prosperous young creator of the column capped 'Green Cheese' absently twirled an inventive pencil between thumb and finger-tips; but he was worried.

His deep-set, gray-green eyes, shaded by a brim-turned felt hat of the same color, were half-closed against the bright distractions, the tiny crow's-feet at their outer corners registering an habitual, detached amusement which he daily sent to market in forty newspapers.

On the broad gravel path immediately before him, perambulators that had cost thrice the price of Uncle Miles's jump-seat surrey leisurely trundled smug, superior kewpies whose interest in the narrow ribbons dependent from their lace bonnets seemed an earnest of future adroitness in the fingering of ticker-tape.

A hundred yards down the slope, kneeling around the lip of a gigantic concrete saucer, small scions of the well-to-do alternately righted unseaworthy sloops and wiped April noses on monogrammed coat-sleeves. Farther down and to the left of this mimic ocean, clumps of tourists, undistressed by the discomforts of their caged kin, idled from the monkey-house toward the bear-pits, pausing briefly to glance up through the untidy steel netting of the squawking, acrid aviary.

Sometimes — as today — the manufacturer of Green Cheese glumly wished he had chosen another vehicle for his syndicated satires than these fantastic 'conversations in the moon'; but they had proved immensely popular and profitable — even more so than his earlier, riskier series of 'Unfrosted Persimmons,' whose astringent quality had so unexpectedly piqued the public palate, jaded by a quadrennium of sentimental superlatives ranging all the way from lush and morbid pathos and the agony of hair-tearing despair to the loud and hysterical hallelujahs of Utopianism at its ultimate peak of drooling idiocy.

Still young in years but prematurely seasoned by cumulative disillusion, Dinny Brumm had been among the earliest to venture a bit of whimsical spoofing, indulgently phrased in the soothing 'Now, now; there, there; come, come,' of the psychiatrist making his afternoon rounds in a genteel madhouse. Dinny approached his increasing constituency gently, regarding them as convalescing victims of a pestilential neurosis superinduced by a long debauch under potent emotional stimulants.

At the outset, his covert fun-poking at the perfervid apostles of idealism who, watch in hand, galloped to catch trains that hurled them from platform to platform, where, daily and nightly, they beckoned and bellowed — saving the world for democracy, for civilization, for altruism, for our children and our children's children, for God the Father and Christ His Son — had been as shocking as a ribald joke told in a funeral address at the expense of the corpse.

But presently it began to appear that a considerable section of the public — weary unto death of the unconscionable nonsense brayed and bleated from ten thousand pulpits, lecture halls, luncheon clubs, women's clubs, open forums, and whithersoever the tribes of salvation-hucksters went up — found itself grinning over the audacities of a youthful cynic who, with no reputation to lose, offered comic relief in the midst of the wearisome epilogue following the final act of a tragedy that had spun itself out overlong.

Two years later, there was none so timid for whom it was not entirely safe and righteous to damn war and invent wry jokes to caricature the apostles and slogans of the noble cause that aspired to world-brotherhood and the Golden Age; but, at the hour, only the venturesome dared apply for such hazardous employment.

Dinny had promised himself the luxury of sweet revenge. Plenty of times he had staggered under the garbage and scoured the latrines for failing to wear the right expression of empty-eyed awe when stiffening to salute the self-conscious lieutenant who, only last winter... or was it the year before? — no matter... used to mince, limp-wristed, to the light of the department-store door, a bolt of silk under his arm, trailed by the plumber's haughty spouse, murmuring, meekly:

'It's a real mauve, madame, as you shall see — and prettuh, very prettuh.'

But the lieutenants and the captains and the majors were not permitted to come to bat every day in the column of 'Unfrosted Persimmons.' The civilian orators had their innings. Dinny was at his best when pitching them a fast one.

The ubiquitous civilization-savers, to whom everybody had listened spell-bound, in a desperate state of finger-gnawing fright, as they luridly depicted the crash and clatter of a blown-up world, were now become somewhat of a nuisance. With the arrogance of Jonah they had howled disaster into the ears of the populace until they, themselves, were fallen afoul of a nasty psychosis unpleasantly akin to sadism.

The war was over that had been so great a Godsend to the large of mouth and small of faith, but the frantic ink and screech of the calamity-merchants was unabated.... Ethical journals of opinion wagged an ominous pen. Prophetic fists pounded verbally inspired Bibles, and cited Jeremiah the empty-umpth chapter beginning at the orty-erth verse. Journeyman seers stamped the rostra of village chautauquas pointing bamboo fish-poles at the seething hot spots on the reconstructed map of Yurrup.... Could civilization survive?... Was not the whole social order on the rocks?... What shall we do to be saved? ... (What's become of the treasurer who was supposed to hand me my check?)... Let us humble ourselves before

God!... Socialize! Evangelize! Fraternize! Organize! Do your bit! Till it hurts! The ushers will now distribute the pledge-cards.

Dinny had a good time.

It pleased his whim, one day, to set the clock back to the closing hours of the fifteenth century. Indulgences were on sale at the tail of a cart.... Step up, terror-stricken, and bail your bloody brothers out of hell!... Yesterday, with valor shining in their eyes, they went forth to make the supreme sacrifice for you and yours... Christ leading on... who had come not to bring peace, but a sword.... Come, now, wipe out this stain... for war is crime, and soldiers are murderers — shame on them!

The more devastating of these ironical gas-bombs, charged from the corroded coils of Dinny Brumm's bitter laboratory, were thrown from the pages of the candidly caustic magazines of protest, the sour humor of the 'Unfrosted Persimmons' being somewhat less diabolical. 'Green Cheese' was even more gentle and conciliatory.

Dinny yawned, and resharpened his pencil. He was tiring of his product. However — one could endure a certain amount of drudgery and boredom over the daily output of Green Cheese, seeing its present market value was two hundred and fifty dollars a week, just as one had endured the tedium of plucking and hurling the Unfrosted Persimmons whose spontaneous acceptance at the hands of the disenchanted had liberated him from his nightly desk at *The Philadelphia Ledger*, and set him loose to live where and as he pleased.

He was not a conscious apostle of common-sense. Had anyone asked him if, in the spirit of a crusader, he were not aware of his mission to a public whose emotions had been scarified and cauterized by the lancets and blisters of the sensation-smiths and calamity-quacks until there wasn't another kick left in them, Dinny would have denied it with a scowl... 'Crusade?... Mission?... Me?... Hell!'

Nevertheless, he daily polished the mirror so that the

people might see themselves almost exactly as they were — a pitilessly honest glass it was, that neither convexed to them a reflection of cherubic amiability nor concaved them to misanthropy.

In these genially mocking 'Green Cheese' columns, synchronous in two scores of widely read papers, the Man in the Moon, ancient, wise, sated as Solomon, drowsily replied to the imbecilic queries and comments of Luna, the Lady of the Moon, an effervescent flapper.

A few experimental lines, raw material to be fabricated for today's output, had been scribbled on the bulky wad of paper reposing on Dinny's lanky knee.

'Lookit, Gramp!' pointed Luna, wetting a finger and setting a curl. 'Lookit what they got now!'

'More progress, I dare say.... Another epoch-making invention.... Civilization at the cross-roads... now marching on, eh?... Heads up... nothing to fear... *altus et altior*. ... What's this, Luna; an electric banana-peeler?'

'Don't be ridiculous, Gramp!... It's a new cigarette-lighter. They're all quite mad about it!'

'Out of matches?'

'Certainly not! — but this automatic lighter's so much more convenient.... It's a little metal lamp — all the way up to sixty dollars. You unscrew at the bottom and pour in a special kind of oil. When you want a light, all you have to do is snap a small iron wheel a few times with your thumb — it doesn't seem to hurt the thumb very much unless you have to do it too often — and it scratches a flint that quite frequently strikes an electric spark that sets off a little wick that's soaked in the oil, and ——'

'How do you mean — it's more convenient?'

'Don't be so grumpy, Gramp!... Aren't you interested in progress, at all?'

* * * * * *

Very shortly after Dinny Brumm, fresh from the pandemonium that was Magnolia, had walked into the office of Mr. Steinberg to inquire what *The Cincinnati Times-Telegram* expected him to do, interesting things began to happen.

The first month — he had been told to 'sub' for Clint Mitchell on 'police and fires' until he learned at least the points of the compass — was too routinish and uneventful for his liking; but presently life was galvanized by the enlivening hubbub stirred when it was announced there would be a visitation from Zandy Craig — *the* Craig, of the Craig Syndicate — first week of May.

The 'T-T' — employees of *The Times-Telegram* always abridged the name — was in a grand state of excitement. Everything was speeded up, soaped, scraped, scoured, scrubbed, sponged, shined. High efficiency prevailed.

Reporters put fresh ribbons on their machines (it was in the uncoddled days when reporters were still able to do that for themselves), cleared their desks, bought a new hat. The girls at the Want Ads counter stopped doing their nails in the presence of customers. Linotype operators tried valiantly to break themselves of the reprehensible habit of tossing pied slugs back into the pot. Windows were washed in the composing-room. The devil wore a clean shirt.

For Zandy Craig saw everything; eyes of a hawk and nose of a hound.... Last time he was here, the entire Circulation was fired in a body, every man-jack of them. Forty salaries were raised. *The Enterprise* was bought in and swallowed up. A new off-set press was installed. Four pages of funnies were added.... The very building had rocked on its bricks for six dizzy days. God only knew — certainly no one else, not even Mr. Steinberg — what might happen this time.... You just kept out of the way, and hoped for the best. If what you were doing satisfied Craig, all he wanted out of you was silence — and damn' little o' that!... So went the tribal chatter out of apprehensive mouth-corners.

It had not occurred to Dinny that the omnipotent

Zandy Craig could be of more intimate concern to him than as the Dread Jehovah of Journalism, his absentee boss. He was related to the great Craig as a blade of grass to a forty-acre meadow. The dim, far-away figure of the contemptible fugitive who had left in the lurch an unsophisticated, over-trustful, little school-teacher, had never been spoken of in his presence as 'Zandy' Craig. He did not even reflect upon the unlikelihood of his unknown parent's achievement of so great prominence. The name roused in him no curiosity, at all.

Everybody spruced up for the big dinner at the Barstow, with Zandy Craig as both host and guest, and all hands present, as was the custom, from the Managing Editor's office down to the coal-bins. The dinner was always an inspiration. Besides, Craig was not niggardly with the fare. You heard what was good for you, and what you'd — By God — better do if you wanted to work for *The T-T*, but you also ate the food of a gentleman, and plenty of it.

Dinny sat by Mitchell, whom he easily liked, far down the T-shaped table seated for six score. The common herd had been settled and was fussing with its spoons.

'You never saw him,' remarked Mitchell, offering a cigarette; 'quite strikin' personality.'

'No,' replied Dinny, furnishing a light. 'He would be, of course.'

'Straight as the scales — and hard as hell.'

A slight commotion at the door of the banquet-room signaled the arrival of the important guest and his retinue. Dinny followed with intent, inquisitive eyes the progress of the tall, dynamic, early-frosted figure, as he strode to the seat of honor, preceded by the Mayor and Mr. Steinberg, and trailed by Mr. Latimer, the City Editor, and Mr. Orton, of the Circulation Department. A genuine outburst of applause acknowledged Zandy Craig's advent. Chairs were pushed back and the company stood, still pounding its hands. Dinny joined in the clapping, through

sheer animal reflex to the racket, hardly conscious of what
he did.

The big man signed to his slaves with a downward push
of the heel of his long, strong hand, and they sat. The
orchestra was off at full gallop. A battery of white-jacketed
waiters trooped in, with soup aloft, a buzz of conversation
broke out, and the dinner was in high gear.

'Dinny,' oracularly observed Mitchell, who was short
and chubby, 'it takes beef to make a big man. You've
gotta be tall if you're ever goin' to look down on 'em.'

'Napoleon was rather — brief, wasn't he?' suggested
Dinny, encouragingly.

'Not on a horse,' defended Mitchell. 'Napoleon never
hollered at his tall grenadiers unless he was walkin' on four
legs.'

'How about us getting a horse, Clint?'

'Us? Me — you mean. You're rangy enough. Tall as
Craig, himself.... Damned if you don't look a little like
him. Same eyes; sort o' navigator eyes — if you know what
I mean.'

Dinny, leaning far forward to gaze down the long table,
was only half-conscious of Mitchell's prattle. Tugging
suddenly out of his mesmerism, he returned to Clint with
an abstracted stare, apologizing for his inattention.

'Beg pardon, old man; you were saying something ——'

'Yeah,' drawled Clint, indifferently, 'you better come to,
and munch your fodder.'

Handsome Bob Moore, Municipal Building and The
Courts, leaned across Dinny to inquire: 'Know if he brought
the angel along, this time, Clint?'

'Haven't heard. She's probably in school, some place.'
Then, for Dinny's enlightenment, Mitchell added: 'Craig's
got a girl, seventeen or eighteen, that left a trail o' destruc-
tion behind her, last July. Moore's never been the same
man. They told him off to show her the finish of a dramatic
lawsuit in Circuit Court — she'd never seen a trial — and he
was so stampeded by her amazin' pulchritude that he for-

got where they were goin' and took her to a ball-game. It was reported the old man asked her, that night, who won the case, and she said, "The Sox."... But, even at that, Bob had his pay raised, when he thought he'd be fired.'

Young Welland, Clubs and Theaters, nosed in from Mitchell's left.

'Yeah, she's here, all right. Saw her in the lobby with Mrs. Steinberg, Mrs. Forsythe, and some other swells. All dolled up to kill and cripple. Very easy to look at.... Guess they were going to a show.'

Dinny was having difficulty keeping his eyes away from the head of the table. It was a curious, unaccountable fascination. Never had he been so engrossed by a personality. He wished he could be close enough to hear Craig's voice as he turned from one to the other of his immediate companions, occasionally putting down his fork to make short, expressive gestures with both hands.

Successive courses came, and clattered away on sagging white shoulders. Coffee arrived, smoke curled upward, chairs diagonaled.... 'Pardon my back, old son.'... Legs crossed, comfortably. Eyes roved to the gavel-zone.

Steinberg hitched about, stroked his chin, rose slowly, pulled down his waistcoat, told an old yarn about Henry Watterson, teased the Mayor discreetly, waited for the polite chuckle, waved a John-Baptist hand toward Craig, and backed out of the picture.

Craig was on his feet quickly.... No stories, no felicitations, no preamble. He strode swiftly, confidently, to the end of the plank and dived off. Dinny never forgot that first sentence — crisp, curt, cold, impudent, kinetic, arresting! With bushy black brows contracted, and narrowing his gray-green eyes, Craig bit his opening sentence into five ragged chunks and spat it, growled it:

'The only chemicals — imperative to evolution — are water, blood, and ink — and the greatest of these —— is ink!'

Craig talked for an hour, his voice rarely rising from the

deep, searching, commanding, dynamic diapason of the dogmatic credo with which he began.

He was speaking to a hard-boiled, blasé crowd, not only fully aware of its thick hide, its cynicism, its fish-eyed challenge that dared any man to speed its heart, tighten its throat, or flush its temples; but unafraid of it. Dinny viewed him as a reckless lion-tamer, stalking arrogantly into the cage, blacksnake whip confidently flicking bristling manes into a corner.... Shades of Nietzsche — but Craig was hard!

Now he had eased up on the old brutes with the long, yellow fangs, and was growling at the cubs; trying to make lithe lions of them.... Dinny responded to the tug. Gad — but life seemed potential, the way Craig talked about it! In his hands, a driving, obsessing ambition seemed august! You wanted to thrust out impatient elbows, crackle your chrysalis, and take wing!

One life!... One chance!... One enchanted youthtime!... Make it pay!... Hurl into it!... Take the cash, and let the credit go!... Be something — quickly!... Let the dead bury the dead!

Dolts and dawdlers, pull up along the right curb and let the unscared strong go by. If you haven't the nerve to pass your sluggish leader, don't hog the middle of the road, but clear the way!... Live precariously! — and like it!... Be sportsmanly; gamble with Life; play for big stakes!... Choose now — whether to scoop or be scooped — all the way to the box that latches on the outside!... My God — but Craig was cruel!

And yet — and yet — Dinny Brumm was drawn to him with an uncanny yielding. Craig had the idea. Craig was a superman, made of superstuff. It was impossible to withstand the attraction of the man's kinetic energy. Dinny's pulse pounded with an admiration close to idolatry.

He shuffled along with short, impeded steps, thick in the ruck that jammed the exits, and cramped with a chunk of the pack into the noxious elevator. The passengers were

silent, a bit constrained. Dinny wanted only to hurry to
his room, twenty blocks away and up the hill, to beat out a
few hot resolutions while they were still malleable with the
glow of the Craig forge.

The lobby swarmed. The revolving, leather-lipped street-
door spun — plop, plop, plop, plop — as the animals, in
line, left for the kennels; the grizzled and mangy, the playful and cocky, the yawning and gamboling.... Dinny
squared his shoulders.

Mitchell was calling from the rear, somewhere. Annoyed,
but complacent, he left the line, sauntered back, inquired.

'Moore's met the Craigess, Dinny.... We're asked to
watch her nibble a rarebit in the grill, and do her a little
genuflection. Want to?'

'Sure... Thanks, Clint.'

The princess was already at court, and presiding uncommonly well. No need to have her identified as the daughter
of Craig; it was on her face, in her eyes, in her hands. She
was Craig — young Craig, drawn to about three-fifths
scale. The Craig *savoir faire* pleasantly veneered what
promised to be — when it matured — a ligneous sub-
stratum of will-to-power. She was not haughty, not arrogant, not vain; but consciously assured. Whatever-it-was-
she-had seemed to be saying: 'It's mine: give it me:
thanks.'

Nobody needed to guess which was the head of the round
table, seated for six. All were standing, for the moment,
surrounded by twice as many more, half of them collected
by Mitchell, en route to the grill. In the polite bedlam of
introductions and renewals of acquaintance, Dinny, with
no responsibilities, stared appraisingly at the self-possessed
blonde, frankly envying her birthright to a magnetic personality that dominated from her gray-green eyes and firm,
red mouth, and pink palms.

'How do you do, Mr. Brumm?' She gripped his hand
like a man, and gave him a steady, smiling look of honest
welcome, same as she had done for young Fitzgibbon,

who had come along with *The Enterprise* since her last visit.

'It must be nice to come back,' said Dinny, 'and find everybody so happy to see you, Miss Craig.'

She had not released his hand. Her smile had vanished. Her eyes had contracted slightly, and shuttled from his brows to his chin, as if attempting to recover a long-forgotten acquaintance.

'You're new, too; aren't you?' she said. 'I'm sure I never met you.... Did I?' She shook her head, still searching his eyes. 'Funny,' she added, half to herself.

He made way for the others behind him. She released his hand slowly.

'Auntie Alison, Mr. Brumm would like to meet you. Mrs. Forsythe, Mr. Brumm.' Her eyes momentarily dropped to the hand he extended, and again swept inquisitively to his face, before she turned to listen to Mitchell's next presentation.

'My son — Mr. Victor Forsythe, Mr. Brumm,' murmured the tall, rather imperious lady in mourning.

'Mrs. Steinberg, this is Mr. Brumm,' reiterated Victor, whose sleek, black hair was extraordinarily long. The tip of a white handkerchief peeped from the sleeve of his dinner-coat.

Mitchell's recruits were insisting that the diners resume their seats, and most of them, waving good-nights with smiles, were drifting away. Dinny followed, laggard, ostensibly lingering a little for Mitchell and Moore, in the process of tearing themselves away from the girl who paid flattering attention over her white shoulders. Something she was saying now made them glance in his direction.

'Dinny!' beckoned Moore.

He obediently joined them, inquiry in his eyes.

'Miss Craig wants you,' explained Clint, adding, with pretended pique and as if the remark were *sotto voce.* 'lucky devil!'

'Mr. Brumm,' she asked, almost inquisitorily, 'did you ever work for any of my father's other papers?'

Dinny shook his head, regretfully.

'Should I have?'

She did not join in the chuckle with which his colleagues rewarded his naïve query.

'Do you mind telling me where all you have lived?' she persisted, as to a witness under cross-examination.

'Well — we'll leave you now,' interjected Mitchell, breezily, laying a propelling hand on Moore's shoulder. 'It would be like you, Dinny, to discover that you and Miss Craig had been schoolmates, or something.... This chap has more lives than a cat, Miss Craig.... Got fired from college for knockin' the steeple off the Y.M.C.A., and made 'em take him back and pay him for lost time.... Good-night!... See you some more, I hope.'

'Nowhere you're likely to have been,' said Dinny, when the clamor had subsided. 'Indiana — and Magnolia College.... We never met before, Miss Craig.... But' — recklessly — 'now that we have, let's pretend we're old friends.'

He had laid his hand on the back of her chair, and when she looked up with still serious eyes to reply, her warm, supple body glowed against his fingers.

'I have never seen the Rookwood Pottery,' she said.

'Would tomorrow be convenient?'

'About eleven, preferably. You work at night, don't you?' She was looking squarely into his eyes, sheltering her voice a little from her table companions.

'And luncheon?'

'Yes — I think so.'

She held out her hand, like a man, without coyness.

'Good-night — Miss Craig,' said Dinny, deferentially, as became an obscure employee taking leave of the magnate's daughter.

'My name is Alison.' Her lips barely moved, as she spoke, making no effort to disguise the fact that their conversation was private. Slowly she disengaged her long, strong hand, gave him another swift, serious scrutiny that circled his face and came to rest, for an instant, on his lips; and rejoined her company.

* *, * * * *

Alison was amazingly direct. The bland candor with which she ignored all the age-old subtleties of her sex, proclaiming in every look, tone, and gesture that Dinny Brumm was hers, by priority claim, all but took his breath away.

It was not brazen, but transparently ingenuous. Dinny was neither amused nor annoyed. Her attitude was that of a willful child daring all-comers to dispossess her of a toy. She had lost no time defining her convictions, indifferent alike to their possible effect on Dinny or any who might discover them.

Even on that first morning, strolling beside an impressed executive, who, learning her identity, had volunteered to guide them through the celebrated pottery, she put herself to no bother of pretense that their interest in art accounted for their visit.

Mr. Dabney would reverently hold up an exquisite vase, turning it, slowly, kaleidoscopically, inviting her to luxuriate in its mellow, parti-colored translucence; but, with a nonchalance so unconcerned that Dinny was half sorry for the fine old pagan, Alison's eyes — briefly, abstractedly regarding the treasure — returned to search his face. She held tightly to his arm. Employees grinned, slyly; exchanged an appreciative wink.... Honeymooners... second day out... utterly dippy... at least, the bride was.

They lunched downtown at the Hofbrau, where Alison expressed no preferences when their fingers touched on the menu-card, and seemed unaware what she was eating. Dinny was surprised to find himself quite unembarrassed by this devotion. It was too genuine to provoke a smile.

When she talked of herself, it was of herself and Geneva, herself and Montreaux, herself and Paris, as if she hadn't had an existence prior to her school-days in Switzerland, begun at fifteen, a few months after her parents' separation. When she talked of Dinny, it was all in the future — hot burning fires of ambition for Dinny. She all but suffocated him with it.

The goal of success was leisure to live, write, and play in Europe. That's what Dinny must live for, look to, as the reward of genius multiplied by hard work. That's what she lived for, looked to — Europe! She implied they were both going there, one day. She did not say they were going on the same ship, but she described moonlit nights on the boat-deck in a dulcet tone and ecstatic mood whose implications were almost shockingly direct.

Whether Zandy Craig was so confident of his dynamic daughter's self-sufficiency or so infatuated with his own business affairs that he gave her no thought, Dinny Brumm could not divine. It was enough to know that Alison's society, for ten memorable days, was not only accessible to him at all hours but flatteringly urgent.

She casually disclosed that Mrs. Forsythe, who lived in New York, was visiting in Cincinnati, hopeful of interesting the well-to-do music-lovers of the city in the budding talent of young Victor, whom Alison catalogued, briefly, brutally, as 'a bit of a cad, too dumb to succeed, and too lazy to bluff'; though she spoke almost tenderly, for her, of Tommy, the eldest, and Grace, who were forever stepping aside to make way for the callow prodigy in whose thin, listless fingers their ambitious mother had placed a fiddle almost before he was able to stand alone.

Alison's disgust and distaste for Victor apparently had wrought somewhat of constraint between her and Mrs. Forsythe. In view of this circumstance, and also the exigent desire of her aunt to promote Victor among Cincinnati's art-patrons, perhaps it was natural that the girl should be independent of much restriction.

After three crowded days in Cincinnati, almost constantly tied up in business conferences, Craig had scurried to Louisville. If Alison had been mistress of her own fate before, she was now even more completely in charge of her time. That time was Dinny's.

At Alison's suggestion, they procured saddle-horses and rode all day in the hills. They ferried to Covington, and strolled in the country. She even had the audacity to call up Mr. Steinberg, late one afternoon, from some undesignated outpost, reporting that she had asked Mr. Brumm to entertain her for the evening, and he would not, therefore, appear at six, as was his custom; to which information Mr. Steinberg replied, dryly, that he hoped she would return him, eventually, to *The T-T*, unspoiled by the honor.

Mulling over the whole tragic affair, later, Dinny found a little comfort in the fact that he had made no effort to capitalize Alison's devotion to the discredit of either of them. Nor was it easy to maintain his attitude of chivalry in the face of her quite abandoned, ruthless, reckless disclosure of a fascination for him to which she had yielded utterly.

Every day tightened their intimacy. Often she hinted of a story she meant to tell him; he would be 'quite frightfully' interested in it, as a scribbler, she knew; a long story, it was; she would let him have it when there was time. Dinny did not press her for it. She had implied that the tale impinged somehow on her family affairs.

* * * * * *

It was Saturday afternoon.... Craig had wired he was returning that night. Alison was to be packed and ready to leave with him for New York, next morning, at ten.

They had tied their horses at the edge of a grove; had sauntered to a favored rendezvous on the rocky lip of a glen; were promising each other more happy days when she returned with her father in the fall.

'I'm going to tell you that story, now, Dinny,' she said, snuggling close to him, and childishly tracing patterns on his lapel with a possessive finger.

'Do,' said Dinny. 'Don't leave anything out.'

They leaned comfortably back against the warm rock, his arm around her, and the story began; just a bit diffidently, at first, for the story was not hers, really, but her father's.

After ten minutes of Alison's calm narrative, paving the way for the most pleasant possible interpretation of her father's youthful tragedy by recalling many of his college experiences, the story abruptly shifted to another locale.

Dinny relaxed his affectionate hold, and fumbled awkwardly in his coat pockets for cigarettes and matches.

'You smoke too much, dear,' said Alison, rather petulantly, annoyed at the distraction. 'It isn't good for you. ... Your hands are trembling.... Look!' She gripped his fingers. He did not reply or smile, but obdurately lighted the cigarette.

'And then,' continued Alison, sinking back against the rock, with a little sigh of disappointment not to find his arm there, 'the most natural thing happened.... You know my father.... He's always been that way.... What he wants, he wants — that same day!'

Dinny sat with eyes half-closed, listening, smoking; lighted another cigarette off the hot end; averted his face, savagely ran his fingers upward through his hair.

Too disconcerted over his unaccountable mood to continue without some explanation, Alison broke off, presently, in the midst of a sentence, groped for his hand outspread on the rock between them, and asked, anxiously:

'What is it, Dinny?'

He did not turn to her or respond to the pressure of her fingers.

'Dinny!' she entreated, pressing her face against his shoulder, 'tell me, dear!... What did I do?... What's come over you?'

'I'm afraid' — he said, hoarsely, after some delay — 'I can't tell you.'

She sat for a moment half-stunned and silent; then, with

a little sob, she wrapped both arms tightly around his neck, and murmured, thickly: 'I can't bear it, Dinny. You must be good to me. You've made me love you. I'm mad about you!'

She raised her face, eyes closed, and offered him her parted lips.

Suddenly haggard, Dinny gripped both her hands and drew them down, holding them vise-like against his knee. He swallowed, convulsively, and when he spoke, his voice was hollow.

'You mustn't, Alison,' he muttered.

'Don't you love me — even a little, Dinny?' she pleaded, with brimming eyes.

'I mustn't!... We can't!' he whispered, staring into her face, the muscles of his cheeks twitching.

'Why?' she asked, inaudibly, her lips forming the query.

He drew her head tightly to him, with a gesture of protection, as if to shield her from a blow, and, after a long minute, measured out the words, dully, one at a time:

'You — are — my — sister.'

* * * * * *

Dinny never pretended this was the reason for his almost immediate decision to join the artillery unit mobilizing at Gettysburg, where the only artillery to be had, at that moment, was in the cemetery, slightly outmoded, as such things went.

Neither did he ever explain to himself — much less to others — that he had waived the exemption Craig had provided somehow for 'necessary members of editorial departments' (meaning everybody on the payroll) out of a sense of patriotic duty.

He wryly, profanely, squirmed into an ill-fitting, ludicrous suit of khaki solely to save his face, and because he was quite too fit a specimen of physical vitality to be at large in civilian clothes at a time when so many hundreds of thousands of inspired patriots were rushing about extolling 'the supreme sacrifice' as a noble privilege dangled before the enchanted eyes of 'our valiant boys.'

Most of this exultant talk was offered by prophets and soothsayers of forty-five and up, who, albeit unable to make such renunciation themselves, were obviously uplifted by the thought that they were not standing in the way or taking the place of some other brother, hungering and thirsting for such righteousness as might be had by blowing a Teuton's head off with a handful of blasting-powder.

Dinny's long, monotonous months in camp never benefited his native land by so much as a feather's weight; and, as for what he himself got out of it, either in discipline, experience, or stimulating friendships, the total result was exactly nil; unless his increasingly bitter cynicism, later capitalized to a monetary advantage, might be said to have fermented a little more through those hateful days.

Even with unpleasant memories as his chief stock in trade, memories fetched to market and savored by the similarly disillusioned, Dinny did not like to cogitate too much about his life at Gettysburg. The revulsion made him ill.

As for 'heroism,' the most heroic act anybody in that camp was expected to perform consisted of the valiant refusal to commit the half-dozen murders for which Justice clamored.

Uniforms played weird tricks on people who, in civies, must have been halfway decent. It seemed to make very little difference about a man's previous character or relation to society, once he had been required to perfect the debasing art of revolving himself stiffly on one heel, by some reflex to a growl that brought the flat of his hand smack against the brim of his cap, the only way he could square with his own soul, for this indignity, was to look promptly for somebody else, even more debased than he, who might be rank-badgered to do him a kow-tow.

Nobody ever saluted Dinny Brumm. Nobody would have saluted Dinny Brumm had he remained in the army until the Dawn of Everlasting Peace. He wasn't the type. According to the letter, he went through all the motions, which largely consisted in offering sustenance to the vanity of suddenly ordained Plattsburgers and surly non-coms; but Dinny's spirit — such as it was — refused to participate. His contempt glared in his eyes, against his will. It was chiseled in the deep lateral cleft between his lower lip and chin, quite beyond his control.

They nearly let him die, during the flu epidemic, for offering frank comments, when half-delirious, relative to the institution with which he was connected, and the important members of its personnel. Before he was able to pull his trousers on again, he had learned a disheartening thing or two about the only profession for which he retained the slightest degree of respect. Always had he venerated the medical profession. Now he had discovered, regretfully, that a few metal buttons, a squeaking new belt, and a pair of spurred boots would frequently play the same amount of hell with the Hippocratic oath that they so incomprehensibly wrought in the disordered minds of formerly gracious grocery clerks and collegiate sons of honest farmers. He saw many a competent, generous, integrity-loving physician degenerate into a pompous, puffy, arrogant ass.

Even the nurses went about, stiff-necked and consciously professional, mouthing the phrase, 'War is no tea-party!'

Dinny Brumm never went over the top, in France, at four A.M., but he spent six weeks in a military hospital, during the flu contagion, which called for almost as much patriotism, and lasted longer.

On the day he went back into civilian togs, he promised himself he would get even with eight anthropoids, to wit; one captain, one lieutenant, two sergeants, two doctors, one orderly, and a nurse. He expected to hunt them down, in their post-war haunts, and pummel them to a jelly — all but the nurse, who was to be enticed to some public place and spanked in the presence of a large, appreciative audience.

The determination to do these animals physical harm cooled, after a while, to an acidulous contempt which he occasionally tapped with a pen for the approval of demobilized thousands who, with ungodly glee, found in his devastating satires a vicarious vengeance.

Alison wrote to him almost every week while he was 'in the service.'

'I am not going to tell father,' she stated, in her first note. 'Poor man couldn't do anything about it, could he?... But, Dinny, darling, it is a frightful thing he's done to us.'

In sober truth, Dinny was incapable of viewing their tragedy with the same despair. Much as he admired Alison, their brief and unfortunate affair had not been of his own contriving. As for permanently linking his life with hers, he would as soon have married a hoisting-engine. Indeed, he had already begun to wonder, before discovery of their blood relationship, by what pleasant, painless process he might adroitly excuse himself from an impending attachment brimful of agony.

He replied to her letters at the rate of one to three, painstakingly shifting their mood, by a calculated katabasis of affection which, within three months or so, had — at least so far as he was concerned — placed their relations on an approximately normal and sound footing.

Angela wrote from the midst of a great revival in Hamilton that the Lord was blessing her labors in a miraculous way. It was not her first important revival, but the first in which she had starred. From now on, she expected to be at the head of her own company. Angela made no effort to disguise her natural gratification over the material features of her success. Dinny was pleased at this honest, albeit unintended, confession, and thought a little better of Angela. She didn't mind admitting that she was in the show business ... on behalf of The Lord, to be sure, but — well — the show business.

Joan Braithwaite was much in his thoughts. Upon the death of her father, he had written her a note. Her reply, some six weeks later (though he had promptly received a black-edged card from her mother, acknowledging his flowers), was post-marked New York. Whether she was there temporarily, or to stay, he did not know. That she expected no further correspondence was implied by the absence of a specific address. There was no one of whom he cared to inquire.

Mr. Steinberg occasionally wrote to him, as became the employer of a volunteer hero, and there was a letter from his father, shortly after he enlisted, commending him on the splendid thing that he had done. The letter was dictated, and signed in a feminine hand, doubtless the same hand that had done a score of them.

'Take this, Miss Rabbit, and make twenty originals for our enlisted employees. Miss Hare has the list of names.'

'Wish to see them, sir?'

'No — you can sign 'em.'

Dinny had chuckled while composing samples of conversation between his father and the stenographer, relative to the issue of Craig sentiments *in re* the war to end war, and save civilization.

The T-T confidently expected Dinny to come back and resume his place, wrote Mr. Steinberg, immediately after the Armistice; but there was to be no more of the family salt eaten; starve first!

With surprising ease, he found a place on *The Philadelphia Ledger*. And then, with no more effort, the bright idea came, the 'Unfrosted Persimmons' offered to be plucked, the mounting wave of prosperity rolled in, and Dinny was at liberty from clocks, bells, and whistles.

He resolved to live in New York. Why not? It was the mecca of journalism and such as do syndicated columns. He did not go there saying to himself that Joan might be accidentally encountered; but, every bus that passed him, as he strolled Fifth Avenue, was thoroughly raked with a questing eye, the roll was swiftly called in the subway-train, traffic-blocked taxis were peered into with undefended impudence, the peacock-alley of the hotel, stuffily scented, was daily, gravely, tallied off — for Joan.

Sometimes, though he was not given to worrying, naturally, Dinny found himself distressed over imagined predicaments in which she was posed in a tragic rôle. He was not quite able to reconstruct the face of a sad or beaten Joan; but, annoyingly often, he had a vision, at night, of lovely shoulders slumped in grief or pain, and the back of a curly head bowed in serious trouble.

It became a mild obsession. He had no use for telepathy, and the slightest hint of any mystical thought-conveyance was, in Dinny's opinion, the sign of a weak mind. But — he was looking for Joan, and the longer and farther he looked, the more deeply he felt that when he found her she would be vastly in need of help.

Dinny wished her well, but honestly wondered whether his anxiety might not be the product of an undefined hope that he could find Joan in a mood to accept his affection, even if at the price of some substantial favor of which she stood seriously in need. Indeed, he brooded so much over the matter that it became a definite fixation. Joan was in some kind of a scrape. Joan was hungry. Joan was walking the streets, looking for a cheap lodging-house. Joan was being imposed upon by some predatory rascal who controlled her rations.

He even tortured himself with fears of which he was ashamed. Joan was, he had discovered, possessed of a pretty active 'temperament.' Could she take care of herself if ruthlessly stampeded?

Today he was weary of the job that almost anyone might have envied him; wearied and worried.

He interlaced his long fingers behind his head, closed his eyes, and re-canvassed all the expedients he had contemplated for the recovery of his Joan.

Budding April in Central Park left him unstirred. Life was stale, flat, and unprofitable.

He began to toy with the idea of a vagabond trip through some foreign country.

CHAPTER XI

'HAD it ever occurred to you,' elaborated Dinny, as the speakeasy waiter made off with their luncheon order, 'that my gifted cousin Victor comes perilously near being an ass?'

Tommy Forsythe traced a brief design on Joe Lombroso's white tablecloth with the tip of his spoon, and grinned wryly. It was not the amiable smile that so readily curved Tommy's lips. The grin threatened a bit of irony.

'I've known that,' he said, slowly, 'for a long time; but — I hadn't supposed *you'd* ever find it out.'

'Thanks,' returned Dinny, dryly, not a little surprised at the satirical come-back. Tommy was always so direct, so honest, so transparently sincere.

'And may I inquire,' pursued Tommy, with an excellent imitation of his cousin's calculated ridicule, 'just when and how you contrived to make this belated discovery of my brother's asshood?... He arrived home only yesterday. You haven't seen him, have you?'

Dinny nodded, sipped his cocktail.

'Last night — down in the Village.... Tommy, he was just a little this side of unbearable.'

'"This side"? — looking from where?' Tommy's sour query rasped and crackled.

'Who's been feeding you raw meat, Pollyanna?... My God — I didn't know you had it in you!' Dinny stared at his cousin with honest amazement.

The Damon-and-Pythias comradeship of Dinny Brumm and Tom Forsythe, which was to rake fore and aft the whole gamut of emotion, from high delight to frantic misery, dated from the latter's receipt of a letter from Alison Craig, written from Seattle in June.

Reticence impulsively discarded, Tom's dynamic young cousin had told him everything, even to confessing an affec-

tion for Dinny out of all proportion to their blood relationship; declared she 'never expected to be the same woman
again'; urged her beloved Tommy to lose no further time in
hunting down this attractive collateral to their tribe.

Before sunset, that day, telephone communication had
been established between Tommy's office in the huge department store on Thirty-Fourth Street and Dinny's bohemian three-room suite in Greenwich Village, the shabby
equipment of which — save for his sturdy typewriter-table,
and his mother's little walnut desk — consisted of ill-related
rubbish that had passed from one impecunious artist's keep
to another's, each piece with a story to tell of battered ambitions, pitiful frugalities, and somewhat of despair.

They spent the evening together in Dinny's rooms; and
when, at midnight, they parted at his street-door, each felt
the other an old friend.

From the first, they were conscious of having little in
common, as to temperament and outlook, Dinny finding his
steady-going cousin amusingly naïve, boyishly enthusiastic
over the elementary simplicities, a 'typical case of arrested
adolescence,' though Tommy was nearly four years his
senior, and had been extraordinarily successful in business.

Tommy, encountering for the first time a determined
cynic, obviously proud of his versatile collection of disbe-
liefs, distrusts, and disenchantments, regarded his new acquaintance with fascinated interest. Dinny Brumm didn't
appear to belong to this world, at all. He had merely
dropped in, as a spectator. He stood on the side-lines, paper
and pencil in hand, watching the human race plod by, making ironical notes and grinning when it stumbled.

In general appearance, the two were strikingly alike; of
approximately the same height, weight, carriage, and pigments. They had the Craig eye, deep-set, searching, flanked
by innumerable, faintly traced crow's-feet. They shared
many an odd little trick of gesture and posture.

Alison's suggestion that Dinny's relation to their clan
should not be disclosed was approved by both of them. Tom

promptly took his handsome new acquaintance home with him, the next Sunday evening, to the Forsythe apartment in White Plains; was pleased to observe how easily his mother accepted him; was surprised at Victor's enthusiasm, for Victor rarely had any use for Tom's friends; was anxious over the eager Grace's frank display of admiration.

'Why — you two things actually *look* alike!' commented Grace, with the half-impudent candor she had learned at the feet of Victor. 'Aren't you afraid you'll quarrel?'

Victor — at that time temporarily home from Italy at the suggestion of his mother, who, as his *impresario*, thought it prudent to have the talented violinist back, occasionally, 'to conserve his contacts,' and give the papers a chance to stir his potential public to remembrance of his existence, progress, goings and comings — instantly attached himself to Dinny with a proprietary air that threatened to elbow Tommy out of the picture.

He couldn't conceive how his unimaginative old drayhorse of a brother, who knew everything about leather baggage and nothing about the creative arts, had captured the friendship of this sophisticate. He must see more of this Dinny Brumm. Brumm had the good sense to live in the Village, too, where everybody who was anybody in the field of the arts found freedom, stimulating companionship, encouragement, inspiration.

It had taken Dinny only ten minutes to discover that the Forsythe establishment operated exclusively to serve the high destiny of Victor.

Grace — dark, swarthy, shiny, with a button popped and loose hairpins — lived solely for the talented fiddler, fetching and carrying for him like an earnest retriever. Tom, nearing thirty, had apparently accepted it as his manifest destiny to devote the bulk of his salary to this lofty emprise.

Once, after three months of increasing intimacy had broken down all reserve, Dinny ventured an expression of his feelings on this matter. He and Tommy were dining together at The Astor. Victor had sailed, that morning, re-

turning to Ghili in Milan, bon-voyaged by a score of friends
from the general vicinity of Washington Square, the family,
and not quite enough inquisitive reporters to satisfy Mrs.
Forsythe.

'If I were you, Tommy, and Victor my brother, I'd request him to unstraddle himself from around my neck, and
try walking on his own feet.'

Tommy had been tardy with a reply; shook his head,
slowly.

'Victor,' he said at length, deliberately, 'was born without feet.... Victor's all soul.'

'But he eats!' persisted Dinny, indignantly.

'You don't understand. It's a long story. You see — my
mother — God bless 'er — managed to make quite an important personage of my father. She married him to make
him, and succeeded. She was so ambitious for his success
that for thirteen years she gave him twenty-four hours a
day; became just a bit obsessed, maybe.

'He died early — as you know — just as her hopes had
been fully justified, and the rewards were rolling in.... It
nearly finished her. I was only eleven, at the time, but her
condition was serious enough to worry me, dreadfully,
though just a kid. I'll not inflict you; but — she was in a
sanitarium for six months.

'Then — with the patience of a spider, she began all over.
With a kind of fierce determination, she set about building
Victor up for a career with a fiddle. Father had left prac-
tically nothing but the royalties on his phonograph records.
This income was pretty good, at first; large enough to war-
rant expensive foreign study for Victor.... Afterwards,
when the records of my father's voice began to slip — well
— I couldn't let my mother down; could I?

'Besides' — added Tommy, brightening — 'Victor might
put it over.... I sincerely hope so — for my mother's sake.'

* * * * * *

That had been in late September. It was November, now,
of the succeeding year.

Tommy Forsythe had just returned from a month in Mexico, full of interesting experiences, though not of the specific business errands that had taken him there. They rarely discussed Tommy's business. His phenomenal rise at Lacey's, from the shipping department up to the leather goods, and from successful salesman to assistant manager of the department, and from assistant to Department Chief, had been achieved in seven years; but Tommy did not often talk about it.

Dinny rather regretted now that he had spoken his thoughts about the asininity of the parasitical Victor. Tommy had enough to bear. It would have been more gracious to keep off it. However, the subject had been pushed into the open: it would have to be discussed.... The picture of last night's affair in the Village drifted unpleasantly across Dinny's memory.

He had been surprised to find Victor at the midnight arty-party in the untidy kitchen of The Red Bear. He had not known Victor was back. But, of course, he would lose no time coming to collect adulation from the art colony to which Dinny, at his fervent request, had earlier introduced him.

Victor — still boastfully giddy from eight nauseous days of hurdling home over a shrieking sea which, he was averring, had put the doctor to bed in his cap and boots, and shattered not only a thirty-year Atlantic storm-record and the captain's elbow, but all the *Vendome's* crockery (not — he languidly chortled — that the latter had been much missed after the first twelve hours out) — had come to The Red Bear in tow of Diane Wimberly, a lanky, pink-haired, lower-case poetess who needed a dickey and a thousand dollars' worth of dentistry.

Dinny had gone late to Felice's party. Once he had thought Felice quite interesting; but, in recent months, she had begun to weary him. In fact — the whole outfit, now that their novelty had worn off, lacked the originality and sparkle he had earlier imputed to the Villagers when, as a lonely stranger in New York, he was in need of quick and easy friends.

Last night's bizarre affair had palled on him. The thing had been carried on in murky gloom feebly tinctured with magenta by a sooty lantern suspended from a peg in one of the massive, ancient, weathered-oak rafters — made of half-inch pine, and installed the previous summer.

Victor — whose voice Dinny instantly recognized, even before his eyes had adjusted to the thick fog into which he groped — was seated in the dilapidated wheelbarrow intended for the 'fagots,' when there were any — The Red Bear, with reckless leanings toward Communism, pretended to be a Russian peasant's hovel — loathsomely detailing his recent discomforts at sea.

Dinny's tardy arrival had not interrupted the undulating flow of his cousin's obnoxious reminiscence, nor was the company much distracted from its wan interest in the nautical narrative.

Felice (Mamie) Manners (Johnson), the hostess, seated on the floor near the doorway, on an outspread newspaper, moved over a little to make room; and, pursing her scarlet mouth in apology for the humble offering, handed him, with her fingers, a large, pallid cream-puff which she ruefully extracted from the bottom of a brown-paper bag wherein the dessert course had been served.

Dinny gingerly surveyed the gift, in the manner of a fastidious dowager examining a freshly exhumed skull, to the considerable amusement of Felice, who, a little drunk was finding Victor tediously verbose, and wished to be playful.

Wanting Dinny to know that she shared his carnival attitude toward her party, Felice strangled the empty bag, put the neck of it to her blood-red mouth, and with many long, cheek-distending, eye-bugging exhalations, proceeded to the task of its inflation; or nearly so, the final blast proving abortive due to her sudden conviction that her employment was ridiculous enough to merit a shocking explosion of suppressed mirth.

Victor reproachfully glanced in the direction of the disorder, but calmly continued his monologue in a marcelled, affected baritone that inspired Dinny — a little drunk, also — to nudge Felice to attention while he feigned to take careful aim at the self-infatuated minstrel with the soggy token of her vanished hospitality.

'Dare you!' whispered Felice, cupping her mouth with her hand, but Dinny reprovingly shook his head, pretending shocked regret that she would entertain the thought of such an effrontery.... Then he had stretched out his long legs, and tried to listen.

Victor had finished with his disgusting *mal-de-mer* and was now in a messianic mood concerning the martyrdom of all true artists, and the tribulations of cat-gut and horse-tail artists in particular. Evidently somebody with a bit of money had recently stepped on Victor's slim, expressive fingers, for he was swishing about with a bare rapier that threatened to annihilate the well-to-do.

Dinny wondered if this were the formal opening of Victor's campaign to impress his friends that he had a good excuse for failure; wondered if Victor was frightened, now that he had finally caught up with his exceedingly bright future, and had it to demonstrate.

'Old Victor,' reflected Dinny, as he sat listening to the makings of an alibi — 'good old Victor knows time's up. He's either got to catch fish, or cut bait, or bail the boat.'

Abstractedly, Dinny had let his heavy eyes rove about the room while his blasé cousin deprecated the necessity for living in a world propelled by the almighty dollar.

He was acquainted with all but two — the youth with the black velvet jacket and negligent Windsor tie, and the thin girl beside the youth, a blue beret drawn down over one eye, and a limp, home-made cigarette dangling precariously from her lip.

The rest of them he knew quite well. Gregory, thirty-five and tuberculous, had confided freely. Gregory was writing an important novel; quite a bit daring, it was; might have to be privately printed. He had been at it now for upwards of three years. It was his first novel, though there had been a slim, mauve, deckle-edged (Gregory was ashamed of the deckle — but Aunt Agatha, of Phoenix, Arizona, who was financing it, quite insisted) volume of unpunctuated verse. Dinny had one of these, a presentation copy, autographed with a scrawl that beckoned the beneficiary to consult the title-page for verification of the little book's parentage.

Vivacious Anne Pelham, who, to better her credit at the expense of her artistic integrity, had confessed her degeneration to drawing for commercial purposes — though what or for whom she drew Dinny had never learned — caught his vagrant eye, smiled, twinkled friendly fingers. The salute would cost him five dollars, thought Dinny. Anne already owed him thirty, not that he cared: the poor little fellow was always hungry.

Sylvia (what the devil was her other name? — He had always thought of her as Carmichael) sang, or was going to ... in opera... once she got a chance. Squat and shaggy Carmichael, next her, did portraits — quite atrocious ones, Dinny thought, though it was out of his line — which Sylvia, who lived adjacent on the fourth floor of a cheap and dirty, gas-reeking, bug-infested tenement house, and shared the bow-legged painter's kitchen, bath, studio, and fatuous ambitions, considered masterpieces.

They had never struck Dinny Brumm quite this way before. He had sympathetically appraised them as a wistful tribe of aspirants to success in creating something interpretative of their thoughts. They had become suddenly ridiculous. There wasn't one of the dozen present, he reflected, who had ever done anything worth a second look. With the possible exception of the gloomy Victor, whose career was unpredictable, not a man or woman of the lot was likely ever to get to first base in the game whose lingo they prattled with such glib familiarity.

At long last, Victor's monotonous harangue was concluded. The audience untangled its legs, milled about the room, yawned toward the door. Felice led Dinny to the little group still clustered about the wheelbarrow.

Victor extended a limp, soft, slim hand.

''Lo, Dinny.... So you're here....Who told you I was home?'

'Nobody... I didn't know you were back.'

Somehow — the raw impudence of the chap annoyed him. His egotism was insufferable.

'In fact,' drawled Dinny, 'we've ventured to have several little social affairs much like this, in your absence; just to keep our spirits up until you returned.... Hope you don't mind.'

No — Victor didn't mind. He smiled, indulgently, and said it was quite the proper thing to do, he was sure; and turned to luxuriate in the twitter of the new girl with the blue beret.

Dinny had slipped out, presently. The Village was beginning to bore him.

* * * * * *

Tommy impatiently shattered one of Joe Lombroso's crusty rolls with his fingers, a bit heated by Dinny's spoofing.

'Ordinarily,' replied Tommy, 'I don't permit myself to become disturbed over anyone else's damned foolishness besides my own; but, now you've invited it, I'd like to tell you something that will be good for your soul — if you still have one.'

'Attaboy, Tommy!' applauded Dinny, merrily. 'Skin 'em alive!'

Tommy drew a heavy frown that Dinny had never seen him wear before.

'This isn't going to be funny,' he muttered. 'After lunch, we're going over to your squalid hole in Daubville, where you're to listen to something I've got for you.... And here's hoping you won't get sore.'

Dinny threw back his head and laughed.

'I'd really like to see you on the war-path, Tommy.'

The subject was not resumed until, having climbed the dirty stairs, and tossing their hats on the littered table, Dinny, amused and expectant, lighted his pipe, and signed Tommy to 'turn it on.'

'As I understand it,' began Tommy, didactically, 'you are one of the most venomous — certainly the noisiest — of all the animals now in revolt against everything your betters have built up over a period of five thousand years, or so.

'You've distinguished yourself as a kicker, knocker, scorner, spoofer, and snarler. Your sour comments on faith, piety, and patriotism are worth a dollar a line.... And, incidentally, I bet you anything you care to put up that the time will come — not long from now — when you've repeated, over and over, all the smart and surly words you know — your stuff won't be worth ten cents a garbage-pailful.... Some of it's beginning to run a bit thin already, Dinny, if you don't mind my speaking of it. I just noticed in the last issue of *The Emancipates* that you used the word "moron" nine times. Better get yourself a new thesaurus. ... You're writing too much, anyhow, my son. Your rhetorical disbursements are so far ahead of your intellectual income that you'll be bankrupt, presently. However — that's your affair.

'You've been the great champion of sincerity. You've thumbed your nose at the hypocritical Bible-whackers, and the gavel-swingers, and the sword-toters. Everybody's an ass but you — and the Villagers; you — and your little hand-picked minority of freedom-fanatics.... Parsons and professors, doctors and lawyers, senators and judges, philanthropists and missionaries — you've had 'em on the grill in a dozen contemptible magazines. You've roasted 'em whole, brought 'em back in a stew, served 'em cold in a salad with sulphuric acid dressing.

'And yet — you'll live down here in this poisonous rat-hole, chumming with a bunch of third-rate, would-be artists, yodeling about liberty to express themselves!

'You rant about hypocrisy! Hypocrisy!... My God!... Can you imagine anything more utterly rotten with pretense than the rubbish that's written and daubed and sculped by these ——'

'Have a light, Tommy,' interrupted Dinny, offering a match, 'and don't yell so loud.... It's Sunday.'

'You wipe that smile off your face, and sit down! I'm not through yet. I mean to tell you some more, and if you don't like it you can go straight to ——'

'I know, Tommy, what you have in mind.... Proceed.... I'm liking it.'

'The new art! Bah! I've been supporting art since I was a youngster; missed college to become an art-patron; had the house littered with artists for years.... Ninety per cent of 'em too incompetent to hold a job, too lofty to earn a living, and too lazy to wash their ears.

'The new literature — realism! Tripe! A lot of dirty stories dignifiedly told by dirty-minded little shrimps, and solemnly discussed by pretenders who make-believe they are enduring the dirt so they can capture the beauty of the "style," when it's plain they're only enduring the "style" for the sake of the dirt.... Kidding themselves!

'Modernism — modernistic painting!... Cubist stuff!... Nobody can fool me, any more, about that.... This latest whelp of modernism is nothing but an idiot begotten of Gin and Geometry.

'And *you* — cramming the magazines full of high-browed sarcasm about the dull slaves of superstition!... chanting about freedom!... yowling about the unpardonable sin of stupidity! Haven't you any sense of humor, at all?... These birds have imposed on you, down here. They've made you believe they were artists — most of 'em clumsy dubs who couldn't draw an honest picture of a long-tailed rat.... Try it out, if you don't believe me. Ask one of these paupers to draw you a picture. Offer this Felice person a hundred dollars to draw — not paint — but *draw* a picture of those two hats on your table, and see what you'll get.... Hypocrisy — hell!'

'Tommy — I've an idea!... Just came to me.... I'm going to write a novel... about the Village.... It's marvellous! Wonder I never thought of it before.'

Tommy scowled, relighted his pipe, puffed moodily.

'What you'd far better do is to let up on mean and surly criticism for a while. There ought to be some kind of a mental laxative on sale for chaps like you. Why don't you treat the world as if you weren't too superior to live in it? Pity there isn't some neighboring planet for you scoffers to go to, once in a while, for a vacation.'

Dinny suddenly recalled himself from the absorbing reverie into which he had drifted. Tommy had been chiding him, pitilessly, and he had missed much of the latter part of it. He reproached himself for his wool-gathering at such a moment.

'You're quite outspoken, Tommy.... But — Boy! — you've given me a whopping inspiration...for the novel, you know. I mean to do it, without delay.... It will be a wow!'

There was no further withstanding the contagion of Dinny's enthusiasm; no use bristling against Dinny's conciliatory smile. Tommy capitulated with a sigh. The chap was incorrigible, utterly inaccessible to reproof.

'Let's go do something,' he said, restlessly, reaching for his hat.

'Young Vladimir Polovsky's talking at three in the Village theater,' suggested Dinny. 'Shall we hear him?'

'Rot!' exploded Tommy. 'Hell of a lot of amusement that would be! More dribble about Communism; eh?'

'It might improve your mind,' exhorted Dinny, paternally. 'I'll bet you never heard a real Communist talk?'

'Don't you believe I haven't. Just got done firing one — a female one — from the store.... Talk? That girl could talk down a Senate filibuster!'

'Yes,' Dinny wagged his head, knowingly, 'that's the answer of capital... big business... to any independent opinion offered by the slaves!... Poor girl airs her theories — and gets fired!'

Tommy chuckled, reminiscently.

'Well — this happened to be the answer of big business to a young slattern who refused to act on the broad hint that she'd be improved by a shampoo. Nobody at Lacey's cared a damn about Sophie's bad opinion of the capitalistic system. It was her revolt against soap.'

Dinny remained loftily skeptical, but willing to grin.

'Lacey's may have pretended that was the reason, but Sophie would probably have been given the sack, just the same. Sophie' — Dinny feigned a sympathetic tear — 'Sophie wanted to be a little candle of liberty — and you snuffed her out!'

Tommy shook his head, laughing.

'We sniffed her out.'

'You've a mean tongue, Tommy.... Suppose we go up to The Capitol and see Hollywood canonize some racketeer who's just come home with his pockets full of money to lift the mortgage off his widowed mother's cottage.... That's about your speed.'

* * * * * *

Dinny began work on his novel, that night. It was his first long story, and he meant to spread it on a huge canvas that would provide plenty of room for the minutiæ of detail.

He knew he could draw Victor — to the life — and meant to make him lead the ludicrous procession of enchanted bums across an elaborate stage set for Art passionate with Revolt.

He believed he would let Victor succeed, at least measurably, and return from time to time collecting laud, honor, and glory from his satellites. As an affected, arrogant ass, Victor would be hard to beat.

There would be room in the story for a bit of honest pathos, too, he thought. These people's ambitions would be vapid enough, and their pretensions no end silly; but there was nothing fictitious about their hunger and heart-break.

Dinny paused in his swift typing of the rough memorandum for the first chapter, and wondered if he would be able to do the *lento* movement, when he came to it. Hadn't he debarred himself from any such excursions into the 'human interest' zone of sincere yearning mixed with tears? He had so consistently mocked at everything savoring of the sentimental that he doubted his ability to write about the deep emotions without inviting a hilarious 'haw-haw' from his cynical constituency.

He settled back in his chair, long hands dangling inert over its arms, and gave himself to sober reflection on this dilemma.

His field had always seemed so pleasantly inexhaustible. Why — a man could keep on spoofing current movements forever! There was positively no limit to the materials at one's elbow. So long as there was an absurd human race, competing in silliness, there would be daily something new to grin at. The satirist's mine had barely been scratched.

Tonight, Dinny's ironically amusing profession seemed suddenly to have walled him in. His field of exploration was quite restricted, after all. Tommy Forsythe had given him an anxious moment, that afternoon, hinting that certain pet phrases of ridicule and contempt, which had served him well, were in danger of becoming tarnished ornaments.

Perhaps he had better stop using the words 'moron' and 'imbecile.' It was a fact that he had called them in to explode disparaging comment rather more frequently than he should.

For a long time he sat meditatively tugging at his left ear-lobe, absently fingering the key-board with the other hand.... Nonsense! He couldn't do a novel! He had had so much highly lucrative sport in ridiculing every phase of tender sentiment — the sickly slobber of penitence, the mawkish drool of the meddling doers-of-good, the exultant imbecility of idealism, the owlish asininity of philanthropic fuss-budgets and sniffling uplifters who loped about crying aloud over the plight of care-free people who desired only to be left alone — that he seriously doubted whether he dared risk a forthright invasion of 'heart issues.'

Viewed from a slightly different stance — Dinny, adroit in metaphor, was fond of considering his problems in the algebra of his craft — the section of the woods where he claimed the right to swing his axe was limited to a very small tract of the forest. It was his job to cut down, chop up, stew, and distill astringents, bitters, and lethals from henbane, hemlock, and wormwood — a sophisticated employment. He would only seem ridiculous tapping maple trees, or sawing down hollow sycamores for their wild honey.

Who would have thought that staid old Tommy would pip off like that?... Talked a little like Joan.... Tommy and Joan would have a good time together, if ever they met.... Dear Joan!

Slowly disrobing and easing himself into dressing-gown and slippers, Dinny recapitulated the strategic might-have-beens of his arrested romance with Joan; relived that passionate half-hour when he had sat, fists clenched, in his dormitory room at Magnolia, debating whether to punish the insufferable Kling.

Suppose he had cooled off, and decided to let Kling go unrebuked.... Suppose the piece in *The Iconoclast* had not appeared at that unlucky moment.... Suppose Doctor Braithwaite had been secure enough in his position for Joan to risk a response to his honest overtures of reconciliation.... He might have had Joan!

And then — what? Joan would have insisted on his living in a Fool's Paradise, no doubt. She would have coaxed and nagged him into a pretense of sharing her ingenuous optimism. He would have spent his life driving spiles into maples, and boiling the sap down to syrup and selling it to the fudge-makers. Ye gods — what a career!... Thirty-five or forty dollars a week, riding up and down elevators, interviewing candidates, magnates, and redeemers who would impressively keep him waiting in their outer offices while they sat hungrily watching the clock, lusting to let him in for a padful of their oracles.... No — it wouldn't have done. There would have been no 'Unfrosted Persimmons.' Joan would have seen to that. The 'Persimmons' would have been brought to market ripe — sticky — sicky sweet — rottenly soft.

And yet ——

Dinny sighed, turned on his bed-lamp, rolled in, and tried to read the current Lawrence; pretty clever dirt, that. ... Rather amusing — Tommy's appraisal of erotica. Tommy was more than half right, of course. Previous to the recent emancipation from superficial prudery, the male youths had climbed up into the haymow to exchange convictions on the ever-exciting subject, and the girls, in threesomes, their arms twined around each other, had taken a nice long walk, whispering with red cheeks.... Something unhealthily furtive about that, of course.

Now the talk was all out in the open.... Lecturers packed hotel convention-halls with rosy-faced, eager, wide-eyed customers who owed it to themselves to post up on psychology as it related to the old, old problem.... No longer was it necessary for the inquisitive youngster to hide his nasty little paper-backed shocker in a corner of the oats-bin.... The subject had been milled up into 'literature,' now.... There need be no further hypocrisy or furtiveness about this matter.... Dinny audibly expelled a contemptuous 'Pish!'... Old Tommy was dead right!

All these college boys and girls swarming into classes on 'Abnormal Psychology'... all these altruistic women elbowing into the Court of Domestic Relations... all these questors of culture, hunting for rhetorical gems in the new, breath-takingly frank, censor-baiting literature of libidinousness!... Same old story... same old furtiveness. But — while the earlier crop of curious youngsters had deceived their parents, the new outfit were deceiving themselves!

Dinny turned a few pages, and pushed the book off the bed onto the floor; snapped the light, closed his eyes, scowled.

And yet ——

Whatever Joan might have been able to do to him and his literary aspirations, it might have been worth the sacrifice.... Gad — what a thoroughbred!

Vivid pictures of her came, lingered, and made way for others even more luminous.... Joan — radiant, supple, agile, tantalizing, generously blending her splendid body with his, that first afternoon on the ice... Joan — demurely eyeing him, and denying it with an indignant toss of the head when he caught her, in silly little Ernie's fussy museum... Joan — warm across his shoulders, her cheek against his, scolding into his ear and hating him with all her might while she drove him nearly mad with her rampant vitality... Joan — gently chiding, tenderly wistful, in his arms!... Joan's kiss!

He must find Joan. Suddenly, the slumbering, half-hopeless, half-abandoned yearning for her almost suffocated him. Whatever it might cost — even to the ruinous price of degrading himself to the maple-sugar business — he must see Joan. They were made for each other. How often he had said 'Rot!' in comment on some such observation made in reference to a congenial pair. But, it wasn't rot. Joan was his — and he meant to have her.

Item by item, Dinny recovered her in every remembered posture, expression, mood, each delicious recollection confirming his decision to track her down and have it out with her.

He reinvoiced all the tentative projects that had occurred to him, earlier, for quests of the vanished Joan. This time he would see it through. He would pocket his prudence, and ask questions of people who might know.

A light suddenly broke. Dinny grinned, nodded, rose, went across to his mother's desk, and began to scribble. For a half-hour he wrote and tore and flung away. At length he was determined to be satisfied with his production, addressed an envelope to *The Times*, Want Ads, enclosed his copy and a five-dollar note.

Dressing hurriedly, he went downstairs, telling himself he was silly to be so precipitate, seeing there was nothing to be gained by posting his letter at two-thirty A.M., but eager to relieve his impatience, somehow.

Wide-awake, mentally turbulent, he walked all the way to The Battery, seeing nothing en route but a stuffy little coffee-shop where he stopped and gulped a cup of scalding brown stuff that had been stained by the original grounds described in the lease.

Now that he had made the adventure, Dinny wondered if he could wait until Tuesday. His ad would appear then. Joan would probably read it before the day was out.... And then what?

Time dragged very slowly, all Monday. It was impossible to concentrate. Dinny was thankful he was a few installments ahead of the game in the manufacture of his 'Green Cheese.'

At seven, Tuesday morning, he rushed over to The Brevoort, bought a *Times*, went in to breakfast, rummaged deep in the advertising pages, found the column of 'Female Help Wanted,' and searched for his request.... It looked a bit crazy.

> RESEARCH SECRETARY — by feature writer. Applicant must be at least casually interested in Indian mounds, preferably of southern Ohio: graduate small college, member sorority; native Wis.; 26, ht. 5:7¼; wt. 125; brown hair and eyes. Experienced ice skater preferred. Excellent salary. Reply in handwriting to Times X29008.

CHAPTER XII

His decision, a fortnight later, to see Angela in action was one of the most unaccountable caprices to which Dinny Brumm had ever yielded.

The sudden resolve to go to Dorchester, New York, and watch Angela heal the sick and cast out devils, was arrived at one Wednesday evening shortly after a casual little dinner with four neighbors at the Purple Pig.

Indeed, the first insistent bleat of desire to do this eccentric thing had whimpered from the depths of Dinny's mind during the dinner conversation when Felice Manners had moodily mooned over her early adventures with religion back in Gimmel, Illinois.

Felice, to judge from the blue circles under her heavy eyes, and the smeary elisions of her thick talk, had been steadily tippling all day. She was now making a muddy landing from her ascension into the upper ether of Bacchanalia.

On such occasions, Felice shamelessly turned her soul inside-out for the edification of whosoever happened to be within range of her appalling self-disclosures.

This time, a brief — and, to Dinny, unwelcome — conversation about Angela, now well on the way to becoming a national figure, had set Felice going about the ponderous piety of Grandfather Johnson's home in frowsy little Gimmel where, at nine, she had been dutifully taken in, after the death of her mother, and had remained until, at sixteen, she had fled unfunded and unpursued.

And while Felice rumbled heavily on, recovering fugitive scraps of a stormy girlhood that had creased the brow and whitened the whiskers of Grandfather Johnson — 'and Grandmothersh, too,' she had added, with an irresistible touch of realism — Dinny, possessed of memories not dissimilar, twirled his own reel back to weedy little Zanesdale.

Now and again, and at briefer intervals, Dinny had been aware of momentary surges — something very like nostalgia. Increasingly given to self-analysis, as life became more and more stale and unpromising, he found this the most singular of his mental phenomena.

It was quite natural, reflected Dinny, that a fortunate man who, in youth, had lived in a congenial home from which he had emerged, at length, reluctantly, would so cherish his memories that there would ever be a strong tug in that direction. It was easy to understand how, across a widening chasm of miles and years, such a man might so long for home and a recovery of its endearments that the yearning would obsess him.

But — as in his own case — for a man who, in youth, had fretted in his home, counting the days which must elapse until he could escape its intolerable irksomeness, eventually rushing out of it without one backward glance, asking nothing but to be spared the necessity of a return, these occasional tidal-waves of homesickness were inexplicable.

Dinny found himself wondering if it might not be true that the homing instinct is universal, omnipresent, inevitable; not very much conditioned by any individual's immediate reactions to his native environment while in it. Why, he even had fleeting seizures of desire to see frumpy old Aunt Martha!

Frequently he told himself that the next time he had an errand in Chicago, he would start a day early and drop off in Zanesdale; he would sit on the fence at the corner of Harsh's melon-patch, and watch the Erie 'fast-lines' whiz by.

These attacks did not last long, however, and when he had regained his sober senses, Dinny would accuse himself of a growing tendency toward weak-mindedness. It would be entirely consistent with his unhappy career, he thought, if, at about forty, he would have to be carted off to a funny-house.

He had rarely thought of Angela for several years. Lately

she was much on his mind. Angela was becoming famous —
or notorious — the choice of an adjective depending on the
mood of the reader who found her startling exploits, at the
behest of Heaven, demanding larger space in the newspapers.

The first important tidings of her spectacular ministry
had broken from Spottswood, Pennsylvania, where for six
hectic weeks she had had that smoky mill-town by the ears.

The revival had begun in the custody of the biggest
church in Spottswood; had rapidly outgrown its quarters
and migrated to the city auditorium; and, because it was
September, had swarmed to the County Fair Grounds
where the Holy Ghost had obliged Angela with a recurrence
of Pentecost.

Hundreds — screamed the big black headlines — had
rushed about, babbling 'tongues' which sounded strangely
even in the ears of a polyglot foundry-town composed of a
little of everything all the way from Mesopotamia and the
parts of Libya about Cyrene to the uttermost jungles of
Siam and the suburbs of Babel.

Still other hundreds, unblest with tongues, had ecstati-
cally rolled in the sacred sawdust, popping out of one trance
into another. In the hilarious 'after meetings,' happy converts milled up and down the aisles, affectionately embracing their fellow-lunatics without regard to age, sex, or color.

After a short interval of recuperation, Angela was reported at Wrayville, Tennessee, from whence the news proceeded of a miraculous restoration of sight to an elderly
woman, nine years blind. A local doctor had verified the
miracle, though there had been some difficulty verifying the
doctor, who, the Wrayville Medical Association insisted,
was not an oculist, but a specialist in botts and glanders.

Presently Angela was again on the hook in twenty score
of composing-rooms, this time at Stillman, Iowa, whither
excursion trains from neighboring towns hurried with
yearning cargoes of sick and afflicted.

'Thish Ashula Brumm' — Felice had thickly inquired,

that Wednesday evening, at the Purple Pig — 'sisher o' yoursh, Dinny?'

The Carmichaels, and the Strothers boy who played Sylvia's accompaniments, laughed.

'Do I strike you as having come from a family of deities?' countered Dinny, rather annoyed that the question had come up.

Felice nodded, thoughtfully.

'Sush ash you, Dinny, alwaysh come f'm holy hillsh.'

'Perhaps Dinny's a fallen angel,' suggested Sylvia.

'No — I mean 't,' persisted Felice, with an expansive gesture. 'If all th' atheish and agnoshish in thish rotten villish were honesh, nine out o' ten would shay... born pioush home.'

'Let's begin with you, then,' proposed Strothers, indulgently. 'You're an atheist, aren't you, Felice?'

'Ever' mornin',' went on Felice, woodenly, 'Grandfa'r took twenty-poun' Bible on hish lap, an' read long chapter f'm Deuteromony er Ebeneesher ——'

'No such book as Ebenezer,' corrected Dinny.

Felice grinned, cannily, over having scored a point.

'Uh-huh! — jushesh I sushpected, Dinny Brumm.... You were brought up on 't. You're f'm holy hillsh — jush like me.'

'Go on, Felice,' urged Carmichael. 'What did Grandfather do next?'

'Well — after he had read longesh chapter he could find, 'bout th' Amalekitesh an' th' Stalactitesh, all eight o' ush shwoop' faish-down into our chair cushionsh, an' tied an' untied an' retied th' yarn knotsh while our Heav'ly Fa'er wush thanked that He had shpared ush to shee th' light o' 'nother day... hell of a compliment f'r Heav'ly Fa'er... Heav'ly Fa'er hadn't murdered ush all in our bedsh.'

Aware, from previous experience, that Felice, at such moments, was very sensitive, Dinny had done his honest best to keep a straight face during this recital; but, having clamped down a bit too hard on his feelings, he now regretfully blew up with a loud report which sent Felice into a pitiable drizzle of maudlin tears.

Dinny had never been party to an event at once so tragic and so devastatingly ridiculous. Felice, barely intelligible, poured out a story that might have made the angels weep while they laughed. As a child, the lonesome little thing had gone out by herself into a far corner of the garden and looked bravely up into the blue, telling God she didn't believe a word of it, and hoping He'd please excuse poor old Grandfather Johnson, who didn't know any better, and meant all right.

'An' God ushe t' talk t' me... Nosshir, I mean 't!... He would jush grin, and shay, "Thash all ri', li'l Felish. You run an' play!"'

Sylvia had taken Felice home when it was generally agreed she had talked enough, and was attracting too much attention.

Leaving the mussy little restaurant, Dinny had gone to his room somewhat depressed. Felice had stirred some quite vivid recollections of his own boyhood. There had been a time when he, too, had been acutely conscious of something — something winged, inside himself — looking up inquiringly, hopefully. Felice had apologized to God in behalf of Grandfather Johnson. Dinny remembered having had much the same feeling as a little boy. God had been maligned. God was their Father... and they had gone down on all fours, twice a day, grovelling like heathen.

But, strangely enough, Dinny wanted to see what was this peculiar energy that Angela had laid hold on. Angela might be no end a mountebank — probably was nothing less or else than that — but thousands were finding something at her hands. Surely she hadn't inherited anything from his smug and stupid Uncle Miles that would stampede city after city into orgies of repentance and hysterias of joy.

At ten-thirty, that night, he was in his berth, listening to the trucks pound the rail-ends as his train scampered up the right bank of the Hudson, and wondering what had possessed him to spend any time or money on such a silly adventure.

* * * * * *

Thursday afternoons — Dinny learned at *The Dorchester Sun*, where he had been cordially welcomed when applying for a press ticket to the Angela Brumm Revival — were set aside for the healing of children.... Lucky, he thought... couldn't have struck a better day!

He lunched with Fred Channing, the editor, after having met a few of the boys at the office, where, as was inevitable, he had been chaffed about his gifted 'relative.'

Channing had slowly closed one eye, impressively, in the midst of the banter.

'You wait!... Some woman!... May be a quack and a faker — but, you take it from me — Angela's got a lot o' *It!*'

They went to the stage door of the big public auditorium at two-thirty. Literally hundreds of people stood about the entrances, hopeful of crowding in to secure standing-room after the ticket-holders had been accommodated. In tow of Channing, Dinny followed through a long concrete corridor, swarming with the surpliced choir, busy functionaries, reporters, parsons, and up the stairs to the large stage, set for three hundred.

The auditorium was packed to suffocation. A tense feeling seemed to pervade the place, as if some astounding event — some sickish tragedy, perhaps — were imminent. Dinny's eye swept the huge hall; raked the galleries into a vertiginous smear of wide-staring, open-mouthed, morbidly curious expectants. Then he analyzed the crowd — small sections of it — item by item; nervously thumbing their paper-backed hymn-books with mechanical fingers, gnawing their lips, apprehensively, as if they had come to a hanging.

The great choir filed in, confident and conscious of its importance, and stood, as in a tableau, until the celebrated

Maurice Manwaring, lithe, athletic, leonine of head, an extraordinarily handsome brute, strode on, raised both modishly white-flanneled arms, and with a commanding gesture that seemed to reach far forward and grab the first triumphant note out of their obedient open mouths, he summoned them to the great declaration that the affair was on, and Heaven was being called in to witness. The piece was Gounod's 'Unfold, Ye Portals.'

Dinny had not been so stirred to the depths — ever! He had come as a spectator; rather a cold-blooded spectator, too. Now he felt himself vigorously pushed into the crowd.

'Un — fo-o-o-o-l-l-ld!... *Unn — fo — o-o-o-ol-l-ld!*... *UNNN–FO–O–O–O–OL–L–LD!!* — YE POR–TALS EV–ER–LAAAST–ING!'

The great crowd couldn't resist the pull of it another minute; came up out of its seat in response to something gripping that reached out, and took hold, and lifted up. Dinny found himself on his feet, his heart pounding, his eyes smarting, his throat dry.

Angela came on, passing him so nearly he could have reached out a hand and touched her black velvet gown. She was an insuperably regal figure, exquisitely formed, incredibly beautiful, with the carriage of a goddess and the rapt eyes of a mystic. Except for the white silk stole which depended almost to her knees, she wore no ornament. Walking confidently to the center of the stage, she rested an expressive white hand on the pulpit and gazed over the multitude with a sort of inspired compassion. Dinny would have given his all for a faithful picture of what was actually going on, at that instant, in Angela's mind.... It was utterly impossible, preposterous, that this woman could stand there, before this yearning crowd, swept by the nerve-tingling influence of such music — and be calmly plotting a hoax!... Angela should have the benefit of every doubt. *Angela was not a fake!*

The anthem rose to a great *crescendo*. The multitude

sat. Angela stood. There was a heavy hush. She prayed. It was a quiet voice, but commanding. Angela maternally gathered up the three thousand in her soft, strong arms, and, having affectionately held them to her ample breast and wiped their tears and fears away, tenderly handed them over into the infinitely stronger arms of their Father.

It was not God's wish that any of these little ones should suffer, or face life unable to savor its sweetness.... Dinny remembered it was a 'Children's Healing Day,' and, glancing about, became aware of babies in arms, little cripples in arms, big-headed, empty-headed, pallid, grotesque *monsters* in arms. Never had he seen such a conglomeration of juvenile misfortune. They seemed suddenly to spring into existence. He had not noticed them before.

God did not want these little ones to suffer.... By faith, they would be healed.... God had promised.... It was enough. We could take Him at His word.

Spontaneously, the choir, as if unable to restrain its pent-up emotions, quietly hummed the old hymn-tune which Dinny recognized as 'My Faith Looks Up to Thee.'

Angela, face uplifted, blue eyes wide, enraptured, called upon her Father, these little ones' Father, to keep His word with her — with them — with us.... Then there began to come from the depths of the auditorium a surge, a sobbing surge of questing song, as if it was welling up out of hearts rather than throats. Dinny's eyes filled. He didn't sing; couldn't have sung; but he was conscious of being in and of that longing multitude whose honest faith — or whose desperate hope, at least — was reaching up.

Dinny never liked to remember, afterwards, the procession that came down the aisles, and up the stairs to the stage, bearing its pitiable freight to the Lamb of Calvary and His calmly confident representative.... Pale, twisted, little children... blind babies... hare-lipped... club-footed ... hunch-backed.

Angela laid her potent hands upon each of them, raised her eyes, murmured a prayer, and a motherly woman in white gently propelled them on, across the stage, to another stairway leading back into the auditorium.

At the foot of this stairway, a huddle of young women, also in white, were receiving the bewildered mothers with encouraging smiles, distributing gifts to the children — gay trinkets, oranges, little dolls for the girls, mechanical toys for the boys.

Dinny began to understand the reason for this quite dismaying anti-climax to Angela's wholesale conferment of God's grace. It was a shock-absorber to provide distraction of the hapless victims' minds from their disappointment in case the power of God was not immediately manifest. There was no question about Angela's excellent intent. Her faith looked up to the Lamb of Calvary. She sincerely hoped — more than hoped; expected — that the Lamb of Calvary would take pity on these wretched. But if, for some baffling reason unknown to Angela, the Lamb of Calvary let her down, there would still be dolls and oranges and toy automobiles, and a red, red rose for mother.

The long procession kept coming on. Dinny was seated where he could observe the faces of the mothers at the moment Angela was in the act of bearing their anxieties to the Throne. He winced as if witness to surgery performed without benefit of anæsthesia. The faces of the mothers seemed strangely alike, the tense, stiff, open lips showing tips of teeth in half-open mouths, as if expectant of sharp and sudden pain; as if Angela were a surgeon, and they had come to have her lance some deep, dangerous infection; waiting, now, for the plunge of the knife. The faces were all set in masks — masks through whose stiff vents, round, wide eyes, and open, straining mouths — the mothers were prepared to shout for joy or scream with despair.

Not often did the mothers immediately inspect their children, after the supplication. They dared not tarry to do that. The thing was to hurry on, as bidden. Dinny suspected the management did not encourage any loitering on the stage, any looking to see.

One mother's trembling hand ran swiftly down the thin leg of her six-year-old boy, and felt for the crooked little foot. The crooked little foot was still there, just as she knew it would be, her tightly pursing lips seemed to say. Perhaps her faith had not been very robust.

One young mother paused, momentarily blocking the traffic, while she lifted her blind baby shoulder high and gazed hungrily into the child's opaque eyes. All the sickening grief of a sickeningly grieving world spread across her face as she slowly turned her head and made a pitiful little sucking noise with her lips as if she had been stabbed. A compassionate hand was laid under her elbow, and she resumed her tramp to the stairs, consulting each step for safe footing as she descended from Calvary's Fountain to have pressed into her trembling fingers an amiable, smiling, wide-eyed, blue-eyed, china doll — the gift of the white-organdied angels, and the black-velveted Angela, and the blood-red Hands, nailed to a Tree. They also handed her a red rosebud. Dinny hoped the management had had the forethought to snip off the thorns.

A bit of unusual stir about Angela detached his gaze from the retreating figure of the blind baby's mother. A nine-year-old boy, with steel braces on his emaciated legs, was being gingerly put down from his father's arms, at Angela's command. She prayed — audibly, this time — in a tone of assurance, of gratitude, as if the boon she asked was already a *fait accompli*.

The silence was absolute, as Angela unbuckled the boy's braces. The clatter they made, as she cast them aside on the floor, had the effect of heavy chains dropped by a prisoner freed. She took the child by the hand, and bade him walk.

He walked! There was a sudden, concerted intake of breath in three thousand open mouths. The father of the boy, an embarrassed farmer, smiled self-consciously, smoothed his tawny mustache, and followed along. The mother stooped and picked up the braces. Angela darted a swift glance, noting the act. She betrayed a faint, fleeting trace of annoyance, but instantly regained her grateful smile, put the skinny little hand of the lad into the big red hand of his unstirred father, and quickly returned to her post beside the pulpit.

Dinny's quick intuition suggested that the little drama had gone bad. The boy's father was a dolt, and his mother was a woman of little faith. Doubtless both of them knew the boy could take a few faltering steps without his braces if someone held his hand. To the vast crowd, however, the miracle was genuine enough. Anyway — the crowd had come to see miracles, and was definitely on Angela's and the Lord's side.

The meeting was drawing to an abrupt close now. The choir had risen and was leading the congregation in praising God From Whom All Blessings Flow, with an unction that certified to the complete success of the demonstration of grace outpoured.

Angela, with face a bit drawn, evidencing that the neural strain of the hour had cost something, raised a graceful, pontifical hand, pronounced a brief benediction, and left the pulpit. As she passed Dinny, she glanced straight into his staring eyes, stopped, searched his face, and spoke:

'Ferdinand!'

Dinny extended his hand soberly, almost deferentially. Angela did not take it.

'Come to the hotel — the Savoy — at five.'

She did not pause for a reply to her command. When Dinny turned, somewhat disconcertedly, to observe what Channing might have made of this revealing episode, his friend had taken prompt advantage of the priestess's exit, and was rapidly escaping. Channing glanced back over his shoulder, drew a quick, non-committal smile, and pointed significantly in the direction of the stage door, as if indicating they would meet there.

He had vanished, however, when Dinny, thick in the exodus, reached the pavement.

* * * * * *

They did not call her 'Miss Brumm,' but 'Angela Brumm,' as if it were a four-syllable word accented on the ultimate.

When the girl at the Information Desk turned to the switchboard operator, relaying Dinny's request to see 'Miss Brumm,' she said:

'Mr. Ferdinand Brumm has an appointment with Angela Brumm.'

She did not say, 'Mr. *Ferdinand* Brumm has an appointment with *Angela* Brumm.' There was only one authentic Brumm, and that Brumm was Angela *Brumm.*

The bell-hop, whom he trailed to the elevator and over the padded carpet of the seventh floor, did not ring, but opened the door to the first room of what proved to be an extensive suite. This first was a very business-like reception office where Dinny stated his errand to a white-gowned secretary.

'Angela Brumm is expecting you, sir. Come with me, please.'

They passed through another room, equipped for secretarial purposes and occupied by three typists zealously tapping noiseless machines. The large sitting-room adjacent was brightly appointed, clearly the boudoir of a woman who knew how to surround herself with the indispensables of the well-to-do; everything in excellent taste, Dinny thought, as his conductress signed him to a rust-silk davenport, and retired.

Angela sauntered in presently, from the opposite door, her shimmering gold hair plaited down her back, dressed in a flowing négligée of unrelieved black silk, black silk stockings, black silk slippers. The high heels added a touch to her regal carriage. Dinny stood, wondering what manner of take-off this conversation might have, after a lapse of more than eight years. Would Angela begin with something conventional — 'unexpected pleasure' — and that sort of thing?

'People call you "Dinny," now; don't they?' she asked,

negligently, as she approached. 'I would have told you to come at once, dear,' continued Angela, putting both hands on his broad shoulders and lifting her face for the kiss which speeded his heart a little — 'but I'm frightfully uncomfortable until I've had a bath and a mauling by my masseuse.'

Dinny understood and expressed his amazement that she could go through so much nerve-wrecking business, daily, without breaking.

'But you're the picture of vitality,' he added, honest admiration in his eyes. They sat, at her inviting gesture, on the luxurious davenport.

'Well?' — Angela glanced up brightly, smiling inquisitively — 'now you've seen it, what do you think?... Is the Man in the Moon disgusted, or amused, or — amazed?'

'He hasn't quite made up his mind yet, Angela,' returned Dinny, thoughtfully. 'He's always reserved, you know; probably a bit over-cautious.... Maybe due to his age.'

Angela puckered her full, red lips into a playful tease.

'I presume Luna thought it a good show,' she ventured, blue eyes widening roguishly.

'Luna leaps at conclusions, of course,' parried Dinny, Angela's woman-of-the-world air and tone mystifying him: he hoped he was keeping his surprise out of his voice. 'However' — weighing his words — 'instinct may be more trustworthy, in such matters, than sheer intellect.... If you don't mind leaving the Moon out of it, for a moment, I'll admit I was never so uplifted, and — expectant, and ——'

'—— and shot down, tumbling, wings broken, scattering a trail of bloody feathers ——' prompted Angela, when he paused, groping for the right word.... 'Am I right?'

Dinny soberly studied her face, somewhat perplexed by her candor.

'Not quite,' he said, indecisively. 'Not shot down, exactly; a little more as if one had risen rapidly, dizzily, in a balloon — and it had sprung a leak.... One had to come down, then.'

'And it was a rough landing,' sympathized Angela. 'I knew by your face.'

'Quite!' admitted Dinny — 'but one still has the balloon. Whether it is beyond repair remains to be seen. I'm afraid I haven't had the courage to look.... Anyway — there's been no time. This sort of thing deserves some — some thinking over.'

She nodded, comprehendingly.

'You may find you've lost nothing by your cruise, Dinny. ... Judging from the things you've been writing — and I follow them closely, dear, laughing and crying, laughing at them and crying for you — it seems you haven't even known you *had* a balloon.... Perhaps it's been worth a trip to Dorchester, just to find that out.'

Which of his sardonic, satirical cronies, thought Dinny, would have had the effrontery to predict that, some day, he might sit in a confessional, unreservedly pouring his sincere wistfulness into the dainty pink ear of an itinerant woman evangelist and miracle-worker? His mood amazed him.

'Honestly, now, Dinny!' Angela had murmured, intertwining her fingers with his. 'Let yourself go — a bit.... It'll be good for you.'

'It has come — only twice' — said Dinny, dreamily — 'in about fifteen years — this strange, brief, uncanny tug; this afternoon, and another time, in a Catholic Church, when I was a freshman.... But — when I was a small boy, Angela, I frequently experienced big, suffocating waves of — of exultation. They never came in winter, as I recall, and never except when I was alone.'

Dinny reclined, staring at the ceiling, and reflected.

'Yes — go on,' said Angela, quietly, patting his hand.

'Only on summer afternoons, flat on my back, looking up into the blue and white, a gentle breeze stirring, bees humming, birds singing, squirrels scampering about — I used to get it, then — just a big wave of it, and it would be gone.... I didn't know what it was, and I can't describe

it now, but — I suppose brave old Walt came about as
nearly ——'

'Walt?' queried Angela.

'Whitman.'

'Oh — I never knew him that well,' confessed Angela.
'Somebody gave me a book of his poems. I've always meant
to ——'

Dinny glanced in the direction of a well-filled book-case.
Angela, following his eyes, rose, and crossed the room.

'Maybe you can find the place, Dinny, and read it to
me. I think I'd like to hear it,' she said, returning with the
book.

'It's pretty long,' warned Dinny, leafing rapidly. 'I'll
try to give you just an idea of it.... Of course' — he laid
the open book face-downward on his knee — 'I'm not meaning to say that I had precisely these thoughts when I was
a little chap, but the thoughts I had have never been put
into words more adequate to describe my feelings than
these.'

Angela impatiently took up the book, and confronted
him with it, nodding her head.

'Just a minute, Angela — and then I'll read some of it
for you.... I think I hated religion, from the start. As I try
to recover my boyish opinions, I think I always knew that
religion was a selfish, ignorant, hole-in-a-corner affair per-
petuated by small people.... God had instantly fallen out
with the world, soon as He'd made it. But He was glumly
allowing the Whole Thing to go on, despising It, deploring
It, enduring It, and wondering how long it would be yet
until all the people became Baptists; and the Baptists,
aware of His impatience, shouted back, "How long, O
Lord, how long?"... Previously — ages before the Baptists — God had wondered how He was going to put up
with everybody but the Jews, who seemed to have caught
His fancy.... I knew, by instinct, that all such stuff as that
was rubbish!... Adam! — and Adam's "fall"! — I think I
knew, even as a freckle-nosed, barefooted, little boy, that

it was nothing but a fairy-tale, and not a very pleasant one, at that. It didn't ring true.... And all that tiresome story of early Jewish magic left me cold. I hated it!

'But — sometimes — on summer days, a wave-like surge of — of gladness, of — of understanding, would sweep over me. I would suddenly *belong!* — if you get what I mean. The Whole Thing was all of a piece, and I was a part of it, and ——'

Dinny took up the book.

'Whitman says he had heard a great deal of talk about the beginning and the end; and he writes' —

There never was any more inception than there is now,
Nor any more youth or age than there is now,
And will never be any more perfection than there is now,
Nor any more heaven or hell than there is now.

In all people I see myself, none more and not one a barley-corn less,
And the good or bad I say of myself I say of them.

I know I am august.
I do not trouble my spirit to vindicate itself or be understood.
I see that the elementary laws never apologize.

I think I could turn and live with animals, they're so placid and
        self-contain'd.
I stand and look at them long and long.
They do not sweat and whine about their condition,
They do not lie awake in the dark and weep for their sins,
They do not make me sick discussing their duty to God.

They show me their relations to me and I accept them,
They bring me tokens of myself...

I wonder where they get these tokens.
Did I pass that way huge times ago and negligently drop them?

Angela sat, with brooding eyes, venturing no comment, when Dinny paused.

'Just for a moment — today — I had one more strong, quick *tug* of that... whatever-it-is! Perhaps you know. Of course you know!'

'Exactly when — Dinny?' murmured Angela, scarcely above a whisper.

'Well — I'd like to say — it would be the most gracious
thing to say — that I got it through something you said,
or did; but that wouldn't be quite true.... It came while
your choir was singing that opening anthem — the Gounod
thing — "Unfold!"... Angela — did you ever catch a big,
fighting trout? — I mean a huge, muscled, determined,
savage trout?... No?... Well — you've been casting, for
three hours; quite confidently, at first, having been told
there's trout in the pool; rather impatiently and exasper-
atedly, after an hour; and then dully, unhopefully, mechanically, half-inclined to quit, scorning yourself for going to
the bother ——'

'I'm following, Dinny,' prodded Angela. 'Do catch one!'

'And then — suddenly — there's a *strike!*... I don't
mean there's a timid little nibble of some sluggish, grubby
four-inch blue-gill.... I mean a swift reaching and grab-
bing and a *tug* that bends the rod to a horseshoe, and the
reel goes "Zzzing"!'

'Great!' shouted Angela, eyes shining.

Dinny stilled her enthusiasm with an outspread palm.

'And then — the line falls limp — and whatever-it-was
had given you that instant's exultant thrill — is gone!...
But' — pursued Dinny, meditatively — 'just to know
you're still capable of a fleeting exultation like that, even
if it's only for an instant — well, as you say, it's worth a
trip to Dorchester.'

'Can't you stay a few days, Dinny?' pleaded Angela.

'No — I'd probably not get it again. In fact, I'm quite
sure.... The physical healing — you know.... It was — do
you mind if I speak plainly, Angela?... It was the most
shockingly cruel affair I ever saw.... My dear—*how can you?*'

Angela's voice trembled when she replied.

'Sometimes I help them,' she said, hoarsely. 'I — I
thought I could at first. I was honest, Dinny.... And then
— they just expected it, and insisted, and there'd been so
much talk about it.... But, Dinny, sometimes I do help
them... a little... Really!'

He shook his head, with a faint, incredulous smile.

'I didn't come here to rebuke you, Angela. You know your own business, and you handle it — *superbly!* God knows I've no right to offer you any counsel — but ——' He hesitated.

Angela gripped his hand in both of hers.

'Say it!' she commanded, soberly.

'Very well — I think you're making a cheap and grotesque thing out of a mystery that's too big for you — too big for anyone!... It's a great pity.'

Dinny rose, laid his long hands under Angela's elbows, looked her squarely in the eyes.

'I'm quite proud of you — all but *that*.'

'Must you go? Have dinner with me. I don't eat — much — but I'll watch you. Please?'

When she saw he was quite determined to leave, Angela gave him her hand, gave him her lips, smiled, pushed a bell. Dinny left without a further word.

* * * * * *

In the morning, he found among the many letters waiting in his box, another package — they came daily — from *The Times*. He opened them without interest, tossing them aside, half-read. Here was one addressed from Pine Hill, Wisconsin. Dinny's curiosity was stirred.

Dear Sir:

This is in reply to your recent advertisement for a 'Research Secretary.' I formerly worked in New York, and the clipping was sent me by a friend.

As to age and physical dimensions, I could qualify for your position, if it is still open.

I know almost nothing about Indian mounds, but am willing to learn from you.

Very respectfully
JOAN BRAITHWAITE

P.S. — I do need a job, Dinny, quite frightfully!

JOAN

CHAPTER XIII

In the pursuit of his singular trade, Dinny Brumm's requirement of a 'research secretary' was about as urgent as his professional need of a trap-drummer or a tea-taster.

At the moment of his frantically impetuous decision to advertise for news of Joan, it had not occurred to him that he might soon be put to the necessity of inventing an occupation for her.

As for the expense involved in taking on an employee, the prospect of assuming such a responsibility, with Joan as the incumbent, filled Dinny with proud delight. He had plenty of money. His residence in cheap bohemian quarters and his association with friends mostly of simple tastes and meager means, while not an intentional frugality, had made but small demands upon his mounting income.

He had preferred that manner of living. Had he possessed a fortune yielding a million a year, his sense of humor would have stood in the way of its distribution by any of the customary tactics employed by the gilded whose alleged exploits in quest of pleasure would, he believed, have bored him to an early and welcome grave.

With the exception of mild extravagances for books, theaters, and clothing — for while Dinny always dressed conservatively, he dressed well — his personal outlay was so trifling that for more than two years his disbursements per month had rarely exceeded his income per week; nor was that quite all of the story, for he had been very fortunate in his discreet speculations.

Tommy Forsythe, whose natural flair for prognosticating movements in the stock market had been capitalized to his own very considerable advantage, was generous with timely tips. Without making much more than an interesting avocation of his investments, at Tommy's canny suggestion, Dinny had been doubling his income. If, therefore, he should find himself disposed to take on a 'research' or any other kind of a secretary, it would be no inconvenience.

It was quite evident from the plaintiveness of her little distress-signal that Joan was in straitened circumstances. Dinny tried to imagine the glorious satisfaction he would experience at sight of the superb creature, exquisitely groomed, smartly gowned, happily independent, with pride in her eyes and money in her purse — himself responsible for her well-being.

For the first hour after his receipt of her letter, Dinny's entire attention had been devoted to the pleasant day-dream of wrapping a probably half-starved Joan around an expensive collation of Vitamins A, B, and C, to the accompaniment of haunting melodies dispensed by the Hungarian orchestra at Dexter's. Joan, stifled and staled by who knew what drudgeries out in little Pine Hill, Wisconsin, should have a sunny, gayly equipped apartment, high up, some-where on Riverside Drive, with a beautiful view. He would show her how a successful young syndicate writer thought his secretarial help ought to be treated. It would be great fun.

But when he tried to construct a tentative portrait of Joan's patrician face, in its response to a detailed statement of his happy plans for her comfort, he found himself dis-mayed. Joan would not fit into that picture. Joan would not consent to become his beneficiary, nor would she accept a penny more than such secretarial services were worth on the open market.... And, by the way, just what would be the nature of such services? Any flimsy subterfuge he might ingeniously invent would only invite Joan's indignation, once she discovered herself in a mere sinecure.

Only one tenable suggestion offered itself. Dinny, as an ardent student of Pepysian lore and the Restoration which he considered the most interesting period of English history, had lately amused himself by tinkering with an idea for a magazine article to be entitled 'Pepys on Lord's Day.' His only reason for not proceeding to the first draft of it, at once, was explained by his own distaste for the considerable drudgery involved in digging out of the diary all of Samuel's chronicles in reference thereunto.

He could set Joan at that. Surely she need not suspect that such employment was mere make-believe. By Gad, he wanted that information. Dinny found himself becoming rather indignant in his imaginary debate with Joan, who had looked him squarely in the eye and accused him of giving her something to do that nobody in his proper senses would ever want done.... What do *you* know about what I want? Maybe I'll ask you to mole out some further data about other people's observance of the Sabbath. Maybe I'm going to write a book — two or three books — on this subject. Maybe I'll want to know how all the characters in Dickens, Scott, Thackeray, Hawthorne, and a lot more, entertained themselves on the Lord's Day.... That's what a research secretary is about! Funny you didn't know that!

By evening, Dinny felt himself prepared to answer Joan's letter. His manner of approach was friendly but dignifiedly business-like. He needed secretarial help, and it had occurred to him that Joan, if footloose and attracted by such employment, would admirably adapt herself to that position.

He didn't mind admitting — this sheet had to be torn up, several times, before it carried just the right degree of restraint — that it would give him more personal pleasure to be working with Joan than with anyone else of his entire acquaintance. (Joan mustn't be frightened off by hints that he hoped their association might be a bit closer than the business relationship contemplated.) ... And he was looking forward with keen anticipation to her arrival; and when might he expect her — for the Pepys matter would not stand much putting off — and might he hand her the enclosed draft to cover traveling expenses?

Eight days elapsed before there was a reply. Dinny's face fell when the money he had sent her dropped out of the letter.

She had not expected, she said, that Dinny would personally engineer a job for her on his own staff. She had written that she needed work, hoping that if Dinny happened to know of anything he would tell her. Her reply to the advertisement in *The Times* 'really couldn't be resisted.' It had so pointedly singled her out as its object.

> You have kindly inquired what I have been doing. Shortly after father left us — we were quite out of funds, mother and I — it seemed best for me to apply for work. That was not so easy, for I had not been trained for any specific kind of employment.
>
> Barney Vaughn's father — he was very kind to mother and me through all that dreadful time ——

Dinny scowled, wondering apprehensively what might be the nature of the obligation Barney's father felt he owed to Joan.

> —— knew a man of influential position with Minch & Grimsby's in New York. I got my position that way; started as a saleswoman; was soon advanced to the Personnel Department. I liked that very much.
>
> How I came to leave there is too long a story, but you will know it wasn't because I stole anything or slighted the work in which I was greatly interested. Is it sufficient to say that I walked out, late one afternoon, nose in air, on receipt of a significant hint that I might have a much larger income by assuming other tasks than I had bargained for? (Now please don't go plunging into Minch & Grimsby's waving a hard fist and offering to kill somebody.)
>
> Mother was far from well. She had gone to live with Aunt Patty and Uncle Jim at Pine Hill, Wisconsin. Uncle Jim Bailey has a furniture store and is the town undertaker. He had wanted me to help him in the store.
>
> So I came to Pine Hill. Mother continued to decline. She was never well after father's death. Three months ago, she passed away.
>
> Since then, my life here has seemed almost unendurable. There is nothing to do that interests me. Uncle Jim and Aunt

Patty are very kind and want me to stay, but know that I am restless and consent to my going to New York.

'By Gad!' shouted Dinny. 'She's coming! She's coming!'

I'm returning the money. It was good of you to offer it. I have saved enough to pay my expenses. If you really think I can be of use to you as a member of your organization ——

'My organization,' chuckled Dinny, a bit worried. 'Wait till she sees it! What could I have said to make her think that?'

—— I'll do my level best. If it doesn't work out, maybe you can help me find something else.

I expect to leave here about the middle of next week. I shall call you up about ten o'clock Friday morning, and get my orders.

Gratefully

JOAN

* * * * * * *

She did not expect to be met at the train, but he would surprise her. Deducing from the time-tables, Dinny hypothetically routed Joan to arrive at six-thirty on Thursday evening. Short of funds, she would not patronize an extra-fare train. Neither would she linger in Chicago. Six-thirty was the time.

Thursday was the longest day he had ever spent. In the forenoon he went up to The Roosevelt and reserved a room 'for a lady who is to be my guest for a couple of days, at least,' the clerk, recognizing Dinny's name, promising every attention and giving definite assurance that the bill would not be presented to Miss Braithwaite. Yes — and he would personally see to it that the flowers would be in her room when she arrived.

A few moments after six o'clock, Dinny was wandering about the huge concourse of the Grand Central, nervous as a cat. He tried to kill time by inspecting the various wares at the news-stand; bought an expensive box of chocolates and the latest *L'Illustration*. At the quarter-hour, he strolled toward the gate. As the minutes slimmed down to four, three, two, Dinny found his heart beating rapidly. The suspense was eating him up.

The straggling group of welcomers began lining up along the ropes. The gate was open now. The train was in. The vanguard of the day-coachers plodded up the incline, bumping their legs with their fat, frumpy luggage.

Here came Joan!... She was carrying her own bags. She looked weary. Now they had found each other's eyes, and her half-reproachful, half-pouting little smile seemed to be saying, 'You really shouldn't have gone to the trouble. I didn't expect it.'

Dinny reached for her baggage and passed it along to a red-cap. Joan put both her hands in his, as his welcoming gesture invited, and lifted her brown eyes inquiringly.

'How did you know?'

'Oh — I meet all the trains,' said Dinny. 'Sometimes people come to New York alone — and appreciate a little friendly greeting.'

'Taxi, sah?' inquired the red-cap.

'No,' snapped Dinny — 'The Roosevelt.'

'Yassah... At the desk, sah.'

'But — Dinny!' protested Joan, as she watched her bags bobbing away through the crowd, 'I can't afford to go to The Roosevelt — even for tonight.'

'We're going there for dinner.' Dinny took her arm, and signified by his manner that there was to be no debate about this.

'Oh, but I've had my — really, Dinny, I'm so mussed and the train was so dirty. All I want is to go some-place where I can clean up.' Joan halted, obdurately.

So — she had made this long journey in day-coaches, and was worn to a frazzle!

'Where had you thought of going?' demanded Dinny.

'Out to the place on Eighty-Sixth — where I lived before.'

'You come with me, and do as I say.... You're my employee, now, and this is an order.' Dinny tried to be very stern.

'I don't begin work until tomorrow.'

'Nevertheless... Let's have no nonsense. You're tired.'

Rather confused and reluctant, Joan demurely consented to be propelled through the throng in the brightly lighted station. Dinny paused at the desk, spoke to the room-clerk, and, turning to Joan, said, in a tone that expected her prompt compliance:

'Follow the boy... Give yourself plenty of time... If there's anything you want, ask for it... I've an errand. I'll meet you here in the lobby at eight.'

Joan shook her head.

'I don't want to, Dinny.' Her eyes were troubled.

'It would be quite embarrassing — if you didn't.'

She stood for a moment, debating, and then said, her voice lowered almost to a whisper — 'I can't pay for it... I'm sorry.'

Dinny looked her soberly in the eyes.

'Please do as I tell you!' he said, biting his words into a crisp command.

She drew a tired little smile, and followed the boy.

'Strike *one!*' said Dinny, triumphantly, to himself, as he watched her enter the elevator... 'The darling!'

* * * * * *

Joan's hour and a half had done wonders for her. When she came down, Dinny, who had been pacing about, rest-lessly, watching the clock and counting the minutes, quickly joined her, wondering if other people were not thinking him a lucky dog.

She was simply dressed in black crêpe, but carried herself with all the poise and confidence of a queen in ermine. Dinny's admiration shone in his face. He was recklessly ecstatic.

'Haven't you grown some more, Dinny?' she asked, taking up her napkin.

'I hope not... I wasn't exactly frail, before, if you recall. ... Remember the trip we took through the ravine, the time Ernie sent us for a key?'

Joan smiled, nodded, flushed a little.

'I'm afraid I wasn't a very pleasant companion,' she said, regretfully.

'You had good reason, Joan... I had been behaving very badly. You'll find I've changed... Vastly improved —— ' Dinny broke off to order their dinner, consulting her wishes, but making it evident that her negatives were not taken seriously when she demurred against unnecessary items.

'What's the nature of this vast improvement, Dinny?' queried Joan, when the waiter had retired. 'I've been reading your articles.'

'Have you?' Dinny's eyes sparkled, appreciatively. 'Then that means you like them!'

Joan pursed a doubtful smile.

'Not necessarily... One doesn't always have to like what one reads... But — I'm an optimist, you know. I keep on hoping you'll write something I'll like, sometime.'

'For instance?' — Dinny was too happy to be dashed by her criticism — 'If you'll tell me what sort of thing you'd enjoy, I'll make a special effort, dear.'

There was a considerable delay before Joan replied, and when she lifted her eyes they did not immediately meet his own.

'Dinny' — she said, as if announcing a resolution that had required some debate, and might not be warmly received — 'let's start right... I've come here to work for you ... Please don't make it awkward for me. Or — I'll not be able to do it, you know.'

'But you *are* my dear, Joan!... You needn't try to reciprocate, the least bit. I'm not expecting it. I'll not worry you with it. You're to think of me as your employer, and you can be assured of the sort of treatment that would be desirable by an employee... But — you will be my dear Joan... just the same!'

'Thank you, Dinny,' she replied, respectfully grateful. 'Now let's talk about something else... Where is your office? Do I come at nine? Are there other — help? How much of my work will be done in the library? I hardly know what you want me to do, you know.'

Neither did Dinny know. He suggested that they eat their dinner untroubled by dull care: plenty of time for that. Her hours would be of her own choosing. There was no office. There were no other secretaries. Joan was to make the researches for him, and report 'from time to time.'

'Once in the morning — and once in the afternoon, maybe?' guessed Joan, vaguely.

'Something like that — or once a week, anyhow,' agreed Dinny, indecisively — 'unless, of course, you were working on an assignment like this Pepys affair, which will probably take you a month, at the least.'

'Then I won't see you for a month — after you've told me exactly what you want?'

Dinny made a quick gesture of protest.

'See me! Of course! Every day! We'll be having dinner together, and there are at least a dozen good shows you'll have to see without delay.... You didn't think I would let you perish of loneliness, did you?... Shall we dance?'

Joan was thoughtful for an instant; bit her pretty lip, and reflected, seriously. Then, apparently coming to an impulsive decision, she nodded brightly, rose, and offered herself to his arms. Dinny held her very close, and whispered, 'You precious darling!'

She brushed his cheek lightly with her hair, and murmured, entreatingly, rather breathlessly:

'Oh, Dinny — please — let's don't — I mustn't.'

But her fingers tightened on his shoulder, and Dinny's happiness was almost more than he could bear.

'You *are* my darling... aren't you, Joan?'

She did not reply, but glanced up into Dinny's eyes, searching them soberly — and smiled.

* * * * * *

Dinny was aroused at eight from sleep, profound because belated, and felt a great wave of happiness breaking over him.

The messenger at his door handed in a letter bearing the device of the Roosevelt Hotel.

Dear Dinny:

I've been thinking things over. I don't see how I can work for you. Maybe you will help me find something else to do. Please don't try to dissuade me. I'll meet you in the hotel lobby at one, as we agreed. Would you like to take me to the Metropolitan Art Museum after luncheon? I'd love it. Thanks for everything.

JOAN

So — that was that. Joan insisted on having something else to do. Perhaps she was right. He would consult Tommy. He would tell Tommy all about it — everything! No — Joan wouldn't like that. He would approach Tommy as if the applicant for work were a casual acquaintance.

At ten, he had Tommy on the telephone. Would Tommy do him a favor? Very capable young woman, daughter of the late president of his little college in Ohio, was in town seeking employment. Yes — she had had good experience at Minch & Grimsby's. Did Tommy know of an opening anywhere?

'Might possibly place her here with us, if she's all you say,' replied Tommy, obligingly. 'Tell her to come in at once. I'll talk to her.'

Splendid! Dinny called Joan, who was in — and delighted. She would go over to Lacey's at once. Mr. Forsythe? Thanks!... Dinny should hear all about the interview when they met. Yes — at one. She'd be waiting. Thanks again, Dinny!

'Such a busy morning!' exclaimed Joan, breathlessly, when he joined her. 'I'm moving back to my old place on Eighty-Sixth, where I lived before. My trunk has gone out there already.'

'How did you make out with Tommy Forsythe?' queried Dinny.

'Beautifully!' Joan was radiant. 'He was so friendly. I'm to be in his department for a month, beginning Monday; and then, after I've learned my way about, as he put it, I'm to be given a chance in the Personnel... I'm so happy... What all did you tell him, Dinny?'

He gave her a proud smile.

'Just that you were an acquaintance, daughter of my college president, fine girl. I didn't add that you were an adorable, lovely ——'

'Tut, tut!' cautioned Joan, softly.

'The taxi-driver won't tell — and, as for Tommy, he'll discover it. Tommy's one of the best there is, Joan. I hope you'll like him.'

She was sure she would. Tommy had treated her as an old friend. She was going to like it at Lacey's.

'And so' — regretted Dinny, dolefully — 'you're not to be my fair employee, after all. I'd quite counted on it, you know.'

'Perhaps I can help you, anyway. I wouldn't mind digging out the story of what Sam Pepys did on Sundays. I might do it, evenings... Any more work on the novel, today?'

'Very little... No composition; just a few more rough notes, and a short cross-section of conversation between Cecil and Margery, who've got themselves in no end of a scrape.'

'You mean you've got them into a scrape,' accused Joan. 'You created them; didn't you?'

'It's a fairly accurate picture of real life, I think,' said Dinny, defensively. 'Such things happen every day.'

They had arrived at a little French restaurant on Forty-Fifth, a favorite of his, and were investigating — Joan with curiosity — their variegated assortment of *hors d'œuvres*. She had insisted on knowing something more about the new story which Dinny had begun to tell her last night.

Throughout the luncheon he talked and she listened attentively, without more comment than little murmurs of encouragement and interest.

When, however, he had brought the narrative up to date with the stark outline of an episode considerably to the discredit of his principal characters, Joan frowned — a little flushed.

'It had never occurred to me before,' remarked Joan, when their taxi had reached Fifth Avenue and had turned north en route to The Metropolitan, 'what a heavy responsibility rests on the shoulders of a story-writer.'

'In what way, dear?... Let's have your theory.'

She hesitated, groping for adequate phrases.

'Perhaps I can't express it, but it's something like this: when a man builds a bridge, or a tower, or paints a picture, or composes a song, he really isn't a creator in the sense that a novelist is a creator.... You — for example — created Cecil and Margery, just as Jehovah created Adam and Eve ——'

Dinny laughed, teasingly.

'That Garden of Eden affair points no moral, Joan. That was just a story — about Adam and Eve.'

She nodded, victoriously.

'Exactly! — and so is this just a story — about Cecil and Margery. Who's ever going to estimate the wholesale damage done to human personality, through the ages, by that Eden tale?... No — I don't believe it, and I know you don't, but millions have believed it, and do believe, at this moment! Think of the centuries of unfair, unjust, belittling appraisals of God — all derived from some ancient shepherd-minstrel's fantastic story, told at an evening campfire on some desert oasis!'

'Bravo — Joan! Proceed! Gad! — that's good!'

'One of the best things you've done, Dinny, is to sneer and scowl at that old story, and its monstrous implications. Many times, in your ridicule of orthodoxy, you've pointed the finger of scorn at a crafty Jehovah who would bring an innocent pair of inquisitive people into the world, and immediately direct their attention to some experiment brimming with tragedy.... But aren't you doing the same thing to Cecil and Margery?'

'How absurd!' laughed Dinny.

'It's too serious to be absurd,' persisted Joan, soberly. 'Your new book will be on the stands in a few months. It will have a great sale among all the restless, scornful, idol-smashers in the land. They follow you as if you were a new messiah. You've never done a novel for them, and they'll grab at this one while it's still damp from the binders.'

'*Laus Deo!*' exclaimed Dinny, fervently. 'I hope you're right!'

'It's a very pretty picture you draw of Margery, innocently yearning for an expanded life. Little Glenville, Missouri, offers security, three meals a day, and a minimum of struggle; but Margery isn't quite satisfied with her easy Eden. She wants a larger life. Well — why, in Heaven's Name, don't you give it to her?'

The taxi drew up at the curb. They sauntered up the steps, momentarily diverted from their serious theme, traversed the spacious foyer, and continued through to the huge chamber of replicas and models of classic buildings.

'Let's sit here a moment, Dinny... I think I want to finish what I was saying... It's quite important — to me, at least.'

She laid her hand lightly on his arm, and swept his face with an entreating query.

'This Cecil — he was so discontented, too, in Sparrow, Minnesota; wanted to go places and do things. Why didn't you let him?'

'Didn't I?' protested Dinny.

'What makes it all seem so pitifully tragic,' Joan went on, unheeding, 'is just the fact that a hundred thousand young Cecils and Margerys, fretting and steaming in their little Glenvilles and Sparrows, are sure to identify themselves with this pair of revolutionists. Can't you think of some better destination for these people of yours, who are sure to be trailed by a nondescript army of admirers, than this degrading wallow you've planned for them?'

'Oh — it isn't quite that bad, Joan... Come now!'

'Dinny — you've a great chance! There isn't a priest or a preacher or a poet or a professor in the whole world who has the opportunity that you have.... You haven't gone in for sentiment. You haven't had any use for religion. You've been a fire-eating iconoclast. Every cynical young fellow, bent on freedom from the old frustrations, is hanging on your words. There isn't one single idealist, in the whole crew of modern apostles, able to command the attention of these discontented people — people like you and me.... Why don't you capitalize this peculiar grip you've got on the imagination of your — your Cave of Adullam, and show them the way out!... *What a chance!*'

'Nonsense, Joan!' scoffed Dinny, superiorly. 'What sort of a figure d'you think I'd cut? I'm not writing Rollo books. There'd be a laugh go up that you could hear to the poles! ... Besides — I'd rather draw honest pictures of life as it is, no matter how ugly, than to paint frescoes and friezes of the heavenly host. I'll leave that job to the parsons.'

Joan smiled a little, her expression reminding him of the gentle dejection she had shown, one eventful night, in her parlor at Magnolia. She snapped the latch of her bag, absently, a few times, and rose.

'Let's forget it — then,' she said, strolling over to the model of the Acropolis.

Dinny joined her, silently, and not a little troubled.

* * * * * *

He had not seen Joan for five days. She had begged off from engagements on the ground of fatigue. Her hours were long, her new work was exacting because unfamiliar, a great deal depended upon the record she might make for herself at Lacey's, especially through these probationary days. The excuse was valid, and Dinny had tried to be patient.

Tonight they had dined at Dexter's and were now en
route to a musical show at The Strand.

'Been seeing much of old Tommy?'

'Of course — every day.... We lunched together, yesterday.'

'I didn't know that was customary,' commented Dinny,
with a surprised little chuckle. 'You might as well have
worked for *me*.' He tried to make this sound like a pleas-
antry.

'Don't be silly. Tommy thinks I've the makings of a
buyer, and wanted to tell me a lot of things there's no time
for, when we're working. It was very interesting.'

Dinny pretended interest in the traffic-jam, ahead.

'That's quite reasonable. Tommy can do a great deal for
you, if he wants to — and evidently he does. You've got on
well with him.... Calling him "Tommy" now, eh?'

'He's just a big boy.' Joan's tone was maternal. 'It's
awfully easy to call him "Tommy," don't you think? It
was you got me into it.... Rather I'd not?'

'Why should I care?' Dinny's magnanimity was almost
militant. 'I just asked out of curiosity. I had hoped you
two would like each other.... Well — here we are, dear.'

The show was good; tuneful, colorful. Joan seemed to enjoy every minute of it. Gad — how vital she was! Dinny
tried to share her enthusiasm, but had to confess to himself
that the piece was dull and tedious. Annoying little dis-
sonances, rasping from deep inside him, shrilled the ensemble
until the clamorous yelp of it tore at his nerves. He was
glad when it was done, and inhaled the first tonic draft of
the outer air with reinvigorated spirits.

Joan was graciously remote, almost too interested in her
distractions to be giving much thought to the new phase of
their comradeship. Whether she was still sensing the slight
constraint which had slowed them up, on that afternoon at
The Metropolitan, or had some other reason for mentally
fending him off, Dinny could not make sure. They were on
the way to her quarters, now — she had insisted, because of

her work — and within another five minutes Dinny would be headed for home tormented by forebodings.

'Can't we take a little spin in the park before we put in?' suggested Dinny. 'It isn't late.'

'If you like.'

He spoke to the driver, who nodded, and slackened the speed.

'Life has become very important, darling, since you came.' Dinny's voice was tender. He reached for her hand.

'I'm glad I came, too, Dinny,' she responded, promptly. 'I never was so happy before... almost as happy as I'd like to be.'

'I wonder if I'm supposed to know what that means — about your — your wish to be happier.... Is it — anything I can do?'

Joan did not immediately reply.

'I — don't — know, dear,' she said, at length, doubtfully. 'I rather hoped you could, but — maybe not.'

He drew her to him.

'Joan, dear — we do belong to each other, you know.'

'Sometimes — I've thought that, too, Dinny.' There was a weary little sigh. 'But — you see — I have to live. I need air, light, sunshine! You don't seem to require it. Sometimes we really do belong — just for a moment... and then... well — we don't belong any more than — than rocks and petunias belong!'

'But, darling, we needn't try to be alike! That's the real beauty of a comradeship like ours. Neither has to sacrifice personality, opinions, or individuality of outlook.'

'No — we needn't try to be alike,' repeated Joan, thoughtfully, 'but it would be preferable if we belonged to the same kingdom of nature. I'm for the world! I like it! It warms me, and I respond to it.... You're at war with it, Dinny.'

'Oh, Joan, dear — can't you forget this silly little difference in our viewpoint.... I love you, darling.'

'I know.' murmured Joan, laying her cheek lightly against his shoulder.

'And you?' he whispered. 'You do care — don't you, Joan?'

'Yes — Dinny — I care.... I care so much that I simply couldn't bear to live that close to perfect happiness — and — and be robbed of it.'

'I'll try — very hard — Joan,' promised Dinny, sincerely.

'Do — please — Dinny!'

Joan's cheeks were wet with tears when he kissed her. He was stirred to an almost painful ecstasy by her response to that kiss.

For a long moment she clung to his lips; then, nestling her face against his arm, with a tremulous little sigh, she said, with passionate insistence:

'Don't fail me, Dinny.... You know — now — how much I love you.'

CHAPTER XIV

JOAN, who had been crying, was mechanically collecting the remains of their picnic; the mockingly gay paper plates, the paper cups, the half-emptied little bottles of olives, artichoke hearts, anchovies, the sandwiches, the deviled eggs, the chicken, the ingenious French pastries.

'Don't bother, Dinny,' she said, pensively, as he ventured to assist.

He put down the salad plate and made quite a task of lighting his pipe, uncomfortably wondering if Joan felt herself not only an object of compassion but of chagrin, too, as she sat, tousled and swollen-eyed, gathering up the pitifully absurd litter of the feast she had spread, an hour earlier, with such a bright, confident air, archly mystifying him with the delicacies she conjured from her wicker basket.

It was rather debasing to Joan, wasn't it, to sit here and owlishly watch her attend to these little drudgeries? Perhaps it was even more humiliating to her if he tried, awkwardly, to share them.

'Go take a stroll and smoke your pipe,' she suggested, divining his perplexity. 'I'm not very nice to look at, anyway.' She smiled, with a sort of childish contrition. 'I'm sure my nose is red... Awfully sorry, Dinny.'

'It was a crime for us to quarrel on a day like this,' growled Dinny. 'All my fault, Joan.'

She shook her head, preoccupiedly.

'I'll divide the honors with you... Run along, dear. I'd so much rather you did... And we won't talk about it again — ever!... Anyone would think we might have learned better — by now.'

'My God — yes! We're a couple o' fools!' Dinny unfolded his long legs and scrambled to his feet. 'I'll be back presently, then. You've the book... Think I'll saunter down and see the chap's sailboat.'

They had left shortly before eight, that June morning, bound for the country in Dinny's new sport roadster which he had bought with just such excursions in view. They had had the streets to themselves. Dinny had called the tubby old Hoboken ferry their private yacht.

Shady, lawn-clipped Montclair was still asleep when they rolled softly through. Except for an ambling group of little girls with long curls and short skirts, three of them walking backwards, obviously bound for Sunday School, and a slim, sedate lady of forty-plus, carrying a black parasol loftily over a high-perched black hat, who was being overtaken and passed by a square, craggy, determined man with a Bible, the residence streets were deserted.

Joan had furnished most of the talk, gayly offering an unpunctuated flow of light persiflage, undaunted by Dinny's silent and studious attention to the road, for he was still far from a competent driver. It was clear, though, that he had something on his mind besides his responsibility at the wheel.

Greenwood Lake, their objective, was all that Joan had hoped it might be when, last night, they had touched heads over the road-map in her little parlor.

The shiny blue car was parked in the grove, at eleven.

Suddenly shaking loose from his dourly reflective mood, Dinny made up for his taciturnity on the road by exhibiting a noisy hilarity as he unloaded their festival cargo and spread the new motor-rug on the grass, fifty yards from the lake-shore. But his impetuous jollity bubbled by artifice, thought Joan. It was not quite spontaneous... Perhaps he would tell her.

They were nearly finished with their luncheon when, Joan having come to a full stop in her narrative of recent events at Lacey's, Dinny, who had been fixedly staring at her face without hearing a word she said, suddenly blurted out:

'I've some news for you.'

Joan nodded, understandingly.

'I knew you had,' she said, playfully, but a little anxious.

'I'm not sure you will approve,' he warned, 'but I've accepted the editorship of *Hallelujah*... Begin in September.'

She recoiled as if he had struck her.

'Oh, Dinny — how could you — after what you'd promised? There isn't a magazine in the whole lot of them that's been so mean — and cynical — and fault-finding... It has hurt me when you even contributed to it. Now you're to operate it!... I'm sorry you told me.'

Dinny did not meet her eyes, but gazed glassily at the lake, scowling.

'Don't my feelings count, at all, dear?' persisted Joan, tenderly reproachful.

He recalled himself, then, as from a distance, and regarded her critically.

'I've never undertaken to discipline your thoughts, Joan,' said Dinny, crisply, 'and — I hope this isn't going to sound too surly — I dispute your right to regulate mine.'

'In other words — it isn't any of my business.'

Dinny leaned back on one elbow, toying with the fringes of the rug.

'I wouldn't have thought of using that phrase, Joan, but — is it?... You see' — Dinny's brows contracted as he felt for his words — 'it's very difficult to refashion another's mind, even if both the — the redeemer and the sinner are ——'

'I don't think that's very kind, Dinny... And I dislike being talked to that way,' interrupted Joan, her lips trembling.

'Well — putting the mere choice of words aside — you've honestly and lovingly wanted to make me over into something other than I am... And I have honestly and lovingly tried to accommodate you. But it's no good. It won't work. I can't do it. If our difference of taste were ——

Look here: if I hated golf, and you liked it, I would go with you and play it — just because it brought you pleasure. I'd learn to like it for that reason. But this is a different matter, dear. This is a problem of work and wages, bread and butter. I'm a journalist. That's my profession. I'm not omniscient, and I can't write about just anything and everything. My line is criticism. And when you ask me to leave off criticism, and go in for hymn-writing and sappy little twitters set to the score of "Buttercups and Daisies," you've asked too much!'

Joan, with mounting indignation, made an impatient little cry, but Dinny raised a hand, briefly, and went on doggedly:

'There's a whole battalion of sugary smilers, rocking and knitting and purring on the front porches of "Houses Built By the Side of the Road." I doubt if there's room in the journalism of loving-kindness for one more dulcet coo; and, if there were, I'm mighty sure I haven't the voice for it. I know you've set your heart on my doing it; and, because I wanted to please you, I've made some sincere experiments in that direction; bought a little volume of verse entitled "Just Folks," and tried to set my big feet in those dainty tracks, but it was hopeless, darling. I put on my starchy white pinafore, tied my little pink sunbonnet under my chin, and went skipping merrily down the road with a nice basket of pansies for rheumatic old Granny MacDoodle, but before I had gone very far I found myself grinning again. I can't help grinning, Joan. You'll either have to get used to that grin — or ——'

'Or — *what?*' queried Joan, soberly.

Dinny was tardy with his reply.

'I'm afraid the alternative is — up to you.'

'May I talk now?'

'Please do. It's your turn.'

'Well — I never asked you to scribble soft sentimentalities. I hate them, too. There's been too much of it. But there's a pretty wide gap between "Pollyanna" and *Halle-*

lujah. It's easy enough to understand why people crowd about the news-stands to buy *Hallelujah*. They've been fed up to the throat on the other thing.... But *Hallelujah* isn't the right answer to their demand for something more sturdy and sensible than mawkish slush.

'There are a few things that deserve better than to be ridiculed. I looked through the last issue of *Hallelujah* — because you asked me to. One article was a reprint of a little booklet some man had written for private circulation among his friends and neighbors. It was dedicated to the Kiwanis Club. He was its president in Littlegrass, or somewhere, Oklahoma. He and his wife had just returned from a six-weeks trip to Europe, and he wanted to tell his friends what they had seen. It was badly written, and full of childish comments; but the man hadn't prepared it for the smart young spoofers who read *Hallelujah*. It was intended for simple-hearted, inexperienced people who own the houses they live in, and pay their bills, and go to church on Sunday, and have only one wife.... And *Hallelujah* — that's always ranting about the bad manners of yokels who eat with their knives, and don't know whether Chekhov won the last Irish sweepstakes or swam the Channel or designed the dome for Saint Peter's — printed that friendly little booklet — mistakes and all — to fetch a chuckle from the really cultured people, the smart people who've been about, and know which spoon comes first — and who wrote "Ulysses."... I don't believe I could bear it to see your name at the top of the staff in a magazine so — so ——'

'Yes?'

'—— so self-consciously clever! So pompously superior! So insolently vulgar!... If that's the kind of company you find yourself at home with, Dinny Brumm, I'm sure you'd never be very happy with me!... You've said you aren't "omniscient," and mustn't be expected to write about everything. That's just where we disagree. You *do* think you're omniscient! *Hallelujah* is omniscient! There isn't anything that *Hallelujah* doesn't know, far better than anyone else. It cackles at theology for being dogmatic, and calls all the preachers idiots and all the creeds rubbish — and after it's through ridiculing them, the all-wise *Hallelujah* proceeds to be just as dogmatic and arbitrary as the people it reviles.... It's always poking fun at Jehovah.... You'd think, from the way it hands down sublime oracles about Art, the Drama, Music, Literature, that it expected the whole world to reserve its opinion about any art-form until *Hallelujah* had spoken.... After that, the wise would know just what it would be safe for them to think.... And now you're going to be the Solomon who supervises the schooling of the sophisticates.... No — Dinny! — I don't believe I could live comfortably quite that close to the summit of Olympus. I'm afraid the bright light would hurt my eyes. I'd always be at a terrible disadvantage!'

'Very well, then,' rasped Dinny, 'that's that — and now we know where we stand.... It would be tragic for us to go on with it.'

'I'm glad you see it, at last,' agreed Joan, in the same tone.

Dinny's lip curled, unpleasantly.

'By the way,' he drawled, dryly, 'speaking of sarcasm and ridicule, you're fairly good at it yourself. I may be bitter enough, but I'd never talk that way to anyone I loved. ... And I don't believe you could, either.'

Joan hung her head, and put both hands over her eyes, and wept like a little child.

'Oh, Dinny, forgive me,' she pleaded, brokenly. 'I didn't mean to hurt you.'

For an instant, he was moved to join her with assurances, but still smarting under the sharp raps, he delayed; and the longer he delayed the harder it was to conciliate.

Joan's little storm of emotion cleared. She wiped her eyes, and tried to smile. Dinny stole a quick glance, and solemnly looked away, heavy-eyed. With a long sigh, broken by little sobs, she began to gather up the fragments, Dinny watching her automatic movements dully. She was a typical picture, he thought, of Woman — instinctively carrying on with the tasks Nature had assigned to her, regardless of what tragedy might rake her heart.... No man would have done it. A man would stalk away — and let the damned dishes go to hell!

He pitied her, and his pity was tinctured with a trace of vicarious mortification. He could have wept, himself. He picked up the smeary little paper plate on which his salad had been served him, and was in the act of passing it across to her.

'Don't bother, Dinny,' she said, pensively.

He walked down to the shore where a tanned youth was untangling some new white ropes in his little sailboat, and was surprised at the steadiness and nonchalance of his own voice as he chatted, amiably, with the young stranger. Here he was — only three minutes and one hundred and fifty feet away from a disaster that had pulled his very house down about his ears — calmly puffing his pipe and inquiring whether the yacht's ropes were the same thing as sash-cord.

Did that mean, he asked himself, that his love for Joan was of less consequence to his happiness than he had thought? Or was his quick recovery due to the fact that he was taking the instinctive course of Man? Woman, anchored to dishes and brooms and beds and babies, always had had time to think — to grieve, to regret, to mope and grow morbid. Man, whacked over the head with a battle-axe, had had no chance to sit down and nurse his hurts. He must instantly be on the alert for another wallop from some other direction.... He and Joan were faithful to their respective atavistic responses to their mutual disaster. She was sitting there on the grass, crying softly, and telling herself her world had gone to smash. He was smoking his pipe, and talking to a stranger about different weights and weaves of rope.... But that didn't mean his little Paradise hadn't been hurled to Purgatory — same as Joan's.... Odd — reflected Dinny.... Elemental forces! — he had never felt their grip, or appraised their long reach, quite so discriminatingly before.

She joined him, after a little; sauntering down to the shore with all the evidences of her grief discarded. While he had been philosophizing over the easy resilience of the male — the quick, decisive rebound of the male who, no matter how strait the gate, how charged with punishment the scroll, would remain the master of his fate, the captain of his soul — the moody, brooding female had deftly repacked the hamper, stowed it in the car, combed her hair, adjusted her swanky little hat at a jaunty angle, powdered her nose, reshaped her lips, donned a smile, and had now slipped a hand through his arm as much as to say to the boy in the boat, 'I've tamed this Animal to drive single or double; rack, pace, trot, run — or what gait would you like to see him do?... I've been training him for fifty thousand years.... He doesn't know it, of course. The silly ass thinks he's the warden of the asylum instead of a patient.'

Dinny wasn't sure he liked to have his theories tossed about in this reckless fashion.

'I've been thinking,' he said, after they had driven a mile without much talk. 'I've had my nose to the grindstone for a good while — in my work, you know — and I believe a change of air would be good for me. I'm going abroad for a few weeks.'

'Splendid!' enthused Joan. 'I wish I could.'

He laid a hand gently on her arm.

'Very well — I'll take you.'

'No, Dinny — we've settled that!' Her voice was casual now.

'I'd be glad to, you know.'

'I believe you would — but it's quite impossible.'

The long silence that followed gave her words a chance to chisel their way quite deeply into her memory. She recalled them, with a start, one September evening, when, in response to a similar invitation as sincerely offered, she used them again, *verbatim*.

A swarthy gypsy girl, one afternoon, last summer, had padded softly back to the little office in Uncle Jim Bailey's dimly lighted, varnish-reeking furniture store, and, pausing before Joan's high desk, had said:

'Your fortune — for four bits?'

Joan had declined.

'Please — I'm hongry.'

The girl had slipped the half-dollar into a dirty, beaded purse attached to her belt, and reached for her client's hand.

'Make it short,' advised Joan. 'I'm busy.'

The girl had stooped over the extended palm, scrutinizing it intently, Joan, with equal interest, marveling at the black, straight, coarse hair on the bowed head, seeming to belong to a well-groomed horse rather than a young woman.

'You are going on a far jorney… on a beeg boat… with a tall man.'

'Is that all?' asked Joan, as the girl moved off, with the slinky gait of something born in the woods.

She paused, spread one brown hand high on her hip tossed her head arrogantly, and retorted, her white teeth gleaming in the twisted, half-envious smile:

'Ees that not enough?'

* * * * * *

According to Dinny's weekly letters, the cynical amusement he had expressed in his first laconic, staccato, dash-sprinkled note, scribbled on his return from viewing the changing of the guard at Buckingham Palace, was giving way to an unexpected admiration for monarchy.

Joan needed never to have been in England to guess what might be Dinny's instant reaction to the ancient shrines and tombs of the departed great. He had a flair for making history vital, and was extraordinarily well posted on the lives of British sovereigns.

As for the bronze and marble memorabilia of departed kings and queens, Dinny's interest was assured, and Joan confidently expected him to relay observations faithfully, interestingly reflecting the half-dreamy mood in which he would saunter through the gloom of the cathedrals.

She was quite unprepared, however, for his comments on contemporary pageantry.

'It will have to go, of course,' ruminated Dinny, in mid-July, writing from the Victoria Hotel in London. 'The general drift is toward republics, and the last of the kings have already been born. There will be no revolution, no choppings-off, no slow tanning of royal heads on iron-spiked towers. The British manage to express themselves with but few gestures. They are not a yelping, mobbish, excitable race. When the time comes, the king will be retired on half-pay and allowed to keep his horses, dogs, and grouse-gun.

'But it will be a great pity when "the captains and the kings depart"; especially the kings, though I presume you couldn't very well have kings without captains. They'll leave the stage together.

'I'm afraid I've become quite a tory, Joan. I have had time and opportunity for a lot of thinking about this. Humanity hasn't evolved out of the king phase. It's a wise, practical government. Republics sound promising enough in their constitutions, highfalutin slogans, apostrophes to "liberty," senatorial oratory, and patriotic verse, but it's no good in practice.

'I'm for the king! I'm for the divinely ordained king who can do no wrong, no matter what capers he cuts. America would be vastly better off topped by a real, honest-to-goodness king, with twenty million dollars' worth of diamonds in his hat, bells on his fingers and rings on his toes, than a harried, worried, temporary president whom any sleek-haired little squirt, paragraphing and cartooning for some impudent, wisecracking editor, can smear with his smartaleckisms.'

'Why — Dinny!' exclaimed Joan, happily, to his photograph on her table. 'Whatever's happened to you?'

'The whole king business is on the skids, no doubt; but it's a great misfortune. So's the Established Church close to the end of the last inning. Nobody on bases, two men out, and two strikes already called on a feeble bat.... But it's a pity. The thing's had a sort of majestic dignity. It's never been in a suppliant attitude, panhandling the brethren and sisters for sixpences to pay the parson's coal-bill. It has been guaranteed by The State, okayed by The Crown. It's been lofty, confident, time-worthy!

'Maybe it hasn't been quite so fussily, busily, frantically energetic, and maybe the rank and file of the people have accepted it rather perfunctorily — about the way they accepted breathing and the circulation of their blood — but it has stood there calmly certifying to an Eternal Fact (or at least an Everlasting Wish). It will be voluntarily supported, pretty soon, I suppose. And that will be the end of its greatness.... Oh — it will still go through the motions; but its dignity will have departed.

'That's what ails the nine score different sects in the States. No dignity; because voluntarily financed by people whose Sunday dime has given them the right to dictate its policies. Even they — especially they — who presume to manage the thing have no respect for it. How could they? Don't I know? Didn't I grow up in it?

'Wormy, shiny-elbowed, little Jonas B. Pring, lifetime errand-boy and cuspidorian for some fusty old firm of lawyers, snubbed by his betters, henpecked at home, hectored by bill-collectors, a measly little nobody, contemptuously snooted by his own dog — he's quite a tremendous fellow at The First Church of Christ.... Only place in the whole world where Jonas can let himself go, and be somebody.... Gets up at the annual business meeting and tells the thirty-six women, nine old men, and four little girls, that the Reverend Blubb is no executive and had best be asked to move along.... And on what meat hath this our nasty, contemptible, little Jonas fed? How came he so important?

'Jonas was a subscriber. For fifty cents a week, Jonas had bought the right to swagger up and down the aisles, distributing hymn-books, himself yelping the tune at the top of his lungs. At the small cost of twenty-six dollars annually, Jonas B. Pring, who everywhere else was dodging sharp elbows, shoe-tips, snarls, and skillets, could fold his important arms high over his inflated chest, tuck in his forceful chin, draw a sagacious frown, and tell 'em all where to get off at when the Lord's business was under discussion at The First Church of Christ.'

Odd, reflected Joan, Dinny's concern about the Church of England. The only comment she'd ever heard him make about the Anglicans was a sour remark to the effect that their chief job was 'to apologize for the Reformation.'

She did not commend him for his slightly altered attitude toward 'institutions,' fearing her approval, however casually phrased, might sound I-told-you-so-ish; evaded discussion of his new ideas; filled her letters with current news, and doings at Lacey's.

There was a great deal in her letters about Tommy, inevitable because her busy life was now bounded by Lacey's, and Tommy was Lacey's so far as Joan was concerned.

She wrote much too much about Tommy without realizing what conclusions Dinny might come to. Tommy's luggage department had been augmented by a line of motor-rugs and other whim-whams relating to cars. Tommy had had a raise. Tommy had been to Chicago, but was back now.

Tommy's brother Victor hadn't been at all pleased with the reception he had received on his Western tour, and was thinking of giving up the fiddle and studying voice. Someone had told him he could sing. Tommy had said he wasn't sure yet whom the joke was on, but suspected it might be on himself.

Tommy had a new eight-cylinder car, very pretty and very easy riding.

After she had mailed her longest and last letter, the second week of August, and recalled what an inordinate amount of Tommy had found its way into her chronicle of current activities, Joan heartily wished she could have it back for revision. However, Dinny would understand. Besides, he liked Tommy; didn't he?

But it was an unfortunate letter to be her last to Dinny, seeing he was so far away, and alone. Joan had expected to write at least once more.

Then the September issue of *Hallelujah* appeared. She bought it hoping to find nothing in it about Dinny's accession to its tripod. The announcement was there — on page one. *Hallelujah* stated, with a swagger, that, from henceforth and until further notice, the increasing success of the magazine was assured, and gave the reason that had all but broken her heart.

Leafing with distaste and disgust through the condescendingly superior titles, Joan presently came upon Dinny at his worst in a venomous attack on a certain great newspaper syndicate.

It was capped 'Greck.'

Soon after her coming to New York, Dinny, in a mellow moment, had confided his story to Joan. It was not told to solicit her sympathy, or to interpret his maladjustment to the normal ways of viewing human relationships; but, with the whole picture of Dinny's frustrated, disillusioned, and embittered childhood, she had tried to understand the savagery of his cynicism.

Sympathetic as she was, however, toward his disaffection in regard to his father, there was no excuse, she thought, for this unconscionable onslaught.

It seemed that some prominent editorial writer in the employ of 'The Greck Syndicate' had caustically criticized *Hallelujah* on much the same grounds as she herself had based her disastrous comments on the magazine in discussing it at Greenwood Lake.

The Craig Syndicate, as everybody knew, had in its

employ, at the top, a considerable number of keen, clever, high-powered Jews. They were forever playing to the prejudices of the vast, unintegrated, dissatisfied, general riff-raff.

Hallelujah was in the same business, of course, but bidding for the interest of a different clientèle. *Hallelujah* and the Craig Syndicate were as nearly alike as identical twins, except for this: *Hallelujah* appealed to the prejudices and dissatisfactions of some fifty thousand self-confessed intelligentsia; the Craig Syndicate appealed to about the same invoice of aversions possessed by ten millions of illiterati.... How natural that they should hate each other!

Some editorial writer for 'Greck'— Joan presumed it must have been the chief incendiary, Enoch Birnbaum — momentarily forgetting, according to Dinny, that he had been divinely ordained to minister unto the feeble-minded, had remarked of *Hallelujah* that it suffered of 'grandiose paranoia in the penultimate phase of that malady, with paresis indicated as the unhappy sequela.'

Dinny, breathing out slaughter, had assumed championship of the besieged *Hallelujah*. Joan, who knew him as well as or better than he knew himself, could easily picture with what lip-smacking, demoniacal glee he had hauled up the drawbridge, dropped the portcullis, and heated the oil he meant to pour down upon the haughty head of 'Greck.'

She did not read it all. Undeniably clever, fantastically cruel, Dinny's indictment of 'Greck' described him in terms of Moses; Moses the law-giver, Moses the sea-cleaver, Moses the manna-man, Moses the medicine-man.

'Greck,' assisted by all Israel, and trailed by millions of uncircumcised, untutored, and largely unwashed hicks and yokels, was headed for the Promised Land. True, he hadn't got any farther than the wilderness, but Jehovah would doubtless look after His People, as was His pleasant custom.

The last paragraph — the one that gave Joan a sickish feeling as if she had witnessed parricide — was a masterpiece of brutality.

'If the great Greek ever made a mistake, he does not recall it. This, too, was a Mosaic gift — forgetfulness. In his youth, Moses ran away and hid himself after having killed a young neighbor; but if he ever remembered, or was regretful, the Good Book — which almost never omits anything resembling contrition — fails to document his misgivings. It is said that Moses' victim was a young man. Had he killed a young girl, he would of course have forgotten the incident utterly, and remembered it against himself no more.'

Joan tossed the nasty thing into the waste-basket and washed her hands.

* * * * * * *

Tommy Forsythe was sailing tomorrow for Lisbon on the *Vulcania*. It was a business trip. He would go to Italy, also, returning to New York in late November.

Joan had lunched with him at Dexter's. He had seemed distraught, probably due to his anxiety that all the last-minute duties should have attention. He had little to say, Joan furnishing most of the talk.

At six, he bade her good-bye as she left the store. It was a casual farewell; a brief handclasp, a bit of banter.

At eight-thirty he called her on the telephone. Might he see her for a moment about something rather important? ... Would she object to a short drive?... He would call in ten minutes.

They headed for Central Park. Tommy was nervous and moody. Joan's curiosity mounted.

'What's on your mind, Tommy?... Anything I can do?'

He was a long time finding words.

'Joan' — the car slowed down to five miles an hour — 'I'm to be away quite a while. There's something I'd like to know before I leave. I have become very fond of you,

as you can't help knowing.... Are you engaged to Dinny
Brumm?'

She shook her head.

'Then I've a right to tell you that I ——'

'No, Tommy, please don't!'

'Will you think about me sometimes, Joan?'

'You know I will, Tommy. You've been such a dear
friend. And I hope you're going to have a wonderful trip.'

'I wish you were going along.... I'd take you if you'd
go, dear.'

'I believe you would — but it's quite impossible.'

There was a long silence.

'Joan — tell me this much. Are you in love with
Dinny?'

'Must I say?'

'No — you needn't say. I understand.'

Joan patted his arm gratefully.

'Tommy — you are a dear.'

He drove her home then, as he had promised, and
soberly said good-bye again at her door. Joan felt very
much depressed. Early in the evening one of the girls
where she lived had suggested their going to a movie.
She should have gone. It was too bad — about Tommy.
She had known he liked her, but she hadn't been prepared
for this.

Now she could not work for Tommy any more. She
would have to leave Lacey's. It was rough sledding... for
a girl... in business; difficult to retain the proper balance.
If you were up-stage and untouchable in your attitude
toward your employer, you had no chance of promotion.
If you were friendly, he made love to you.

Old Mr. Abercrombie, of Denver, with business at
Lacey's in July, had spent an hour with Tommy. Evidently something pleasant had been said to Mr. Abercrombie about her, for when Tommy introduced him, he
said:

'If you're ever tired of New York, and want to live in a

really good town, where the air is pure and the wages are
right, wire me.'

'Maybe I'll do that, Mr. Abercrombie,' she had said,
accepting it as a gracious little courtesy.

Then Mr. Abercrombie had met several others of the
department, and was about to leave, but had returned to
her, saying, seriously:

'I meant that, Miss Braithwaite.... We would like to
have you at Abercrombie's.... Here's my card.'

By midnight, Joan had dismantled her room of everything that belonged to her, and was ready to be off, pending
instructions. She called a taxi at midnight and went to the
nearest Western Union branch on Broadway. After dis-
patching the night-letter to Denver, she returned to her
room and slept — badly.

At ten-thirty, next morning, there was a wire telling her
to come at once. The telegram expressed delight. Joan was
cheered.

'Where shall we send your mail, Miss Braithwaite?'
asked the mystified Mrs. Higgins.

Joan hesitated, and impetuously resolved upon a bit of
bridge-burning.

'I'm not looking for any,' she said.

'Are you going far?' inquired Mrs. Higgins.

'Very — and I shall not be back for a long time.'

The train left at noon. Joan, feeling like a fugitive, was
glad when it was in motion. Once through the tunnel and
out into the sunshine, she had a pleasant sensation of
freedom from an accumulation of perplexities. She dallied
long over her lunch. They had passed Poughkeepsie before
she had finished.

* * * * * *

The *Berengaria* docked at ten on Friday. Dinny, who
had never asked himself whether he felt at home in New
York, was glad to be back. England had done his mind a
few small services. The passionate impatience with which

he had viewed nearly all the traditional reliances — now that they were outgrown, outworn, and anachronistic in a new, mechanized era — had tempered considerably.

There was an assuring solidarity in the massive gray stones of England, poise in the recumbent, armored effigies that lay in single-file through the vaulted transepts of her quiet cathedrals, peace in her tranquil greensward.

On the homeward voyage, with much time for thinking, Dinny had determined upon certain changes in his manner of living. He would take life a little more comfortably, for one thing. He would live less feverishly, as became a balanced mind. The thought of returning to his shabby little suite in the Village was distasteful. He would move uptown, equip his bachelor apartment with a few solid comforts, and make a less hectic and hurried thing of his life.

Now that he was actually home again — his light baggage had been quickly inspected by customs — he was eager to carry out his resolution. He would proceed to it without delay. Joan would be happy to see him well out of the Village and its associations. How pleased she would be when he told her!... He had quite abandoned his novel. Joan would be gratified.

The rooms were shabbier than ever. The few pieces of furniture that were his should be sent out for redressing. His mother's walnut desk had had no attention ever, for all that it had been knocked about from pillar to post for a quarter-century. Its legs were scratched and scored and its body bore many scars. He must not trust its rehabilitation to any but an expert in such matters.

Why not get going on it at once? He called up Becker's, who dealt in antiques, and inquired for Mr. Becker himself; explained who he was, what he had, what he wanted. The elderly Becker, with an errand in the vicinity of Washington Square, said he would run in and have a look at the desk himself.

Dinny was sorting over his books when old Becker arrived, having found it important to occupy his mind with such diversion as was to be had. He knew Joan did not like to be called to the telephone during business hours. It would be a long day.

Old Becker was a thin, wiry, little man with a gray beard and pale blue myopic eyes that peered at you in an absurdly childish fashion.

'Lofely!' murmured Becker, caressing the rich wood with an appreciative palm.

'My grandfather made it a long time ago for my mother, when she was a young girl,' explained Dinny. 'The old fellow was quite handy with tools, I've been told; though, of course, the value of the desk is largely sentimental.'

Becker drew down the lid, almost reverently.

'Handy mit tools!' he muttered, ironically. 'Handy mit tools? Mein Gott! A greadt ardtist! Und you say — handy mit tools; hein?'

He peered inside the desk.

'Vas iss dat?... Mueller?... Mueller!' His pale little eyes searched Dinny. He poured out a torrent of queries. Where did this grandfather live? Was that his name — Mueller? Indiana? Gott in Himmel — no!... Where had he lived before that?

Dinny said his grandfather had migrated from Dresden as a youngster.

'Ah — so!' Becker wagged his head and tugged at his straggling whiskers. 'Der Muellers made no desks... but your grandvadder Mueller — he made a desk for his childt.... It iss very lofely!'

So — Aunt Martha's occasional vague, proud references to the glory that was Mueller, back in 'th' old country,' had some substantial basis of fact. He had always thought the story an exaggeration — one of Aunt Martha's pipe-dreams.

Old Becker was grinning mysteriously, and Dinny regarded him inquisitively.

'Leedle secret, too; hein?' He significantly tapped the

exquisitely crafted little pilaster between the center pigeon-holes with an understanding thumb.

'I'm afraid I don't understand,' said Dinny, stooping to inspect the pilaster critically. 'Secret?'

Becker's expression was a study. He had stumbled upon two secrets — a secret drawer — a mystified owner.

'What makes you think so?' inquired Dinny.

The old man was slow with his reply; looked Dinny up and down, searchingly, as if wanting to satisfy himself that his client was really entitled to know what an owner of such a treasure should have known. Apparently assured on that point, he explained that the central pigeon-holes were an inch wider apart than any of the others. Back of the ornamented pilaster there was a narrow drawer.

Dinny was on the point of suggesting that they experiment, but on second thought decided to make the exploration alone. He quickly came to terms with Becker about the expense, and the old man left, saying: 'Ve vill treadt it vell.... Mein Gott!... a *Mueller!*'

With the point of his knife-blade, Dinny endeavored to loosen the pilaster and start the alleged secret drawer. The little pilaster was unbudgable. Doubtless something else had to be pushed, pulled, moved, before the drawer would open. He inquired of every nook and cranny for a suspicious knob, button, or unexplained gadget. The desk remained calmly innocent of any duplicity. He would have to fall back on old Becker, after all.

Tommy Forsythe would hardly have gone out to luncheon by now. He wondered if they might not go together. Perhaps he might find Tommy free to do so. He called Lacey's and connected with Tommy's department.

No — Mr. Forsythe was not in. Mr. Forsythe was out of town. Who was this — please? Oh — Mr. Brumm. Mr. Forsythe sailed for Europe on Wednesday. Yes — Wednesday noon.

Dinny decided to risk asking for Joan, so long as he had the connection.

'May I speak to Miss Braithwaite?'

There was quite a little pause.

'Miss Braithwaite isn't with us, any more, Mr. Brumm.'

'You mean she's not with Lacey's? Since when? Where's she gone?' Dinny tossed his prudence aside, and fired his questions as if he'd the right to ask them.

'She's not been here since Tuesday — closing time. We do not know where she is.'

'That's strange!'

'Yes, sir... Is that all, Mr. Brumm?'

Dinny's hands trembled as he hunted for the telephone number of Mrs. Higgins. His voice was unsteady when he asked his questions.

No — Miss Braithwaite wasn't there any more. . Yes, she had taken all her things and left shortly before noon on Wednesday.... No — she hadn't said.... No — they positively did not know!... And who was this, talking?

Dinny slammed the receiver back on the hook, and sat for a long time, lost in moody thought, wondering if it were really so. He brought both long hands down with a despairing slap on his knees, rose with a sigh, caught up his hat, went downstairs, and strolled down the street, hands deep in pockets, his mind in a tumult. He had lost Joan!... Damn Tommy Forsythe!... Damn Greenwich Village!... Damn *Hallelujah!*... To hell with Everything!

CHAPTER XV

A RAGGED, rumpled, yellowed scrap of paper, solidly printed on both sides in nonpareil, fluttered to the floor.

Dinny picked it up and held it between his fingers while he unfolded the bulky letter from which it had fallen. The fragment could wait. He laid it on the desk.

It had taken him an hour, that night, to open the narrow little drawer faced with the miniature Corinthian pilaster.

In the afternoon he had dragged the desk to the window and painstakingly inspected every square inch of its surface. Nothing had come of it. At nine he had laid aside his coat, emptied the desk of its meager contents — for he almost never used it — and set about his task determined to see it through.

The long, shallow drawer below the lid which, when let down, was the writing-table, he removed. This operation promised little, for the drawer was a full fifteen inches below the pilaster and clearly unrelated, but he had done everything else and had now arrived at the phase of his exploration where the incredibilities were being examined.

Taking up this skillfully mortised drawer in his hands, Dinny scrutinized it, inch by inch. In the center of the back panel there was a notch in the top, half an inch deep and three-eighths of an inch wide. It excited his curiosity. Perhaps there was some small projection in the depths of the desk, at the rear of the aperture from which this drawer had come, something articulating with the unobtrusive little notch.

Aware of his inability to thrust a well-muscled forearm into this shallow drawer-space, he inserted a walking-stick and probed about with the tip of it until he found a small, squared, wooden tongue. He pushed up on it gently. It instantly responded with a sharp metallic click that seemed to come from higher up in the region of the pigeon-holes.

The quick, decisive tap, unquestionably the release of a spring, startled him; for, upon having reached the path of discovery, Dinny's nerves had keyed to the sensitiveness of fiddle-strings.

Lowering the hinged writing-table, which he had been supporting on his arm, he glanced toward the little pilaster. It was protruding about three inches. Attached to it was a narrow upright drawer. He drew it farther out. It contained a thick letter which all but filled its limited space.

With rapidly beating heart, Dinny held it closer to the desk-lamp, for the writing on the sealed envelope was faded almost to illegibility, and read the words written in a sprawling feminine hand: 'Confidential — To my child — from Julia Miller Craig.'

The letters were so large, and growing larger as the end of the sagging line was reached, that there had been no room on it for the 'Craig,' which was written below 'Miller,' almost as if it were an afterthought.

Dinny drew up a chair to the desk, sat down, and, with a strange sensation of having stepped into the presence of a disembodied spirit, he carefully opened the brittle old envelope with his paper-knife. A ragged, crumpled fragment of paper fell out. He picked it up from the floor without regarding it closely. Doubtless the letter would explain.

It was not easy to read even the first page on which his girl-mother had clearly spent the best of her waning energy. This fact she recognized at the outset. She was writing in bed; she was very ill; she would do her best. She was burning up with fever, and things were all 'out of drawing.'

'God!' muttered Dinny.

She had seemed rather remote — a mere sacred symbol — until he came upon that little phrase.

Why — that was exactly the way he would have said it, himself! He and this girl, nearly ten years his junior, were not only of the same flesh and blood; they were mentally, temperamentally kin!

For the first time in Dinny's life, his mother assumed

definite reality. She came alive in this letter — in this single phrase — and spoke as clearly as if she were at his side. He had a curious feeling that he was not alone. He drew a quick breath, and slowly turned his head, glancing up over his left shoulder. Then, pulling himself together, resolutely, he returned to the letter. A wave of tenderness swept over Dinny; something other than a feeling of filial reverence; rather the sense of desire to lend her his strength, as if she were a young sister in dire need of his protection.

Things were all 'out of drawing' because she was so hot and weak. Yesterday she had been quite excitable from the fever, and had wandered a little. She would speak of that, later, if her strength held out, she said —

I'm not out of my head now. In fact — my wits seem to be speeded up by the fever. Everything's so much brighter and louder. Father is working, out in his shop, and when he lays his chisel down on the bench, I can hear it drop, both ends of it, the wooden end and the iron part. Each leaf on the maple — I see the tree through the window — is twins, after I have looked awhile. One of the twins is blue, the other yellow. At first, when I look out, each leaf is green. After I have looked hard, for a minute, the leaves are twins, like I said, one blue, one yellow. Then my eyes hurt, and I stop looking. At noon I heard the cracked school-bell over at Hinebaugh's. That's four miles. You can't hear it this far. That's how sick I am, and that's how this kind of sickness sharpens you till you're sharper than you want to be, and it hurts. You don't hear things with your ears, when you're this way, but with your eyes. Every tiny noise is big, and pounds in your eyes, deep behind them.

So, if I say anything queer, you will know why, if you're old enough. But I'm not crazy, and I know what I'm doing. I hope you believe this, for I'm going to tell you something very important before I am through, if I can still hold my head up that long. It's pretty dizzy.

'God!' muttered Dinny, half-sick.

If I only knew how to talk to you, dear, it would be easier. I can't quite place you. You're not a baby. I know that. I'm never going to have a baby. One minute, you seem a boy about fourteen that looks ever so much like Zandy, and next minute you're a girl about my age, and look a little like me. I expect they will put me by mother, near the fence, close to where Zandy first told me. There will be some comfort in that — at least there is now.

Dinny's eyes were smarting; his throat ached.... 'God! — what a cruel thing for the dear little chap to endure!' He read on.

The Dresden part of it was difficult to interpret. It demanded hours of study, later, and the utmost concentration, for Dinny to disentangle the crashed and telescoped detail of the jumbled memories. The narrative resembled nothing so much as a cycloned house, with the refrigerator upside-down on top of the piano, and a large, ragged chunk of identifiable dining-room plastering — wall-paper holding it together — in the kitchen-sink alongside a gift copy of Maeterlinck's *The Life of the Bee* and an old wreath of immortelles. The stuff was all there, but out of normal juxtaposition, by no means easily put to rights.

But for the fact that Dinny had already been given reasons for respectful credence in the Mueller tradition, his mother's confused reference to Dresden would have been too fantastic. The things he most wanted to know about that were absent. The superficial detail was highly elaborated; the garden, the garden-wall, hollyhocks, the door in the wall and the wrought-iron hinges on the door, the grassy-banked river, the boats, and a punt with a red-and-blue canopy — but almost nothing about the life of the place.... The cushion on the window-seat in father's room was of rose velvet, but there was not a word about father's reason for running away from home to America or what had become of the people left behind.... There were lily-pads on the pool in the garden and goldfish under them.

The part about his own father was in keeping with the lyrical quality of the Dresden story — a girlishly romantic reminiscence of tender things said and done. Dinny felt, at this point, that the letter had drifted slightly away from the original intention of confiding to a child, and had taken on the style of a personal journal quite too private for any other eyes than the writer's. He was reluctant to read certain parts of it.

Dinny found it very difficult to reverse the career of the spread-eagle, dictatorial, dominant Zandy Craig, of the Craig Syndicate, and return him to the bewildered, gentle, downy fledgling that had been the 'dear, dear Zandy' of his mother's memoirs.... He would have given ten thousand dollars for the unpublished manuscript of 'Greck.'

Perhaps he had misjudged his father. After all, Zandy — Dinny found himself thinking of this man as 'Zandy' — had been but a youngster when it happened. If he had had it to do over again, five years later, he might have shown up better. There was no doubt Julia — Dinny was thinking of her as 'Julia' now — loved him, trusted him. Surely that was worth something. You could mark that up to Zandy's credit.

But — all the same — By God! — Craig had killed her! You had that to remember, too.... Well — we could think that over — later.

Dinny turned to the next page, and continued. The writing was even less legible now. What with the cloudiness of the composition, and the almost indecipherable script, his mother's attempt at a discussion of an apparently bizarre theory she had arrived at, in her disheveled mental condition, was not a thing to be read with full understanding.

The curious metaphysics she seemed trying to express, phrased in whatever naïve terms a country school-teacher might catch up hastily in the exigency of her fatigue and fever, was still further enshadowed by the increasing uncertainty of the nervous pen. The faded letters were so ill-formed that a given character might be *h, n, u, r,* or *v,* with the adjacent vowel offering you your pick of *a, e,* or *o.*

* * * * * *

It was nearly three o'clock before Dinny had reached the reference to the little scrap of crumpled paper which, in the stress of translating the letter, he had all but forgotten. He took it up, and read it now, but it seemed strangely irrelevant to the matters his mother was treating with such a valiant struggle to make herself understood.

Dinny went back a few paragraphs, and re-read. Julia had written this at mighty cost. She deserved his best efforts to interpret it.

Long before this trouble came to me... don't feel badly, child, it wasn't your fault... I had been frightfully bitter about lots of things. I was lonesome, and didn't belong in this house. I had never been taught anything worth knowing. I didn't even know how to eat. If it hadn't been for the books I read about the habits and little courtesies of refined people, I would have known no more about how to do at the table than old Florrie.

I got so I hated the sight of them. Father, poor old darling, I loved him with my pity, but that was about all. The girls — Martha never was a girl — were so silly and coarse and ignorant that I despised them with all my heart, hating myself for feeling better than they were. For I was not naturally conceited. I am shy and bashful, really. But I was always ashamed that I was related to Susan and Greta.

I hated Martha. I got so I hated everything she said and did. Since I've been sick — up to yesterday... I'll tell you soon about that, dear... I couldn't bear even to have her touch me. The sound of her voice, down in the kitchen, made me want to get up and shout that she was nothing but a sour old simpleton, even when I couldn't hear a word of what she was saying — nothing but the nasty noise.

I hated the boys. I think I had always hated them. They were dirty, inside and out. They were exactly the same as the rest of the loafers that sat along the porch at Baber's store, and got all quiet when you came, and, after you had passed, there would be a rough rumble of a dirty voice, and then they would all spit and laugh a dirty laugh. If you're a girl, maybe you'll know what I mean, though I hope not much. If you're a boy, and you ever laugh just like that, I hope there'll be no chance

for me to hear it wherever I'm going to. I'd rather die like a
dog, and stay dead forever, than endure such shame.

I don't know what's going to become of you, child, but I do
hope you'll never have reason to hate things and people the way
I have.

Then — when this trouble came, and lately when it's seemed
pretty doubtful — I got to hating the whole world until I was
just as sick from that as this other trouble. It was just like a
poison that was eating me, burning me on the inside. My hate
hurt clear up in my throat. I hope you'll never know what that
kind of hate feels like.

'God! — don't I know?' muttered Dinny. 'You poor
little thing!'

Well — yesterday a queer thing happened. Part of it was
awful, and I hope you won't think less of me. Martha came and
wanted to read the Bible to me, and I wouldn't let her. She put
it under my pillow then, and went away. I was so angry at her
and it that I tore it up. Maybe you'll be shocked. It was too
bad, and I'm sorry. But I tore it up because it was full of what
Martha called 'precious promises' — and look what had happened to *me!* This was God's Book, and He had been mean to
me. So I tore up His Book. I'm ashamed to tell you this, but it
gave me a kind of terrible pleasure to do it — a kind of hot joy
that I used to think the Devil had when I was a little girl and
believed there was a Devil.... You don't believe there's a Devil,
do you, child? I'm thinking of you as a little girl, now, about
the size I was when they used to frighten us at revival meetings.
I hope you're not living with ignorant people who believe in
hell and devils. Surely you've a right to a little better raising
than that. I couldn't bear it if I knew you were that poor and
degraded.

I quit tearing at the Bible only when my hands were so tired
I couldn't move a finger. Pretty soon I fell asleep. Father
found the awful mess I had made and cleaned it up before anyone else saw. But there was a little piece left. The next time I
was alone I read what it said, and it seemed so different, maybe
because it was all there was left.

It seemed to be intended for me. Maybe it won't mean just
the same thing to you, because you're not all full of poison and

hate and mean feelings toward almost everybody and everything, the way I was. At least I hope you're not, for it's dreadful and worse than any sickness. It really *is* a sickness!

This little piece that I read wasn't like religion at all. I hated religion. You did something wrong, and had to go crawling on your hands and knees to be forgiven for it. You had to cry and beg and whine like a dog. But this wasn't like that. It wasn't anything to sniffle about the way they have to do in church when they are sorry for hating people who have wronged them. I always despised whiners. They said in church that God wanted you to whine, for He liked to hear sniffles from scared people. So I despised Him for that. He wasn't my sort.

Dinny put down the letter, rubbed his tired eyes, and shook his head. His mother's reminiscences were his own. Again he felt that strange kinship between himself and this unhappy girl who had given him birth. Her blood coursed through his veins. Her queries were his. His criticisms were hers. It was in the blood-stream! His temperament was a biologic inevitability. You grew figs on fig-trees. You grew thorns on thistles. Didn't you? Well — there you are, then! Nothing to be done about it! Is there?

Julia had despised whiners. God liked whiners. 'The sacrifices of God are a broken spirit.' God liked broken spirits; liked to hear 'em wail; liked to see 'em wring their hands, and pour ashes on themselves. That had been his own chief objection to the whole structure of traditional theology. He wanted to be a man. He wanted to stand upright and face the sun. God wanted him to grovel like a cowed animal. Dinny knew now how he'd come by his passionate aversion to such self-abasing, personality-destroying, soul-defiling ignorance! He wanted to reach across the Border and clasp the hand of this fearless, unfettered spirit. He was proud of his Julia. His eyes were wet with emotion.

This little piece of religion that I had left, lying under my hand as if it was meant for me, doesn't whine at all. It doesn't ask you to whimper for mercy.

It's just a business proposition same as if you owed a thousand dollars to Mr. Smith, and ten other people owed you a hundred dollars apiece, and Mr. Smith said, 'Pay me that thousand dollars,' and you said, 'I can't — with all these people owing me.'

And Mr. Smith said, 'I don't need the money so much, but I like you and want to be friends with you, and as long as you are owing me you'll be keeping away from me for fear I'll ask you for it and make you ashamed. And it won't do any good for me to tell you just to keep the money and forget it, because that would make you ashamed, too, and you would always feel in debt. So — I'll make you a proposition. If you will cancel all the debts of these people who owe you, and are afraid to face you, so that they can afford to cancel the debts of the people who owe them, I'll call it square with you. Then we can all be good neighbors again, and nobody will be afraid of anyone else, or shy, or ashamed.'

This all sounds so much more sensible to me, dear, than the way they talk about it at the meetings. It's just as if God wanted us to do business with Him about these things that have kept us strangers.

Maybe this will sound silly to you, but I closed my eyes and said, down inside myself where there seemed a little spot that brightened up, 'Please forget that I tore up Your Book, and help me to forget it too, for it makes me very sorry to remember.' And God said, speaking from down inside of me, just as plainly as anything I ever heard, 'Will you forgive your father for drinking up the opportunities you might have had, and Susan for refusing ever to come into your room on account of the desk, and the boys for being rude, and Martha for not wanting you to have any fun?'

And I said, 'Yes — I will.'

And then He said, 'Will you forget everything they ever did that has made you disappointed and sorry — just as I'm going to forget everything you've done to disappoint and sadden Me?'

And I said, 'Yes — I will.'

Of course I can't expect you to understand the strange feeling that came over me, but it wasn't like anything else that ever happened. Please don't think I'm telling you something I dreamed, I was quite wide awake. The queer thing that happened was just as if some wonderful doctor who knew how to cure any disease instantly had given me a powerful medicine that cleared out all the poison! I felt all *clean* and *new!* ... Then I found myself smiling, and I laughed. And — this was because I am so weak, I suppose — I cried a good deal; but not for being unhappy or afraid or ashamed. Maybe I can't explain this very well, but I felt proud, just as if I had been promoted or had won a great prize, or had discovered I was a princess or something!

It's awfully hard to try to make this sound the way it actually was. For I don't know whether I'm talking to a little girl with a doll in her hand, or a big boy old enough to go to college, but this thing that I've got is a sort of *power!*

That's the best I can do to explain it. When you get it, you'll know. I want you to have it, for there's no other feeling like it. I believe that if I could get well, now, I could do almost anything!

It's great to be able to talk to God, now, any time you want to, and say anything you like, and know that you're fast friends. It would be wonderful to get well, and see Zandy again; but if I don't, I'll see God exactly as He is; and I'm not afraid.

I thought about it nearly all night — and kept talking to Him, and He would answer me. Please don't think I'm out of my head. I'm awfully tired. That's what makes the writing so bad. And I said I was dreadfully sorry I had misunderstood Him so, and he said, 'Well — Hiram and Elmer misunderstand *you*. They think you consider yourself too nice to have anything to do with them. And Susan and Greta think the same thing, that you're above talking to them about their little troubles.'

This morning Susan came to the door and looked at me. She seemed so shy and scared, as if she had never seen me before, and I motioned to her to come in, and she sat down on the little chair by the bed. And it was just about as easy as it had been, last night, when God and I made up. I just reached out my hand and rubbed my fingers over Susan's face, softly. It was the first time I'd intentionally touched her for years, and we almost never had anything to say to each other, not for years and years. And Susan slipped down on her knees by the bed, and put her arms around me, and we both cried, but I was happy, and I loved Susan for the first time in my life.... Dear Child — the poison is all out of me now. Of course, I'm too sick of the other trouble to get well — but it doesn't really matter. I'm happy. I love the boys, too, and I'm going to let them know. And poor father — he does feel so badly about everything.

Dinny put down the letter, and paced the room, unable to endure another line of it. Of course, poor Julia was laboring under intense emotion, terrific neural strain. A great deal of her experience could be charged to an hallucination easily explained. Naturally, the whole family would be wrought up. Susan would have been a beast to remain cold and aloof under the pitiful little tender of affection. Nobody was normal at the time.... But — God! — suppose such relief and release were real! Suppose that for the mere act of unloading one's memory of all the bitter hatreds and cankered grudges, one might feel free to lift one's eyes and smile into the face of God — as dear Julia had — and be cleared of all the 'poison!'

Suddenly there came a definite surge of such painful wistfulness to lay hold upon some strength beyond his own as had never possessed him — not even for the instant when Angela's choir, bursting forth with an exultant 'Unfold! Unfold!! Unfold!!!' had tugged at his soul — not even in that brief, boyish quest of The Mystery when he had sat in church with the Timmy Fagans.

In those fleeting experiences Dinny had glimpsed the possibility, resident in him, for rapture and radiance. For these ecstatic instants, the Light had broken through, certifying to two facts: there was a Light, and he possessed the spiritual retina to see it. The shutter clicked — and for that one little split-second the Light poured in; but, afterwards, the darkness settled again.

Maybe Julia had found the way to a permanent possession of that spiritual illumination which, rarely, he had sensed with a brief ecstasy that stirred him to the depths, and promptly left him cold.

If Julia had found it, and in such high degree that she was undaunted even by the impending tragedy that stared into her girlish face, might he hope to capture that strange magic for himself? Why not? They were the same sort of people; weren't they? Julia and he were kin. Her queries were his queries. They had shared much the same dilemmas of frustration, disillusion, disappointment. They had shared the same hot hate of a world that had consistently let them down…. Julia had never 'belonged,' but, at last, *she had 'belonged'*!

* * * * * *

Slumping down in his chair, taut with the emotional tension of the past half-dozen hours, Dinny covered his face with his outspread hands, and muttered, half aloud:

'I'll give it a trial!… God! — I wonder if I'm losing my mind…. I'm going to make the experiment, and see what comes of it.'

He reached for the crumpled scrap of paper, and sat staring at the well-remembered words which he had heard Uncle Miles read, monotonously, scores of times, words now highly charged with energy. He felt himself studying a formula in Physics. Again Dinny returned to his mood of deep meditation.

God! — suppose the thing were real!… But, if it was real, why didn't more people know about it? If there was anything to it, surely the religious would have practiced it. A man who possessed this dynamic joy that Julia had found — why, you could spot him at a thousand yards by the light in his eyes!

That was the appalling obstacle in the way of Dinny's confident belief in the reality of the mysterious 'lifting power' that had caught Julia up, and held her, in an hour of crisis.

Would she have discovered it, at all, had she been well, mentally sound, physically fit? According to her own documented testimony, she was upset to the point of having to plead with her child for belief in her sanity. Was she any too sure of it, herself?

Sane people had no capacity for permanently possessing

this uncanny spiritual strength. They had brief experiences of ecstasy. He had had them. Doubtless everyone, according to his temperament, had felt these occasional tugs from Otherwhere. Perhaps every inquisitive person nourished the vague dream of making lasting connections with this strange energy of exultation. That's what the religious were out after. They wanted to 'fix' their idealisms on the highly sensitized plate, and make them permanent... But — with what success?

Dinny found himself recalling instance after instance, in the little churches he had known as a growing boy, when the activities of a congregation of alleged Christians seemed actually to interfere with the personal peace of the individuals thus brought together. Not only did their religion fail to illumine them: it quite definitely got in the way of their self-confessed aspirations.

He remembered his own grinning, as a lad, over the celebrated rumpus that had rent Uncle Miles's little church at Zanesdale. Mrs. Bilger wanted the Sunday School chairs for the Eastern Star banquet on the same night that Lida Kronk had promised them to the Modern Woodmen of which her Claude was the Chief Axe-Swinger, or whatever it was. And before they had done with the acute phase of the battle, not only was the whole congregation lined up in two hostile camps, but the town itself was involved. Uncle Miles had raced frantically back and forth across No Man's Land, pleading for arbitration, meanwhile being himself potted from both sides. Even as a small boy in short pants, Dinny had considered the affair a howling farce.

Now — in the light of what Julia said she had found, Dinny knew that the vulgar and noisy controversy over the church chairs hadn't been funny, at all. The whole matter had been tragic beyond the telling. Was it not just such small-minded jealousies and stupid little exhibitions of egotism brazenly flaunted by persons conspicuous in the business affairs of country and village churches that had made the general public laugh the whole institution to scorn?

Surely, thought Dinny, he had done his bit toward making such *gaucheries* ridiculous. Conventional religion, in the custody of the typical church of his own acquaintance, was not merely banal, farcical, impotent. By Gad — that sort of thing was definitely blocking our evolution! It was shutting off even such fugitive glimpses of the Light as a man might find for himself if left to his own devices as an untaught pagan!

Of course, reflected Dinny, here and there, even in the stifling antagonisms forever on display in Uncle Miles's little churches, a rare spirit contrived somehow to grow.

There flashed across his mental screen the picture of 'old man' Houk. They never referred to him in any other way: 'old man' Houk, who kept the light hardware and notion store near their church on the edge of Fort Wayne. There was a peculiar light in the old fellow's eyes. There was the quality of thermo-dynamics in his smile. How good God was to him, 'old man' Houk was always saying in that gentle voice of his. How 'blest' he had been. And sometimes the people laughed a bit when they talked about 'old man' Houk's gratitude, for if ever anybody had his nose to the grindstone with nothing tangible to show for it, Houk won the prize. The two girls had married early, one bringing a worthless husband home to live; the other had abandoned hers, returning with three small children. As for the boy, he was no end lazy, impudent, and always in trouble. But 'old man' Houk had something!... However — he may not have been quite all there. Even Uncle Miles had said that the old chap had a loose screw.

Now the question arose, in Dinny's mind; was 'old man' Houk a bit unhooked mentally, or had he managed to 'lay hold' on the energy that Julia had found? Were these occasional mystics inspired or demented?

Pursuing his recollections of Uncle Miles's ugly little churches that seemed bent on nothing but trivial expedients to pay their insignificant bills, in the course of which silly endeavors — rummage sales, ice-cream socials, and shockingly dull home-talent plays — they generally stirred up fresh rows, Dinny's honesty forced him to concede that you really couldn't expect much fineness to develop in the weedy Zanesdales and Ungers, where there was nothing to think about but one's treadmill and the callosities worn thick and hard by one's ill-fitting harness. It wasn't quite fair to judge religion, as an institution, by what one observed of it in Zanesdale.

But then — there was Magnolia! Magnolia had been the mecca for a religious cult whose constituency in that zone numbered well into six figures, a cult that regarded its neighbors with sour pity. Had not smug and pious little Magnolia excoriated and discharged the only Christ-like personality on her staff — the only man in the whole outfit who had had the valor to stand up and say that the Master he followed was an uncompromising apostle of peace?

Dinny remembered how they all used to laugh over the perennial feud between the factions that backed Professor Strickler, who taught Hebrew, and Professor Munger, who taught Homiletics, each of whom had been trying for years to discredit the other in the opinion of the parsons over a region five hundred miles in diameter.

But here, again, fairness demanded that Dinny take account of all the facts in the case. Magnolia, after all, was but a little tea-pot. You couldn't appraise religion at large by the disgusting envies that stood out awkwardly, like sore thumbs, interfering with everything the college and seminary aspired to do.

Who were Professors Strickler and Munger — for all their unctuous mouthings and frock-coated pomposities — but grown-up farmer lads, innocent of any experience whatsoever in an outer world of urbanity and culture? Dinny knew their story. Having graduated from the seminary, they had been fortunate enough to marry the daughters of well-to-do lay members of the Board. After a few years of inconspicuous paddling about in the mud and dust of small-town parishes, their fathers-in-law had engineered them into seminary chairs (rocking-chairs), where, between venomous thrusts at one another, they had taught the young fry what they ought to know about the Old Testament in the original, and the theory of preaching the gospel of peace and salvation. Admittedly, that was pretty bad; but you mustn't judge all institutionalized religion by the performances of fat and furtive little Stricklers or lean and malicious Mungers.

No — to be decently fair, you had to look at The Thing higher up. But what results did you get from such investigation? What spirit had actuated the organization of the greater sects in Christendom? What ghost had haunted the passionate conclaves in which reformations, reappraisals, and re-evaluations had taken wing? Surely not the Holy Ghost! Which one of them had walked out of a Mother Church because it wanted a better chance to believe and exemplify the theory of whole-hearted forgiveness, tolerance, sympathy, and 'second-mile-ish-ness,' which had constituted the vary solar plexus of the Galilean gospel? Stand 'em up in a long row and demand their reply to this question, and see what you get: 'Do you believe in the celestial commerce whereby you, yourselves, come into the possession of permanent power and radiance, in exact proportion to your ability to condone and explain and forget other people's " trespasses"?'

And yet — here stood this Ancient Thing.... By Gad — everything else in the world, by comparison of age, reeked of fresh paint, green lumber, hot rivets, and perspiration. It had outlived every other institution on earth, despite the fact that its early death had been forecast by the wiseacres of each generation for nearly two millennia. A new day had come. The arm-wavers were saying that more had happened in the past twenty years than in the preceding five thousand. Radical changes were tearing down yesterday's customs, mores, laws, dogmas. Religion was on its last legs. But was it? Not so you could notice it. The Thing had as much vitality as ever.

What, actually, did it stand for? You had to explain its enduring life somehow, didn't you? Had it arrived at this apparent guarantee of perpetuity by virtue of its high achievement in promoting the world's peace? — Nonsense. It had been a notorious fighter.... Had it offered notable service in encouraging scientific progress? — Ha! ha! Now you tell one!... Had Rome shown much inclination to walk a second mile? Had Calvinism presented the other cheek? Had Wesleyanism handed over its cloak when sued for its coat? Had the Anglicans agreed quickly with their adversaries, 'whilst in the way with them?'... Hosts of them were unquestionably excellent people, the majority wanting to improve themselves; occasional individuals, in all the cults and sects, contriving to 'lay hold'; but, considered as institutions — considered as An Institution — exactly what did it stand for? How, in the face of all the dismaying facts, had it earned its evident immortality?

It had always done a bit of philanthropy, yes; but so had the 'unredeemed,' for that matter. Its sporadic efforts at charity were always being outranked in volume and administrative acumen by secular agencies. It had always pretended to educate, but was without caste in the opinion of high-powered schools. Sometimes the parsons made a great to-do about the imposing array of North American Universities, all of which had been founded by preachers, and backed by churches. Even so, at the beginning; but such of these institutions as had actually won high recognition had long since lost their original religious affiliation.

In short — what was religion good for? What did the Ancient Thing stand for? What made it last? Dinny thought he knew. Organized religion stood for the people's *yearning!* It was a costly monument to the people's *wistfulness!* All the people, considered as individuals, felt occasional little clicks of the camera shutter: the Light poured in on them for an instant: they kept hoping to make these fleeting surges of ineffable luminosity permanent, good for all weathers!

But, in the face of this testimony of religion — intolerant, irascible, pig-headed, hair-triggered — was it really worth the effort for a person so materialistic, so critical, so unsentimental as himself, to hope that he might find the spiritual dynamics which had come to the rescue of his disappointed and embittered girl-mother?

Dinny looked at his watch. It was four o'clock. He had exhausted the last tag-end of his mental resources. Any further thought about these matters, in his present condition of fatigue, would be merely exasperating. He threw off his clothes, snapped out the light, and slept.

* * * * * *

Street noises roused him at nine from a deep sleep, and he sat up dully trying to remember where he had left off. There was an odd sensation that the day promised to be eventful, though in what manner Dinny had no definite idea. The best he could make of it was a nervous tension of expectancy, anticipation, novelty, somewhat as he had felt when he awoke on the day he had sailed to England, and on the day Joan was to arrive. Something was going to happen.

Tuning himself up with a cold shower and ten minutes of vigorous calisthenics, he dressed carefully and walked over to The Brevoort for breakfast. There were several important things he had planned yesterday to do today. He must go up to the *Hallelujah* office for a bit of conference, for one thing.

On his homeward voyage, Dinny had looked forward to this new position with interest; hardly with pleasure, for it had been difficult to feel quite satisfied over it while haunted with the memory of the hurt look in Joan's eyes. And even now that she had run away, and didn't belong to him any more, and was probably pacing the deck of the *Vulcania*, at this very moment, fondly arm in arm with Tommy Forsythe, Dinny still sensed a feeling of unrest and dissatisfaction over the whole *Hallelujah* business, heartily wishing he had never gone in for it. Perhaps tomorrow would be soon enough to report there.

He had planned also to go uptown and look at a few bachelor apartments somewhere in the west eighties, but there was really no hurry about it.

Well — then — what *was* the important thing he had on his mind? — this something that had to be done without delay.

Dinny never wearied of analyzing his own mental processes. He had learned that it was no longer considered scientific to speak of one's 'subconscious mind.' The new Psychology said there wasn't any such thing. 'Subconscious mind' was as obsolete as 'Soul.'

But you could call it what you liked, or refuse to call it at all; the fact remained that two distinct mental processes could be carrying on at the same time in one individual's head. Dinny often marveled at this queer phenomenon. Here he was, this morning, rumpling his hair with his fingers and trying to remember just what it was that so urgently demanded his attention, and, all the time he was wondering, his subconscious mind — which was mere nonsense, of course; for he didn't have a subconscious mind, there being no such organ now recognized by science — was quite certain that he would return promptly to his room and attempt an experiment based on Julia's letter.

While he was drinking his second cup of coffee, Dinny rather reluctantly admitted to his subconscious mind — which he didn't have — that such had been his intention from the moment he had wakened, an hour ago, and that if it would just have the decent courtesy to wait until he had finished his breakfast, he would do as he had planned to do, anyhow, without benefit of such counsel. In these occasional interior conferences, Dinny's subconscious mind always seemed much older and more mature than the rest of him, which he was inclined to resent. There was something a bit too paternal and hortatory and all-wise in the advice offered from that quarter.

This morning, the distinct identity of his two minds seemed more clearly defined than ever in his experience. Perhaps he had been thinking about that one matter, bringing both his conscious and subconscious minds to bear on it, until they had temporarily lost their capacity for integration, like the green leaves on Julia's maple tree that she had stared into twins — one blue, one yellow. It was almost as if he, himself, were facing a battle with a very mature and omniscient ghost who, normally benign and approximately acquiescent, had suddenly decided to say: 'Yes — you will!... And I'll see to it that you do!'

Dinny was determined, however, not to give in too promptly. On his way back to his rooms he decided not to take another look at the gripping letter until he had done at least one 'Green Cheese' essay. He always tried to keep about three weeks ahead of the release date, and was now four days behind his schedule, due to indolence on shipboard.

Taking every advantage of current and seasonal topics, Dinny's theme for this morning's composition would relate somehow to the national observance of Columbus Day. He had scribbled a few rough notes, yesterday; nothing of value, however. All he had was:

'Lookit, Gramp!... They got the flags out again!... Some festival or other.'

'That doesn't mean anything, Luna. The Ku Klux have terrified them into buying flags. They're flying almost every day now. Hadn't you noticed?'

'Yes — but the Knights of Columbus have run one up on their buildings.'

'Humph! — it must be something else, then. What happened on October twelfth, Luna? You wouldn't be likely to know, would you?'

Dinny typed this much, and, thrusting his hands deep in his coat pockets, appraised it with a critical eye. What was the good of it? Many people would grin, no doubt. Some of them would be sore. All of them would again be made aware of the widening rift between the 'One Hundred Per Cent Americans' and the field, embracing other pigments, other creeds, other nativities, than the increasing organization of sheeted patriots who had bought their right to hate their neighbors for Ten Dollars and the price of a white cotton disguise.

He drew the paper out of the machine, and crumpled it in his fist. Why not try to do the thing constructively once. Surely the readers of his 'Green Cheese' column would forgive him a wee digression from his habitual spoofing, scoffing cynicism. They might even enjoy just a tough of sincerity; not too sentimental, of course: that would spoil everything.

Why not try it? It would be in line with the experiment he hoped he was going to make, wouldn't it?

Dinny inserted a fresh page into the typewriter, and wrote the opening phrase which always distinguished his feature article.

'Lookit, Gramp!'

And then he sat for full five minutes, absently toying with the keys, utterly unable to proceed.

But — I can't do anything like this, reflected Dinny. If there's any substantial fact in what Julia says, there are a few things you have to do first before you can take an affirmative position. You've got to 'un-bitter' yourself.

He grinned, rather foolishly.

'Very well, Mr. Smith,' he soliloquized, half aloud, 'we'll say I've owed you a lot of money; and Zandy Craig, and gloomy old Aunt Martha, and the Reverend Miles Brumm, and Spike Davis, and Major Clemens, M.D., and Barney Vaughn, and Orville Kling, and — and Tommy Forsythe — owe me. And you're prepared to call it square, and sweeten me up, if I stop despising these other people.... All right, sir, I'll take you up!' Dinny made a sweeping gesture of dismissal to the imaginary company of his enemies.

'I'll forgive the outfit at one swoop. Or, if you'd rather, I'll forgive 'em one at a time. Here they go. I'll forgive Uncle Miles, first — the damned old embezzler.'

Suddenly the sardonic grin left Dinny's face, and a wave of self-disgust swept him. What a cad! — to let his chronic cynicism defile a situation that had been brought about by a farewell message from the dear girl who had died to give him his life!

There would be no more of this vulgar sacrilege, he could promise himself that much. He would give up all attempts to do the impossible thing, of course. It was not for people of his type. He had carried his load of aversions too long. It had grown fast to him. But, at least, he could honor Julia's faith by refusing to make a travesty of it!

That much settled, then, Dinny lighted his pipe, and drew up to his machine, quite confident that he had shaken off this strange temporary psychosis that had been playing the devil with his thoughts. The page wasn't quite straight, and he made himself a great deal of bother adjusting it. The machine needed a drop of oil, and it took quite a while to find it. The ventilation in the room wasn't very good, and he opened both windows. Having sat down again, ready now to go at his task in earnest, he felt a draft and got up to close one window partly. His coat cramped him, and he took it off.

And then — from far in the depths of himself, where his subconscious mind might have been, had he had one — there welled up a solid, substantial, mature thought, as definite as if it were actually phrased in a spoken command: 'You may as well proceed with the thing you are going to do. You're wasting your time. You've lost your knack at Green Cheese. There'll never be any more; not from you. You've gone into this liberty-quest too far to back up! Admit you're beaten — and see what you can make of the other thing.'

Dinny rose, with a sigh, went to his mother's desk, and sat for a half-hour with his elbows on the writing-table, his head in his hands.

Rousing, at length, with an air of determination, he went to the telephone, called a familiar number, and was almost startled by what he found himself saying.

'*Hallelujah*?... Mr. Brumm speaking.... Is Johnny Keaton there?... Please.... Johnny?... Dinny Brumm.... Very good. How are you?... I'd rather expected to be in, today, but I've just had word that I'm required to make a business trip West. May be all of a couple o' weeks. Wish you'd carry on without any coöperation from me until you hear from me.... That's fine.... And Johnny — how would you like to do my Green Cheese stuff for a while. You can, you know. Better than I.... If you like it, and can get away with it so everybody's satisfied, it'll be a nice thing for you. I'm tired of it. And I may have to do quite a little traveling for a few weeks. Might even have to go to Europe. You take over all the editorial responsibility up there until you see me again.... No — this is something sudden; more or less personal business; emergency stuff.... Thanks, Johnny. I'll write you more in detail.... Yes — tonight; if I can get a reservation. Just now learned that I had to go.... Goodbye.'

Dinny turned to his clothes-closet, reached to a high shelf and threw down the bags he had put away yesterday.

'There may be nothing in it,' he muttered, as he began peeling his clothes off their hangers and tossing them onto the bed, 'but I'm going to give it an honest work-out.... God! — if the thing should be true!'

CHAPTER XVI

'I'M A-GOIN' out that way myself soon as this here gol-darned loafer changes my oil,' volunteered the middle-aged farmer, who had taken his foot off the hub and sidled up to help answer the query about transportation to Oak Grove. 'Yuh c'n come along, if yuh don't object t' ridin' with a hawg.'

'Bet you'd raise hell if anybody else called yuh thet, Jase,' drawled a voice that apparently belonged to the pair of legs protruding from beneath the truck's engine.

Jase spat, nonchalantly, grinned, and rubbed a stubbly chin; then winked companionably.

'If yuh ever wants t' take one o' them slow movin' pitchers,' he advised, elaborating a confidential air, 'yuh can't do better 'n t' come t' Larwill. These here fellers in Lije Hinebaugh's garage has been a-practicin' till they's purty good.'

'Thanks for the offer of a lift. I'm wanting to go out and see my Uncle Miles Brumm. That's my name, too — Brumm.'

The obliging farmer left off his bantering attitude, stared hard from under his shaggy brows, and rubbed his palm on his blue denim pant-leg before presenting it.

'Yer Julia's boy, mebby?'

'Yes. Did you know her?'

'Reckon I did. My name's Schrofe. We was neighbors like. She taught our school fer a winter — er a part of it. You ain't never been out here afore?'

'Once,' said Dinny, shoving his bags out of the way, as the legs began to wriggle out from under the engine, followed by a large pan of spent oil. 'I was about seven. Aunt Greta was being married. We were here only for a day. How long have my Uncle Miles and Aunt Martha

lived up here? I'm afraid I had almost lost track of them,
for a while.'

'Well — it's about two years, come Christmas. I've
owned th' little place fer quite a spell. Angela writ a-askin'
could her folks come back 'n' live there. 'Pears like th' ol'
man 'd had a stroke, er somethin'.'

'How's he now?'

'Oh — he gits about.'

'And Aunt Martha?'

'She's well as common. Makes a little garden, 'n' that.
Chickens, 'n' that... Yuh ain't seen 'em lately?'

Dinny shook his head, waiving the opportunity to explain.

'Guess we c'n go now,' said Jase, pulling out a fat roll
of soiled money. 'Here's yer filthy lucre, Lije. I'll be
gol-darned if that ain't what it is. Time a dollar bill's
made a dozen trips t' one these here little garages ——'

'We don't have no trouble a-gettin' people t' take 'em,'
drawled Lije. 'Better have an understandin' with this
feller, Mr. Brumm, afore yuh start north, er he'll charge
yuh th' price of his dang truck fer th' ride.'

'Any time I'd take a dime offen Julia Miller's boy ——'
said Jase, soberly. 'Climb in, won't yuh, and we'll go down
t' th' express office fer that Berkshire shoat. Bought 'er last
week over at th' fair in Wayne. Wasn't fixed t' take 'er
home with me. Had th' family along — pap 'n' th' girls.
Ain't got none o' my own. I'm a old batch.'

They were rattling down the dusty street toward the
railroad station, Jason waving a hand to the hicks idling in
front of the implement store.

'I s'pose yer married, this good while, eh?' he shouted.

'No,' replied Dinny, adding, 'The only girl I wanted
wouldn't have me.'

Jason made a careful job of backing the truck up to the
station platform, turned off his engine, and climbed down.

'Same as me,' he said, grinning mysteriously. 'The gal
was yer maw.'

There was a little surge of resentment in Dinny's mind over the impudence of this untutored old yokel. He didn't like the idea of Julia's having been admired to this extent by a person so far beneath her. What right did this fellow have to cherish the memory of Julia?

The rough wooden crate scraped into the truck with a screech accompanied by the pig's shrill squeal of alarm. Jason climbed up, started the rackety engine, which added to the pig's consternation, and they rumbled through the village, and out upon the highway, driving at a snail's pace.

'This damn pig cost four hundred and twenty-five dollars,' explained Jason, ''n' she's got t' be handled with care. I spect yer quite anxious fer t' git up there, too, seein' it's been so long since yuh heared from 'em.'

'I hadn't supposed pigs were so expensive,' commented Dinny, hoping to distract attention from his obvious lack of knowledge about his relatives. 'How much is pork worth now?' He tried to make the query sound as if he had at least a passing interest in such matters.

Jason guffawed loudly.

'Well — pork ain't a-bringin' much, just now; but this here shoat ain't pork, 'n' when she has pigs, 'bout a year f'm now, they ain't a-goin' t' be pork, neither. I got a Berkshire boar over t' our place that I'd like fer t' show yuh. By Golly — nobody's ever called that feller pork. Say — if yuh was t' slit that there big boy's belly up intuh bacon, I guess it 'd cost yuh 'bout fifty dollars a slice. It's easy fer t' see yuh ain't no farmer.'

Dinny listened with a pretense of interest, but conscious of an uncomfortable irritation over the fact that his Julia, once upon a time, had been the object of this crude old chap's attentions. Somehow it pushed Julia farther away from him, even if she had been unaware of this devotion. This pig-fancier had unwittingly thrust his rough, unrefined bulk between him and the idealistic image of his mother.

'I've saw pieces o' yourn in th' papers,' Jason went on, grinning broadly. 'Seen 'em in *Th' Tribune*, when I've went t' Chicago. Our papers 'round here don't seem t' take t' 'em like. I brung a couple o' 'em home once f'm Chicago, 'n' I thought pap 'd laugh hisself t' death. Pap says, "Gol-darned if that ol' feller in th' moon ain't about right." I mind one time yuh writ a piece 'bout them flossy automobiles a-splashin' mud on people 'long th' sidewalk when there wasn't nothin' in th' car but a poodle dog a-ridin' by hisself in th' back seat. Yuh oughta heared pap holler 'n' laugh. He likes 't when yuh git 't on 'em, 'specially th' tony folks. Pap's always a-braggin' 'bout yuh, 'cause yer Julia's boy, 'n' he set such store by her. He says, "Gol-darned if Julia's boy ain't a sharp feller that they's got t' leave alone, fer he's got a mean tongue, 'n' enough pizen in him t' start a bran' new hell." '

'Was that what he said — "poison"?'

'Yeah... 'Course pap was only a-foolin'. He likes yer pieces. Pap didn't mean 't harmful. It was just a joke, 'n' that.'

'It's no joke with me, Mr. Schrofe.' Dinny was surprised to find himself saying this. He had blurted it out, impulsively. Now he would have to explain, best he could. 'Your father's quite right. And he meant what he said as a friendly joke. I know that. But — there's been too much poison in me, and it's not good for me. I don't mind telling you that I'm taking a little treatment for it.'

'Pills — 'n' that?' inquired Jason, interestedly.

'The equivalent of pills — yes. I'm going to look up a few of the people I've had occasion to despise, and see if I can't come to terms with them. Perhaps that will do the trick. Just confidentially — I haven't seen my uncle and aunt for many years; not since I started away to college.'

'Forgot 'em — mebby?'

No — Dinny hadn't exactly forgotten them. It was not easy to explain, but he had gone away to school, and then the war had come along, and then he had gone East, and always his time and mind had been occupied.

'Yeah — I reckon,' agreed Jason, indulgently. 'But I bet there's more to 't than that. We always thought Preacher Brumm was a kind o' slippery ol' cuss. Mebby he done somethin'. As fer Martha, she prob'ly wouldn't a-done nothin', a-bein' what she is, so pious 'n' that.'

'I thought it would be good for me to see them again.'

'Yeah — that's proper — 'n' let bygones be bygones, eh?'

'Exactly.'

'Well — that's proper like, if yuh can do 't. Pap's always a-sayin', "Fergive 'n' fergit, 'n' like th' ol' Indian says, 'Always remember!'"'

Dinny indulged in the first hearty, spontaneous laugh he had had for several days.

'That's the only brand of forgiveness I've ever carried in stock, I'm afraid.'

'Well — there's only just one feller in th' world I ain't never a-goin t' feel right about, I guess. They's lots o' people what I don't care fer, not special, but this here feller I hate. I ain't never got over 't. Long time ago, come winter, 'n' nothin' much t' do, nights, but set 'n' think, I used fer t' do a little plannin' how I c'd go out West where he lived, 'n' stick a knife in him.'

'I don't suppose I could guess his name,' ventured Dinny, half-suspecting Jason would not be averse to a confidential chat on the subject.

'Reckon yuh could. That's th' feller, all right. He prob'ly never done nothin' fer t' help yuh. Gol-darned selfish brute! By Golly — I'd like t' kill him!'

'It's been a sore spot with me, too, Mr. Schrofe, though I think it's only fair to say that he made an honest effort to show an interest in me. I suppose it was my own fault that his generosity was unrewarded. I didn't care to take anything from him. However ——'

'By Golly — I honor yuh fer 't. So'll pap.' Jason idled the truck to a stop on the grassy roadside, and pointed across the highway to a barbed-wire gate fronting the

dense woods. 'Mebby yuh'd like t' see th' ol' path. Let's
git out, 'n' I'll show yuh.'

They ambled across the road, and Jason hooked an
elbow over the top rail of the gate.

'Julia used fer t' leave th' road, right here, 'n' take that
there path through th' timber, when she was a-teachin'
th' Schrofe school. It used fer t' b'long t' ol' Squire Craig,
damned ol' hawg.' Jason drew a bunch of keys from his
pocket and unlocked the gate.

'Apparently it belongs to you now,' observed Dinny, as
they entered the woods.

'Yeah — I bought 't. Didn't rightly have no use fer 't,
er nothin', but ol' Craig was purty hard up afore he died,
'n' was willin' t' sell.'

Jason stooped and picked up a dead branch that had
fallen across the almost obliterated trail.

'Right along here she come, ev'ry day.'

Dinny felt sobered in the chilly shade. Hardly conscious
of his act, he removed his hat. His resentment over Jason's
attitude toward Julia was quite gone now.

'Yeah — yer Julia's boy, all right,' muttered Jason,
candidly studying Dinny's face. 'That there little point
where yer hair sort o' grows down like, right in th' middle.'

'You have asked me several personal questions today,
Mr. Schrofe,' said Dinny, seating himself by Jason on a
fallen log beside the grassy path. 'Would you object to
my asking you one?'

Jason's eyes crinkled with understanding.

'Yeah — I guess that's the reason I bought 't. That's
what yuh was a-goin' t' ask, eh? I kep' 't secret from pap
fer awhile. But when he found out I'd bought 't, he said,
"Glad yuh done 't, Jase. No use fer ev'ry Tom, Dick, 'n'
Harry to be a-trampin' through them woods."'

Dinny impulsively laid a hand on Jason's knee.

'Julia would have appreciated it, I know,' he said, a bit
unsteadily. There recurred to him certain fragments of
adroitly crafted ridicule he had hurled at the insensitive-

ness and general stupidity of the hicks and yokels who composed so large a percentage of America's population. What could you expect, he had often queried, of people who never went anywhere, never saw anything, never read anything? What did a ballot amount to in their hands? What did they know about the type of government that speeds the spread of culture?

Here was a hick, sitting beside him on this log. He talked like a hick, dressed like a hick, and was on the way back from a hick town with a pig in a crate. The hick was just now in the act of rummaging in his overall pockets, with clumsy fingers. His big brown thumb had a purplish-black discoloration at the root of the nail. Now he was bringing up in one hand a huge jack-knife and in the other a soggy plug of chewing tobacco. Typical hick! Cow-companion! Pig-comrade!... But he had bought a twenty-acre tract of second-growth timber that he didn't need or want, because there was the faint trail of a path through it that a neighbor girl had traveled on the way to her school, more than a quarter-century ago... Ignorant hicks! Country full of them! And what could you expect — Dinny had often inquired, superiorly, in the smart journals of sophistication — of a civilization so loaded down with dull dolts who spent their lives wading about through the ooze of the barnyard?

'Want a chew?' inquired Jason, hospitably.

'I've never been quite brave enough to do that,' grinned Dinny. 'I'll smoke a cigarette. Would you like one?' He tendered his gold-lined, monogrammed, silver case.

Jason chuckled quietly and shook his head.

The unexplained chuckle was just a bit disquieting. Dinny had long been of the opinion that yokels possessed no sense of humor, at all. Evidently this one had what passed for that, though it was odd what things amused him.

'I want to tell you a secret,' said Dinny.

For ten minutes, he reviewed the peculiar circumstances which had concealed Julia's letter from him, until now.

Jason's eyes interestedly followed Dinny's long, slim, well-kept hands as they brought out the leather wallet containing the precious legacy. He took the letter, rather timidly, and turned it over and over in his calloused palms, before handing it back.

'I'm going to read you some of it — all of it, if you wish. I believe Julia would want me to.'

'I'd like fer t' hear 't,' replied Jason, huskily. 'That is,' he added, admonishingly, 'if yuh don't think she'd mind — my knowin'. We was never close like, yuh unnerstand. It wasn't her, yuh unnerstand. It was just me. Julia never knowed, not proper like, 'bout my feelin's 'n' that.'

Dinny nodded, comprehendingly... Hicks and yokels couldn't be taught good taste, he had said, in the ultra-refined pages of *Hallelujah*. All these silly attempts to add anything to their culture were wasted time. You only made them restless, self-conscious, and ridiculous. They didn't have the *savoir-faire!*

'I know Julia would want you to share this secret, Mr. Schrofe,' reiterated Dinny, impressively. 'Some of it I found just a bit difficult to understand — but you're the kind of a person to see through it... Much more clearly,' he added, 'than I.'

* * * * * *

An hour had passed. They had been dimly conscious of dinner-bells. Through the latter part of Dinny's reading, Jason had made no further effort to conceal his emotion, trumpeting into his voluminous red bandanna with an abandon of restraint. It was as if Julia's tragedy had occurred only yesterday.

'I s'pose there must 'a' been somethin' to 't, like she says,' he remarked, thickly, as Dinny folded the letter. 'She c'd forgive 'em all, and get th' power like, 'n' that. But Julia wasn't just ordinary folks. You 'n' me, we couldn't. 'Tain't in us. Leastwise — 'tain't in me. D'yuh think yuh c'd do 't?'

'I don't know,' said Dinny, soberly. 'That's what I'm trying to find out.'

The wrinkles around Jason's eyes deepened as he candidly studied Dinny's face.

'Not meanin' any offense,' he ventured, 'but I sure w'd never 'a' picked yuh fer th' part. Yuh don't 'pear t' be th' kind o' feller that c'd make a go of 't.' He rubbed his knee and grinned, broadly, hinting that a new idea had struck him amusingly. 'Say — if yuh do get this here big power t' be free 'n' happy like, yuh'll sure have a hell of a time writin' them sassy pieces, won't yuh?'

Dinny stared, amazed at the old chap's quick deduction. 'You've touched a mighty live wire. I'll tell you something about that. It's a queer story.'

'No — I don't think that's s' gol-darned queer,' decided Jason, after Dinny had spent some time explaining how, since finding Julia's letter, he had been unable to get himself into the mood for composition of 'sassy pieces.'... 'Yer handlin' dynamite, by Golly! Julia said 't was a sort o' power, 'n' yuh c'd always count on what she spoke. She's put this stuff in yer hands, 'n' told yuh how t' shoot 't off. Gol-darned if yuh hadn't better do 't th' way she says.'

'You're joking. It's serious with me. I've ruined myself for my work. I've lost a taste for the only thing I know how to do.'

'Like hell I'm a-jokin'!' protested Jason. 'It's just like I said. Julia has handed yuh some high explosive! Yuh c'n either blow stumps with 't, 'n' clear yer ground so yuh c'n raise somethin' — er yuh c'n leave 't a-lyin' around, and take th' risk o' a-blowin' yer brains out... Ain't there nothin' else yuh c'n do b'sides make snoots at people in the papers 'n' that?'

This last was too much for Dinny, and he laughed, Jason joining, apparently well pleased that he had lifted his young friend from his gloomy mood.

'I learned to handle a chisel, a little, when I was a lad.'

said Dinny, reminiscently. 'I think I could make a living.'

"'Pears like th' more sensible thing t' do is t' carry on, now yuh've started out t' experiment with Julia's idear. Mebby, if yuh git that there power, what she talks about, yuh c'n write anything yer a-mind t'.'

'I'm afraid I've a long way to go.'

'I know I couldn't do 't. That there one feller'd always be in th' road. I'd fergive 'n' that — but I wouldn't stop a-thinkin'. What he done t' our little white stone, what pap 'n' me put up — I'd never fergit that, not in a thousand years.'

'What was that?' asked Dinny, sympathetically.

Jason busied himself for some time, breaking a handful of dead twigs into little pieces of equal length.

"'Twouldn't do yuh no good t' know 't. Yuh got a big job afore yuh, anyways. 'Twouldn't help yuh none — yer knowin'.'

'Very well — if you'd rather not tell me.'

'Julia's name really was Mueller, after all,' soliloquized Jason. 'We thought they'd made a mistake on th' big stone what he had made fer her. But this here letter looks as if he was right. We always thought 'twas Miller... Well — sh'll we go now?'

Jason had leaned forward to turn the ignition key, after they had boarded the truck, but, apparently impressed with a fresh idea, straightened to offer a further comment on Dinny's problem.

'Just now come t' me — somethin' mebby yuh hadn't thought about much. If yuh did grab on t' this here power o' Julia's t' be steady 'n' happy like, 'n' begun a-writin' afterwards, yuh c'd write about that! By Golly — I bet lots o' folks 'd read 't. Gol-darned if they wouldn't eat th' paper 'twas writ on, a-thinkin' 'twas medicine. 'Course — if yuh'd been a parson, always a-snifflin' 'bout fergiveness, 'n' that, 'n' a-gettin' paid fer bein' friendly with God like, that'd be differ'nt. Th' people'd all say, "Aw — hell!" — 'n' turn over t' th' funnies... But if ever a feller like yerself took t' a-writin' that he'd rech up 'n' got some power f'm on high what had cleaned out all his pizen 'n' made him happy 'n' that, fer keeps, by Golly, there'd be a million folks a-wantin' th' recipe fer 't!'

Jason felt satisfied with this long speech, finishing it with vigorous nods of his head and convincing smacks of his brown fist on the steering-wheel. He drove the truck back onto the road, and began making up for lost time without concern for the comfort of the indulged shoat. Dinny was thinking. The old fellow might be a hick, but he possessed extraordinary native sense.

In a few minutes, they had turned to the right, and were nearing the little white Baptist Church. Jason pointed it out, as they approached, but did not slacken speed, nor did he turn his head as they passed it and the quiet cemetery that lay to the rear. Dinny suspected that the treasured path through the woods had come to be the hallowed ground in Jason's opinion, rather than the grave where, apparently, some misunderstanding about a monument had seriously embittered him.

'Not very fer now,' he shouted. 'Just b'yond that there little holler. Yuh c'n see th' chimbly. There's yer Aunt Martha, a-pickin' up them winter pears... Well — I'll set yuh down. Wish yuh c'd come over 'n' see pap, whilst yer here. I c'd come 'n' fetch yuh.'

'I think I would like to,' said Dinny, gratefully. 'Could you come over in the morning? I want to see your father.

Aunt Martha was shading her eyes with both hands, her inquisitive grimace distorting her face into an expression of naïve perplexity. The vanished years spun like a top. Dinny felt eight, as he lifted his bags down, and started toward the house. Uncle Miles, shaggy, seedy, and minus the short burnsides of yesterday, appeared in the doorway. He had drawn the well-remembered, benevolently patronizing smile.

'Well, well, well!' boomed Uncle Miles.

*   *   *   *   *   *   *

'Would yuh care fer another piece, Ferdinand?' Aunt Martha was saying primly.

'By all means, Ferdinand,' heartily seconded Uncle Miles, taking up Dinny's purple-stained pie-plate. '*Absolute*ly!'

It had been amazing to Dinny with what ease and dispatch he had fitted back into the environment he thought he had outgrown.

Aunt Martha was a little grayer, and laid her thin hand on the backs of the familiar chairs as she moved about. There were nice new teeth, but she still shielded with the corner of her lip the area where once there had been a missing right upper canine. One of Uncle Miles's legs was not quite so up and coming as the other. The shoulders sagged, the least bit, making the shiny black coat a size too large. Otherwise, they were the same people; mellower, perhaps; a little more subdued.

Dinny had feared a painful constraint. As he had neared the house, bags in hand, his heart had pounded. For the moment he would have given much to efface himself from this awkward reunion. But there had been no dilemma. Uncle Miles was as openly cordial as if he were welcoming home a son in whom he had invested his all. Aunt Martha murmured little tendernesses as she nervously clutched at his sleeves.

He had lied effortlessly when they inquired whether he had had his dinner, and responded with enthusiasm when they wanted to show him 'th' place.' He was shown the chicken-coops, the barn, the little shop that had been his grandfather's. Dinny lingered there for a time. It was long since it had been in use, but it smelt of good, sound wood in process of fabrication, as if fuddled old Ferd had just stepped out of it.

They did not hint to know why Dinny had come. So far as he could observe, they were not craftily concealing that query. He was not asked where all he had been, or what he had been doing. They made no comments on his

success. The fact that he had withdrawn to another world
with which they were totally unacquainted, and now
belonged to it as he had never for one moment belonged to
them, gave them no apparent sensation of diffidence.

Uncle Miles rigged two cane fishing-poles, later in the
afternoon, and invited Dinny to go with him down the hill
to the little stream where they caught a few small perch
and talked freely about Angela, of whose celebrated exploits her father was gratefully proud.

At supper, served shortly after five, to Dinny's high
satisfaction, Aunt Martha accounted for the scattered
family whose ghosts vaguely hovered about the well-worn
door-steps, the old-fashioned thumb-latches, the paths to
the shop, the pump, the barn. Poor Susan, of course, was
dead. Ferdinand knew that, didn't he? Yes — she had
worked fer the Squire Craigs, and died there. Greta was
still out in Californy. They had an orange farm and three
fine boys. Yes — Greta wrote, about twice a year. No —
she had never came back. It was purty fer. Elmer was
still down at Lafayette in 'th' Home.' Hiram was up in
'th' Thumb,' a-workin' at a sawmill... Dinny followed the
Miller saga, at a distance, interested mostly in the fact
that these people and their affairs were as remote as if
Aunt Martha had reported on the goings and comings of a
family in Zanzibar.

He waived his proffered right to a second helping of
huckleberry pie, and, having easily gained the floor in the
process of graciously declining their hospitable entreaties,
Dinny ventured, without preamble, to account for his
unexpected visit.

He had become convinced, he said, that his life was not
being very well lived. The phrase struck him oddly, once
he had uttered it. Doubtless it had been shaped by this
environment. It was the way Uncle Miles might have said
it, had he been in a mood of confession. Life had lately
seemed to lack fulfillment, he said. He had felt a desire to
make peace with the few people whose relations to him had

been a source of 'disquiet' to himself — and doubtless to them also. He paused.

'So yuh've been 'n' got converted, Ferdinand,' murmured Aunt Martha, sanctimoniously. 'Bless th' Lord fer that!' She lifted the corner of her white apron, and, raising her spectacles, wiped her eyes. 'Miles,' she said, brokenly, 'our prayers has been answered. Our wandering boy has at last saw th' light. Praise t' His Blessed Name!'

'Abso*lute*ly!' ejaculated Uncle Miles, smiling approvingly, and hitching his chair back to cross his legs. 'And your aunt and I are very glad you came. How long can you stay, Ferdinand? Hope you won't have to hurry away. There'll be lots to talk about, now you're here after such a long time.'

'Thanks, Uncle Miles,' returned Dinny, in a brief aside. 'As I was saying, it has recently distressed me that I had permitted certain misunderstandings to ——'

'That's all right, Ferdinand,' broke in Uncle Miles, 'and there's nothing to forgive. You're as welcome as — as the flowers in May.'

Aunt Martha was crying now, noisily. A sudden wave of distaste for the whole adventure flooded Dinny's spirits. His old repugnance claimed him. He might have known there would be just such a calamitous scene. It had been his hope that there might be a calm, conciliatory talk. The tension would be eased. But clearly it was hopeless. Uncle Miles wished only to dodge the issue that had hurled them apart, offering an effusive and blustery hospitality as an alternative to the air-clearing discussion which the situation so urgently called for. Uncle Miles was extravagant with his tender of huckleberry pie, but winced at the thought of an honest invoice of their disaffection. It was somewhat like Angela's gift of an orange and a doll to the baby whose eyes she could not open. Aunt Martha, as usual, had taken refuge behind a tear-drenched apron.

'I shall be leaving, in about an hour,' said Dinny, calmly, 'and it would please me greatly if we three could have a quiet talk.'

Aunt Martha left off sobbing, wiped her eyes, and listened. Uncle Miles broke out with vigorous protests. Dinny raised a hand, insistingly, and the old man subsided, rather crestfallen.

'I don't mean to make a long story of it,' pursued Dinny, 'but something has happened to make me quite seriously anxious to be on the very best of friendly terms with everyone. You have wondered, Aunt Martha, if I had been converted. Probably not — in the way you mean. I don't feel any more religious than before. It's only that I have discovered myself to be thoroughly poisoned with aversions, disgusts, and bitter memories, which are making a sorry mess of my life. I want now to rise above all that, if I can.'

'But that's conversion, Ferdinand!' exclaimed Aunt Martha, fervently. 'It's th' workin' of th' Spirit! Blessed be His Holy Name!'

Uncle Miles nodded, sagaciously, and his lips formed the large word that denoted unqualified endorsement.

'And so — I'm here to ask you to forgive me, my dears, for putting myself completely out of your lives. I would like also to be forgiven for all the hot, hateful thoughts I have had in regard to you both — especially toward you, Uncle Miles, and for the bitter contempt that has swept through me whenever I thought of you. I'm asking for your pardon. I want to be at liberty. I'm weary of carrying that load.'

Aunt Martha was crying softly. Uncle Miles's face impulsively brightened, wreathed with an absolving smile. He cleared his throat, and stretching out a hand, patted Dinny assuringly on his coat-sleeve. Dinny took the old hand in his, and, observing that Uncle Miles was in the very act of booming out a volley of gallant 'abso*lute*lys,' leaned far forward, stared questioningly into his uncle's eyes, and slowly, meaningly, shook his head.

'No, Uncle Miles — not that! It's your turn to talk — but not that! Say what you're thinking! You'll feel much better afterwards — I can promise you.'

The old fellow slowly withdrew his hand, and with the back of it rubbed his forehead, beaded with perspiration. Then he swallowed hard and essayed a grisly yawn. Dinny had once seen a man die who, after the exhalation of his last breath, had yawned just that way — a yawn with no breath either coming or going.

They waited — and Uncle Miles spoke, hollowly.

'Well — it was like this, Ferdinand. At first, you were only a baby, and had no use for the money. Our salary was too little to live on, comfortably. What came in for you was a great help — a great help. Your income was larger than mine — than ours. I suppose I must have had a worldly pride, and dreaded to see the time come when you would be better off than the rest of us.' He hesitated, rubbing his eyes with his knuckles.

'I can understand that perfectly, Uncle Miles,' declared Dinny. 'It must have been a very real problem.'

'Well — then I saw how you felt toward your father, and knew you would never accept any help from him. That's when I should have ——'

Dinny nodded, comprehendingly.

'It was a great temptation, I am sure, Uncle Miles.'

'Yer Uncle Miles kept a-sayin', when he went into that Holstein cattle business, out in Ioway — and lost ev'ry cent to that rascally, thieving ——' Aunt Martha's voice was growing shrill.

'Yes — I had the thought that perhaps I could invest your money so you could ——' Uncle Miles groped for the right word.

'Don't spoil it, Uncle Miles,' admonished Dinny, hardly above a whisper. 'It's a great sensation, let me tell you! I hope you can have it! You'll find it's worth it, sir!' Dinny's voice had risen to his exultant words. Aunt Martha murmured, 'Bless th' Lord!'

'No!' shouted Uncle Miles, in a tone that explained how much effort that one agonized little bark cost him. 'The fact was — I wanted to put away something. I wasn't saving it for you... Now — you know all about it!... God — help me!' The brave old head sank, lower and lower, there came a sort of inhuman guttural cry from his tight throat.

Aunt Martha rose, with a little whimper of alarm, and put her arm around him, pressing her cheek hard against his.

'Miles — my *dear!* Yuh done it — at last! Bless th' Lord! Bless th' Lord!... Oh, Ferdinand, you've been sent f'm God to help your poor uncle — 'n' me.'

Dinny was deeply moved. He did not attempt to analyze his strange sensations, but, eclipsing the surge of sympathy for these repentant, broken-hearted old people, there rose in him a consciousness of an almost uncanny vitality — the 'will-to-power' consciousness, as nearly as he could define it at the moment. He felt suddenly matured! It was as if his permanent mind — what he was always thinking of as his 'sub-conscious mind' in spite of anything the new Psychology might say — had not only ceased complaining at the decisions and intentions of his 'conscious mind,' but had actually taken charge of the whole enterprise! He knew now what Julia meant, though he had fresh reasons for understanding her lack of words to explain her strange sensation. She had called it a *power!* Well — that's what it was. It would sound trite and sentimental if he attempted to elucidate. But — what he had come by was not a sentiment — any more than the roar of the turbines beneath Niagara is a sentiment. Julia was right! *This was a kind of power!* God only knew what all you could do with it — but here it was!... Power!

Uncle Miles rose, his old face twisted in a pathetically tearful smile, and offered Dinny his hand, Aunt Martha still hugging his arm.

'Seems like we ought to have a word of prayer,' suggested Aunt Martha, when they had passed through the doorway to the little sitting-room.

'We've just had that, Aunt Martha,' said Dinny —

'the real kind. Now — suppose we sit down and talk a little more about this. Did I understand you to say that some man, out in Iowa, had defrauded you of — of that money?'

They told him the story in relays, Uncle Miles becoming so excited over the rank injustice they had suffered that Aunt Martha tried to calm him.

'Yer uncle gets almost sick, sometimes, a-thinkin' and a-talkin' about it. I do wish he could ferget it.'

'That's why I asked,' said Dinny. 'Uncle Miles — whatever became of that fellow? Do you know?'

'The last I heard,' growled Uncle Miles, 'he was back on a rented farm not far from Unger, where I first met the dirty skunk. He broke up, out there, as he deserved.'

'Broke up — did he? Perhaps he did not intend to cheat you. Probably he was a poor business man. Chances are he's burning up his insides hating the people who took his property away from him. Knowing what I do now, Uncle Miles, if I were you I'd write him a friendly letter — you and he were once good friends, weren't you? — and ask him to come up here, this fall, and spend a Sunday. Tell him you and Aunt Martha have a big, fat hen that ought to be stewed. Noodles, too, and huckleberry pie.... Treat yourself to a thrill! Set yourself free!'

'Ferdinand,' said Aunt Martha, smiling pensively, 'it sure does sound queer — yer a-talkin' like this — when yuh look so worldly like 'n' all.'

'It doesn't sound a bit queerer than it feels, I can assure you, Aunt Martha.'

'You'll stay the night with us now, won't you, Ferdi-nand?' entreated Uncle Miles.

* * * * * *

Old Abner was leaning on both elbows, his boot on an inverted three-gallon tin swill-pail, gazing down into one of the pig-pens. He turned his head as Jason and Dinny approached. His jaw sagged, and chopped up and down, nervously, as he stared. The worn tabs of his ancient coonskin cap lopped his ears. Had Dinny seen a faithful photograph of him, a week ago, he would have identified the subject as the patriarch and original founder of The Hicks.

He came slowly to meet them, rubbing his gnarled hand on his short, stuffy, leather coat. There was no introduction.

'Take off yer hat,' requested Abner. 'Jase says yuh've got that funny little point o' hair, like her'n.'

Dinny obliged.

'Powerful funny 'bout that, Jase,' drawled the old man, pointing a crooked forefinger at Dinny's head, as if inspecting an animal. 'Her pap had that there, same as her, same as him. The old feller always had his cap on, mostly, 'n' I never rightly noticed 't until he was a-layin' on th' coolin' board, next mornin' after he hung hisself. Gol-darned if he didn't have 't, too! Danged if he didn't look like a 'ristocrat, a-layin' there!... Well — come in t' th' house, son, 'n' be welcome.'

'I never knew before that my grandfather had taken his own life.' Dinny became aware that many mysterious silences and evasions of Aunt Martha's had now been explained.

'Well — it won't hurt yuh none t' know 't. Yuh c'n be proud o' your grand-pap, son. Gol-darned if 'twasn't purty fine 'n' brave o' th' old codger. I sure never'd a-thought he had 't in him. Ev'rybody was a-moonin' around, that night, a-feelin' scared like, 'n' kind o' shamed fer the Millers. Gol-darned if I wasn't proud o' th' old cuss!'

'You have some unusual ideas on the subject of — suicide, Mr. Schrofe.'

'Well — o' course — I wouldn't 'xac'ly recommend 't t' nobody, but, all th' same, if I'd knowed yer grand-pap had 't in him, I'd 'a' had a lot more respect fer him whilst he lived.'

They drew up their chairs before the grate — stiff, prim, narrow rocking-chairs that had a tendency to creep about

on the worn rag carpet — and spent two hours talking about
Julia's monument.

Old Abner's bitterness about Craig's shocking discourtesy
in having their little stone cast aside had obviously become
an obsession. Once he had launched upon the painful topic,
there was no distracting him.

'Guess we'll have t' start now,' admonished Jason, consulting his big nickel-cased watch. 'I'm a-drivin' him over
t' Wayne, pap, to ketch a train fer Cincinnati.'

''Pears like I done all th' talkin',' regretted Abner.
'Lot o' things I wanted t' ask yuh, too. Seems like when I
get a-goin' 'bout that there feller, I can't stop.'

'Yes,' said Dinny, 'it's too bad. I'm sorry. I am on my
way to see him, and I mean to ask him about it. I don't
believe he ever knew the particulars. It must have been a
terrible mistake. Would you be glad if you found out it
was a mistake, and that he was not really to blame?'

The old fellow slowly nodded his head.

'Gol-darned if I wouldn't give ev'ry one o' them Berk-
shires, out there in them pens, t' hear that feller say he
hadn't knowed, 'n' was sorry 'n' that!'

'Like hell yuh would, pap! Half o' them hawgs b'longs t'
me!' Jason, vastly pleased with his joke, gave the old man
an affectionate whack between the shoulders.

'All fun aside, Mr. Schrofe,' said Dinny, seriously, taking
his hand, 'I hope to find out that my father never meant to
do you generous people this harm. I believe it would hurt
Julia, terribly, if she had known about the misery it's
caused you.'

As they sauntered toward the sedan, standing by the old
hitching-rack, Jason said, 'Would yuh mind if I told pap?'

'About the letter?'

'Yeah — th' letter 'n' that.'

'I believe Julia would want him to know about it, don't
you?'

'Yeah — I'll tell him.'

CHAPTER XVII

ALTHOUGH aware of the curious phenomenon of familiar streets narrowing, during one's extended absence, to about three fourths their previous width, and tall buildings shrinking to a mere travesty of their former stateliness, Dinny Brumm was unprepared for the shock when, at midnight, he followed his bags from the taxi to the desk at The Barstow.

Even allowing for the fact that when he had first timidly ventured through its spacious, shriekingly ornate lobby, as an untraveled youth, The Barstow was vain-gloriously, self-consciously new, it seemed impossible to believe that a few years could have so tarnished its gilt and frayed its cushions.

The once impressive gargoyles still reared on their hind claws to support massive old-worldish lamps, but the awe-inspiring challenge of their 'How dare you, worm?' that had darted from their shocked, staring eyes, was now replaced by a simpering, apologetic servility. Their orbs were dull, their flanks were lean, their talons had straightened out as if to ward off a slap.

The desk, formerly to be approached hat in hand and with regret that one had not brought a joss-stick, had had its stinger pulled, too, its smile resembling the conciliatory smirk of the urgent driver upon invitation to pull up at the curb and state his name and address for the augmentation of certain statistics in process of assembly at Police Headquarters.

And yet, barring the normal wear and tear of a half dozen prosperous years, The Barstow, Dinny knew, had not altered appreciably. The change was all in himself.

But whatever of modified outlook had been gradually coming to pass in his mind, due to the liberating experiences of the years, to the tarnishment of earlier glosses

and glitters, and the reduction of once astounding dimensions, it was nothing compared to the uncanny magic that
had suddenly recreated him into something so different
from the self whose habitual deductions and reactions had
been stabilized — so utterly different that he found it difficult to recognize his attitudes and opinions as his own.
His habitual responses were inactive, as if he had been
smitten with an amnesia.

Yesterday's experience of complete reconciliation with
Uncle Miles and Aunt Martha had performed some queer
tricks on Dinny's mind. He had not been surprised at the
sound of his own words soliciting pardon for the bitter
animosity he had nourished in regard to them. That was
what he had gone there to do, and he had meant to see it
through, hoping for no further results than the satisfaction of getting it off his chest. Down inside himself, whatever he might say to Uncle Miles, there would unquestionably remain the private opinion that the pompously
pious old fellow was a piker.

All that Dinny would have to show for his strange adventure in the voluntary enterprise of crow-eating would be
a sense of having made an honest experiment with Julia's
theory for the purgation of poison. He did not expect that
his estimate of Uncle Miles would be in any way reappraised.

But when he had finished with them, last night, he had
not only told Uncle Miles that he fully forgave the wrong
he had done; he really had forgiven the old man and was in
a mood of sympathy for him. Uncle Miles had faced an
odd predicament as custodian of a child's annuity exceeding
his own salary. Dinny could understand how his uncle had
postponed doing the thing that required to be done, saying
to himself, 'Next year I must tell him,' but always fearful
of the consequences. What indeed would become of a
small boy, living in a frugal home, were he suddenly handed
an allowance in excess of the family's total income? Uncle
Miles had drifted into an unhappy perplexity, but not because he had the instincts of a thief. And Aunt Martha

had consented to it, ruefully, no doubt, believing that Uncle Miles knew best.

Once upon a time Dinny had felt that if ever the occasion arose when he could back the old weasel into a corner and force him to confess himself an unmitigated fraud the sensation of seeing his despised pomposity shrivel and peel off like snake-skin would be worth all the mental torture he had suffered.

Uncle Miles had crumpled to a degree surpassing the most extravagant hopes Dinny had sourly cherished, but there was no diabolical pleasure afforded by it; Dinny had shared the old man's sorrow with an understanding that seemed to enhance the value of his own personality. He began to appreciate what Julia had written concerning her altered estimate of herself, after sincerely making peace with Susan. She had felt 'promoted.' It was as if she 'had won a prize.' It was as if she had discovered herself to be 'a princess.'

Throughout today Dinny had reviewed last night's strange experience in Julia's room where he had slept.

At ten, Aunt Martha had lighted the way up the steep, narrow, uncarpeted stairs, piloting him with a reeking kerosene lamp.

'Almost nothin's been changed in here since it was her'n,' said Aunt Martha, turning down the patchwork quilt. 'Hiram had a sale cried when him 'n' Lucy moved to Michigan, but Jase Schrofe, who had previous bought the house, bid in these here things o' Julia's and had 'em left where they was. Exceptin' fer the desk, it's the same.' Aunt Martha patted the pillows. 'Yes,' she sighed, reminiscently, 'dear Julia died in this here old bed.'

So it was here that Julia had summoned her slimming strength to write the letter that was 'promoting' Dinny to something of the lofty dignity that she had won 'like a prize.'

Ordinarily, he thought, it would not be much of a recommendation for a bed to say of it, five minutes before one climbed in, that someone of far-reaching posthumous in-

fluence had died in it, in a lugubrious tone hinting that the
departed spirit might be within earshot; but if Julia's
ghost haunted the room, so much the better, thought Dinny.

He was a long time going to sleep, and even when, from
sheer fatigue produced by the emotional strain of the day,
he drifted into semi-consciousness, there was a strange
sense that Julia was coming along into his dreams.

There never had been a photograph of her except a cheap
little tintype of a group of girls taken at the county fair.
The cheeks had been tinted to an unhealthy flush, and the
mouth had been drawn into a prim little pucker. It was
unfair to Julia, of course, as even Aunt Martha admitted to
whom beauty was but skin deep.

In his half-somnolent state, Dinny conjured a portrait of
Julia, the radiant. It was a satisfyingly clear picture, and,
as he half-consciously brought it alive and put it through a
variety of moods, he felt he was recovering his girl-mother.

The dream, if it was a dream, was not altogether pleasant,
however. Julia seemed to proceed into an attitude of entreaty as if he had done something to make her very unhappy. And when, at length, sitting opposite him on the
grass, her feet folded under her short skirt, she began pensively gathering up the little paper cups and plates, her
eyes downcast and swollen with crying, Dinny roused with
a painful recurrence of the one tragic mistake that could
not be mended.

He had made peace with Uncle Miles to their complete
mutual satisfaction. And tomorrow he would have an interview with his father who, he had learned by wire before
leaving New York, was in Cincinnati for a week on one of
his periodical inspection visits; doubtless that interview
would lift the burden of misgiving he had carried in respect
to Zandy Craig. He had it in mind to stop at Magnolia,
also, and attempt to revise his opinions of that institution,
in the light of his new flair for sympathetic understanding.

But there was nothing to be done in the case of Joan.
She had made it quite impossible for him to repair the

damage he had done to an affection which, instead of relaxing its grip, seemed to be mounting!

He tossed about for an hour, worrying over the utter hopelessness of his longing for Joan. Conceding that their romance was a closed incident, what might still be done to insure her happiness? For, surely, Joan could not feel satisfied with the manner in which she had left him without a word when she had decided — quite impulsively, he presumed — to run away with Tommy. What a dismal honeymoon for Joan! And for Tommy, too, who couldn't be expected to be pleased with himself.

If they weren't on the other side of the Atlantic, reflected Dinny, he would go to them with his comradely congratulations and the assurance that he not only bore them no ill-will but sincerely wished them great and lasting joy. It would be worth almost any length of journey to replace, in his memory, a contented and joyful Joan for the torturing image of her tear-stained face as she collected the pitiful little remains of their picnic luncheon. It would be a quite dreadful thing to have that picture of Joan's dejection and disappointment increasingly menacing his peace.

His decision to mend matters with Joan in so far as might be achieved through a friendly interview with her and Tommy involved a long series of imaginary circumstances in which they were brought together now at a little dinner he would give for them at Dexter's, now at their own table in an apartment somewhere up town. But — by Gad! — why wait? Lacey's had said Tommy was to be in Europe until early November, hadn't they? Why shouldn't he slip over there, directly, and give the poor things a chance to enjoy their honeymoon, undistressed by the remorse which Joan would inevitably feel? By Gad! — he would do it! As soon as he had finished with his father, and the intended visit to Magnolia, he would sail. He would make his relations to Tommy and Joan so pleasant for them and him that they could expect to be comrades forever! That would take but a day. Then he would go to London for the winter, and try to write. He had no notion what he would be writing, but there was a sensation of desire. That was good: he had quite lost it.

It was a great idea! He would sail next week. That would solve the problem. He couldn't have Joan back, but he could do his utmost to make her happy. Dinny had gone to sleep constructing scenes and dialogue for the little play that was to dispose of the paper dishes.

* * * * * *

At ten, next morning, Dinny telephoned up to the suite which Zandy Craig occupied on the ninth floor, requesting an interview.

A male secretary informed him that Mr. Craig's day was entirely engaged. If Mr. Brumm wished to confide the nature of his business to Mr. Craig's assistant, Mr. Effelbaum, an appointment could be arranged.

Dinny sensibly refused to be irritated over this slight delay. It was consistent with good business that Zandy Craig should not be open to the importunities of any bore or beggar who happened to drift in. He said he would be glad to see Mr. Effelbaum and explain his errand. The time was set for eleven. That was excellent. Mr. Effelbaum would quickly clear the way for him. Perhaps he and his father might lunch together.

With keen anticipation, and not a little nervous excitement, Dinny dressed carefully, and, at eleven sharp, took the elevator to the ninth floor, where he was shown into the suite, the secretary taking him immediately into the presence of the bright-eyed, urbane, little Jew who served as the last barricade between his exalted master and the public.

'So you would see Mr. Greck?' began Mr. Effelbaum, tapping his desk lightly with a long steel paper-knife.

Even making due allowance for Mr. Effelbaum's Hebraic handling of gutturals, there was something rather ominous in the manner of his pronunciation of 'Greck.'

'Mr. Craig is my father,' replied Dinny, suddenly resolved to make his story short and come to the point without circumlocution.

'Mr. Greck has no son,' said Mr. Effelbaum, stiffly.

Instantly Dinny understood. Effelbaum, resentful of the 'Greck' article in *Hallelujah*, was treating himself to a helping of revenge.

However, Effelbaum was acting according to his best knowledge, no doubt. He was honest in his belief that Zandy Craig had no son. Dinny was a mere impostor, so far as Effelbaum's information went.

'Perhaps you had better ask him. He is in, I presume?' Dinny was patient, respectful.

'There is no needt I should inquire, Mr. Brumm.'

Dinny reached in his pocket for a card, scribbled a line on it, and handed it across the desk.

'Would you mind giving this to Mr. Craig?'

Effelbaum read the brief message and returned the card with a crooked smile.

'Mr. Greck will nodt see you, sir. You may tell me whadt you want.'

Dinny flushed uncomfortably, and leaned forward with an elbow on the mahogany desk.

'Is he in?' Dinny's tone hinted at an impatience that was rapidly getting out of hand.

Effelbaum, savoring the situation, grinned sardonically and nodded.

'Budt not to you — Mr. Brumm.'

Impetuously, Dinny rose, and observing that Effelbaum's hand was moving toward the row of ivory buttons on the left corner of the desk, quickly grasped him by the wrist.

'You may think you're doing your duty,' he growled, 'but this time you're exceeding it. I came here to see my father, and I mean to! Understand? Which of us takes that card in — you or I?'

To Dinny's surprise, Effelbaum glanced up with a taunting distortion of lip, and laughed.

'You take idt in to Mr. *"Greck!"'* He wagged his head in the direction of the adjacent door and shrugged a shoulder, self-absolvingly. 'I haf triedt to spare you a bainful moment. You are determinedt to haf it... Go — and haf idt!'

Dinny released his grip on the unresisting hand and searched Effelbaum's sneer with eyes suddenly nonplussed.

'Do you mean to infer that my father has given instructions I am not to be admitted?'

Effelbaum's brows, lips, shoulders and palms raised, concertedly, in a gesture that wished himself well out of the awkward *contretemps*.

'Mr. "Greck" toldt me he had no son. If you can convinze him to the contrary, I shall nodt detain you.' He rose, opened the door, and bowed Dinny in, with an elaborate gesture.

'Mr. *"Greck"* — Mr. Brumm.'

The stenographer at Zandy Craig's elbow rose and retired. Craig pushed in the slide on which her notebook had rested, leaned back in his opulent swivel-chair, folded his arms, and regarded his intrusive caller from under lowered brows.

'You may sit down, if you like,' he said, coolly, dashing Dinny's intention to offer his hand. 'I assume you are my son. In fact — now that I see you, I know you are. There is a certain likeness. And you have something of the facial lines of your mother.'

Dinny smiled, half-heartedly, wondering, as his father paused, whether it was time for him to speak.

'May I inquire why you came, and how I may serve you?' continued Craig, steadily.

'I came to ask your pardon.' Dinny's voice was sincerely contrite.

The big man slowly raised both long arms, clasped his hands behind his leonine gray head in a pose that Dinny recognized as a natural posture of his own when in a quandary, and closed his eyes.

'I am sorry I have waited so long,' added Dinny.

'Yes — I'm afraid you waited... too long!' Craig looked squarely at the tardy prodigal, his expression severe.

Dinny nodded.

'I never thought I wanted to see you, sir, until lately. Something quite important has altered my opinion. I would like to tell you about it.'

'That can wait,' said Craig, folding his arms on the desk. 'I'll talk first, if you're agreed. I've probably thought more about this matter than you have; and, anyway, I'm your father. It's my right to speak first, is it not?'

Dinny smiled approval.

'When you were a lad, young fellow, I made many efforts to show you that I meant to do everything I could for you, in face of the circumstances that kept us apart. I could not hold it against you when you resisted my attempts to ——'

'I did not understand, sir. I had been led to think that ——'

Craig signed that he did not wish to be interrupted.

'Yes — I know, or can surmise, what you were led to think. Your Aunt Martha would have seen to that. And as for your parson uncle, I dislike to think of him. But — to continue — I did indulge the hope that once you were away from that atmosphere, it might please you to reflect that you had a father who had tried to do what is customarily thought of as the right thing.

'After Mr. Brumm had informed me you had a job and were on your own, I still waited. Sometimes I hoped that you would be moved to write me at least a note of appreciation. I disliked to think that I had bred a child who, in his later teens, had not managed to develop as much common courtesy as would have seemed to demand some sort of response.'

Dinny's chagrin and remorse were painful. He lowered his eyes, and nodded, slowly.

'Through that period when you would have been going

to college like a gentleman, and backed by the full support of your father, I happened to be heavily worried by a variety of cares, by no means the least of which — though I'm damned if I know just why I'm telling you this, for you have no right to my confidence — was my wife's separation from me. She had found me incompatible, though I was very fond of her. My duties required a great deal of my time. I was much away from home. We drifted apart. She left me.

'My daughter Alison was shortly sent abroad to school. Had you come to me, in those days, informing me that you had been an ass and an ingrate, I should have attempted to dissuade you of that estimate of yourself, I think, just from sheer loneliness and a natural wish for a reconstruction of my family ties.

'Eventually, Alison comes home, and accidentally encounters you here, though I was not informed of that until much later. Why she did not tell me, at once, I do not know, though I have surmised, and if that unfortunate accidental meeting brought either of you any unhappiness — and I rather suspect, from chance remarks of Alison's, that it did — I am sorry. She did not tell me until the appearance of your assault on me in that damned dirty little rag which, I am told, you are now editing.'

Craig's voice had risen, indignantly, with the last few words. His eyes were full of pain and his big fists clenched. He pushed back his chair, and rose, thrusting his long hands deeply into his trouser pockets.

'That day,' he shouted, savagely, 'whatever desire I still had for a sight of you — my son — was utterly abandoned. God knows which one of your ancestors you may resemble, but you're not like your charming mother, and I have the self-esteem to think you're not like me!'

Craig had flung the chair back against the wall, and was pacing up and down behind the desk, biting his words into hot bits.

'If you had come here shabby and broke, I would instruct

my secretary to draw you a check. That would be for the relief of my own mind. You do not appear to be in want. You are well dressed and apparently have had your breakfast. I presume your position as the editor of a filthy magazine devoted to sophisticated blackmail and parlor socialism puts you beyond the necessity of my alms.... So — there is nothing you are likely to want that I can give you. As for this belated request for pardon, suppose we don't go into that, at all. I am not a sentimental person, either by instinct or practice. Neither are you, if I have correctly interpreted your temperament as reflected in your writing. Whatever made you come here, I don't know — and I don't care to know! If you have any remorse, run along with it! If I have any regret, it's my own business.... Now — I think that's all, and if you're sure you are in need of nothing but my pardon, may I ask you to excuse me. This is a busy day, and, as you know, this interview was unsolicited by me.... Mr. Effelbaum will show you out.'

He pushed a button, and Effelbaum appeared as if he had been waiting, hand on knob, for his cue.

This sudden move of his father's had been so unexpected, so ruthlessly conclusive, that Dinny was at a loss to know what, if anything, to do.

The door was wide open, Effelbaum was in the room waiting, Craig had readjusted his gold nose-glasses and was busying himself with the papers on his desk. Dinny had been definitely dismissed, and nothing remained for him to do but leave. He felt himself chastised like a half-grown boy. This man was his father, in very truth. Dinny's complete breakdown of self-possession was obviously an automatic response demanded by filial instinct suddenly recognizing the paternal authority of this man who, a stranger, had now loomed large as the sire.

For a moment only Dinny hesitated, took one step forward, was on the point of entreating for a chance to be heard. His father did not look up. Effelbaum fiddled with his watch-guard. Dinny turned slowly away. At the doorway he paused.

'I am very sorry, sir,' he said, respectfully.

There was no reply. Effelbaum was at Craig's elbow, receiving a handful of opened letters. The trim stenographer was waiting for the retiring caller to make his exit. Dinny's interview with his father seemed to be over.

* * * * * *

Magnolia was only fifty minutes away, but in those fifty minutes Dinny carefully examined his own mind in respect to the adventure on which he had launched, a few days earlier, and was delighted to discover that the unfortunate meeting with his father had not dashed his interest and belief in the thing he had set out to do.

A week ago his mind would have been tempestuous with bitter hate and stormy schemes for reprisal. He could easily picture the nature of his burning thoughts as he rehearsed, item by item, the progressive phases of his defenseless humiliation in his father's office. No! — By God! There wasn't a man alive who could put Dinny Brumm into such a debasing predicament and expect to get away with it unscratched! Least of all the man who had been responsible for so much of his mental torture, all through the years! Craig should have his pay with usury! Damn him! *Damn him!*

Dinny was surprised, this afternoon, at his mood; not surprised so much over his attitude of sympathetic understanding for Zandy Craig who had waited and hoped for some manner of response from his disaffected son — waited until the wound had healed and left an impermeable scar. The thing that amazed Dinny was the nature of this new serenity. It was not a mere hand-folding inertia. He tried vainly to define it in a phrase, and could arrive at nothing more adequate than 'dynamic peace.'

As he sat looking out at the window of the club car which served as a hub for the revolving wooded hills, faintly tipped with early autumn tints, Dinny's mental state was a novelty to himself. Whatever description his mood deserved, it was certainly not apathy. There was something vital, vibrant, kinetic in it. Jason Schrofe had not been far afield when he thought of this peculiar energy as 'dynamite.'

Always Dinny had entertained varying degrees of contempt for the unworkable theory of non-resistance. Sometimes he grinned when he saw the word in print. What sort of people were advocates of non-resistance? Strong men — likely to make some constructive contribution of skill or genius? Not at all. The non-resisters had had their frail, other-cheeking, boot-licking program of life handed to them at birth. It was less a sublimity of soul than a feebleness of body.

As for organized warfare, that was quite another matter. That was a mass-madness inspired by predatory bankers and swashbucklers, diabolically unconcerned about the cost of their greed and pomposity to the drafted and driven who were herded into the tragic hoax by the stimulating rattle of brave drums, stampeded into indifference to the likelihood of their being ushered out of it to the depressing tune of scalpels and saws and forceps tinkling metallically on glass-topped, rubber-castored tables. That was, indeed, another matter!

But non-resistance, attemptedly practiced by an individual, was sheer cowardice. How idiotic — for a churchful of people to stand up, of a Sunday morning, and bellow their lungs out for a theory that none but the sick, crippled, and undersized actually believed in to the point of practical demonstration.

How deliciously absurd — when some hollow-cheeked, hollow-chested, dreamy-eyed, five-foot-four, one hundred and nineteen pound Christian boosted himself up at prayer-meeting to declare, in a thin, piping squeak, that, as for him, he believed in non-resistance.

The only sane answer to that, offered by the people who really had the world's work to do, was a laughing 'By Gad — you'd *better!*'

'But,' shrills the altruistic little fellow, 'this is my honest conviction! I sincerely believe that it's more sensible never to fight back!'

'Doubtless,' grins the ham-handed six-footer. 'You would! You're a wise little man. You just keep on thinking that, if you know what's good for you!'

Invoicing his own feelings, today, Dinny marveled that the hymns and liturgies and homilies of Christianity had taken so little account of the fact that non-resistance, far from being a state of supine lethargy, was a dynamic of high potentiality.

Why didn't the Church leave off singing, 'I am Jesus' little lamb,' and recognize the very substantial and demonstrable power of *the spirit in action!* Dinny had never felt so alive, so alert, so energized in all his life. His compliant understanding of his father's rudeness and refusal to conciliate was accompanied by a rising tide of personal poise and power. Perhaps this serenity was at least approximately denoted by the ancient phrase — 'the peace that surpasseth understanding.'... By Gad — it was a fact!

For a moment there was a flash of belief, as if he had discovered a universal cure-all for every possible anxiety, that the potent sentence printed on Julia's salvaged scrap of scripture was possessed of magical properties. But, of course, even this formula for power was conditioned somewhat by circumstances. He could forgive Joan for running away from him without a word of regret or explanation. Doubtless he deserved it. She had given him his chance. By what right could he expect her to live interminably on the hope that he might wear himself out with hateful cynicism, and, having eventually burned up all his carbon, ask her to take charge of the ashes! The girl had her life to live; hadn't she?... Oh, yes — all that was plain as a pikestaff; but the fact remained that no length of his love, no depth of his understanding, no dynamic of forgiveness could restore Joan to him. Some mistakes were irrevocable! ... He could forgive — had forgiven — his father for the savage rebuff, but that would not give him back his father.

* * * * * *

Magnolia was a mere pocket-edition. The clangor of the gong with which the motorman cleared the track, as the Sunnyside Avenue car demanded her right of way at the corner of Main and Broad — busiest spot in town — was surely redundant, seeing how little traffic she coped with. All activity on the streets had been slowed down to the tempo of Zanesdale and Unger.

Dinny watched the familiar shops amble by, smiling unconsciously at their decrepitude. Had the town built nothing new? Yes — here was an important replacement; a full half block of glossy yellow brick six stories high! The car had stopped on the red, and there was ample time to read the names of the businesses that occupied the imposing new building. Some of the names he recognized. There was Hunter the Hatter which he had always considered a choice bit of alliteration, often wondering whether Hunter's selection of a vocation had been influenced thereby. Some of the names were unfamiliar. The whole transparent corner of the ground floor was occupied with swagger motor-cars — 'Spencer Davis, Manager.'

Was it possible that this was 'Spike'? That was his name — Spencer. It would be interesting to see what manner of man Spike had evolved to. Dinny impulsively strode to the rear platform as the car started forward, and swung himself off. He had all but forgotten Spike. Once upon a time, he had hated him with all his might, but in recent years nothing had been left of it but a dulled, dispassionate aversion.

The place was empty except for the display cars, a workman with a chamois-skin, and a neat girl with an adroit nail-file who was advertised as ready to furnish 'Information,' in case — as appeared unlikely — anyone should desire it.

'Yes, Mr. Davis is in,' replied the girl, indifferently, as if the fact could scarcely be expected to interest anybody. 'Through there,' she added, pointing over her shoulder with the nail-file, and resuming her occupation.

It was Spike; no question about that. There was a symmetrical bald spot on his crown about the size of a tonsure, but it would hardly have been mistaken for that if the picture of it had included the ears which, viewed from the rear — he was bent over a desk telephone — were built rather for enduring combats than confessions.

Dinny waited, just inside the door, for Spike to finish and greet him. Becoming aware that the conversation was embarrassingly private, for Spike was in an attitude of frantic supplication, he quietly backed out, but in that moment he had accidentally heard enough to inform him that his erstwhile opponent was in difficulty.

'Yeah — but see here, Mr. Amberly, I simply can't do it today! Maybe I can by Monday or Tuesday, if I can make some collections. Give a fellow a break, can't you? Yeah — I know it's a sight draft, but I can't raise seventeen-fifty this afternoon, and that's all there is to it!... Hell! It's impossible!'

The receiver had banged back on the hook, and Spike, considerably shaken and distraught, was moving toward the open door. Dinny was occupied with reading a large bulletin pasted on the glazed partition setting forth the merits of a new oiling system that had just made over the whole motor industry into something theatrically other than it had been. Spike looked his age — plus.

'Do you remember me?' asked Dinny.

Spike stared hard for a moment; then grinned as amiably as his perturbation would permit, and nodded, extending his hand.

'Y-e-a-h!' he marveled, as the light slowly filtered through. 'Dinny Brumm! I'll be damned! What are you doin' here?'

'A little business trip, Spike, and' — a sudden impulse

prompted Dinny to rush on into an unintended remark —
'I have decided to buy a car here and drive back to New
York. Thought you might be willing to talk it over with
me.'

'That's what we're here for, old-timer,' rejoiced Spike,
noisily. 'About what are you looking for, Dinny? You're
turning something in, I suppose.'

'No — I disposed of my car some time ago when I was
to be out of the country for a while.'

'That's good — and unusual.'

They stepped out into the show-room, where Spike, who
knew his business, proceeded without delay to an energetic
sales-talk, utterly oblivious of their earlier antagonism and
the marked changes wrought upon each of them by the
intervening years.

Dinny was only a half-hour making up his mind to purchase the dark blue coupé with the gray whipcord uphol-
stery. It was, he said, about what he wanted.

'How soon can it be ready for the road, Spike?'

'It's ready now!'

'How about plates?'

'I'll get 'em for you. You can take it along with the
demonstration tags; they'll be all right for today.'

They returned to the office desk and sat down.

'The usual terms — over ten months?' Spike straightened the carbon in his order-book and prepared to write.

'No — I'm going to pay cash for it.' Dinny produced his
check-book, and unscrewed the top from his pen. 'Seventeen hundred and fifty — right?'

'Yeah — that's right,' repeated Spike, with a combination gasp and sigh that struck Dinny as one of the most
startling expressions of surprise and relief he had ever
heard.

'There you are,' said Dinny.

Spike fanned his shoulder with the unblotted check, and
laughed nervously.

'By God, Dinny, you don't know it, but you've damn'

near saved my life. I don't mind telling you that if I hadn't
sold you this car — right now — for cash — I likely would
have lost my agency!'

'Glad I happened in, then, at the opportune moment.'
Dinny tried to make the comment sound casual.

Of a sudden, Spike's face grew serious and he gnawed his
lip, reflectively.

'Just when did you come in, Dinny?' he asked.

'Two-forty — from Cincinnati.'

'Yeah... No — I mean, how long had you been here
when I found you outside the door?'

'Only a moment... It's quite all right, Spike. I can use
the car. I had expected to buy one, sooner or later.'

'Well — it's pretty damn' decent of you — I'll say,'
muttered Spike, in a tone of mingled gratitude and contrition.

'You would have done the same thing, doubtless, if you
had accidentally stumbled in on me and found me in a
jam.'

'I doubt it!' confessed Spike, brusquely. 'What's come
over you, Dinny? You sure weren't that sort of a chap
when we were in school, and' — he chuckled, dryly — 'nobody would think you were a Fairy Godmother, to read
your ——'

'It's all happened just lately, Spike. Like to hear about
it?'

'Yeah — if it isn't private. I sure would... Wait till
I tell that boy to put on a new spare. The one she's carrying has had couple o' hundred miles about town.'

It was not an easy task to confide the secret to Spike.
He was quite unprepared for such thinking, and he had
important matters on his mind. He had first to talk to Mr.
Amberly. Dinny could not help being amused at the vast
alteration of tone with which he informed Mr. Amberly,
crisply, that he would be over presently to take up 'that
little matter' in full. It called to mind the story about the
rabbit that found the whiskey.

'Well — I'm damned if I ever thought you'd get religion,' observed Spike, after listening, rather absently, for some minutes. 'You're the last man in the world.'

'I don't think it is that,' said Dinny. 'I've discovered that it's impossible for a man to be healthy and up on his toes with his system poisoned by old grudges. I suppose it's like arthritis. The poison's all through you, though the focal infection may be in one place and the pain in another.'

'Yeah — I see. You've got an infected back tooth, and a pain in your shoulder. Is that what you mean?'

'Precisely! You've an old grudge against your uncle, and — and take it out on your girl.'

'Married — Dinny?'

Dinny shook his head without looking up.

'You must have had a grudge against your uncle. Have you fixed it up?'

'Yes — but I waited too long.'

'Lost the girl, eh?'

'Quite definitely.' Dinny rose, and they went out to the curb where the new car was parked.

'I suppose you'll be driving over to the college,' wondered Spike. 'Lot o' changes over there since you ——'

'Since I was fired,' assisted Dinny, smiling.

'Yeah — I wouldn't blame you if you never wanted to see it again. They sure did give you a rotten deal.'

'I thought that, too, until just lately.'

'By God! — I believe you're in earnest! Do you honestly think that it would make a fellow more efficient in his business if he made friends with all the people he despised, and everybody that had got his goat, and not given him a break?'

'Well — if he went into it for the sole purpose of selling more cars — that's what you mean, don't you? — I doubt it very much. But if he made an honest stab at it, with the hope of cleaning out his poison and promoting himself to a higher class of animal, his increased efficiency would inevitably follow, don't you think?'

'It sure sounds sort o' moonshiny. God! — I'd feel silly going into old man Kennerly's place, for instance, to ask him to be friends. Couldn't, if I wanted to, now,' added Spike, with apparent relief that a good excuse had occurred to him, 'The old double-crosser's laid up at home, I understand, with some kind of a heart attack. Damned if I knew he had one!'

Dinny smiled broadly.

'Maybe he's poisoned. Why don't you go and help the doctor pull the old bird through?'

'How would that help *old Kennerly* get rid of his poison, if I went to see him with the idea of getting rid of *mine?*'

Dinny shook his head, admitting his perplexity.

'Funny thing about that,' he said, thoughtfully. 'It's true, though: this stuff's contagious, Spike.... You know' — he went on, after a momentary reflection — 'I didn't come here today to do anything for *your* poison. I'm trying to be free of *mine*. If you go to old Kennerly to be free of *yours*, I dare say that before you're done with it, Kennerly will have unloaded *his*. Might save his life! Or — if it didn't, he might at least be able to die like a gentleman.'

Spike stood staring.

'My God! — Dinny! Do you believe there's anything in this?'

Dinny took Spike's coat lapel lightly between thumb and fingers, looking him steadily in the eyes.

'Yes — and *so do you!*'

He opened the car door, and climbed in. The engine responded smoothly to the starter.

'You remember the way, don't you?' called Spike.

'Yes... But I'm not going out there, just now. How's the road down to Pinckney?'

'Perfect! And pretty, too. Remember the cliffs and mounds, down there?'

Dinny nodded, let in the clutch, rolled slowly down the familiar street. In his present state of mind, he wondered if he was really competent to drive. His hands were trembling.

Old Jason was right. This stuff — whatever it might be — was like dynamite. You had to handle it with care... Sentimental moonshine? My God! The stuff acted like radium! It didn't go off with a bang — but you had to look out! There was no question but it would destroy a man who trifled with it! He decided he would think twice before he told anyone else. A conviction was taking form in his mind that hadn't occurred to Dinny before. An energy as potent as this mustn't be trusted in the hands of people without definite instructions concerning its nature. He must find out a little more about it before he passed it on any further. Canny old Jason had seen the dangers at a glance. *Anybody who tried to use this dynamic for his own material advantage would almost unquestionably burn his fingers!*

* * * * * *

'Yes — poor old Clancy had to give up the battle,' drawled Mr. Brophy, pushing the mustard-pot across the table. 'The beer was no good, any more, and cost too much, and, anyway, the old chap had a certain self-respect; didn't care to be associated with the young crop of bootleggers. So — he closed up.'

'If they could have had Clancys dispensing beer, all over the country, perhaps we would never have come to this pass,' observed Dinny. 'But the thing had got out of bounds, most places. The Clancys were in the minority.'

'But there were enough Clancys to justify a bit of steady thinking on that subject before the whole liquor industry was turned loose to be operated by pick-pockets and safe-crackers!... Well — it's too late to be owling over that tragedy. It's done; we're in for it!... Let's talk about *you!* What brings you here?'

Dinny had strolled into *The Star* office at midnight, finding Mr. Brophy taking his coat off the peg preparatory to going out for lunch. After a warm welcome, or as warm as was to be expected of the unexcitable editor, who was not given much to hysteria, Dinny went back into the composing-room and renewed old acquaintance with the four or five who remained. Old Timmy Fagan had died.

'Shall we go over and see Clancy?' asked Dinny, when they were out on the street.

'No — that's a speakeasy now,' growled Brophy. 'I don't like the people who run it. They'd sell you a stroke of paralysis for a dollar. We'll drop in here at Ketolphus's place. You like Greeks, I recall.'

'I came out this way on several errands,' said Dinny, replying to Mr. Brophy's inquiry. 'I'm on a sort of peace commission.'

'Didn't suppose you went in for that kind of thing, Dinny.'

'No — it has been rather out of my line.'

Brophy grinned.

'Out of your line!... You've been a young hell-cat! Whoever sent you out with the impression that you were a cooing dove? You've been a storm-center so far back as I can recall... Well — let's hear all about it.'

It would be interesting to try it out on Mr. Brophy. The chances of his accepting it, to his damage, were as nothing is related to everything. Dinny, somewhat obscure and hesitant with the preliminaries — for his auditor's impassive face held out no promise of sympathetic comprehension — reported quite fully on his strange legacy and his recent experiences in so far as he could without violating confidences.

Brophy had smoked, stolidly, and listened.

'My son,' he said, gravely, when the narrative had reached the point of highest ecstasy for Dinny, and highest density for the white-haired Brophy, 'you've been working too hard. It's a natural penalty for philosophizing. You've made it your job, for years, to find out how much is the matter with the world. You never tried to treat it for its diseases; you just diagnosed, and shook your head, and telephoned for the undertaker. Now you've tired of that and are looking for some kind of a patent medicine. I think you're crazy as hell, and ought to be in a sanitarium.'

Dinny laughed, heartily, and tapped the end of another cigarette on the table.

'I never felt so well in my life, Mr. Brophy.'

'Any lunatic will tell you that. You'd better have a nice, long talk with a reputable psychiatrist. What do you suppose Beaton and those other chaps on *Hallelujah* would think if they knew you were cruising about in this state of mind? Why — you talk like this what's her name... My God!... she's no relation of yours, is she?'

Dinny's attempt to defend himself and his theory was not very satisfactory, chiefly for lack of time. Brophy had pressing work to do before *The Star* was put to bed, and made no disguise of his urgent necessity to be off.

When they parted, he was not only cordial but rather disconcertingly solicitous. Dinny must have a bit of rest. It was clear he had been working too hard, and had let things get on his nerves.

Back in his room at the hotel, Dinny suffered a moment's reflection that people victimized by psychoses are usually unaware of their misfortune. However, Spike Davis didn't think him crazy... or did he? His father didn't think him crazy, or he would hardly have thrown him out so indifferently. Old Jason didn't think him crazy. By Gad — he was never so sane in his life! Of course Brophy couldn't see it. Suppose Brophy had come to *him*, a month ago, with a similar story: what would he have thought of *Brophy?*

* * * * * *

It was an exquisite chapel, the gift of Mr. Joel Day in memory of his mother. Expense had not been considered. It was a work of art.

Recalling the general stampede of the old days when the ten-fifty bell summoned all Magnolians to compulsory prayers in the barn-like, taffy-colored assembly-hall, Dinny was amazed at the apparent reverence with which the students filed into the beautiful Gothic structure, dimly lit by mellow tints sifted through windows of unquestionable æsthetic value. He was struck by the fact that the current crop of Magnolia students was vastly superior in appearance and bearing to the hicks of his own collegiate generation; then promptly decided that the change was probably within himself. His appreciation of almost everything was on the rise; why not his respect for Magnolia? There was a rightful place for the little college, after all. His long-time disdain of it had been unjust.

But, even allowing for his own alteration of outlook, Magnolia had broadened. There were candles on the altar, and when the college choir appeared in the stalls it was appropriately vested. The organ, concealed behind chaste grillwork, was playing *Ein Feste Burg* with skillfully conceived variations. It was a good place to be. All the old feeling of antagonism toward everything that was Magnolia had vanished. She had suddenly become Alma Mater.

A tall chaplain in academic robes had followed the choir into the chancel, approaching the lectern where he stood for a moment with bowed head. Even in the uncertain light, Dinny recognized him at once. Doubtless Kling was a professor in the Seminary now; a commanding figure, obviously deserving of the confidence they had in him. After the service, Dinny would seek him out, and the old constraint would be lifted.

The *a cappella* choir sang, very impressively, one of Tschaikowsky's haunting anthems. With dignity and feeling, Kling began to read the last chapter of Ecclesiastes.

It was as if Dinny listened to the majestic thing for the first time. Often he had made some ribald joke that played on 'the grasshopper' who, perhaps through overindulgence, had become a 'burden.' That this ancient confession of a cynic was great literature had never occurred to him. What a superficial, heady fool he had been! What insufferable impudence! Speaking of hicks and yokels, who but an ignoramus could have been guilty of impertinences so raw?

Here was an incomparable pen-portrait of the penalties of such sophistication as had all but quenched the springs of Dinny's life. In this drab picture, the shutters had been closed, the garden had dried up, the porters at the gate sat dully oblivious of the world's activity. In the adjacent mill, the sound of the grinding was low. Things were so quiet that the voice of a bird startled one. The great palace was all but dead.

Once upon a time, fountains had played, flowers had bloomed, the spacious corridors had been flooded with music. The whole institution had throbbed with vitality. The joy of life had been drawn up from the inner spring of the luminous spirit as if by a silver cord attached to a golden bowl.

But the magic elixir had not been valued for what it was worth. The silver cord had slipped through unheeding fingers and *the golden bowl had been broken!* It was necessary now to go outside one's own gates and seek the fountain for one's water-of-life, using the communal pitcher that served other unfortunates who had broken their golden bowls. One day *that pitcher was found broken beside the fountain!* There was nothing left, now, but to go to the public cistern and stand waiting one's turn; and finally there came a day when *the wheel was found broken at the cistern!*

It was at that exact moment in Orville Kling's sonorous reading of this ancient cynic's lament — as Dinny often confessed, later — that the inspiration suddenly came which produced his monumental story, *Thirst* — a book so gripping that it was carried to the farthest corners of the literate earth; laughed over, wept over, prayed over by hundreds of thousands who, though hosts of them may have broken their golden bowls, or had been so unfortunate as to have found the pitcher broken at the fountain, resolved they would see to it that the wheel was not broken at the cistern!

When Kling had finished his reading, and closed the Book, he prayed. Every head was bowed; Dinny's, too. He found himself simple-heartedly grateful for the mental guidance of the man for whom he had long nourished a sullen hatred. There was a benediction while they sat in reverence; then, after a moment's absolute silence, the congregation stirred, rose, and quietly departed. But Dinny was too deeply moved to lift his head. A feeling of great exultation swept the strings of his soul. There had been laid on him a commission. He had been appointed an apostle to them whose gardens were wilting, whose silver cords were slipping, whose golden bowls were in danger of breaking.

The organ had returned to its versatile adventures with the courageous score of 'A Mighty Fortress is Our God.' Dinny's eyes were suffused with a rush of hot tears. His heart was pounding. His consciousness of his new responsibility was almost more than he could bear.

'Lookit, Gramp!... at *Dinny Brumm!*'

'What's the matter... Did he upset his vinegar jug?'

'No!... Lookit!... *Lookit!*'

CHAPTER XVIII

IT WAS not an ideal evening for a stroll. The air was damp and uncomfortably chilly. Apparently it had been raining very hard, a little earlier, for the wet leaves on the sidewalks were laid in semi-circular festoons as if swept there at the turn of a tide, and the gutters were filled with tight-packed, soggy piles of them.

But Dinny wanted to move about under his own power. The rough voyage had been tedious, and the trip from Cherbourg had tried his patience, for now that he was nearing his journey's end he was eager to have done with it and proceed to the singular errand that had brought him so far.

It was too late to locate Tommy and Joan tonight. To-morrow, pursuant to the advice he had secured from Lacey's, he would endeavor to connect with Tommy through their Paris office. If lucky, he might have the contemplated visit with the honeymooners before the day was out. Next morning he would run up to Calais, and so to London, where he had already engaged a room at the Victoria.

Descending the steps of the Continental, Dinny sauntered up and down the arcaded block, strolled over to the Place Vendôme and back again to Rue de Rivoli, wondering how he might amuse himself for the remainder of the evening.

On impulse he took a taxi and drove across the river. On Raspail, a little below Saint-Germain, he decided to get out and walk. After ten minutes of aimless rambling, he sighted a café that seemed more active than any he had seen.

Pleasurably recognizing its name, for he had often heard of 'The Dome' and its popularity with Americans, he turned in among the little iron-legged tables that cluttered the sidewalk, found one unoccupied, ordered a glass of sauterne to ensure his welcome, and leisurely took stock of the amiable crowd, most of whom were youthful, many of whom were reminiscent of the Greenwich Village habitués, and all of whom — with one single exception in sight — appeared to be in a more or less festive mood.

The unaccompanied woman who sat facing him, a little distance away, took no interest in her neighbors. She did not appear to be in acute trouble, but was downcast, meditatively toying with a half-empty glass of something that looked like cognac. Hers was not a problem of poverty, for she was the best-dressed person there. She could have pawned the silver mesh handbag on her table for enough to put her up at the Ritz for a few days, and the price of her black fur coat would have kept her in good comfort for six months.

In a moment their eyes met briefly, and, because hers were unmistakably American eyes and full of loneliness, Dinny was faintly conscious that his face must have reacted a bit to his recognition of the fact that they were fellow-countrymen. If she noticed the fleeting smile in his eyes, she made no response to it, abstractedly returning to her pensive fingering of the glass.

Dinny found it difficult to detach himself from her, and studied her face with interest. In her depression, she looked forty. Later, when she smiled, five years vanished magically. She was a lady — with a story; no doubt of that. But it was not necessarily a sordid or discreditable story, for though her face was sad, it was not hard and it was not ashamed.

She glanced up now, smiled faintly as their eyes momentarily met again, drained her glass casually, and drew the collar of her fur coat more snugly about her neck. Doubtless she was on the point of leaving now, and Dinny was half-glad. Her dejection was dampening his own spirits, already low enough, for, as the distance lessened between him and the courage-testing event that had invited him to Paris, the more sensitive he became to his irreparable loss. He had moments when he wondered whether he would be able to go through with it.

Rising slowly, she took up her expensive bag from the table, and, with eyes regarding him inquisitively, came over to Dinny, paused, laid a black-gloved hand on the back of the vacant chair. He rose instantly, and invited her to sit down. She did so, with entire self-possession, folding her arms on the table.

'Were you surprised, Dinny, when you found my note?'

'Janet! — my dear!'

He reached out both hands to hers.

'You didn't recognize me,' she said, ruefully. 'I must have changed more than I had thought.'

'But it has been so long, dear, and of course I wasn't expecting to see you, and — you've bobbed your hair, haven't you? It's quite becoming, Janet.'

'No — I've changed. I know that, Dinny. The game I've been playing alters one.'

'How does it compare with — wheel-barrow?'

'Less exciting. Much slower than chess; and if you win, there's no prize.'

'It wears the players out, you mean?'

She nodded, with just a faint recovery of the Janet look of quick understanding.

'Exactly. The players are worn out, and it's after midnight, and finally one of them makes the last move, which both had seen coming for an hour, and — the game's over. The guest yawns and goes, and the drowsy host calls in the cat and puts out the milk-bottle. And that's all. Not very stimulating, would you say?'

'Where is he now, Janet? Want to talk about it?'

'As for wanting to — no. But I'll tell you. We separated more than a year ago. Oscar returned to the States for a while. He is in Florence now; or was, the last I heard from him.'

'Who won the game?'

She shrugged slightly and dismissed the query with a lazy little flick of her fingers.

'I believe I made the last move, but by that time we were

both too indifferent to care, or to remember — certainly not with any pride of victory, or ——'

'Humiliation of defeat,' assisted Dinny, comprehendingly.

'I'm not so sure there wasn't some humiliation,' confessed Janet, after a pause, 'even for the winner — if I won.'

'The money part — maybe?' Dinny wondered.

Janet nodded.

'Why do you ask? The story will surely bore you, and it makes me unhappy to remember.'

'Sometimes it helps a little to talk things over, dear.'

'Well — I fancy you know that Mr. Day divorced me, as of course he should. Along with word of that came notification that he had made over a great many valuable securities to me. I declined them, through our attorneys, but Mr. Day's decision remained unchanged. You may recall that Mr. Day's temperament was not to be described as — as vacillating, or volatile.'

Janet's drawling understatement left so very much unsaid that Dinny laughed, appreciatively. She had not changed, after all.

'The dividends kept coming along,' continued Janet, in an even tone, 'and I used them, reluctantly at first.... And then, when Oscar and I parted — it was mostly my fault, for I think I was the one who remarked that we both knew we were weary of each other — he gave me his blessing and three thousand shares of T. and T.'

'You're well provided for, dear.'

'Oh, yes — I have almost everything anyone would want except self-respect, and I've been doing without that for so long I hardly miss it.' She had tried to make this last sound dryly cynical, and ended it with a twisted little smile.

'Janet,' said Dinny, soberly, 'you've broken your golden bowl!'

She lowered her eyes, and nodded; then glanced up, inquiringly.

'What's this — about a golden bowl, Dinny?'

'It was attached to a silver cord,' he explained cryptically. 'And whenever you wanted happiness, you drew it up from the spring. I'm afraid you've let the silver cord slip through your hands.'

'Is that what that means — "Or ever the silver cord be loosed, and the golden bowl be broken"? I never knew.' She laughed, quietly. 'Since when did you go in for such philosophy, Dinny? I've read enough of your hellish satires to know that you're not in the golden-bowl business.'

'I'd like to tell you all about it, Janet. You say you've changed. I wonder that you recognized me! It's quite a long story.'

She pushed back her chair.

'Suppose we go over to the Crillon — I live there — and sit in the lounge. And you can begin at the beginning, and tell me everything.... But you won't scold me; will you, dear?'

* * * * * *

Dinny's heart was beating furiously, and his mouth was dry, as he paced nervously to and fro near the little elevator. The shaft of it, rising from the lobby, was a mere skeleton of ornamental wrought-iron curlycues, and one could see the descending occupants long before they arrived on the ground floor.

At any moment now, Tommy would be coming down, and Joan, too, more than likely, for it was nearly ten and she would undoubtedly be up and dressed for the day.

They would greet him with a brave show of cordiality, trying hard to cover their mystification with a rapid fire of questions. 'Why — of all things! — Dinny Brumm!'... 'How lovely to see you here!'... 'Where are you stopping? When did you come? How nice of you to look us up!' But underneath all the friendly racket, how much of constraint would there be?

It had not been difficult to locate them. At nine-thirty, Dinny had telephoned Lacey's office. Yes — Mr. Forsythe was in town, stopping at the Regina. Perhaps he had not left yet; might catch him there. It was only a step over from the Continental.

'Down in two minutes, old chap!' Tommy had answered, on the house telephone. 'Powerfully glad you're here! Delightful surprise!'

Was it, really? Dinny wished he could be more certain of that.

The little elevator had again slipped slowly upward through the gold ceiling. And now — a few frantic weeks of waiting having elapsed — it was coming down, bringing Tommy's long legs, broad shoulders, expectant smile. Dinny was steadied and comforted, a little, by the smile.

'This is certainly a great treat, Dinny!' Tommy gave him a comradely thump on the shoulder, and beamed.

'I'm on my way to London,' explained Dinny, hastily, as if his train were waiting. 'It occurred to me I'd like to have a glimpse of you and Joan — for old sake's sake ——'

'Joan?' echoed Tommy, happily. 'Is she here, too?'

'My God — Tommy! You don't mean to tell me ——'

Tommy stared, uncomprehendingly, for a moment, and then grinned.

'You didn't think we were here together, did you? The last I saw of Joan was the night before I sailed in September.'

They were standing near a little gilt and scarlet divan; and Dinny, whose knees were shaky, sat down, Tommy joining him, much amused by his sudden collapse.

'The fact is,' resumed Tommy, 'Joan has been much on my mind, these past few weeks. She vanished, the same day I left. She did not show up at the store, next morning. They made inquiries without results.'

'Had anything happened,' inquired Dinny, huskily, 'to account for it? Do you suppose some harm has come to her?'

'I'll tell you all I know,' said Tommy, soberly, after a

moment's delay. 'I suppose you've a right to all the information there is.'

* * * * * *

'Her Uncle Jim ought to know where she is!' shouted Dinny, excitedly. 'Perhaps she's there! She went to him once before when she was in trouble. I'll cable!'

'I'll go along. You're not fit to be at large, Dinny. You'll get yourself run over. Buck up now! You look like a ghost. We'll find her. Uncle Jim will know — if you can get it out of him.'

* * * * * *

He knew that Janet and Tommy were amusing themselves at his expense, as the boat-train started. Tommy had said something funny to her, and nodded toward him, as he waved from the window of his compartment. She had laughed, gayly. Had anyone ever heard of so good a joke? A round trip from New York to Paris for information about his girl! — information he might have had for ninety cents if he had queried Uncle Jim in the first place.

The three of them had lunched together, Dinny well satisfied over the prompt congeniality of Janet and Tommy, whose amiable chatter left him without much responsibility for the talk. He had never been in such a state of utter rout, mentally. Uncle Jim's cable had not arrived until nearly four. After that there had been a great panic about getting Dinny aboard the first ship. The Olympic was due to call at Cherbourg at eleven. He could just make it.

The train was increasing its strides now. Dinny's hands trembled as he took the cablegram from his pocket. Bless old Uncle Jim! He had come through without a moment's delay. The message was brief, but illuminating.

ABERCROMBIES DENVER

Tommy had fortunately been able to fill in the details. He remembered Mr. Abercrombie's call at Lacey's, and his unusual interest in Joan.

It was a long trip to Cherbourg, and the Olympic was exasperatingly slow getting herself persuaded to draw up the anchor and amble on toward the west. Dinny wondered, as he stood at the rail, whether it would help things along if he volunteered assistance.... What? Another big netful of mail-bags? What did so many people have to write about that was so important?

* * * * * *

There was a telegram from Janet at the purser's office when he called to arrange for his passage.

TOMMY TELLS ME MUCH TO DO FOR SHOP GIRLS IN NEW YORK STOP PERHAPS CAN USE MONEY MENDING BROKEN BOWLS PITCHERS CISTERN WHEELS STOP THANK YOU DEAR FOR COMING STOP KISS JOAN FOR ME STOP TOMMY ADJACENT SAYS ME TOO STOP LUCKY DEVIL

* * * * * *

Every day en route Dinny composed radiograms to Joan by the dozen, informing her he was on the way and hurrying as fast as possible. None of them was sent. He couldn't explain, by radio, that he was ready now to keep his promises, several times broken, nor dare he risk frightening her away from Denver with the announcement that he was about to press his claim.

The Olympic might have been an old square-rigged threemaster from the way she wallowed and plodded as if it was of no concern to her whether she ever reached New York or not; but one morning, after ages and ages, she nosed her way into her berth, and at two Dinny was on the train, composing speeches for Joan... The *darling!*

* * * * * *

He had firmly decided, after much debate, that he would not attempt to see Joan at the store. He would call on Mr.

Abercrombie, briefly explain his mission, and Mr. Abercrombie would give him Joan's street address. From what Tommy had said about the fine old fellow, that seemed quite reasonable.

The train arrived shortly after three, and Dinny went directly to the big store. Mr. Abercrombie listened with interest.

'We should be very sorry to lose Miss Braithwaite,' he said. 'But I'm afraid I couldn't stop you, even if I tried. So — find her, my boy, and good luck to you.'

He sent a message to her house from the Blackstone, asking her to give him a ring at the earliest moment, and waited in a state of near-lunacy. Six-twenty! — twenty-five! — thirty! Joan should be at home by this time. He sat near the telephone, ready to leap to it.

At seven, unable to endure another minute of this torture, he called her house. The voice replied cheerfully, 'Hold the line, please,' and a little later said sympathetically, 'Sorry — but Miss Braithwaite is out.'

He sat for a long time with the telephone in his hands, wondering what next to do. His hopes were tumbling to pieces.

At eight, he resolved that nothing was to be gained by moping in his room, and was putting on his coat to go down when a letter was delivered by messenger. He opened it, in a panic of apprehension.

Dear Dinny:

You and I have caused each other a great deal of misery. And nothing could be easier for us to do than keep on making ourselves and each other utterly wretched until one of us died or ran away.

I'm not going to pretend that I'm happy, but I'm busy, and I like my work. It cost a good deal to decide that it was better for us never to see each other any more. But, having made that decision, I know it is to your best interest, and mine, that I stick to it. You know I would love to see you; but, Dinny, I can't go through it again!

Please don't try to persuade me. Here is once when I'm
certain that I know what's best for us.

Ever yours

JOAN

After a half-hour of suffering, Dinny resolved to play the
last card in his hand.

He went to the desk, and wrote:

Dearest Joan:

I'm not asking you to renew friendship with the Dinny
Brumm of the Green Cheese and *Hallelujah*. It may be
hard for you to believe, but I'm definitely done with all that.
I am just learning to walk. I need you as never before, and I
love you desperately.

You will find enclosed a letter that I found secreted in an
old desk that was the property of my mother. Please read it,
dear. I have made the experiment that Julia recommended to
me. And it has worked!

Do let me see you, if only for a moment, tomorrow!

Loving you dearly

DINNY

Having dispatched the letter to Joan's address, he went
down and walked the streets for an hour. He remembered
that he had had no dinner, but was not hungry enough to
care. Returning at length to his room, he went to bed, and,
utterly exhausted with the long strain, drifted off into a
troubled sleep.

How long the telephone had been ringing he could only
guess. The insistent demand had been punctuating a series
of dreams in which he was being entreated, urged, bela-
bored, to respond to some desperate situation. Half-awake,
he groped for the instrument, noting, as he turned on the
light, that it was half-past five.

'Dinny!' Joan's voice was very low, and broken.

'Yes, darling.'

'Dinny — I'm afraid I can't wait till morning.'

'Come on down here, then... I'll meet you in the lobby.'

'Would that be too dreadful?... What would people think?'

'Hang the people!... Oh, Joan!... My dear!'

There was a considerable pause.

'Very well... I'll come... Half an hour... Good-bye.'

Dinny found himself laughing aloud, half-hysterically, as he dressed. He bet his last dollar nothing like this had ever happened before. His fingers were clumsy as he wrestled with his collar. Joan was coming! He glanced out of the window. There was a faint dawn-glow.

The lobby of the hotel was deserted except for a sleepy clerk at the desk, and two old fellows with damp mops scrubbing the tiled floor.

Dinny stood just inside the revolving door, and waited.

A taxi drew up. He rushed out to meet it, opened the door, stepped in.

After a while the taxi-driver closed the door with a bang, but whatever hint it was intended to convey had been too subtle for his passengers.

Five minutes later, he opened the door again, and said:

'I'm goin' across here for a cup of coffee and a doughnut. And if the cop gives me a ticket for parkin', I'll expect you to pay for it!'

* * * * * *

There was a very simple little wedding that afternoon at five. Joan had made no objection to its immediacy. She was beside herself with happiness, and whatever Dinny wanted to do, no matter how impetuously arrived at, was acceptable.

At breakfast, Dinny said:

'What would we be waiting for, I'd like to know, if we waited another day?'

'That's so,' agreed Joan. 'It would be silly, wouldn't it?'

'This afternoon, then?'

She nodded, enthusiastically.

'And go away — directly afterwards.'

'As you like, dear.'

'Far off... somewhere on a ship... around the world, maybe. That's a great thought, Joan. We'll go 'round the world... Want to? We can, you know.'

'I'd love to, Dinny.'

'Why are you smiling?'

'I'm happy.'

'No — it was something more than happy. Tell me.'

'I was just remembering,' said Joan, 'what a gypsy girl told me, a few months ago. I was soon to go on a long "jorney" with a tall man on a "beeg" ship.'

'By Gad, Joan, I was afraid you had!... We'll take the first train out, after we're married. Right?'

'Yes — we couldn't go any sooner than that.'

'To San Francisco... and sail! Agreed?'

'Let's!'

* * * * * *

The lobby of the Saint Francis was astir with dinner guests arriving for a banquet when Dinny and Joan came down from the room they had occupied for an hour. It was a newspaper affair, they learned. Zandy Craig was meeting the entire *Enquirer* outfit and a score of prominent citizens.

'There's Alison, darling,' exclaimed Dinny, as a half-dozen modishly gowned women stepped out of the adjoining elevator. 'We must speak to her.'

She turned as if she had overheard her name spoken, and joined them with a little ejaculation of happy surprise.

'Dinny!... You don't mean to tell me you've managed to persuade this lovely ——'

'Joan, please meet my sister.' Dinny was ecstatic.

'I would give anything for a couple of minutes with you, Alison,' murmured Joan. 'But you're going to the dinner, and I mustn't detain you.'

'No — I'm not. Father couldn't be bothered with mere women at his parties. Do you want to tell me something that won't keep another minute?'

'We're sailing in the morning. I may not have anothei chance.' Joan seemed much disappointed.

Alison searched her eyes with an inquisitive glance, and fleetingly regarded Dinny with a similar inspection.

'Very well. I'll talk to you now. We'll step over into the lounge.... Will you wait for me, a few minutes, Mrs Baumgarten? I'll not be long.'

They disappeared, Joan's hand tucked under Alison's arm. Dinny was very proud of them. They were thoroughbreds!

Ten minutes later, when they rejoined him, they were smiling as if the interview had been mutually pleasant. Alison collected her party and hurried away.

'Big secret, Joan?' queried Dinny, consumed by curiosity.

'Don't try to make me tell you, dear; not yet.'

'I'll wait, but don't keep me at it too long!'

* * * * * *

Returning from the theater, which they had found ratner tame, for it had concerned itself with the tribulations of a pair who were put to tremendous bother and expense to find each other after a long misunderstanding, they went to their room and were bending over an array of cruise literature, outspread on the table, when the telephone rang.

'It's for me,' said Joan, taking up the instrument... 'Yes, Alison... That's wonderful!... Now?... Nine-sixty-seven?... I'll be up in two minutes!' She put down the telephone on the table, and smiled into Dinny's eyes. 'I've an engagement, dear, for a little talk with — can you guess?'

'That's marvelous, Joan. Hope you'll not be disappointed.'

'May I take Julia's letter along?'

'I don't know who has a better right to it.

* * * * * *

Joan had been gone for more than an hour. Dinny had

tried to pass the time by studying the itinerary of the long journey on which they were about to embark.

Utterly unable to command his thoughts or concentrate his attention on the gaudy promises of the illustrated prospectus, he sat staring at the wall, wondering how Joan was making out with her strange adventure. It would be quite a monstrous pity if anything had happened to distress her. She had been barely touching the ground with her toes. Never had he seen anyone so radiant!

There was a peremptory summons from the telephone. Joan's voice sounded as if she had been deeply stirred.

'Come up here, dear, please... Room nine hundred and sixty-seven; I'll wait here for you.'

Joan and Alison met him at the elevator, when he arrived. They had both been crying recently, he thought. They parted as he came toward them and, turning, each took an arm. He waited for them to speak, but they had nothing to say as they piloted him down the long corridor.

At the door they stopped, and released him.

Dinny looked inquiringly from one to the other.

Alison turned the knob, pushed the door open a little way, patted Dinny affectionately on the arm, and stepped aside.

'He is waiting for you, Dinny,' she said, softly.

Joan put her arm about his neck, and, standing on tip-toe, whispered, brokenly:

'Be very tender, dear.'

THE END